My
Husband's
Lie

BOOKS BY EMMA DAVIES

Lucy's Little Village Book Club

The Little Cottage on the Hill
Summer at the Little Cottage on the Hill
Return to the Little Cottage on the Hill
Christmas at the Little Cottage on the Hill

The House at Hope Corner
The Beekeeper's Cottage
The Little Shop on Silver Linings Street

Letting in Light
Turn Towards the Sun

Merry Mistletoe
Spring Fever
Gooseberry Fool
Blackberry Way

My
Husband's
Lie

EMMA DAVIES

Bookouture

Published by Bookouture in 2020

An imprint of Storyfire Ltd.
Carmelite House
50 Victoria Embankment
London EC4Y 0DZ

www.bookouture.com

ISBN: 978-1-83888-600-4
eBook ISBN: 978-1-83888-599-1

PROLOGUE

Thea

Looking back, I wonder whether our holiday had been to blame. Two weeks of unexpectedly perfect weather at Easter, when the girls had gambolled like lambs in the fields surrounding the farm where we had stayed, and even Drew had lost the pinched look he so often wore. His stride had lengthened, his shoulders had relaxed, and he just looked… content. As for me, I'd found a freedom I hadn't experienced in years. Something stirred in me that holiday and, whatever it was, it wouldn't lie back down. Was it just nostalgia, or something deeper? I don't know, but it grew inside of me just as surely as the two girls I had once carried.

It wasn't as if we were unhappy. Sure, things had been difficult when Chloe and Lauren were little, but show me a family with young children where things don't get fraught. We got through it and, although the girls and our lives filled our three-bedroom terrace house to the rafters, I never thought I hated it, not really, not until two weeks of space and fresh air and love, actually, made me realise how cramped we all were. Not just our house, but us, everything that made us who we were, was being slowly crushed to death. So when I stumbled across the details for Pevensey House I knew I had found a way for us to be free, to settle the thing that had stirred inside of me, and I didn't hesitate. I should have done, I realise that now.

Drew

I should have been firmer. I knew it was a mistake to go back, but I was kidding myself too. I wanted it just as much as Thea did. She hadn't had an easy time of things after Lauren was born. The birth was difficult, and it drained her, robbing her of her usually sunny disposition for months, but she never once complained. Even when Lauren's temper tantrums reached their peak, aged two, Thea looked after us all, juggling things, balancing; everything in her life a trade-off for something else. And I guess I just wanted more for her too.

Seeing her on that holiday reminded me of the Thea I first met, the one who walked barefoot everywhere, the one whose fits of giggles exploded out of nowhere. It made me realise how beautiful she was, how much I loved her. And her work? It came to life during those two weeks, the best she'd ever produced – winning the commission was evidence enough of that. So how could I possibly hold her back, just when she had found her wings.

Besides, who wouldn't want to live at Pevensey? It was gorgeous. Warm mellow stone, huge windows letting in more light than you knew what to do with, and space, so much space... No, I was yearning for the change just as much as she was, anything to be free from the tyranny of the commute and Roger's caustic comments day in, day out. But I knew the danger and I let us walk right into it. So if anyone was to blame it was me, but instead I blamed Thea. And, when it came down to it, that's what everything was about, wasn't it? Who was to blame...

CHAPTER ONE

The photo is a little bent now, but it's one I remember well. I've looked at it many times over the years: two children playing almost naked in the garden – him, with a face smeared in mud and missing at least four teeth; and her, long straggly hair, a little on the pudgy side, holding up a worm for inspection. Me and Drew. Drew and me. Scarcely one without the other.

I angle the photo a little more toward the light, trying to see the detail, smiling as I wonder how Drew could ever have fallen for such an unremarkable child as me. But he had. We'd grown up together and somehow we'd never stopped. Back then we lived next door to one another, and even when one family moved, the other followed so we managed to stay in each other's orbit. I'm thirty-four now and so is Drew and, apart from five excruciating years when we were both studying at different universities, we've always been together. I'm still unremarkable. A little on the short side, with chin-length, dark, bobbed hair which spends its day tucked behind my ears, and only a smattering of freckles to bring my face to life. I have nice skin though, I've always liked my skin. Drew, however, is far from unremarkable. Drew is simply gorgeous. In the right light he can pass for Jude Law, but more important than the way he looks is the way he makes me feel.

The Celts have a term for it – *Anam Cara*. It means 'soul friend' and that's exactly what we are. Drew teases me when I say such things, rolling his eyes in mock exasperation as he walks away. But I catch the little smile on his face as he does so, and I know he feels the same way.

I drop the photo back in the box, resisting the temptation to take out another. I'm supposed to be working, or packing, or both. But instead I've been sitting here for the best part of an hour, sifting through the recorded moments of our lives before my parents moved us away from Pevensey House and our sleepy corner of Shropshire. There were plenty more photos from the years after we moved, but these have always been my favourites. Pictures from a golden childhood.

My legs have gone to sleep from kneeling on the floor and I get to my feet, trying to work some feeling back into them. I know I've wasted too much time and a glance at the clock confirms it, but I couldn't resist this trip down memory lane. We move in just over a week's time and I'll be able to pack most of our things methodically and efficiently, but somehow all these mementoes, all these feelings, needed one last airing before I temporarily shut them away. One last stocktake of the past before we start our new adventure.

It's a Friday in late July and our girls finish school today for the summer. In fact, for our youngest, Lauren, it's the end of her infant education. In September she'll be moving into the juniors, but it will be a new school for both her and Chloe. They're growing up so fast that some days I feel like I can't keep up with them, but I'm hoping that once we move we'll all be able to slow down. Time moves differently in the country somehow. I'm so looking forward to long, carefree summer days, away from noise and bustle, perhaps more for Drew's benefit than anything. I'm looking forward to seeing the crease above the bridge of his nose soften. To seeing the slightly distracted air he often wears to dissipate, and to see him reading a book of an evening, just like he used to before his grinding days and the commute rendered him senseless.

I still can't quite believe we got so lucky. But that's how I know how right this is. Things don't fall into place quite so easily unless they're meant to be, and six short weeks was all it took. I guess our holiday, deep in the rolling countryside back at Easter, was the start of it, but as soon as we came back things were different. It was as if I'd learned how to magically turn on the tap of my creativity; my work seemed brighter, more confident, more alive. I know winning the V&A Illustration Award last year helped enormously, but my submission for the Kathryn Talbot series was the best work I've ever produced. When I found out in June that I'd gained the commission I knew that something magical was about to happen.

Three days later, Drew came home and dropped the bombshell that he'd applied for and been granted voluntary redundancy. He'd worked for Franklin and Wilks since gaining his degree, it's the reason we moved to London in the first place, but he'd done all he could there. He'd started as an architect's assistant and had risen through the ranks, making partner three years ago. Except that Roger, the colleague who thought he should have got the promotion instead of Drew, had made his life hell. And Drew isn't a pushover by any means, but it was wearing, constantly trying to parry Roger's pathetic attempts at undermining him. While we were on holiday Drew told me that the company was going through a tough time and might have to make a couple of junior architects redundant, but perhaps our holiday had ignited his yearning for freedom too. Or maybe it was just the boiling-hot June day that had finally brought him to the end of his tether, I don't know.

The thought had terrified me at first but, as we'd lain together that night, trying to block out the noise of the near-constant London traffic, he'd confessed that what he really longed to do was start his own business. He'd been working on and off for the past couple of years on designs of his own, what he called his honeycomb houses: low-cost, flexible pods that could be built singly or attached to each other to give an infinitely increasing space. It was a project he was passionate about developing. He had the money from his redundancy and we had a home in London that was worth far more than it should have been. Perhaps now might be a good time to make some changes, he'd said.

Spotting my old family home for sale only a week later had surely been the hand of fate at work. I'd been sitting in the dentist's waiting room of all places, flicking through the glossy magazines, when there it was – in the Fine & Country section. Pevensey House. The last piece of the jigsaw fell into place and the rest, as they say, is history.

I close the box lid and pick up a roll of Sellotape, ripping off a section with my teeth and sealing our memories shut. I need to get a move on or I'm going to be late picking up the girls. Then it's on to their last piano lesson, a dash to the market to grab what I need to make dinner and then, finally, I can wait for the sound of Drew's key in the door and we will all be home. The end, but also a beginning.

It's only when I move that I realise how stifling it is up here. This tiny attic space is where I work, illustrating children's books, and the only place in our house where my drawing board doesn't need to be tidied away, leaving it ready to pick up where I left off. It's cosy in winter but, with only two small roof lights, it gets hardly any breeze and it's a relief to descend into the lower part of the house. I grab a glass of water from the kitchen, holding it for a moment against my pink cheek before swallowing the liquid in one continual motion. I pause to mentally gather myself for the onslaught outside and then, flicking a glance at my reflection as I pass the mirror in the hallway, I pick up my bag and let myself out into the busy street.

It wasn't always this way. Or perhaps it's just that my perception of it has changed. When we first moved here the street was wide and tree-lined and at times seemed quite peaceful. But now, although the street is just as wide, the trees just as present, it thrums with a restless energy that never stops. There are cars and people and buses and dogs. Noise from traffic, radios, the odd shout, babies crying, and I swear today I can hear the pavements creaking with the heat. And in among this, incongruously, slotted between a gap in the buildings, is St Hilda's Primary School. The metal is hot to touch as I push open the gate into the playground.

Despite my panic about being late, I'm somehow earlier than usual and I stand in my habitual spot, nodding at my tribe as they pass. It isn't long before I spot Rachel and I move slightly to accommodate her beside me. She blows a puff of air up her face, trying to get her fringe to unglue itself from her forehead.

'I am so glad I won't be doing this for a while,' she says.

We all are. I can see it on everyone's faces around me; the relief that the summer term is over and with it an end to the ceaseless clock-watching and monotony of the drop-off and pick-up.

I grin at my friend. 'And I'm so glad I won't be doing this *ever* again – well, here at least.'

She pulls a face at that. 'What am I going to do without you?' she wails, and I slide an arm around her waist, squishing her into a sideways hug. We stand that way for a moment, both thinking about our respective futures, until I pull away, turning to face her.

'What you are going to do is make sure you find the time to come and visit us. I mean it, Rach. Properly visit us. I know we're going to be just that little bit too far to come for the day but, if you think about it, that makes it even better. You can come and stay for the weekend, or even longer. We can be your holiday home in the country.'

I mean it and she smiles, but we both know it probably won't turn out like that. Not because we don't want it to, but because life has a habit of getting in the way, and what seems easy and simple often turns out to be difficult and complicated. And time just slips past. Before you know it, you haven't seen one another in so long that it becomes embarrassing and so more time goes by. But I hope not. I don't know what I'd have done without Rach.

I know nearly every single mum standing in this playground, and some of the dads too, but none of them are my friends, not really. We've shared conversations, and jokes, had coffee together even, but I wouldn't cry in front of any of them like I have with Rachel. You know, the kind of crying where snot pours out your nose and you don't care. Like the time when we thought Chloe had meningitis and when my father died. I got chatting to Rachel about a week after Chloe first started school and we've been friends ever since. Her husband, Gerry, is great too. Maybe it's because he's a paramedic and deals in death and destruction on a daily basis, but he has the most wicked sense of humour; it's positively evil, but I love it and I'm going to miss them both so much.

Rachel squeezes my arm. 'I'll let you get settled in first…' But then she gives a cheeky grin. 'How about the week after you move in?'

'Deal.'

She runs a hand up her arm as if brushing away an insect. 'Seriously though,' she says. 'You know how pleased I am for you, Thea. All that space for the girls, a brand-new studio for you and Drew, and a new business for him too. It couldn't happen to two nicer people. You deserve it, you really do.'

I run a finger underneath my eye. 'Don't,' I say. 'Or you'll have me blubbing like a baby.' And I think I detect a little gleam in her eye too.

Rachel sighs. 'I can't imagine ever having memories like you have. My childhood was just a series of almost identical houses on whichever air-force base my dad was working out of. I've always longed to have roots…'

'You'll get your dream, Rach, I know you will. Two years from now you'll be running your catering business from a big old farmhouse with roses round the door. And Jamie will be skipping around with bare feet and permanently sun-kissed cheeks, you wait and see.'

Rachel grimaces, eyeing the other mums on the playground. 'Meanwhile, I'd better hope this lot keep having dinner parties, anniversaries and *just a little evening soiree, Rachel, you know the kind of thing.*'

I grin. I do know the kind of thing. It's one of the reasons I like Rachel so much; she hates the London social scene just as much as I do.

A shout catches her attention and she looks up to see Jamie hurtling across the playground. His breaking free from the ranks of his other classmates draws a look of consternation from his teacher, but it's the last day of term and she clearly hasn't the energy left to remonstrate with him. Rachel gives a little wave, acknowledging the receipt of her child as he barrels into her, and the teacher continues releasing her charges to the waiting parents.

Chloe is in the same class as Jamie, and Lauren is in the one below, and eventually all three children are present and correct and we're able to make our way to the school gates. It always amazes me how quickly everyone disappears and today the process seems faster than usual, people melting away, eager to get their holidays started. Chloe tugs at my sleeve.

'Look at what I got, Mum,' she says. She fishes in her backpack and pulls out a carrier bag filled with presents. 'And Emily Hewson's mum made me a cake, but we ate it all at break.'

There's an assortment of girly wrapping paper but among it are rubbers, new pencils, a pencil case, some lip salves and three little notebooks tied up with ribbon.

'And Mrs Stenning got me a card.' She fishes back in the bag, her lip caught between her teeth. 'Oh... I can't find it. Never mind, I'll show you when we get home. Have we got time for an ice cream?'

It's the first time her sister's face lights up. Lauren probably has a similar assortment of going-away presents from her friends, but she's never shared Chloe's penchant for sparkly new possessions and so the prospect of an ice cream is far more appealing.

'A promise is a promise…'

The girls squeal, Chloe thrusting her school bag at me and linking arms with Lauren. I throw Rachel a look and she laughs.

'I'd better let you go,' she says and we hug again but, almost immediately, her face falls slightly. 'I'll see you soon, yeah?'

I nod, realising the girls are already walking away.

'Yes, soon,' I reply, knowing that the countdown has begun, the times we'll be together becoming fewer and fewer until there are none left. I wave as we slip through the gate and then suddenly we're back out on the busy street.

'Hold my hand!' I call to Lauren, waiting until she does as asked, her hot fingers slick in mine. I need a cool shower and a glass of something even colder, never mind an ice cream.

It's nearly six o'clock by the time we push open our front door and the day still hasn't relinquished its grip on the heat that has built up. The girls run for the kitchen as soon as we arrive and I juggle with the shopping for a moment before hanging up their book bags on the hallway pegs one last time. Just off the kitchen, the tiny back garden is in full sun but I push open the door to it anyway, hoping that a breeze might find its way into the house. Then I turn on the cold water tap and let it run.

'Uniforms!' I shout at the girls' retreating backs, ten minutes, a glass of water and a biscuit later. It's our Friday-night routine, and has been for so long I scarcely even think about it. But we are home and my stomach flips in excitement at the thought of the coming day.

*

Drew returns home even later than usual. He looks hot and battered, the end of a week which, given the fact he's leaving, has probably been much worse than normal. His face shows a mixture of things: an overarching tiredness, the release from the enforced patience that the commute requires, the lowering of the shields that life in London necessitates and, perhaps, pleasure at having accomplished all that he needed. Relief is not there, not yet. But it will come. Probably not straight away, but in the next few weeks, slowly, as the realisation of a life left behind steals over him. For now, the house is quiet, the girls away in their rooms, and that is all he needs.

He sits on a swivel chair at the breakfast bar, his leather case on the counter, and I move so that I'm standing beside him. I turn his seat towards me, catching at the ends of his tie, sliding the knot even further down its length until I can remove it completely. I drop it next to his bag. I run my hands through the wavy tendrils of his hair, pressing my fingers into his hot scalp in a way I know brings relief, and gently pull his head towards me so that it rests against my chest.

'Done?' I ask.

'Done,' he replies. And for a long moment there is nothing else to say.

When he finally raises his head, a small smile has formed on his face and he gets to his feet, sliding a hand around the nape of my neck and kissing my lips. He's at least a foot taller than I am. There's a cool drink waiting for him on the side and by the time he reaches it, drinking steadily and gratefully, he is already coming back to life.

'Where are the girls?' he asks.

'Upstairs.' They've already had their tea and a bath and are now cooler in clean pyjamas, waiting patiently for their storyteller to arrive.

He nods, grinning, as he makes his way to the door. He turns at the last minute. 'Did you manage to get the broadband sorted out?'

'I did. Pevensey House will be fully connected by the time we move in.'

'Thanks, love.' He's too tired to tick anything else off his mental list, but this is important.

'And I've got someone lined up to give us a quote for the work that needs doing in the studio. Even better is that he has a free couple of weeks so, if everything works out, he can get things underway almost immediately.'

Drew grins. 'Studio,' he says, blue eyes twinkling. 'I like the sound of that.'

I like the sound of it too. Of course, it isn't a studio yet, it's just an old garden room that adjoins one side of the house, but it will be. A place to begin work on my new commission. It's big; illustrating the books of one of my favourite children's authors, and important too. Getting this right will open all sorts of doors for me and I know Pevensey will be just the place to make this happen.

Drew holds my look for a moment, reflecting my own excitement back at me. And then he is gone, leaving me to finish preparing supper.

It's only just gone ten when we get to bed, the room muggy and barely even dark. I turn down the sheet and climb in beside Drew, the soft light shading the contours of his body.

'Did you ring your mum?' he murmurs, as I lean in to kiss him goodnight.

'No, not yet… I got busy with something else.'

His eyes open a fraction. 'Thea…'

'I'll do it tomorrow, promise. There's plenty of time.'

He nods, his eyes locking with mine and, despite the heat and our tiredness, there is a moment when I think that we're not going to leave it there. And then Drew lifts a hand to the side of my face.

'I don't think I can, sorry…'

But I don't mind because, as I turn, his hand snakes over my hip to rest in the dip of my waist as it always does, and his foot slides against mine. I am home with the man I love, and who loves me.

Minutes later we're both asleep.

CHAPTER TWO

Pevensey House is showing its age a little, but it's still beautiful. Built during the Victorian era, it spent a good portion of its life as the village rectory but has long since relinquished that role to the much smaller, more modern – and inevitably cheaper to run – vicarage at the other end of the village. I'd no idea as a child, and still don't, how long ago Pevensey became a family home, but I'm not really interested in its history today, just how it makes me feel.

There's a whole kaleidoscope of butterflies in my stomach as we navigate the narrow lane beside the church. We'd only made one quick visit to the house before we bought it. A little foolish perhaps, but it really hadn't seemed necessary given that I could still remember every inch of it. In fact, I think we'd only gone in the first place to check that the estate agents weren't lying about its condition after all these years. Not surprisingly, I'd taken nothing in on that occasion. I'd been far too excited and overawed to be back and I'd let my memory be my guide. Today, I'm terrified that my eleven-year-old eyes have lent my thirty-four-year old ones an impression of the house that bears no resemblance to reality. But I needn't have worried, it is just as I remember.

The lane widens just beyond the church, sweeping around the rear boundary of the graveyard to the left, and the beech hedges and horse chestnut trees that border Pevensey's gardens on the right. At the top of the lane lies Rose Cottage where Drew and his parents used to live. Someone has painted the outside a pretty shade of pale pink since his time there, but everything else about the setting is achingly familiar, right down to the row of hollyhocks that peep over one side of our five-bar gate.

Drew brings the car to a standstill just in front of it and we tumble out, stretching and happy to be freed from the confines of the hot vehicle. A breeze lifts a line of dust from the road, scattering leaves as it goes, and the dappled light from the trees overhead paints the lane with moving shadows. But other than that, all is still. There are no other cars and no people, birdsong the only noise. I can feel the tension sliding from me with every breath.

Drew opens the gate and I get to look properly at the house that was home for the first eleven years of my life. It sits at the rear of a gravelled forecourt, warm mellow stone softened even further by a Virginia creeper that will need a very good prune come the spring. There is a wide porch, with two windows to the right – the dining room – and three to the left – the study and the bigger of the two sitting rooms. The roof is slate with a chimney at either end. Away to our left is a timber car port with a shed attached and, to the right, gardens as far as I can see. My breath catches in my throat.

With an excited cry, Chloe streaks away from me, heading for the open space that must seem even more enormous from her child's perspective. Compared with our tiny garden back in London this is a paradise and the thought of what we've given our girls blossoms inside of me. I wait while she runs a wide circle on the grass before returning to us, panting slightly, and gazing wide-eyed at the house.

'Right then. Who wants to look inside?' I ask.

We sprint for the door as if the driveway has suddenly become a mass of boiling lava and fidget impatiently while Drew tries to find the right key.

'Daddy, come on…' whines Chloe. 'I want to see my bedroom.'

I look down at Lauren. 'And how about you, sweetheart?' I say. 'What do you think?' Up until now she's hardly said a word.

'Will Scampers be all right?' she asks. 'Do you think he'll like it here too?'

'I think Scampers is going to love it,' I reply. What self-respecting rabbit wouldn't?

Her face lights up. 'Then I definitely want to see my bedroom.'

Drew pushes open the door and stands back while our two excited whirlwinds make a mad dash for the stairs.

'And how about you, Madam?' he asks me, a glint in his eye. 'Are you wanting to see the bedroom too?'

I feel a surge of warmth at his suggestion, the familiar pull of desire that could so easily consume me, but instead, I skip out of his way.

'Plenty of time for all that, Sir. Come on, I want to see the studio.'

But even as I say it, I know I can't go there yet – the house has just pulled me in and I'm enveloped in memories. In front of me is the same wide black-and-white tiled hallway that I remember from all those years ago. In fact... I cross to its threshold with the dining room, looking down as I do so. 'I don't believe it, Drew, look...'

The tiles are a little grubby but, given their age, still in excellent condition – all except for one. It's tucked in the corner by the skirting, and is cracked clean in half. I hear my father's voice in my ear, telling me a story I'd heard so many times and yet would willingly hear two hundred times more. Right on this spot is where Mum's waters broke when she was carrying me. She'd been about to serve dinner, carrying a thick casserole dish full of beef stew, which hit the tile with an explosive noise that brought my dad running. There had been gravy, carrots and chunks of potato everywhere, so he'd said, but I can't believe the broken tile is still here, untouched, marking the very first day I entered the world. There are tears in my eyes before I even have time to draw another breath.

Drew pulls me close and we stand for a moment letting our memories wrap around us. It feels like the very first time he put his arm around me, when we were ten, and he'd come inside to find me crying because I'd dropped the baton during the relay race at Sports Day and my team had lost as a result. He'd hugged me and told me that, even if I had butterfingers, I was still the prettiest girl there. I think that might even have been the very day I decided I was going to marry him.

He slides his fingers into mine. 'Come on,' he whispers. 'Let's see what else we can find.'

Footsteps thunder above our heads but the girls can't come to any harm and so we leave them to explore. We cross the hallway to poke our noses into the study and then the sitting room, which is tired and dated but looks out onto the garden from two huge bay windows. Just beyond it is the old conservatory, butting up against the side of the kitchen which runs along the back of the house. Once another door has been knocked through at the far end it will open into both rooms, making it a perfect studio with plenty of space for us both. It makes my fingers itch just looking at it.

Drew goes to stand inside, gazing out into the garden, and I leave him for a moment, retracing my steps through the living room to inspect the kitchen. The front door is still open, the double-height hallway turned golden by the afternoon sun, which gilds the mahogany panelling and staircase. Lazy dust motes float on a beam of light and I watch them for a moment before a faint clicking noise draws my attention. A tentative nose pokes around the doorway as the most beautiful Dalmatian slinks inside, his claws tapping on the tiles. Almost immediately a whistle sounds from outside and the dog is gone, its feet skittering on the fore-court's gravel. It's out of sight by the time I reach the door, but our encounter leaves me with a smile on my face. I haven't discussed it with Drew just yet – one thing at a time – but, now that we've moved, I would love to have a dog.

I think it's fair to say that the kitchen hasn't fared as well as the rest of the house. When I was a child it was a big, warm and friendly room, with a huge Rayburn, a stone butler's sink and an assortment of wooden cupboards. It had suited the room and the style of the house, and its unfitted appearance is quite sought after today. However, at some point it has been replaced with an oak monstrosity which is dark, heavily carved and now stained and sticky with grease. There is still a Rayburn but, unlike the lovely cream-coloured one we had, it's a dreary and sombre green. But, it's all fixable and remains a huge space which, once it's had its veil of gloom lifted, will be warm and cheery once again.

'Oh…' Drew's voice comes from the doorway. 'I don't remember it being this bad…'

I'm determined to look on the bright side. 'No, it needs gutting, doesn't it? But if we're going to rip a hole in that wall anyway, what does it matter?'

'No, I guess it doesn't. But you're going to have to live with it like this for a little while… until we can get a bit sorted.'

I know what he means of course. The studio has to be a priority – without it there can be no work, and with no work there will be no money coming in, and no new kitchen.

'Drew… have you seen the size of this room? I don't really care what it looks like right now because at some point in the future I will be able to cartwheel down the centre of it if I choose. Of course I can live with it,' I add, grinning. 'Muppet…'

'Just checking,' he says lightly.

I cross the room to give him a hug. 'This is absolutely, one hundred percent the right thing for us to be doing,' I say. 'Don't you dare doubt yourself.'

And then he gives me that look, the one that still makes me go weak at the knees. He doesn't say anything, but then he doesn't need to. We've always supported one another – he took the strain financially when I was just starting out and looking for freelance work, and he knows I'll do the same for him now, if necessary. I glance at my watch.

'The builder chap should be here soon. Let's go and suss out plug sockets.'

'I love it when you talk dirty...'

*

Derek is an absolute godsend. In his mid-fifties, wearing a no-nonsense white polo-shirt and a pair of black utility trousers that have so many pockets I'd be surprised if he can ever remember where he's put anything. But the fact that most of his work is undertaken in the area speaks volumes. If the locals are happy to keep him in business then so will we be.

We're standing in the conservatory and he immediately crosses to the windows to stare out into the garden. 'Crikey, it must be ten years or more since I did any work here, but I've always liked this place.' He flips open a page in the notebook he's brought with him. 'So don't you go believing any of the stories you might hear.' He looks around. 'Anyway, what's the thinking here then?' he continues. 'You're planning on using this as an office, I gather.'

Drew slides a look at me as I frown, but anything either one of us might want to say is immediately lost in Derek's series of rapid-fire questions. He removes a pencil from his top pocket and starts sketching.

'So, the kitchen's that way isn't it, if I remember right?' he asks, waiting for the answering nod. He pauses for a moment. 'If it were me, I'd put a door through there,' he says. 'You won't want to be going all the way around just to get a cup of tea, will you?'

I smile at Drew. 'That's what we were thinking, yes.'

The pencil scratches across the page. 'And both of you will be in here... Only I'm wondering about sockets, you see... You'll need more if you have separate desks, but if it were me...'

I stand in the centre of the floor. 'We had wondered whether we could have a work bench right down the middle of the room,' I explain. 'That way we could have cupboards along the rear wall and we'd be facing out into the garden. The light is what's important.'

Derek peers at the tiled squares beneath his feet. 'And are you wedded to these?'

I hadn't really thought.

Drew shrugs. 'Thea?'

'I don't know, maybe carpet will be nicer.'

'Warmer certainly,' answers Derek. 'If it were me,' he begins again. 'I would have your bench down the middle, facing the garden like you said. Run the cables under the floor and have a bank of sockets at either end of the bench. A small radiator at either end of the room, and your cupboards and whatnot along there. It will add to the price but I'd think about a motorised blind system, too, for the sunnier days – you'll struggle with the light in here otherwise.'

He looks up, frowning for a moment. 'Folks don't always realise, but you can have too much light in a place, especially if you're working using screens and such like. Plus, you'll boil in here otherwise. Have a run of them, across the ceiling and down each window in separate strips. That way you can have each strip set differently according to how you like it and, as the light moves, you move the blinds.'

I hadn't even thought of that, but Derek is obviously convinced.

'Sounds good,' says Drew. 'We're going to be in here a lot, we need it to be comfortable.'

'Right then.' Derek's pencil stills. 'Leave it with me, I'll get a few quotes to you by Tuesday afternoon if that suits. I know you want things underway as soon as possible.'

Drew is working incredibly hard to keep from laughing. Not because it's funny but because he's as amazed as I am. Nothing was ever this easy in London.

'That would be absolutely perfect. We do need to get everything sorted as quickly as we can… Buying this place all happened a bit out of the blue and we haven't had much time to think, or plan.'

Derek nods and replaces the pencil in his pocket. 'Well, it's still a lovely house, I'm sure you'll be very happy here.'

I grin at Drew. 'I always was…' I reply.

Derek gives me a quizzical look.

'I grew up here,' I say. 'So did Drew actually. We lived next door to one another. He was at Rose Cottage… just down the lane.'

He looks us up and down. 'Well, I'll be damned. Drew Gordon…!' He taps his finger against his notepad. 'And Thea! – Bradley, you would have been back then, wouldn't you? Blimey, everyone knew your folks. I even did a bit of work for them when I first came to the village. Hadn't long started my own business and grateful for anything.' He narrows his eyes. 'It was only a couple of extra sockets in the kitchen… and an extension into the pantry for your mum's chest freezer… but then of course your dad got me the job doing the renovations up at the village hall. It properly put me on the map, I can tell you. So it wasn't just the village that was grateful for everything your dad did for them, but me as well. The work just flooded in after that and I've never looked back. In fact, I'm probably still in business thanks to him. How's that for a story?'

'I'm impressed,' replies Drew.

'Aye, those were good times before…' Derek breaks off to peer at me, eyes weighing something up. 'And so you two got married, had kiddies of your own and now you've come back here…' But whatever he was going to add remains unsaid. 'Right, well the very best of luck with everything, and, like I said, give me a day or two and I'll let you know how I'm fixed.'

Two minutes later he's gone, and we're left staring at each other, speechless.

'Well, how lovely was that? Meeting someone who knew our parents on the day we move in. What are the chances…?'

Drew gives me a wayward glance. 'All I'm really concerned about is whether he does a good job and so I'm happy to find out he's been in business a long time. He must be well respected.'

It isn't what Drew wants to say at all but it's just like him not to draw attention to anything negative.

'It was an odd comment he made about the house though, don't you think? About not believing any stories we hear.'

'Not really. I imagine we've probably picked up a ghost or two through the years. It's a big old house, I guess it's almost mandatory.' He grins suddenly. 'My money's on a pale grey lady…'

I slap his arm playfully. 'Stop it,' I say, wriggling my shoulders as a sudden shiver ripples through me. 'You heard what Derek said, he thinks the house has a lovely feel to it. Anyway, *we* already know that.'

'Of course we do,' he replies, plonking a kiss on my nose. 'I'm just teasing.'

'Plus, Derek is going to get our studio sorted out for us in record time. If it were me… I'd say we just struck lucky…'

Drew is just about to reply when a piercing scream echoes down the hallway.

CHAPTER THREE

Drew gets there first, clearly imagining, as I am, a scene of devastation or at the very least bloodshed.

Instead, facing each other across the hallway are Chloe and the same Dalmatian I'd seen earlier, come back for a repeat inspection. Chloe is three steps from the bottom of the stairs and the dog is a foot from the front doorway, its whole body waggling in nervous excitement, not in the least bit put off by Chloe's dramatics. Lauren, I notice, is peering shyly through the banister from the galleried landing above.

Seconds later, a harassed-looking woman appears and makes a lunge for the errant canine.

'I'm so sorry,' she blurts out. 'I don't know what it is about this house, but he's been trying to get in here for days.' And then she stops dead. 'Oh… You must be the new people.' She has a hand on the dog's collar and straightens up. 'I'm the incredibly embarrassed woman from next door… Erm… Anna… Grainger.' She pauses to smile up at Chloe who is now staring, transfixed. 'And this, very friendly, but rather naughty dog, is Fergus. I'm sorry if he scared you, I promise he didn't mean to.'

Drew takes Chloe's hand and leads her from the stairs. 'Come and say hello, Chloe. I think poor Fergus is probably a bit frightened too. I don't suppose he's used to little girls screaming at him.' He mouths the word 'sorry' at the woman, as he leads Chloe forward, bending down to fuss the dog.

'Hi, Anna,' he says easily. 'I'm Drew. This is my wife, Thea, and this is Chloe…' He turns and beckons. 'And her little sister, Lauren.' He drops to his haunches. 'Oh, you're beautiful, aren't you?' he adds to the dog, as Fergus quivers in ecstasy.

I wave at Lauren and wait for her to come down the stairs, smiling at the woman as I do so. 'The girls don't really mind dogs at all, so please don't worry. It's lovely to meet you.'

The woman is about my height, and age too, I reckon, with thick sandy-coloured hair tied up in a loose ponytail, half of which has come loose. It trails around her shoulders in wisps. Her face is a little pink, but she's not wearing any make-up and I get the feeling that she rarely does. She wouldn't need to, she's incredibly pretty, with huge almond-shaped grey-green eyes – but there's not a trace of artifice about her. I know instantly that I'm going to like her.

'I can't tell you how much I've been looking forward to having proper neighbours,' I add.

She gives me a quizzical look.

'I mean, we had neighbours before,' I explain. 'Just, it's different in London; people keep to themselves and I used to say hello to our neighbours on the one side, but the people on the other…'

Anna laughs, smiling down at the dog who is trying to lick Lauren's face. 'Oh well, you'd best be prepared for village life then. Everyone knows everyone and, if you've got dogs, or children, that process takes all of about ten minutes. Actually I think someone mentioned to me that you had girls…' She pauses. 'I can't think who it was now, but I was rather relieved when I heard. The couple here before you were lovely, but older…' She grins. 'Much, much older… and not a fan of Fergus…'

She pulls a face and then looks down at Lauren. 'I've got a little girl about the same age as you. Her name's Tilly. Would you both like to come and meet her? She's just at home with her dad – that's my husband, Rob.'

I exchange a look with Drew, not sure what to say. I don't even know Anna, not yet, and I'm sure she is lovely but... She interrupts my thoughts.

'Oh God, sorry! Listen to me. I have a terrible habit of not thinking before I open my mouth. You'd really think I'd know better, especially where children are concerned, given what—' She stops suddenly. 'Never mind... Besides, you'll be far too busy to visit today, won't you? But, I'd love for you girls to meet Tilly. All I've heard since she finished school for the summer is "Mummy, Mummy, when will the new people be here?" She's desperate for some new playmates.'

She checks her watch. 'If you have time, maybe you could all pop over later? I expect you've brought stuff with you, but I can at least ply you with tea and cake.' She turns to look back through the front door. 'Oh, I do hope your removal van hasn't got lost?'

'No, don't worry, it won't be here for a little while yet. The lads were going to stop off for lunch first so that they could work through once they get here.'

But I'm still not sure. The girls' eyes lit up at the mention of cake, but it seems a little too soon; I'm not sure if I'm comfortable with things moving this fast. Plus, given that Drew used to live in their house, isn't that just a little... weird?

'Actually, we're at a bit of a loose end now until our worldly goods get here. So we'd love to come if that's still okay,' says Drew, giving me that look. The one that says, 'You know I'm right, when have I ever let you down?' And so I smile and nod happily, because he will be right. He always is.

'And as long as you're sure you have the time?' I counter, just to be polite.

Anna nods. 'I've just finished putting up the parish notices so that's my chores done for the day.'

'Then that settles it,' says Drew, fishing in his pocket for the house keys. 'Shall we follow you over?'

I fall into step with Anna as she heads out across the gravel forecourt, while Chloe and Lauren dance about with Fergus somewhere in between us and Drew, who lags behind, locking up.

'Have you lived here long?' I ask, as we walk.

'Not really. Five years,' replies Anna. 'So only another forty to go until we're considered local.' She grins. 'Actually, no one's really like that here, thank God, I can't be doing with all that. In fact, it's one of the reasons we moved this way. I'm from Kent originally and by the time Tilly was two I'd got so fed up at how competitive everything was, I thought I was going to go mad. There was a three-year waiting list for the nursery I wanted her to go to, and don't get me started on primary schooling. I'd have had to put her name down several years before she was even born and well…' She breaks off, pursing her lips for a moment. 'Don't judge me, but Tilly wasn't planned.'

I look at her in surprise. 'Why would I judge you? That's hardly a crime…'

Anna doesn't answer straight away. 'Well, anyway, we decided that we'd prefer Tilly was allowed to be a child, rather than a commodity, so we moved up here. She went to the village playgroup when she was three and then to the primary school up the road, which she loves.' She stops for a few seconds as we pass through her gate. 'Best decision we ever made coming here. Will your two be going to the local school?'

'Definitely.' I smile. 'We were lucky where we lived in London. Purely by chance, because it had never occurred to us otherwise, we ended up living in the catchment area for a great school, but I know of parents who did all sorts of things to get enrolled there. And the school itself was jammed between buildings, had virtually no outdoor space, and was a fifteen-minute walk away through roads gridlocked with traffic. Believe me, the village school is a thing of my dreams.'

I've been so busy talking that I've just carried on down Anna's driveway without thinking and I stop suddenly. I've walked up here so many times in the past, but Anna must think me very rude. I'm about to apologise and explain when she turns and looks back at Chloe and Lauren.

'I'm just wondering what class your two will be in. Tilly's eight.'

'Yes, Lauren's eight too, only just. Chloe's nine, so classes two and three, the secretary said. A Mrs Hollingsworth and Miss Butler, I think?'

Anna nods. 'Yes, that's right. There are only four classes – it varies, but at the moment it's Reception and Year One, Years Two and Three with Mrs Hollingsworth, Three and Four with Miss Butler, and then Year Six with Mrs Speed.'

I try to commit the information to memory. 'We didn't get a chance to look around the school before we bought the house, but I'm sure they'll love it. I have such happy memories myself, so I hope it hasn't changed too much.' I grin at Anna's astonished expression. 'I grew up here,' I explain, loving the way it feels to say this. 'In fact, so did Drew.' I point back towards Pevensey. 'That's where I lived, and Drew lived next door…'

She nods, a round 'O' of surprise on her lips, and I wait for the information to catch up with her. 'But…' She turns to look at Drew. 'Oh…' And then she bursts out laughing. 'That's amazing and very weird! I dread to think what hideous architectural crimes have been perpetrated at Rose Cottage; it's been pulled about a bit over the years.'

'Well, it wasn't pink for starters,' answers Drew, catching up with us. He appraises the building, a broad smile on his face. 'But the rest looks as I remember it, from the outside at least.'

Anna whistles for Fergus and leads us to the back door. 'Then you'd better come on through and get reacquainted,' she says, laughing. 'And I'll go and see where everyone has got to.'

It's even more bizarre standing in the hallway of Rose Cottage than it was at Pevensey and I'm conscious of how Drew must be feeling too. At first glance not a lot seems to have changed over the years, apart from the decoration of course, but, as he looks around, he studiously avoids my eye. Anna is gone only a matter of seconds, however, before she returns with a tall, athletic-looking man and a mini version of herself trailing at her side.

'Girls, this is Tilly…'

On cue, Tilly steps forward. 'Would you like to come and play? We can go outside if you like.'

Lauren looks up at me, a query on her face, and then back down at Fergus who clearly knows when he's on to a good thing. 'Can the dog come too?'

'Of course,' answers Anna, seeing my nod. 'Tilly, why don't you show them the Wendy house. I'll bring you out some drinks in a bit.'

They don't need a second invitation and, with a flurry of scampering legs, all four of them barrel through the door. There's a sudden increase in space in the hallway and an awkward pause for a second before Anna's husband holds out his hand.

'Well, that's them sorted,' he says, smiling, relief showing on his face. 'I'm Rob, it's good to meet you.'

Rob must be at least six-foot-two and, like Drew, is wearing the regulation uniform of men in their mid-thirties: jeans, tee shirt and shirt worn loose over the top. But even the relaxed cut of his clothes can't hide the tautness of the muscles beneath them, and I can feel the two men sizing each other up, subconsciously or not. Rob has a wide, friendly face, however, with smiley eyes and longer than average dark hair, already threaded through with grey at his temples.

'It's good to meet you too,' says Drew, shaking his hand and waiting while I do the same. 'And we were hoping to find children on our doorstep, so it couldn't be better.'

'Lauren is the same age as Tilly,' explains Anna. 'And her sister, that's Chloe, is a year older.'

Rob nods approvingly. 'Tilly will be made up to have some new playmates.'

There is an unspoken question in the air but we avoid it for now and instead smile at one another.

'Well, let's not stand on ceremony,' says Anna quickly. 'Come into the kitchen and I'll put the kettle on. I promised you cake as well – don't worry, I haven't forgotten.' She flaps her hand at Rob. 'You'll never believe this, but Drew used to live here, when he was a child. In this very house. And Thea used to live at Pevensey… So you grew up together and now you're married…' She gazes around her kitchen. 'Come on then, how does it feel to be back?'

'Weird…'

'Amazing…'

I answer the same time as Drew, my eyebrows meeting at his reply, which is so different from mine. But Anna laughs and, just like that, the conversation begins to flow. There's something very down to earth about both Anna and Rob and their house is as unpretentious as they are.

'Of course, I'm being incredibly nosey,' starts Anna. 'But I thought I saw Derek Hardcastle's van outside yours a little while ago. Are you having some work done?' She brings a big pot of coffee to the table which sits in the centre of their kitchen.

'We're hoping to,' I reply. 'What's he like?'

'Not the cheapest,' replies Rob, picking up the question. 'But he does a good job, and he does it quickly and when he says he's going to, which is why he's rarely out of work. It's too small a community to mess people around.'

'Yes, we hoped that might be the case. He certainly seemed to be on the ball. We're both going to be working from home and the old conservatory on the side of the house will be just perfect for us once it's converted. The sooner the work's done the better.'

Rob is nodding. 'It can be tricky combining work alongside home life, can't it? But that sounds ideal.' He leans forward as if to speak confidentially. 'I probably shouldn't even admit to this, but I'm rather envious; Pevensey is such a beautiful house. My own office is tiny, too small really, and I sometimes wonder if we wouldn't be better off living in the vicarage. But it's such a soulless house, if you'll forgive the pun.'

'The vicarage?' I look up in surprise, noting that Drew has done the same.

'Oh…' Anna looks at her husband, a little confused. 'Didn't I say? Rob's the local curate.'

Rob's eyes dance with amusement. 'At least have a piece of cake before you run off,' he says, grinning. 'It's the most brilliant conversation-stopper I know, guaranteed to put the fear of God into people, literally…!'

I cover my mouth with a hand, embarrassed at the look of horror that has undoubtedly crossed my face. 'Sorry… it's just that you don't look like… I mean…'

'I'm glad to hear it,' replies Rob. 'And I shall take it as a compliment. I'm not sure what the look is for a stereotypical curate, but I suspect it's not good.' He takes a sip of his coffee. 'But, whatever your views on the church, I can guarantee that, unless it's a subject you wish to talk about, it will remain off the list of conversational topics. Neither will you be coerced to come to the Sunday service.' He grins at us. 'So, now we've got that one out of the way. What is it that you both do?'

Drew is first to answer. 'I'm an architect,' he says. 'And have just given up my safe and comfortable job in London to start up my own business, moving halfway across the country first – just to add a little extra frisson of terror into the mix.'

'Which is obviously going to go extraordinarily well,' I add, poking Drew in the arm. I catch Anna's eye and smile.

'What sort of work are you hoping to do?' asks Rob. 'Because if it's small-scale stuff, you could do worse than have a chat to

Derek actually. He knows absolutely everyone and is as straight as they come. I'm sure he'd be happy to spread the word for you.'

'Well, the plan is to concentrate on designing and selling modular homes. I've been working with several overseas charities the last couple of years supporting low-cost housing initiatives, but now it's time to take my ideas even further. It's a pretty radical concept as far as building construction goes and could revolutionise the industry if I get it right. No one else is really working in this area either so it has the potential to be the tip of what I hope turns out to be a very large iceberg. Still, thanks for the tip-off. At the end of the day I need money coming in, and, if it's wall-to-wall extensions and barn conversions that pay the bills, so be it.'

'Well, good luck,' says Anna. 'That sounds fascinating.'

'I might come and pick your brains actually,' adds Rob. 'When you're a bit more settled. There are a few projects I've become involved in where that could be of interest.'

Drew nods. He's had no end of conversations with people who say similar things and nothing comes of it. But who knows, something has to stick some time.

Anna busies herself with an enormous Victoria sponge and waves a cake knife at it. 'First rule of village life,' she says. 'If you don't already know, learn how to make one of these.'

I laugh. 'I shall remember that,' I reply. 'Although I confess my baking skills are a bit rusty. Not an excuse, but I never seem to find the time.'

Anna expertly deposits a slice of cake onto a plate and passes it to me. 'So apart from looking after two lively children, a husband and a huge house, what is it that you do, Thea?'

We are so going to get on. 'I'm an illustrator,' I say. 'Children's books mostly.'

'I'd love the chance to be creative like that,' says Anna. 'But I work part-time as a piano teacher, mainly for the council's local music service. It's really not as much fun as it sounds and, incongruously, not creative at all. But it's not all bad. It's a term-time-only job so I'm on holiday now!' And a heartfelt sigh floats across the table. 'Would your girls like some cake too? And a glass of squash, or milk? Water if you prefer.'

I smile back happily. 'The girls would love some cake, Anna, thank you. But only a small slice; Chloe's very excited and can be quite spectacularly sick if she has too much sweet stuff.'

I help her carry the things outside to where the children are playing happily inside a large two-storey playhouse. It connects to a turreted fort-style climbing frame that sits alongside it by means of a curvy crawl tube from the upper story of the house. A slide and two swings complete the ensemble.

'Oh my God, that's brilliant!' I exclaim, without thinking. Our small garden back in London simply wasn't large enough for anything like this and another set of possibilities opens out in front of me.

Anna smiles. 'It might seem a bit much for an only child, but it's good for Tilly, you know…' She comes to a halt, the slight reticence from earlier returning.

I'm not quite sure what to say, but Anna and Rob's welcome couldn't have been more perfect and I'm hoping they're going to be our neighbours for a long time to come. I decide to bite the bullet. Anna doesn't strike me as the sort to mind, and it's probably a discussion we should have sooner rather than later, otherwise I fear it might never happen at all.

'I can imagine,' I reply. 'Was Tilly born with just one arm?'

Anna is watching the girls' antics and she turns to me, a grateful smile on her face. 'She was. It's a hereditary defect.' She pauses for a moment. 'That's what I meant when I said earlier that Tilly wasn't planned. We weren't going to have any children, you see, but then I fell pregnant and…'

I nod and smile. 'She's beautiful,' I say. And there's no need to say any more.

Fergus is first to notice the arrival of the cake and gives a slight woof which brings Tilly running, Chloe and Lauren following close behind. My girls are rosy-cheeked and slightly out of puff, but look so happy my heart swells.

Lauren approaches shyly to take a drink from the tray that Anna is holding. It's blackcurrant squash and she prefers orange, but she takes it without question, saying a polite 'Thank you.' The drink disappears in seconds and she replaces the glass and comes to me to claim her cake.

'You look like you're having huge fun,' I comment.

Lauren just beams and nods her head. 'We've been climbing,' she says. 'And running, a lot.' She drops her head a little, looking up at me. 'Mummy, Tilly only has one arm.'

'Yes, I know, sweetheart.'

'But she's ever so good at climbing.'

I nod. 'Has she been teaching you?'

Lauren takes a bite of her cake, nodding. 'A little bit. I got my leg stuck going backwards in the tube but Tilly came and helped me. And I've been telling her about Scampers too. Can she come and help me with him?'

'As long as it's all right with her mummy, yes, of course she can.'

Lauren weighs up my response. 'I think it's going to be much better for Tilly with us living next door,' she says. 'Because I don't think she needs any help but, just in case she does, then Chloe and me will be here, won't we?'

I feel a surge of pride at her words. 'Yes, you will,' I say. And I'm suddenly reminded of the photo I held only a week or so ago, of my younger self playing in this garden, muddy, and happy, just like a child should be. I'm so happy we're all here.

CHAPTER FOUR

Derek drinks an awful lot of tea. In all other respects he is the perfect builder: methodical, efficient, hardworking and clearly skilled in his work. But he is also a serial downer of mug after mug of weak-as-dishwater tea, and I'm getting through milk like there's no tomorrow. Which is where the village shop comes in so handy.

It's doubled in size since I was a child, by way of a small extension at the back, and this extra space means the shop now sells a range of local gourmet produce alongside the usual array of necessities. As Derek is particularly partial to cake, I'm now lingering over these exorbitantly priced items far longer than I should be. Anna's right, I really do need to find the time to make my own. My eyes drift to a shelf of baking materials – perhaps I should start as I mean to go on – but almost immediately I discount the idea. I've got far too much to do.

It's as I'm standing, deep in thought, that the weirdest feeling comes over me. As if time has somehow wound itself back to the years of my childhood. The impression is so sharp that if I were to reach out my hand, I swear I'd feel my mother's solid presence beside me. And I'd touch her arm, for reassurance, just like I used to. I look up, startled and confused by what could be making me feel this way. And the instant that I do so, I realise that every sound in the shop has fallen away; the hum from the chest freezer that stores ice creams, the sound of voices from over by the till, the shuffling footsteps, all gone. It's their absence I'm feeling now, and it feels disconcertingly like an echo of my past.

But the next second everything restarts, picking up where it left off. As I snatch a cake from the shelf, heedless of its flavour or cost, and scoop up milk and an extra packet of biscuits, my movement further breaks the mood and I make my way quickly to the till.

'Morning!' The greeting from the woman behind the counter is bright, the face in front of me smiling. Another, to its left, wears a slightly more cautious welcome. Both women are about my age.

'How are you getting on?' asks the first. 'Settling in okay?'

And then I realise. These women know far more about me than I do about them. I push down my vague sense of panic and brighten my own expression.

'Morning,' I reply, laying my purchases down on the counter. 'Never seem to have enough milk, but otherwise, yes it's all been lovely. Still not found a home for everything of course, but we're getting there.'

The smiles continue. 'Well, welcome to the village. I'm Jackie and this is Stacey.'

I nod, noticing that Stacey is empty-handed and doesn't appear to be buying anything. 'Thanks, I'm Thea.'

There's acknowledgement but I'm not telling them anything they don't already know.

'Yeah, Anna said you've moved in next door to them.'

'Yes, although funnily enough—'

'Is it right you used to live there before?' asks Stacey. 'Only…' Her mouth closes abruptly as if she's changed her mind about what to say.

'Yes, that's right, when I was a child. It's so lovely to be back.' I look from one woman to the other, searching their faces for any features I recognise. 'Were either of you…?'

'I've lived here my whole life,' replies Stacey, eyes narrowing. 'I don't recognise you though…'

I smile, far more brightly than I'm feeling. 'I got old, I expect. Sorry, I don't remember you either…' The woman has bleached blonde hair, it's almost impossible to tell what colour it would have been originally.

'No, well you can't remember everyone, can you?' And she clearly isn't going to tell me any more.

I fish for my purse. 'I'd better get back,' I say. 'I've got a builder doing a few alterations for us and it's at least ten minutes since he had his last cup of tea, he'll be desperate for another.'

I roll my eyes, but I'm met with what my mother would call surface-only smiles and Anna's comment about what it takes to be considered local flashes through my mind. I've clearly got a way to go yet.

Jackie rings my items through the till and two minutes later I'm back out into air that feels wonderfully fresh after the claustrophobic atmosphere of the shop. I stand for a moment, staring down the road I must have walked hundreds of times in my life. But it seems different somehow, as if my perception filters have been reset. I had the oddest feeling of déjà vu just now but, as I look at the straggly line of houses, the trees, the church and school in front of me, I realise that I'm suddenly looking at them with my own eyes, and not those of my younger self, the one wearing the rose-tinted glasses. However, the view in front of me is still pretty, it's still a glorious summer day. Maybe I'm just finally beginning to understand that I'm here in my own right, a thirty-four-year-old wife and mother, not a primary-school child. I give an involuntary shiver and start walking. It's different now, that's all; which is a good thing, I remind myself.

I've just passed the school when the door of a cottage to my right opens and I ready a smile to greet whoever emerges.

'Thea, hi!' Anna gives a little wave from the threshold, motioning that I should wait for her, before turning back to the person behind her in the doorway. 'Thanks, Mary, Rob will be so happy

to hear that you're going to do the flowers for us again this year.'
She takes a step forward into the front garden and is followed out
by a much older woman. She's very tall and thin and, even with
the barest of glances, there's something about her that I recognise.
I'm still trying to figure out what when her voice booms out from
behind Anna.

'Thea Bradley, well how about that.'

If her use of my maiden name didn't clue me in on her identity
then the way my body stands to attention certainly does. I've heard
her say my name in that manner far too many times for comfort.

Anna does a double take as the woman moves past her, arms
outstretched to greet me.

'Mrs Williams?'

Her laugh is loud and rich with warmth. 'Mary,' she tuts. 'I
haven't been Mrs Williams for a very long time, not to you anyway.
Come here and give me a hug.'

I meet her halfway up the path, where she crushes me against
her with surprising strength, and total disregard for the shopping
I'm carrying.

'I'd heard you were back at Pevensey,' she says, scrutinising me.
'And Drew, too. You always were inseparable.'

Behind us, Anna laughs. 'Of course! Mary must have been
head teacher when you were at school here.'

I disentangle myself. 'She was. And, as you can see, I still jump
a foot in the air when she says my name like that. However did
you know we'd moved?' I ask.

'From your mother of course…' Mary replies. 'Who, I believe,
is still waiting for a phone call.' Her raised eyebrows speak volumes.

I stare at her, astonished. 'I will ring her, I promise. It's just
that what with one thing and another it's been incredibly busy.'

I'm trying to avoid Mary's stare, but it's impossible. She might
be an elderly woman now, but she still has mastery of the steely
gaze that was so effective in my youth. 'Which I'm sure she

appreciates. But you know, Thea, nothing will ever get better if you keep skirting around the issue…' Her face softens. 'But I was so incredibly sorry to hear about your father's death. It must have come as a horrible shock for you.'

I manage a nod, just.

Mary clears her throat as if she, like me, has just become aware of Anna's presence. 'So your lovely neighbour and I have just been talking about the flowers for the Harvest Festival service,' she says. 'Which I shall have the honour of attending to again this year, even if I can't make the service itself.' She beams proudly. 'I shall be in Devon for my granddaughter's christening, but I shall make sure the church looks beautiful before I go.'

Anna smiles. 'And now all I need to do is find a few more volunteers to help with the supper.'

'My God, is that still going?' I reply. 'It used to be such fun. Every year, without fail…'

Mary Williams beams. 'I'm happy to say it is. And in no doubt partly down to your father of course.' She turns to Anna. 'You might not be aware of this, dear, but it was Thea's dad who rescued our village hall from demolition, and saved the allotments behind it too. I dread to think what would have happened to the village if the developers had their way, but they didn't and, thanks to his efforts, the village not only raised the funds for the hall's repair but put into place a proper committee to look after it, which they've been doing ever since. The Harvest Festival Supper is still one of our biggest fundraisers.'

'Do you know, I'd practically forgotten that,' I reply. 'Probably didn't take much notice, I expect, too busy being a child.'

'Well now that you're back with us, perhaps you could follow in the family tradition and lend a hand?'

I look helplessly at Anna, wondering what exactly I'll be letting myself in for. 'We need a few more volunteers to help run things this year,' she explains. 'And you'd be brilliant, because you already know how things work.'

I pull a face. 'Hardly. I was all of ten years old the last time I went, but…' Mary has that look on her face. The one she always used when I argued that Drew and I weren't talking in class. 'I'm sure I could do something. Just as long as it's not baking cakes; it's not exactly my forte.'

'Done,' says Anna happily. 'I'll sign you up.' She looks back at Mary, grinning. 'Well, that wasn't so hard. Let's hope I can get a few more people on board just as easily. I'll be in touch anyway.' She moves away from me, back down the path.

Mary smiles. 'It's good to have you back, Thea. Your mum and dad did a huge amount for this village in all sorts of ways. I know you wouldn't have been aware of much of it, but they were well thought of, and there are lots of us here who still think that way. Always remember that. Now, I'll let you get on but, once you're a bit more settled, perhaps you could call in for a cup of tea? I'm here any time you feel like a natter about the old days.'

'I will, thank you. And it's so lovely to see you again. I didn't even realise you were still living in the village.'

'Didn't you?' She's watching me again. 'Perhaps you've just forgotten.' And then her face brightens. 'No matter, you know now. Give my best wishes to Drew, won't you?'

I nod, trying to grasp the faint flicker of a memory that fires inside me. 'Of course… well, bye for now.'

Anna has already reached the road and I join her, turning at the last moment to say a final farewell, but Mary is already facing away from me, her back bent to a rose beside the door. As I watch, she snaps off a dying bloom, folding it inside her hand as she retreats back inside.

'Is everything all right?' asks Anna, as I turn back towards her.

'I think so, why?'

'Nothing really, you just looked a bit worried when I first saw you.'

'Did I?' It takes me a minute to think back. Seeing Mary has stirred up a whole host of memories and their faltering pictures in my head are distracting. 'I think it might be because I've just come from the shop and had one of those moments where conversation stops dead around you. At least I think that's what it was; I might be just imagining things.'

I stop to look at her. 'It was weird, a bit like déjà vu… Do you ever get that? When something feels familiar but you can't say why? I was definitely under scrutiny though… and I'm really not sure if I passed the test.'

Anna pulls a face. 'Oh, I think that might be my fault, I'm afraid. I was in the shop earlier and, as the curate's wife, I'm expected to provide information wherever I go. On anything, or anyone. No one ever seems to think that I might not want to. So Jackie obviously quizzed me about you, and she's a bit of a gossip, but mostly harmless. Anyway, I only said nice things about you, I promise.' Anna breaks off to grin at me. 'Don't worry, she's only being nosey because you're new to the village, or rather not new, but you know what I mean. They'll be talking about something else by lunchtime.'

I smile back. 'I expect so, we're really not that exciting… I did meet someone else though. Stacey, I think her name was.' I wait for the answering nod. 'She grew up here too apparently, but I think she was a bit disappointed she didn't remember me. But then I didn't remember her either so…'

'It must be weird,' muses Anna. 'Having everything look the same, but be different. Always wondering who you're going to bump into…'

I look at her, puzzled. How did I not realise that things like this were going to happen? It's as if I imagined that we would just move in and pick up where we left off, like we were in some kind of a vacuum. But I must have thought about it, surely…

'Well, I hadn't expected to bump into my old head teacher, that's for sure. I can't decide whether that's a good thing or a bad thing.'

'I guess that rather depends on how naughty you were as a child.'

I slide Anna a glance. 'That's the problem,' I reply. 'I definitely had my moments.'

She laughs easily. 'Didn't we all? It must be quite nice though; the fact that she's here to reminisce with.' She pauses for a moment. 'I don't mean to pry, and you can tell me to mind my own business, but she obviously thought the world of your mum, and your dad… Did you lose him recently?'

I stare down the lane ahead. 'Three years ago,' I say. 'But sometimes it feels like it was yesterday. Strangely though, since we've been back, all the memories I'm having seem to be of my mum, and yet I wasn't as close to her.'

We're walking side by side and, as I turn to look at her, I realise that she's deliberately keeping her eyes straight ahead too. Giving me space to talk.

'I'm still not. Actually, I had thought that when my dad died things might get better between us, but so far that hasn't been the case. If anything, it's made it worse.'

Anna stops suddenly, turning to look at me square on. 'Maybe that's why you've come back then. Don't they say everything happens for a reason?'

'Hmm, maybe. Although moving here hasn't helped our relationship either.'

'Is that why Mary said you owed your mum a phone call?'

I sigh. 'I should have thought about coming here in the first place, that's the problem. I just got so caught up in the excitement of finding out Pevensey was on the market and getting the move organised that I didn't stop to think how insensitive it would appear. Mum always loved the house, we all did, but for her this place must be absolutely awash with memories of my dad. It's bound to hurt.'

Anna nods. 'So how long did you live here for then?'

'I was born here, well not here, in the local hospital, but we were here until I was eleven. We moved the summer before I went to secondary school.'

'Oh, I see. Is that why, so you could go to a different school?'

I stare at her. 'No, I... Actually, I'm not sure I know why.' I shake my head. 'I think my memory must be playing tricks on me.'

But Anna just shrugs. 'You probably didn't even think about it,' she replies. 'I know what I was like when I was eleven – so caught up in my own little world I hardly noticed what was going on around me.'

I'd like to believe her, but she's wrong. It isn't as simple as that. I'm standing just a few yards from the house I grew up in. A house I adored. It should be teeming with memories from the time we left, but it isn't. The space where those memories should be is just a big, black, empty hole.

*

'Mum?'

'Thea! Darling, it's so lovely to hear from you. How is it all going?'

'Great... bit weird, but oh, you should see the house, Mum, hardly anything seems changed at all and—' I stop suddenly, remembering the purpose of my call. 'Well anyway, we're in, still trying to get a few things straight but the studio is underway, which is the main thing. So we wondered if you might like to come and visit in a few weeks' time. Once we're a bit more settled.' I'm wondering quite how to phrase my next sentence. 'And also when you've had a chance to get used to the idea of us being here a little more... I'm sorry, Mum, I really didn't really think how it would feel for you hearing we were coming back to Pevensey.'

I can sense the intake of breath from the other end of the line. 'Well, it was a huge shock, Thea, I'm not denying it wasn't, but perhaps... well, I didn't handle it quite the way I should have. It's just that I thought you were happy and settled in London – so hearing you'd decided to up sticks and move for no apparent reason seemed odd. But maybe that *was* a rather knee-jerk reaction.'

'But, Mum, it wasn't a complete whim to move here… not entirely. The change gives us so many of the things we wanted, things we've discussed before: more space, peace in which to work, an end to working tyranny for Drew, the kind of environment we want the girls to grow up in. In fact, the list is endless…'

'Yes, and I can see that now I've had a little more time to think. But Thea, picking Pevensey in which to do that seems… I just don't want you to get hurt, that's all.'

'Why ever would I get hurt?' I'm trying hard not to let my voice rise; we've both just apologised for goodness' sake.

'No, I just meant…' She pauses for a moment. 'Sometimes we have such fixed memories, particularly childhood ones, and over time they grow and distort so that they become something much more than they ever were—'

'But—'

'No, let me finish. I'm not saying that our time at Pevensey wasn't special, it was, but when you put things on a pedestal—'

'Like Dad, you mean?'

'Thea, I didn't say that.' She lets out a sigh of frustration. 'Nobody needed to put your father on a pedestal, he was quite the most wonderful man, as well you know… No, all I meant was that when you attach a certain importance to things, particularly things from your past, you can fool yourself into thinking that they were better than they were. I just don't want you to think that way about Pevensey and be disappointed if it doesn't live up to your expectations.'

'Mum, I'm not daft, I…' But then I stop, because I can so easily see that I've been in danger of doing that very thing. 'Anyway, I'm sorry for the way I sprung our news on you without thinking first, but I hope you still want to come and visit. You'll be very welcome and it is beautiful, even after all these years…'

I think I hear her breath catch in her throat as if she's about to speak, but nothing comes.

'Oh, and I bumped into Mary Williams today,' I add, hoping to move on to somewhat safer ground.

'Mary…?' She sounds distracted now. 'Oh yes… I'd quite forgotten… I might have mentioned you were moving. Well, how lovely. I expect she was pleased to see you, all grown up.'

'Well, she still manages to put the fear of God into me. Hardly changed at all. She invited me round for tea as well but I'm really not sure I'd have the nerve to go. I hadn't realised you still kept in touch.'

'Oh yes, we… Not often, birthdays, Christmas, that kind of thing. But she always was a good friend, despite being your head teacher.'

And I realise that there's a whole other side to my parents' life in the village that I'd failed to notice with my young eyes. They were just my mum and dad; I'm not sure I even considered them as people in their own right and perhaps I'm just as guilty of that now.

'I've been roped into helping with the Harvest Festival Supper too, can you believe that?'

She laughs. 'Heavens, is that still going? It certainly brings back some memories but I'm glad to hear the old traditions are still in force. Listen, see how things go, Thea. You'll be busy with your work, I know, but yes, perhaps in a few weeks I could visit… You and Drew are both well though? And the girls? How are they settling in?'

'Oh Mum, they absolutely love it. They spend all day in the garden, just like we did. Not a care in the world. And I know we haven't been here long, but I really can't picture us living anywhere else. How on earth did you bear moving?'

She clears her throat. 'Well I'm pleased, that all sounds wonderful.' There's a pause of a few seconds. 'Sorry, Thea, I'm going to have to go. There's a bowls match on this afternoon and…'

'Yes, yes of course. I didn't mean to hold you up. But you're okay, are you, Mum?'

I hear the smile in her voice. 'Darling, I'm fine… Now, give my love to Drew, won't you, and the girls… And Thea, if you ever want to just… chat… you can always call me, you know.'

'I know, Mum, I will.'

'Bye then…'

'Yes, bye…'

I hang up, lips pursed. And it's several seconds before I place my phone back down on the counter.

'Penny for them?'

I look up to see Drew in the kitchen doorway. 'Sorry, I was just thinking…'

There's a sharp intake of breath. 'Steady on,' he says, grinning. 'You'll do yourself a damage.'

'I just rang Mum… Drew, did we do the right thing, moving here?'

His face falls as he moves swiftly towards me. 'Thea,' he says, taking hold of both of my hands. 'We were very happy in London. But somehow over the years our house shrunk to half its size. There was no room to breathe and we outgrew London too. The things we want are different now, and I don't think either of us realised how much until we were given the opportunity to consider them. Had Pevensey not come up on the market, then we may not have thought about them for a good while yet, but it did and so we have. What we didn't have is any time to consider other possibilities before we moved, that's all. Maybe that's why you're feeling it was a bit rushed, but that doesn't mean in any way that it's the wrong decision.'

I stand back a little. 'Do *you* think we rushed the decision?'

'Thea, I didn't say that. I was suggesting that you might think it was a slightly rushed decision... and so that now, when you're a little... stressed by it all, that's what you're fixating on.'

'I'm not stressed, I'm just...'

He slides a hand around my waist, pulling me closer. 'Yes, you are,' he says. 'Because you're doing that distracted thing with your hair. Pulling it out from behind your ears and then tucking it back again.'

'Am I?' I'm buying for time. I know I've been doing it, it's driving me mad too. 'It's not that I'm getting second thoughts or anything, but it's still a big move for us. And talking to Mum just now made we wonder why we ever left in the first place. We will be happy here, won't we?'

'Yes, Thea.'

'And you don't think it was the wrong decision?'

'No, I don't think it was the wrong decision,' he repeats, and there's an amused twinkle in his eyes. 'What are you like?' he asks, smiling. 'The girls are going to have an absolute ball here. Your work is going to go from strength to strength, and I've already got a few potential clients lined up courtesy of Derek. It's all going to be wonderful, Thea, just relax.'

'I didn't know you'd got work lined up,' I say, surprised. 'What kind of work?'

But Drew refuses to acknowledge my concern. 'Architectural work,' he says with a grin. 'Just like Rob suggested, one or two things for local people. Nothing might come of them, but if it does, great. It will tide me over until I'm able to forge ahead with my own stuff. The last thing I want is for us to be worried about money now we're here. Nothing will taint the experience more.'

'But we discussed this,' I press.

'Yes we did. And I'm not going back on what we decided, Thea. I don't have a problem with you keeping us financially for a little while, but if I can bring in a bit too that has to be good news.'

I hold his look for several long seconds but Drew doesn't look away. He has nothing to hide, and I'm reminded yet again how lucky I am to be in a relationship in which communication is so open.

I smile. 'I know. I just don't want you to lose sight of your dream, that's all.'

'Thea, I'm closer to my dream now than I've ever been. My honeycomb houses are going to be a thing, I promise you, and I'm not going to lose sight of that.' He pulls me towards him again. 'And especially not when I have you to remind me.' He rubs his nose against mine. 'Stop worrying. It's all going to work out wonderfully.'

CHAPTER FIVE

I can't believe the rest of the holiday has already gone. We've been busy of course; working in the house, having fun and exploring our old neighbourhood, but even so the last few days have ended up in a frantic chase around trying to get everything ready for school. New uniform, the dreaded new shoes... rubbers, water bottles, the list is endless. And, despite loving the attention from their new-found friends, Lauren and Chloe are still nervous at the prospect of a different school. As am I.

It's ridiculous to be worried what people think about you when you're thirty-something years old, but I guess the new-kid-in-the-playground feeling never quite leaves you. I can still vividly remember my first day at this school; standing in the grounds, clutching a tight hold of my mother's hand, Drew's too as I recall, and feeling sick with fear. I'd been perfectly happy at home, playing in the garden, baking with Mum, or drawing and painting – there had been lots of that. But, in the end, I'd had such an amazing time that I'd raced out to meet my mum at the end of the day, running so fast that my brain couldn't keep up with my legs, and I'd fallen in the playground and taken all the skin off my knee. I think I still have the scar.

I'm so grateful to be walking down the lane with Anna on this first morning, because even if I'm not a new child here today, as far as everyone else is concerned, I am a new parent. And I'm about to run the gauntlet of a new playground, with its cliques, and everyone standing in their particular spot. It's enough to have any woman quaking in her boots and I'm having to remind myself that it's the children's first day at school, not mine.

But it's very strange to be back here today, holding my own children's hands as I look around from the viewpoint of my much older self. Everything is different, yet achingly familiar; the poignancy of those early days, and what they meant for me, incredibly powerful. It's a visual marker of how far I've travelled in my life, and I can't help but wonder what the future holds for my girls. Will they be standing in a playground thirty-odd years from now with their own children? Will the intervening years have been kind? Will they be fulfilled in their jobs, with loving partners? Will they be as happy as I am now? The questions come thick and fast and I have to remind myself that none of us have a crystal ball, and a happy past is no guarantee of a happy future.

There's a palpable sense of nervous excitement as we enter the playground. While the traditional calendar doesn't show it, it's still the start of a new year and even the old hands are aware of the unfamiliarity of new beginnings. The teachers are catching up with their pupils' news, the children's faces animated and fresh from the summer break, and I hang back a little not quite knowing what the form is. Tilly has a firm grip on Lauren's hand though, and immediately takes her over to their teacher. Mrs Hollingsworth bends to say hello and, looking up, catches my eye with a bright smile. She moves through the crowd.

'I see Lauren has already found a good friend,' she says, smiling first at me and then at Anna. 'So, I know she's going to be well looked after. But if there's anything you're unsure of, do please come and ask. It's always a little bit mad on the first day back, but I'll be around at the end of the afternoon if you have any questions, or just want to chat.'

I nod, grateful for her words. Lauren can be quite shy to start with and often has to be reminded to voice what she's thinking, but she has Tilly by her side and I'm not so worried about her. Chloe, on the other hand, doesn't really know anyone in her class yet. She's standing looking around her, clutching her new lunch bag to her chest. But I needn't have worried. Mrs Hollingsworth has already spotted her difficulty and I remind myself that this is only a small school; everyone will be known here; brothers, sisters, possibly even nieces and nephews, every child will have an identity.

'So you must be Chloe,' she says, waiting for the confirmatory nod. 'Shall I take you over to meet your teacher, Miss Butler? I know she's got two lovely girls ready to show you where everything is. Come and say hello.'

I'm relieved when Chloe follows her without so much as a backwards glance. I'm turning back towards Anna, intending to share my relief, when I catch sight of the woman from the shop, Stacey, standing a little way from me. Her open stare challenges and it's me who looks away first; as if I'm the one embarrassed to have been caught looking and not the other way around. I feel my skin prickle. Another mum steps between Anna and me, breaking my line of sight, touching Anna's arm to get her attention.

'Anna, sorry, I've been meaning to get in touch. My sister-in-law is driving me nuts about this christening, but we're still harvesting and it's not like I haven't had one or two other things to do…' She pulls a face and then continues in similar fashion.

I look around, wondering if there's someone else I can make small talk with; I don't want to seem as if I'm hanging on the end of a conversation that clearly has nothing to do with me, but neither do I want to stand immobile knowing that Stacey's gaze is still trained on me. Gratefully, I see someone moving purpose-fully towards me, head down and holding tight to the hand of the toddler beside her. It takes a moment to recognise her, but I remember her as the other woman from the shop just in time.

'Hi, Jackie.' She's wearing jogging bottoms and a tee shirt stretched tight across her chest. She is also fully and immaculately made-up, even down to the thick mascara-covered eyelashes that blink up at me. How she's managed to get that lot on and get ready for school is beyond me. I barely had time to brush my hair this morning.

'Does your daughter want to come back to ours after school? She can stop for tea if she likes. I'm Jasmin's mum.' I look to where she's pointing – at the two girls who are now chatting away to Chloe some distance from us. 'The one with the French plaits,' she adds.

The invitation is so out of the blue it surprises me. I'm trying to work out what Chloe's body language is saying as she talks to two girls she's only just met, but she seems happy enough. Before I can answer, however, Jackie raises her arm.

'Jaz!' she shouts across the playground, beckoning her daughter over once she has her attention. All three girls move as one. 'Would you like to have your new friend back after school?' She smiles at the second child. 'You can come as well, Beth, if you like, if your mum will let you.'

I'm stuck. I have no idea whether Chloe would like this or not, and I really don't want to answer for her. But either way, she seems to be caught in the middle of something that could easily be a little awkward. I remind myself that both Chloe and Lauren ran off quite happily to play with Tilly on the day we met her, but somehow this seems different. Jackie is looking directly at Chloe and waiting for her answer, and I see the hesitancy in my daughter's eyes as she flicks a glance at me. But then she smiles.

'Can I, Mum?' she asks. Her eyes look a little over-bright.

'Yes of course,' I reply, thinking. 'Although maybe not for tea, Chloe, not tonight. I'm sure you're going to have a brilliant day, but you'll probably be quite tired too.' I'm not sure why but I'm keen to give Chloe an out. 'Why don't you see how you feel? I'll be coming up later anyway to pick Lauren up so you can decide then if you want.' I turn to Jackie. 'Would that be okay?'

'Course.' She looks at her watch. 'Right, I need to get this one off to playgroup. Come on, Shannon. I'll see you later.'

Shannon doesn't look like she wants to go anywhere much but, after dragging her feet a couple of steps, the toddler is soon persuaded to pick up the pace a bit.

I smile reassuringly at Chloe. 'Have a lovely day, sweetheart,' I say, but she is already being ferried away, all three girls giggling at something. I look around for Lauren, spotting her and Tilly sitting on a bench at the back of the yard. They look like two old women who have been there for hours, chewing the fat about anything and everything. With Anna still chatting and me happy that both children are not about to have a wobble, I realise there's nothing else for it but to go home.

I've only taken a couple of steps, however, when Anna comes back over. 'Everything okay with Jackie?' she asks. When I nod, she continues. 'That's good. It can be a bit daunting, can't it? Until you know who's who and what's what.'

And as the curate's wife, Anna knows everyone. I'm about to ask her a question when I stop myself. Probably best to go with the flow, for now at least. 'I'm just relieved that there are no tears. Both girls went from Nursery straight into Reception at their old school, so this is the first new school they've been to. They seem all right though.'

'Water off a duck's back,' says Anna, smiling. 'They're lovely girls, and I'm sure they'll fit in just fine. Every school has its characters of course – there are one or two of Tilly's friends that I'm not so keen on – but in the main, they're all very nice. And, now you've survived that ordeal, do you want to come back for a cuppa?' She looks across at me and then laughs. 'That's a no then. I'd forgotten today's the first day you can get in the studio. You look like you'd run home given half a chance. Don't worry, we can catch up any time.'

A surge of excitement fills me at her words. The building work in the studio was only finished yesterday, but it's not quite ready yet. I still need to unpack everything and get it straight and the lure is almost impossible to resist. 'Would you mind?' I ask.

'Don't be silly,' Anna replies easily. 'We can have a coffee any time. I'm not back to work until Wednesday anyway.'

Other parents are leaving now and, as we pass through the playground gate in single-file, I hold it open for the next in line. I meet the same intense eyes that were looking at me earlier but, despite Stacey's muttered thank you, her cold expression doesn't alter. A second later she's gone and Anna's bright chatter chases away the feeling. The road ahead is golden with autumn sunshine and I have work to do. It doesn't get much better than this.

Except that when I push open our front door, there's a new feeling, something other than the comforting familiarity that usually greets me. I pause in the hallway, feeling the space around me but, despite the fact that I'm alone, I know there's someone else here with me. My younger self is sitting midway up the stairs, just on the turn to the left behind the newel post. It was a favourite resting place of mine, and I have no idea what has made me think of it now. But I can't resist the pull of memory and I slowly climb the steps until I'm sitting beside her, my feet on the tread below, hugging my knees which, in my adult body, are bent double. And I suddenly remember why it was I used to sit in this spot.

It's the very centre of the house. And from here the whole ground floor seems spread out beneath you. If anyone was downstairs you knew exactly where they were – in the dining room or the sitting room to your left, the study or the drawing room to your right, or the kitchen behind you. Every movement and every sound could be tracked, everyone's passage around the house, and even the conversations floated upwards so you could hear them. And all the time you remained hidden from sight. But the house is silent now, it's empty, so why am I here? Just what am I listening for?

An involuntary shiver ripples down my back and I suddenly have a longing to throw off the past and return to my warm and sunlit studio and the task that is waiting for me. I stand decisively, realising as I do so that today is actually the first day I've been alone in the house. Drew is out, gone to Birmingham for an early morning meeting, so it's just me. No wonder I've been catapulted back to my childhood – my memories have all just been biding their time, waiting to jump out on me when my mind is not occupied by other things. I stroke a hand fondly along the banister and walk back down the stairs, tutting. What am I like?

I give a wry smile, amused by the ease at which I'm able to spook myself, but I'm no longer a child; I'm an adult with a lot to accomplish before Drew arrives back. He'll be home just after lunch, which gives me about four hours to get everything shipshape. I want our studio to be perfect by the time he returns and, with my mind now focused, I practically run to the kitchen to make a quick coffee.

Derek has done a brilliant job and he seemed to know almost instinctively what we were after without us having to explain the vagaries of the creative mind. In fact, he even came up with several suggestions for fittings that are going to make life so much easier. The old and tired conservatory has been transformed.

A custom-made workbench now runs down the centre of the room. Divided into four sections, the surface of each of these lifts up, resembling an old-fashioned school desk with storage space beneath. And, although two of the desks are flat, the other two are fitted with an ingenious mechanism that allows the lid to tilt at any angle. Fixing it in place with a simple catch provides a sloped working surface which is perfect for both mine and Drew's work.

We face the garden and, as well as the amazing light which falls in exactly the right place, it means we have a beautiful outlook too. Having installed the system of blinds that Derek recommended also means that we can block out both the sun and the view should we wish to, either partially or completely. Having been forced to move around my previous workroom simply to follow the light source, this is going to feel like the height of luxury.

Behind the workbench is a row of fitted storage units along the rear wall, incorporating both shelves and drawers, and it's these that I really want to turn my attention to this morning. I've never had enough space before to have all my art materials around me. Mostly they were packed away in boxes, brought out only when needed. Now though, there is room for everything – all the bits and pieces that I've hoarded over the years, never knowing when they might come in handy. Old sketchbooks, papers, design books, my inks, wonderful old drawing pens that I couldn't bear to be parted with, now they will all have a home; neat, tidy and organised. Almost as important is the ability to be able to keep the rather more practical side of my work under control as well – all the administrative details that get so easily out of hand and make filing my tax returns a nightmare. I feel almost giddy with excitement at the thought of becoming the efficient grown-up I've always longed to be. 'A place for everything and everything in its place', so the saying goes, and I'm just beginning to understand how gratifying that is.

On an impulse, before I start, I raise every blind as high as it will go and fling open the doors to the garden. It's still a warm day, but the breeze is fresher than it has been of late and feels lovely blowing through this airy room. I drag through the boxes which have been waiting patiently in the study and open all of them at once, trying to get a feel for the amount that needs to be re-homed. Then I set to work, filling drawers, cupboards, lining shelves, jiggling things around and then putting them back where they were. Gradually, as the morning ticks by, it begins to take shape.

By the time he gets back, I've set up Drew's PC and added a row of his architectural prints along the wall by the door. There's a vase of huge sunflowers on the small table in the corner and next to it his incredibly comfortable, but very shabby, leather chair which, if I ever threw it away, would be almost certain grounds for divorce.

I'm so lost in my thoughts that I don't even hear him come in the house until he appears, grinning, in the studio doorway. His hands slip around my waist from behind, lifting the edge of my tee shirt and sliding over my stomach. His head dips into the gap between my shoulder and my ear as his lips graze my neck. He smells of lemons.

'Someone's been busy,' he whispers, as he presses his length against me.

I turn in his arms. 'Do I take it you've had a good morning?' I ask, pulling away slightly to resist his kiss, although we both know what's coming next.

His eyes are dancing with amusement. 'Do I take it you've had a good morning too?'

'It's been lovely,' I reply. 'Can't you tell?'

'It looks amazing…'

'Fibber, you haven't even looked.'

'I don't need to…'

'Yes, you blooming well do…' I slap playfully at his chest. 'I haven't slaved away all morning for you not to notice how incredible all this is.'

Drew holds my look for a moment, his eyes a teasing reflection of mine, but then he does release me and, taking a step backwards, looks slowly around the room. His eyes widen as he takes in everything, and sees for the first time how this room will work in practice.

'This is going to be amazing, isn't it?' he says.

'Yes,' I reply, inching closer. 'If past experience is anything to go by…'

He laughs. 'Thea Gordon, whatever do you mean?'

We stand looking at each other, in the silent, almost-empty house, where no children will be around for several more hours yet.

We barely make it up the stairs.

CHAPTER SIX

I don't even notice how dark it's become until a sudden cloudburst flings rain against the window. There's a clatter from downstairs and a window bangs somewhere as the wind rises to meet the storm.

I scramble from the bed, pulling myself out from under Drew's arm as I hurl the bedclothes aside. We were both dozing, warmed by the glow of our love-making, but now the downpour outside feels as if it's in the room, running down my skin in icy rivers.

'Where are you going?' Drew's voice is confused.

I'm already halfway to the door. 'I left the doors open,' I yell as I race across the landing and hurtle down the stairs. I can hear the rain thundering against the front door and pray I'm not too late.

The studio door is swinging on its hinges, the source of the banging noise I heard, and the wind lifts the papers on my end of the desk. But, mercifully, apart from a few spots of rain on the carpet by the door, the room is untouched, the rain driven in the other direction, across the garden and not towards the studio with its invitingly open doors.

I drag them shut, feeling the icy splatters of rain against my warm, still-naked body, and shiver violently. The sky is a murderous colour, pouring a deluge onto an already drenched garden, threatening to snap the heads of the hollyhocks with its furious pummelling. But it isn't this that makes me feel cold. It's the thought of the damage that could have been wreaked on the room, the newly polished wooden surfaces splattered by water drops that would have leached the colour from them, soaked the carpet and stained the walls. How could I have been so stupid? Except that…

I peer up at the sky, jumping as a crash of thunder fills the room. Half an hour ago it was a high, almost cloudless blue, with only wispy streaks of white. Just a gentle, mild, autumnal day. Where on earth has the storm come from? The glass is running with rain, the noise almost deafening, and a touch on my shoulder has me jumping from my skin.

'Thea, for goodness' sake, I thought something terrible had happened.'

Drew's pulled on his boxers and is holding out my robe and I stare at him, perplexed.

'Something terrible nearly did happen,' I reply, reaching out to take my dressing gown. 'If the wind had blown the rain the other way, the room would have been soaked.'

He suddenly pulls the robe out of my reach, amusement flickering in his eyes. And a slow smile begins to curve his lips upward. 'Have you any idea what you look like?' he teases, and I'm suddenly aware of the ridiculous picture I must be painting. 'God, you look wild.'

'Ten minutes ago that would have been a compliment,' I complain.

'It still is, but…' He opens out the robe so that I can step into it and pulls it around me, loosely tying the cord. Then he tucks my messy bed hair back behind my ears. 'It's just a storm, Thea.'

For some reason his words make me shiver again but, even as I do so, I can feel the growing warmth from my clothing and I smile and lean against him.

'Sorry,' I murmur. 'I was just terrified that all this loveliness was going to be ruined.' Even as I speak I can hear the rain lessening and see the gradual lifting of the gloom. I turn to look back outside where the sky is now streaked with light. 'It was a bit apocalyptic, you have to admit.'

Drew grins. 'Perhaps. But I'm just mightily relieved that the garden isn't overlooked.' He stands back and looks pointedly at his bare legs and chest.

I draw the robe around me and fold my arms over my breasts. 'Oh my God, what must we look like?' And I burst into sudden giggles. 'Imagine if we did have close neighbours. What on earth would they have thought?'

Drew raises an eyebrow. 'I'd love to know, wouldn't you?' he replies, eyes twinkling. 'But you really must stop your boobs bouncing everywhere, Thea, or we'll never get any work done...'

'It wasn't my fault,' I say, pretending to be miffed at the suggestion. The sun is already beginning to peek back through the clouds. 'So you can make me a cup of tea to atone for your scandalous behaviour, while I go and jump in the shower. Alone,' I add, pointedly. I've been caught out like that before.

The water feels good at first. There's something very decadent about taking a bath or shower in the middle of the day but, as I begin to rinse the soap from my skin, I catch sight of the rivulets of water running down the shower screen. I'm not afraid of storms, I never have been, but there was something about this one that unnerved me. Perhaps it was the suddenness of it that caught me unawares, the loud banging noise that woke me from sleep, like a portent, or... an echo, I realise, a door slamming shut. But its power was unmistakable and, although I can't articulate why, it leaves me uneasy. I'm glad when I can step free from the water and wrap myself in the biggest, fluffiest towel I can find.

*

By the time I have to make the return journey to school you'd hardly even know it had rained. In fact, the lanes look beautiful, the gardens freshened by the downpour, their colours rendered vivid.

'It's a miracle it didn't happen at home time,' remarks Anna as we walk. 'That's what normally happens.'

I laugh, because she's so right. 'I pity the teachers,' I reply. 'Can you imagine the noise of twenty five-year-olds screaming during the thunder?'

She grimaces. 'It makes them wild,' she says. 'I work with a lot of teachers and they always say the one thing they hate more than anything is the wind. It bedevils the kids apparently. I don't know why, but it's a fact. Are your girls bothered by storms?'

I shake my head. 'No, fortunately. In fact, I think they quite enjoy them. But I would imagine there will be some tales to tell,' I add. 'As first days go, it's been a bit dramatic.'

As it happens, Lauren and Tilly are scathing about the reactions of some of their more hysterical classmates. 'Honestly, Mum, it was ridiculous…' says Lauren when I ask her. 'Mrs Hollingsworth had to get quite cross, but I don't blame her, they were making a right racket.'

I smile and nod at my ever-so-grown-up daughter. 'But you've had a good day though?' I ask.

'Yeah, brilliant. They've even got chickens here,' she replies, as she and Tilly walk past us to wait a little distance away.

'Chickens?' I query, looking at Anna for confirmation.

'All true,' she says. 'Three of them at last count. There's a garden area at the back of Miss Butler's class and the children get to decide what they want to grow. And one of the things they picked was chickens…' She raises her eyebrows.

'You make it sound like they're being fattened up for Christmas.'

'No, they're just kept for their eggs.' She flicks a glance towards Tilly. 'Although… let's just say that one or two of the chickens are on their second reincarnation, if you know what I mean.' There's a faint wink. 'And no questions asked.'

I grin at her. 'Well, chickens or no chickens, I'm glad Lauren's had a good day.' I scan the straggles of children still coming out of the school. 'Just Chloe to go now...'

I spot her walking out with her classmates a few moments later and give a little wave to let her know I'm here. If she does want to go home with Jasmin then I don't just want her to rush off without speaking to me first. I've already clocked Jackie, standing a little distance from us, and I look across and smile, ready to confirm arrangements. Chloe hasn't quite reached me, however, when a boy streaks past us, rushing for the gate. He clips Tilly on his way past, crashing against her shoulder and almost sending her flying. It's one of those moments when, as a parent, you don't know what to do first – rush to the potentially injured child, or chase after the boy. I don't want to overreact, but my danger-sensing radar is bleeping loudly at the possibility that he could run straight out into the road. I recognise the lad from this morning – it's Stacey's son – and my heart drops.

Tilly is fine, more startled than anything, and Anna very sensibly doesn't make a big deal of it. Stacey, however, is obviously going to make a fuss. She strides past me, bellowing at her son and, although she drops her voice as she reaches him, it's obvious by their body language that he's getting a good telling-off. One that isn't going down at all well. He throws off her arm, looking petulant; wriggling as she pulls him back towards us, where he stands, head down.

'Say sorry to the little girl, Leo,' she demands. 'How many times have I told you to be more careful, especially around people who are—' She stops dead, and I'm grateful that she bit her tongue. I'm almost certain that what she was about to say would have been horribly inappropriate and I wince on Tilly's behalf. She's such a sunny-natured child but she's probably been on the receiving end of some pretty nasty comments in the past due to her disability.

'It's fine,' answers Anna easily, stepping in. 'No harm done. I expect you were just excited, Leo, weren't you?'

He half looks up, grateful, and is about to answer when Stacey interrupts. 'I said, say sorry, Leo...'

His head drops again and his muttered apology sounds sulky and insincere.

'It's really okay,' reiterates Anna. 'Please don't give it another thought. I'm sure it was just high spirits.' Beside her Tilly is smiling happily, just as keen as her mum not to make an issue of it.

'Yes, well, he needs to learn some manners. I keep telling him he can't go around treating people like he does, but he doesn't listen.' A rather defiant note has crept into Stacey's voice.

'I expect it's just the relief at having the first day of the new term over and done with, isn't it?' I say. 'Even if you love school it's always a little strange after the long summer break.'

Stacey's eyes narrow as she looks at us in turn, and I see a sudden flicker of unease. Perhaps it's just that with Anna and Tilly, me, Lauren and Chloe and now Jasmin and Jackie too, there are seven of us all gathered around, but I can see she's feeling uncomfortable, threatened even. It's unfortunate, but it wasn't deliberate.

She lifts her chin a little and looks back at me. 'What's it got to do with you?' she sneers. 'I should keep your nose out if you know what's good for you.'

I catch Anna's eye but she looks just as uncomfortable as I'm feeling and I'm at a loss for what to say. Jackie, on the other hand, is leaning in with interest. I'd only been trying to lighten things up and I certainly wasn't trying to stick my oar in. I'm desperately searching for something to help the situation when Stacey clutches at Leo's arm.

'Right, come on, you,' she says. 'Before you cause any more upset. And, like I said before, stay away from them lot up at the big house.' Soon she's melted away, lost in the still milling gaggle of parents and children.

There's a rather subdued hush until, seconds later, Lauren, bless her, breaks the silence, the slightly sticky conversation thankfully flying right over her head.

'Mum, can Tilly come and play with Scampers for a bit?'

The tension eases and I smile brightly. 'Yes of course, sweetheart. As long as that's okay with Anna.'

Anna smiles too. 'Just until dinnertime though. No late nights now it's back to school.'

Tilly gives a predictable groan, but she links arms with Lauren in acceptance of the situation.

'And how about you, Chlo? Have you had a good day?' It feels late to be asking her now and it's not the way I wanted to greet her at the end of her first day. In many ways I wish she'd just come home but I don't want to stifle her potential friendships either.

'It's been okay…' She trails off and then looks at Jasmin who's standing by her side, chewing the end of her plait. 'Can I go back to Jaz's, Mum? Please.' I can see she's not keen on having a public discussion on the merits or otherwise of the day.

'Of course,' I reply, looking across at Jackie, who nods in confirmation. 'What time shall I fetch her?' I ask, smiling. I don't even know where Jackie lives.

'No problem, I'll drop her home. 'Bout six be okay?' She's already moving away. 'Come on girls.'

And just like that they're gone. Chloe doesn't even say goodbye.

'It reminds me of that song,' remarks Anna with a sympathetic smile. 'They're slipping through your fingers all the while.' She pauses for a moment, weighing up what to say. 'Jackie lives on the estate up at the far end of the village, so does Stacey,' she adds. 'In case you were wondering. But I'm sure Chloe will be okay.' There's a lot more she could have said and we both know it.

'Sorry… it's just in London, well, it's different there, I know. But the girls never went on play dates anywhere without me knowing exactly where they were and having contact numbers too.

It's been a long while since I lived in a village. I guess it's going to take some time getting used to a more relaxed attitude.'

Anna nods. 'There's no need to apologise, Thea. Caution isn't a bad thing and definitely not where your children are concerned. I think it took a while for things to get back to normal here after what happened, but it was a long time ago now and eventually you have to put things like that out of your mind, don't you? Otherwise you'd never let your kids do anything. But if it helps, Jackie's okay. A bit rough and ready, likes a gossip, but otherwise nice enough.' She's looking at me carefully and I realise I'm staring.

'Sorry, Anna,' I say, confused. 'I think we're talking about two different things here. I just meant that maybe folks in London are a bit more cautious. We didn't live in a rough area by any means, but it's generally not as safe there as in the country. Or maybe that's just our perception of it, I don't know. What did *you* mean?'

Anna bites her lip. 'Oh… I thought you knew, when you said… But it really was a long time ago. Forget I even said it.'

'Forget what?'

She looks to where Lauren and Tilly are standing a little distance away before leaning in slightly, lowering her voice. 'The girl that went missing in the village… Georgia Thomas, the one that was assaulted…'

The hairs stir on the back of my neck. The name means nothing. 'I'm sorry, Anna, I haven't got a clue what you're talking about.'

There's an anguished look on her face. 'Oh dear, I shouldn't have said anything. Please don't worry.' She tuts. 'I've made it sound like you've moved into the middle of some awful drama on the television. You haven't. It was an isolated incident, fifteen, maybe twenty years ago, and nothing like it has happened since. I really don't know the details anyway, I don't want to. There's too much goes on in the current world to pay attention to something that happened so long ago. But you know what people are like, long memories, especially over a story like this.' She lowers her voice even further. 'A girl from the school went missing for a few hours and when she was found she'd been... assaulted. The person that did it was never caught apparently, but, like I said, nothing else ever happened.'

'Oh I see,' I say quietly. 'Well no, I didn't know about that...'

I'm not sure what I think, but it happens, I'm well aware of that, and Anna looks so anxious that I don't want to make a big deal about it. In fact, why would I? It's ancient history now and for goodness' sake we'd lived in our house in London for eighteen months before we found out that the chap at the end of the road had attacked his wife one night when he came home drunk and found she'd burned his dinner. It made no difference to *our* lives at all. I brighten my expression.

'Don't worry, Anna, I don't think we'll be needing to pack up and move back out just yet, but I appreciate you telling me. I'm glad I heard it from you and not someone else.'

She smiles in gratitude, motioning ahead to where Lauren and Tilly are waiting patiently by the gate. 'The village must feel very different from when you were a child, but it's still a great place to live, and I think it's lovely that you're back here with your own children, growing up somewhere that has such fond memories for you. None of that has changed.'

She nods her head firmly as if judgement has been passed, and I realise that she's right. There's always a period of adjustment moving anywhere new, so why should here be any different, just because it's where we grew up? We're adults now and the circumstances aren't the same. I start walking, grateful to have Anna as a neighbour – and as someone who's rapidly becoming a friend too. 'Have you got time for that coffee?' I ask. 'I'm dying to show you the studio.'

'I thought you'd never ask...' she replies, rolling her eyes.

Drew is hard at work when we arrive back and it's good to see his desk covered with papers, a mug standing to one side. It looks like the room has always been this way and the day like any other.

'You look nicely at home,' I say as Anna and I walk through the door. 'How does it feel?'

'Wonderful!' he replies. 'I don't know why we didn't do this before. Working for yourself, from home, versus being in a huge, noisy, artificially lit office and just a part of the food chain… no contest, is there?'

'Well, put like that…' Anna grins. 'But it's incredible in here.' She looks around, taking in all the changes to the room. 'Besides, you don't need to convince me about the benefits of working from home. Rob loves it.'

'It certainly has a lot to recommend it,' agrees Drew, with an amused expression on his face as he looks directly at me.

I blush slightly, knowing exactly what he's referring to. 'Anyway, we had better not hold you up,' I say, moving towards the kitchen door. 'Anna and I are just going to have a coffee, would you like a refill?'

His eyes flick away as his laptop makes a pinging sound. 'No, no thanks, I've not long had…' Whatever it was has captured his attention.

I smile at Anna and a complicit look passes between us. She's just as used to this as I am.

Once in the kitchen I open the back door to the garden, knowing that it won't be long before Lauren and Tilly come in seeking a drink and something to eat. Plus it still feels nice, leaving doors open, letting them come and go. And Scampers has never eaten so much fresh grass. I put down a tin of biscuits on the table where Anna is sitting.

'I still haven't quite got around to making that cake,' I say. 'Shame on me.'

Anna pounces on a cookie. 'I don't know why. I mean, it isn't as if you've had anything to do… Seriously though, the studio looks amazing. And I know you've got lots planned for the rest of the house but it already looks heaps better – alive, does that make sense?'

'Yeah, lived-in…' I look around the kitchen, every surface of which is covered with the detritus of a busy family life.

'No,' replies Anna, deliberately dismissing my remark. 'Come alive, more vibrant.' She takes a bite of her biscuit just as Lauren and Tilly race past the open door, Lauren shrieking as Tilly chases after her.

'That'll be the screaming then.'

Anna laughs too. 'Maybe. But the couple who were here before you were so…' She casts around for the right word. 'She wasn't so bad, but he was incredibly grumpy, and very negative. It was as if he sucked the life out of things, brought everything to a dead stop. When we first moved in I used to pop over from time to time – you know, curate's wife and all that. And they were elderly, I thought perhaps they needed the support. But I had to stop coming after a while; it made me feel depressed.' She gives an involuntary shiver. 'Actually, it was more than that – he gave me the creeps, just something… off about him. But I think the house likes having children here; it feels lighter somehow.'

I can see she's wondering if I think her comments strange, but I don't, I know exactly what she means. The house always felt happy to me as a child, even at the age when I was especially susceptible to things that went bump in the night. I never felt scared here, despite the creaking floorboards and gurgling radiators. The thought brings to mind something from earlier that I've been meaning to ask Anna about.

'Our builder said an odd thing when he first came around, about not believing the stories we might hear about the house. Has it attained something of a reputation?'

Anna shakes her head. 'Not as far as I know. I can ask Rob, but I suspect it's just because it's old and big – if it were in an Agatha Christie book it's definitely where the murder would take place.'

I smile, shrugging. 'You may well be right. Perhaps that's what Stacey meant when she said to stay away from them lot up at the big house. Maybe she thinks we're all up to no good.' I roll my eyes. 'I don't know what we've done to deserve her snide remark, but perhaps just living here is reason enough. You know, I get that this is a large house, and I know we're very lucky to be able to live here, but I think I'd rather she called me a snobby cow or a rich bitch or something and be done with it, instead of making silly comments.'

Anna sympathises. 'The whole thing this afternoon was really awkward. And it wasn't as if you said anything wrong.'

Anna looks across at me and I pull a face. 'Stacey probably didn't mean what she said. I expect she just felt we were being judgemental and wanted to retaliate.'

Anna blinks. 'Were we being judgemental?' she asks. 'I didn't think we were.'

'No,' I say decisively, picking up my mug. 'We weren't. It was her that made a massive drama out of it, not us.'

CHAPTER SEVEN

'For goodness' sake, Thea. It was just a stupid comment. You don't need to get so het up about it.' Drew's gaze slides away from me and back to his laptop.

But I'm not getting het up, I just mentioned it because it *was* a silly thing to say. That's exactly my point. And I'm wondering why Drew, one of the least argumentative people I know, is suddenly looking like he's spoiling for a fight. Even at this angle I can see how tight his jaw is clenched.

Anna has gone home, but the girls are still playing in the garden. I'm sitting with Drew in the studio and I can hear them now, the odd shriek every now and again that always seems to accompany girls at play. Perhaps it's this that has darkened his previously sunny mood.

'I can ask the girls to keep it down a bit if you like.'

'What?' Drew looks up at my comment, clearly irritated at having his concentration broken. 'No, they're fine. Just leave them be.'

Once again I'm dismissed as his keyboard claims his attention, a small sigh betraying his frustration, and something else too. I notice the slight droop of his shoulders.

'What was your email?' I ask. 'The one that arrived when I was in here before with Anna.'

And, finally, the Drew I know and understand returns to me with a sheepish look. 'I didn't get the job,' he replies. 'Sorry.'

I hate it when I'm right.

'The one you went to see about this morning?' I clarify. 'That was a quick decision.'

He sits back, spinning his chair to face me. 'Yeah, too quick. There was another guy just leaving as I arrived, with a lot of handshaking and backslapping; clearly someone who'd had a working relationship with them before. No prizes for guessing who got the job.'

There's still something not quite right about his reaction. 'Well at least they let you know quickly. Not ideal, but I guess that happens all the time. And you're used to that, surely? Didn't you always say when you pitched for commissions before that it was as much to do with if your face fit or not?'

'Yes, but in case you hadn't noticed, I'm not in my old job now. And I understand full well the point you're trying to make, but what if my face never fits? It mattered if I lost a job before, of course it did, but I still got paid regardless. I don't have that luxury any more.'

Drew's voice has risen while he's been speaking and he suddenly vents a breath. 'Sorry,' he says again. 'You deal with this all the time, don't you?' His tone is back to its normal timbre. 'You've been dealing with it for years...'

I smile and reach out my hand. 'Yes, but I'm not going to say welcome to my world, Drew, and you'd best grow a pair. Being self-employed is tough, it takes a lot of getting used to, reminding yourself over and over that rejection is not personal, and really...' I pause to think for a moment. 'Really, it doesn't get much easier. But I'm a good illustrator and you're a good architect, you'll get there. You'll pitch for jobs and you won't get them. Then you'll pitch for some more and you might get one... But gradually the yesses outweigh the noes and then… well, then your dreams start to come true.'

I squeeze his hand. It's a rather cracker-box philosophy but that doesn't mean it isn't true. Nor does it mean that I haven't turned the air blue, screaming obscenities at my laptop when I didn't win a commission, or, by contrast, danced around the kitchen crying with happiness when I gained the most trivial or boring piece of work. But there's also a lot of truth in the old adage 'If you can't stand the heat get out of the kitchen.' At its worst, working for yourself can be the loneliest, most soul-destroying, self-doubting existence on the planet, but when it's good… there is a soaring freedom and armour-plated feeling of invincibility that I wouldn't swap for anything.

Drew is still looking at me. I mean, really looking at me.

'I don't think I ever truly appreciated that,' he says. 'All those years when you were first starting out, juggling your work with feeding our babies and keeping our home the place I longed to come back to every night.' He drops his head a little, ashamed. 'I'm sorry if I never gave you credit for what you were going through. Or didn't listen to your doubts, or fears. I don't think I can recall you ever complaining and yet, here I am, a couple of months into working for myself, and already behaving like a spoilt child.'

You'd think I'd know Drew by now, but he never ceases to amaze me. How he can be so incredibly honest and candid about his shortcomings. It's something I'm rubbish at. In Drew's case, though, he invariably has nothing to apologise for.

'I never felt like that,' I say softly. 'But don't forget we're our own harshest critics too, we have to be. Besides, you're a man, you're bound to behave like a spoilt child.'

There's a moment when I think he might take me seriously, but then he catches the twinkle in my eye and he pulls me closer. 'Thank you,' he says. 'For being you.'

He drops a kiss on the end of my nose and I glance along the desk to my own workspace. This latest project is so special it makes my heart bleed. I want to start work so badly my fingers are beginning to itch and yet I know that once I start I won't ever want to finish it either. There simply hasn't been time today, but tomorrow is another matter; that's when I can really begin to live my dreams.

For now though, domesticity must take centre stage and I'm already drifting back through to the kitchen lost in thoughts about what to cook for tea, when my phone begins to ring.

'Is that the countryside?' asks the voice when I answer.

'Rachel!' I exclaim. 'Hello. It's so lovely to hear from you.'

'Are you sick of the smell of cow poo yet?'

I laugh. 'No, but the sound of pheasants making out at five in the morning takes some getting used to.'

'I bet… Anyway, how are you all? Wasn't it the first day back to school for the girls today?'

Bless her, Rachel never forgets anything important.

'It was… and I don't want to jinx it, but so far, so good. And we're all doing great…' I glance at the calendar on the wall. 'Is it really two weeks since we last spoke?' I add. 'That doesn't seem right.'

Rachel groans. 'Tell me about it,' she replies. 'Jamie isn't back until Wednesday and so we've been what's euphemistically called "making the most of the remaining holidays". I'm shattered.'

There's a shared empathy that I can feel even through the airwaves. 'Aw, not long to go now though; you'll be fine. And by the end of the week, you'll be kicking around the house wondering where Jamie is and missing him like crazy. How's Gerry?'

'Actually, that's why I'm ringing.' She probably senses rather than hears my sharp intake of breath. 'Don't worry, everything's okay,' she adds quickly. 'It's just that by some miracle he's been given this weekend off and I haven't got a job on either. So I was thinking maybe we could invite ourselves down to yours and—'

'Yes!' I interrupt. 'Oh, please come. That's such a brilliant idea, Rach.'

'Well, otherwise I can see it being Christmas before we get to see you and I can't wait until then to see your new house... old house. Besides, I'm dying to get out of the city. It's still so boiling hot here.'

'Well, we haven't done much, but the studio's finished and—'

I break off as a loud knock sounds from the hallway. 'Rach, sorry, can you hang on a sec? Someone's at the front door.'

I'm still thinking about the possibility of seeing Rachel again at the weekend, so I'm momentarily taken aback to find Jackie and Chloe standing on the doorstep. It's nowhere near six o'clock. There's no sign of Jasmin either, but I can hear what I imagine must be Jackie's car, running in the lane outside.

'Oh, hi Jackie,' I begin. 'Come in.' I dart a glance at Chloe, who looks, not upset exactly, but confused more than anything. 'Sorry, I'm just on the phone to a friend. I'll pop and tell her I'll ring her back in a minute and then...'

But Jackie has already taken a step backward. 'No, don't worry, I don't need to stop. Something's come up and I've had to bring Chloe home.' She certainly looks flustered.

'Oh... is everything okay?'

But Jackie won't quite meet my eye. 'Yeah... it's just, well anyway...' She takes another step backwards as if making sure I've understood she's handing Chloe over. I don't want her to feel embarrassed though, these things happen.

'Is there anything I can do to help?' I offer, smiling. I don't know what else to say.

'No, no... it's fine... thanks.' Jackie is already on her way back to the car.

'Okay, well, thanks so much for having Chlo... and for bringing her home.' But by now I'm talking to Jackie's back.

I smile at Chloe. 'Oh, well, never mind, sweetheart. Is everything okay?'

She nods with a slight smile.

I place a hand on the back of her shoulder. 'Come into the kitchen and have a drink or something. I'm just on the phone to Rachel.'

Chloe heads straight for the biscuit tin and I haven't the heart to say anything. I pick up my phone.

'Hi Rach, sorry about that. Just Chloe being returned home. So where were we?'

'Coming to see your gorgeous house,' she replies. 'But listen, rather than chat now, why don't I ring at the end of the week and we can talk arrangements then? That way we can save all our news until we see one another.'

'Sounds good to me,' I reply. 'We're still a bit rough and ready though, Rach. You'll have to bear with us.'

There's a loud tut from the end of the line. 'As if that's going to put me off,' she says. 'Don't be silly. It will just be wonderful to see you… I've missed you,' she adds, a little tentatively, clearly wondering whether she should have said anything.

'Aw, Rach, I've missed you too…' Except that I haven't, not really. I would have, if I'd stopped to think about it, but I've been too busy getting things sorted here. And it's a stark reminder that I've been neglecting her. It's been all well and good for me, excitement by the gallon fuelling my days, but it's been different for Rachel, her life continuing as if nothing has changed, except it has. How would I feel if I were in her shoes, my closest friend suddenly gone from my life? The thought makes me feel suddenly emotional.

'But I hope you know you can always pick up the phone, Rach. I know we're all busy, but never too busy for a chat,' I say. 'Oh, I can't wait for the weekend now…'

She sighs. 'Me neither…'

We ring off after another minute or so and I turn my attention back to Chloe, who is hovering.

'Well, that was a bit odd, love, wasn't it? Was everything all right at Jasmin's?'

She nods. 'Yeah, it was okay…'

'And you had a good day at school?'

'I didn't know anyone,' she admits. 'Not really.'

'No, I know, but soon you'll know everyone. Then you won't feel quite so awkward.'

'Suppose…'

'And people here seem really friendly.'

'I like Beth,' replies Chloe.

I wrack my brains, trying to recall which one she is. But then, I remember – the other girl alongside Jasmin who'd been charged with buddying Chloe today.

'Oh, but I didn't see her at the end of school.'

'No, she left a bit early. She had a dentist appointment.'

'That's a shame. Well, perhaps she could come back and play after school one afternoon when she's free. Or Jasmin could, they both could actually.'

Chloe nibbles at the edge of her biscuit. 'I'm not sure I'm going to be friends with Jasmin, after all,' she says.

'Okay, well… you can't be friends with everyone, can you? In fact, you wouldn't really want to be, and it might take a little while to work out who's going to be your best friends.'

Chloe looks up and nods, but then drops her head again, studying the toe of her shoe.

'Chlo, did something happen at Jasmin's this afternoon?'

There's a tiny pause and then a change in expression on my daughter's face. If I know her, it's all just about to come tumbling out.

'Mum, it was really weird… I like Jaz, I mean, she's okay… a bit… you know, pushy, but we weren't doing anything wrong, just playing in her room…' She bites her lip. 'We were probably a bit giggly, but we weren't making tons of noise or anything, and when I got there her mum was fine. We had some squash and biscuits and she said we could play upstairs, but then she just came up and said I had to go. Even Jaz thought it was odd. And her mum nearly bit her head off when she asked why.' Chloe looks as if she's about to cry. 'So, now I don't think I'm going to be friends with her, after all.'

'But I don't see any reason why not… I think Jasmin's mum just had some bad news or something,' I say, trying to make Chloe feel better.

'But it didn't feel like that, Mum. It felt like it was something I'd done, like it was my fault.'

My heart goes out to her. It's a horrible thing to have happened, today of all days, even though I'm sure it's entirely innocent. I hold out my arms and Chloe slides inside, resting her head against my breasts, as she has done countless times in the past.

After a few minutes she straightens up. 'What's for tea?' she asks, and I know we're almost out of sticky territory.

'Macaroni cheese.' It's her favourite and she flashes me a smile.

'Thanks, Mum. I'll go and get changed. Is Tilly still here?'

I nod. 'They're in the garden, playing with Scampers, I think.' She's about to go when I call back to her. 'If you see Beth tomorrow, ask her if she'd like to come round,' I say. 'Any day is fine.'

She smiles and moments later I hear her music start playing upstairs. She's okay.

CHAPTER EIGHT

I can't believe how much work I'm getting done. Or how wonderful it feels while I'm doing it. There's a lightness to my touch
that seems to spin around me from the moment I sit down in the
morning, to the minute I have to stop to pick the girls up from
school. And I'm absolutely convinced that the setting has a lot
to do with it. Why on earth did my parents ever leave this place?

The weather has been glorious. Perfect autumnal days where
the air has been gentle and the colours languid and golden. The
garden looks beautiful, still massed with flowers, but I think what
I notice most of all is the peace. It worried me slightly at first; that
I was spending too much time looking up from my work, lost in
thoughts as I soaked up the quiet, still, magic from outside. But
then I realised that all I was doing was charging that part of me
where my creativity comes from. I was conjuring dancing images
in my head of how I wanted my illustrations to look, and the
moment I picked up my brush they flowed from its end straight
onto the paper.

So now, I just let go. I stop watching the clock and breathe,
feeling the joyful ease of what I'm doing wrap itself around me
as I paint. And the more I feel it, the more attuned I become to
the feeling, until I know the path to it so well that it takes only
seconds to return there.

Even Drew has noticed. The days of the week have whizzed by as we've established our working routine. The space never feels crowded with us both in here and, although we talk, there's mostly just a companionable silence as we lose ourselves in our work. Drew says that he's looked up several times to see me staring out the window with an expression on my face that he can only describe as bliss. I like that.

I smile across at him now as his brow furrows, leaning forward to concentrate on a detail he's adding to the plan in front of him. It's a bread-and-butter job, as he calls them – drawings for an extension to a small cottage in the next village, which came about courtesy of Derek – but Drew doesn't seem to mind. He can do this kind of stuff almost in his sleep, but the fact that it's personal, the fact that he's going to see the results of his labours every time he drives past that cottage, makes up for the fact that it's not what he ultimately wants to be doing. His hair has grown slightly longer over the summer, but I like it; the length encouraging it to curl over the nape of his neck, which is smooth and tanned. I look away. Sometimes too much looking at Drew really isn't good for my work ethic.

I've almost finished this illustration, the first of about thirty which will be needed for Kathryn Talbot's new book. It's a full page and exquisitely detailed. The stories feature two mice, a dormouse and three rabbits who, of course, are all the best of friends, alongside a villain who is a rather naughty weasel. But each has its own individual characteristics and every child who reads these books will end up having a favourite, just as I did when I was a child. Of course it wasn't Kathryn who wrote the stories back then, but her mother, yet Kathryn has carried on the family legacy with a sure and certain voice that still captures their very essence. That I should be illustrating them here, in the house where I first read them, is the proof of how right this all is.

I lean back slightly to get a better overall impression, tutting as the phone rings. The one in the hall, not my mobile, which will doubtless mean that it's someone trying to sell us something. I look across at Drew but he just grins, even though he doesn't even look up from his laptop.

'Nah-uh,' he says. 'It's your turn…'

He's right, it probably is. I slide off my stool and hurry through the living room to catch it before it stops.

'Mrs Gordon? It's Eloise Faulkner here…'

I frown. I should know the name, but it seems out of place somehow.

'From Wood View Primary?'

The girls' head teacher. The breath catches in my throat. 'Is everything all right?'

'The girls are fine,' she replies, each word clipped neatly from the next. 'That is to say there's no emergency. But I wonder if you could come into school, please. I'm sorry to have to tell you that Lauren has been in a fight and we don't allow fighting at Wood View, Mrs Gordon…'

'No, well… I should hope not,' I manage faintly, my head spinning in confusion. How on earth could Lauren have possibly been involved in a fight? They must have the wrong child. 'But, yes… yes, of course I can come in. When would you like? At the end of the day?'

'I can see you now,' she replies, leaving no room for negotiation.

I check my watch. 'Yes, well, I can be there in about ten minutes or so and—'

'That will be fine, thank you.' She hangs up before I've even had the chance to finish what I was going to say. I haven't met Mrs Faulkner yet, but word on the playground is that she's firm, but fair. From what I've just heard I'd say she's well suited to her job. She has a knack of making even grown adults feel like a naughty six-year-old.

I realise I'm still staring at the phone and return it gently to the receiver on the hall table. My first emotion is disbelief, followed quickly by anger that Lauren should behave in such a way. But then, almost immediately, the doubt reappears. Lauren has never put so much as a foot wrong at school. In fact, neither has Chloe, whose only misdemeanours have been for incessant talking. But Lauren has never even had that accusation levelled at her. It just doesn't make any sense and I can feel my hackles beginning to rise. I know my daughter and there's more to this than first appears, I'm sure of it.

I drift back through to the studio in a daze. I've never experienced anything like this before, and I'm not sure how to deal with it. Drew doesn't even look up as I reappear, probably convinced, as I was, that the call was from a salesperson. It's only when he realises I'm still standing in the doorway that he looks up.

I stare at him, open-mouthed. 'That was the school,' I say. 'Lauren's been in a fight…'

His face registers his shock.

'They want me to go in,' I add.

'I'll come with you,' he says, immediately. 'Is she okay?'

'Oh… I don't know,' I say, ashamed. 'I didn't even ask…'

We look at one another. 'It won't be Lauren's fault,' I say. 'It can't be.'

Drew nods. 'I know… but let's wait and see, shall we? I'm sure it's something or nothing, but the sooner it's nipped in the bud, the better.'

'I'll just go and put on some lipstick…'

Ten minutes later we're ushered into a small waiting area in the school by a receptionist who looks even more stressed than I feel. We sit on two small plastic chairs and it's alarming how insecure I can feel in such a short space of time. I've sat in this space before, many, many years ago, waiting for Mrs Williams, and I have to remind myself that, today, I've done nothing wrong. Drew squeezes my hand and I'm so grateful he's here. We're the epitome of responsible parenthood surely, as if that counts for anything.

A door opens from further down the corridor and I can hear the noise of a crying child getting steadily closer. I look up at Drew in horror. It's Lauren; I'd recognise her cry anywhere. But she isn't just upset, she's hiccupping and sobbing like her heart's about to break. I feel it like pain.

Moments later she spots me and hurls herself headlong at my skirt, as I stand to catch her. She buries her head, clutching at me. This isn't a child who is afraid of being told off, or who is contrite at having done something wrong, but one who is utterly distraught, and anger rises inside me like a swelling tide.

Drew also gets to his feet, just as the teacher following Lauren reaches us and, by her bearing, I realise this must be the head. She smiles briefly.

'Mrs Gordon *and* Mr Gordon. Thank you for coming.' She glances at Lauren. 'Do come through.'

I'm not sure what to do. I can hardly walk into her office dragging Lauren with me, but she's still clinging to me like a limpet. I'm also furious that Mrs Faulkner doesn't seem to have acknowledged the state Lauren's in and I'm now more determined than ever to have my say. I know Drew is more than capable of dealing with this himself, but for Lauren's sake I want to fight her corner too. There's no way I'm sitting outside with her.

Drew bends down, his hand caressing Lauren's head as he murmurs against her hair. Then in one smooth motion he lifts her from me, holding her close as her arms slide around his neck and her cheek seeks out his bare skin, drawing comfort from it. He nods at me and I'm suddenly ready.

'Mrs Faulkner?' I begin, as we walk into the room. 'Could I just ask when this fight happened?'

She glances at her watch, clearly surprised by the question. 'At morning break, so a little over an hour ago. Have a seat.'

'I see,' I say quietly, holding her look for a moment longer than strictly necessary. I bend to Lauren as I reluctantly take my seat.

'It's all right, sweetheart, we're here now.' There's a shuddering intake of breath but I doubt if Lauren could even string a sentence together just yet.

Mrs Faulkner clasps her hands together loosely on her desk. 'I'm sorry to have to ask you to come in, particularly this early on in the term, but I wanted to discuss Lauren's behaviour with you today. We don't tolerate violence of any kind here at Wood View and this kind of behaviour is simply unacceptable. Now, obviously Lauren is new to us here and, up until this point, I would have said that she'd settled in very well. However, it would be helpful for us to get a picture of how things are… going forward, so that we can manage them better.'

I exchange a glance with Drew and he looks just as astonished as I am. I can't believe she could make such an assumption. 'Sorry, but that sounds as if you're expecting this kind of thing to continue and I can assure you that Lauren—'

'Perhaps I had better explain what happened, Mrs Gordon.'

I sit back in my chair, knowing that I need to try to keep calm.

'As far as I'm aware there have been no problems up until this point, but at break, Lauren's class were let out into the playground. About halfway through, one of our very experienced teaching assistants clearly saw Lauren punch another child. He was very upset and—'

'He?' I query.

'Yes… a boy, also from Lauren's class, very deliberately punched.'

Lauren hasn't mentioned any boys in her class, only… My eyes narrow. 'Was anyone else involved, other than Lauren and this boy?' I ask.

There's a very slight pause. 'Another child was there, yes. Who also became very upset. But she did confirm what Lauren had done.'

I'm beginning to get an inkling of where this might be going because, if Lauren was outside playing, there was only one person she'd be playing with. 'And was that other child Tilly, by any chance?'

Mrs Faulkner looks slightly irritated to have to admit it, but she nods. 'Yes, it was as it happens.'

'And so what did Tilly say?' I ask. 'Did she shed any light on why Lauren thumped this boy?'

She nods. 'She said... actually, that he had asked Lauren to hit him, which sounds a little far-fetched to me, but Mrs Gordon, this really doesn't change anything. *We* don't allow physical violence for *any* reason.' She breaks off to give a small smile. 'And I'm afraid that in the absence of any other information, I'm at a loss to explain what would have made her do such a thing. The teaching assistant did do her best to find out what had happened, but Lauren admitted it, so...'

Lauren's head is still buried in Drew's shoulder, although her sobs have quietened. She's listening, I realise.

'And have *you* asked Lauren what happened?' It's pretty obvious that Lauren is guilty as charged, but that's rather missing the point. Lauren shouldn't have resorted to violence, but what concerns me is that she should do something so completely out of character. That, and the fact that the head teacher doesn't know Lauren well enough yet to be aware of this – and worse, seems quite happy to label her as a troublemaker.

Mrs Faulkner looks a little uncomfortable. 'I have tried to, yes, but she's been...' She unclasps her hands and makes a small gesture towards Lauren. 'Not altogether easy to talk to.'

'She's been like this, you mean? For over an *hour*...'

'I do understand your distress, Mrs Gordon. It's hard when a child misbehaves, but I have spoken to both the other children concerned, and I'm afraid there's no doubting the fact that Lauren punched another pupil.'

I lay a gentle hand on Lauren's back. 'Is that true?' I ask her. 'Remember how we always tell the truth.'

She turns a tear-stained face towards me and nods sadly. My heart goes out to her, she looks so forlorn. 'But Mummy, Leo was hurting Tilly! And he wouldn't stop even when I asked him to. He's been doing it all day!'

'I know that you were only sticking up for your friend, Lauren. But hitting people is wrong, you know that… You do know that, don't you?'

There's a barely perceptible nod as her lip starts to tremble again.

'Then why did you do it?'

'Because *he* wouldn't stop!' she blurts out. 'Yelling at me all the time. *Wotcha gonna do about it?* she mimics. 'Wotcha gonna do about it, *little* girl. You gonna make me stop? *Go on, hit me, I dare you.*'

I have an almost uncontrollable urge to laugh at the expression on my dear, darling, fierce and courageous daughter's face. Except I know it's not funny. Because however much I want to applaud Lauren for what she did, that's hardly the thing to do when you're a responsible parent, especially not when you're sitting in the head teacher's office. But I have no idea what to say either.

Lauren looks angry now, as if she's just worked out the injustice of it all. Why she's the one getting the blame when all she was doing was what Leo had goaded her into.

I look across at the head, who's frowning slightly. 'I'm sorry,' I say. 'It's very obvious what's happened here, but I can assure you that it won't be repeated. Lauren and Tilly have become very close over the summer… and it's in her nature to be protective and stand up for her friends. I happen to think that's a commendable trait, and Lauren wouldn't normally hit anyone. She does know right from wrong.'

'Yes, but I only have your word for that…'

'Shouldn't that be *enough*?' I counter.

She falters slightly. 'I don't mean that it isn't,' she says, calmly. 'It's simply that, in my experience, parents aren't always that keen to admit when their children are in the wrong.'

'Not in this case.' I'm finding her placatory manner more than a little condescending. 'We fully accept what Lauren did, and we'll certainly be having a chat at home to reinforce that violence isn't the answer.' It's killing me to say these things when the situation seems so unfair. 'But I'm sure you'll agree that Lauren isn't the type of child to go around thumping people. She's obviously been very upset by this.'

Mrs Faulkner nods. 'I do appreciate that but, unfortunately, this is a very serious matter and there are clear guidelines for situations such as this. The normal procedure would be to exclude Lauren from school for a day—' She holds up her hand as my mouth drops open. 'However, given what you say and the fact that we don't as yet have Lauren's records from her previous school, on this occasion only, I'm going to err on the side of caution. However, should there be another occurrence of this type of behaviour, I will have no hesitation in issuing an exclusion.' She raises her eyebrows. She doesn't say *I trust that won't be necessary*, but she may as well have.

'Thank you,' I say. 'We appreciate that. We've always seen the relationship between home and school as a partnership and certainly wouldn't want to undermine the authority of the school if there were any issue. In fact, we'd expect to work together to find a solution. However, in the case of both of our children there has never been an occasion when this has been necessary, not in the past and I wouldn't anticipate one in the future either. I'm sure this is just a one-off.' I clear my throat. 'Incidentally, is Tilly okay?'

The Head looks as if she's chewing on something rather unpleasant. 'I don't think Tilly's made any complaint,' she replies.

I try to look as if I'm sympathising. 'Yes, that makes it difficult, doesn't it? She obviously has a lot to contend with, but she doesn't strike me as the sort to make a fuss. Such a lovely girl.' I glance at Drew and see my own expression mirrored there. Neither of us is about to make an issue of this but whether we're about to make an enemy of the head or not, there's a point to be made here.

'Right, well, thank you, Mrs Faulkner,' says Drew. 'We'll be sure to have a chat to Lauren this evening and make sure we're reinforcing the right messages.' He gives Lauren a squeeze and runs a hand affectionately over her hair. 'Well done you, for sticking up for Tilly, but if Leo or anyone else does anything to hurt her again, you need to tell the teacher, okay? Or a teaching assistant, and then they can help.' He checks his watch and smiles. 'It's nearly lunchtime, so I guess we'd better let Lauren get back to class,' he says.

'Actually I did wonder if you wanted to take Lauren home. Given that she's been… rather upset.'

Which is exclusion by any other name. Not bloody likely. I refuse to let Lauren think she's being punished. She loves school and I'm not about to let anyone change that for her.

'What do you think, sweetheart?' I say. 'You can come home if you want, or stay with Tilly and the other children?'

It doesn't take her long to make up her mind. She gives a big sniff and nods. 'Can I stay with Tilly?' she asks. 'I'm sorry, I promise I won't hit Leo again.' I lean forward and take a tissue from the box on the head's desk and pass it to her. 'Good girl,' I add. 'Now, have a good blow.'

Drew is getting ready to leave. 'Is there someone who can take her back?' he asks, turning on a full-wattage smile.

'I'll ask my secretary.' There's a perfunctory nod as the head gets up to cross to the office next door.

I take the opportunity to look at Drew, eyebrows raised. He's got very good at holding his tongue over the years, a skill he developed from working in a large organisation with too many aspiring managers. I'd give it ten seconds once we get outside before he starts venting his feelings.

Within a minute, Mrs Faulkner is followed into the room by a woman who looks old enough to have been at the school when Drew and I were pupils. She stands in the doorway, a set expression on her face which looks like it could curdle milk. I really don't want to release our daughter to someone who looks so harsh and unwelcoming, but I guess we have no choice. I beckon to Lauren who, after a kiss goodbye from us both, walks slowly to the woman's side. It's as she does so that the secretary meets my eye for the first time. I had expected to see some compassion, or perhaps empathy on her face, but instead there is open disdain and a supercilious look that almost takes my breath away.

It's only Lauren's small wave that jerks me back to the present. 'See you later, sweetheart,' I say as she leaves, waiting only a second or two more before getting to my feet. Drew does likewise.

I hold out my hand. 'Thank you so much for asking us to come in,' I say. 'I'm glad we were able to sort everything out.' Pretending to be so reasonable is killing me.

But Mrs Faulkner has somehow ended up on the back foot and she doesn't want to lose face either, so she's prepared to play the game and be gracious.

'No, thank you for coming,' she says. 'I do appreciate your understanding.'

Oh, I understand all right. Leo's a bully. She knows it and we know it, just like we know she's not going to do anything about it.

She shows us to the door. 'Moving is such a tricky time, isn't it?' she says. 'How are you settling into the village?'

'It's just so lovely to be back,' I say. 'Everything we hoped for.'

She looks at me for a second, eyes slightly narrowed. 'Yes, my secretary mentioned you had lived here before…' It's all coming back to her now. 'Years ago… In the same house, in fact.'

'Thanks again,' says Drew, holding out his hand. The other is resting lightly on my back and I feel the slight increase in pressure. Clearly Drew has no wish to entertain her small talk.

Moments later we're back outside. I don't say anything immediately, putting some distance between us and the school as we walk back down the lane. But I also want to give Drew the opportunity to have his say first. When he doesn't, I glance across at him. He's angry – I can see the hard line of his jaw – but he's staring straight ahead and doesn't look like he's about to engage. Perhaps he just doesn't feel like this is the most appropriate place to do so. Yet the lane's empty.

'Sanctimonious, bloody…' I trail off when I can't think what to call the head that isn't very rude. 'And what was all that with the secretary as well? Jesus, did you see the look she gave me, like I was an axe murderer or something?'

Drew frowns. 'She wasn't the friendliest of souls, but I don't think—'

'And as for that jumped-up… Who the hell does she think she is?'

'The head teacher,' replies Drew.

'*We* don't tolerate violence of any kind,' I say, repeating her words. 'As if *we* do… And to make a sweeping assumption that Lauren is some sort of troublemaker when she knows nothing about our family. Hardly professional. Worse, she's using that as an excuse to cover up her complete lack of interest in actually getting to the truth. Either doesn't want to know, or doesn't care, I'm not sure which I hate more. For goodness' sake, it's not as if we're disputing the fact that Lauren hit Leo, but talk about asking the wrong questions. I know it's a new school for Lauren and all that, but I'll be damned if I let her be tarnished with a reputation as a troublemaker just because Mrs Faulkner isn't doing her job properly.'

'I think you got your point across,' replies Drew mildly. 'And she's in a very difficult position, Thea. As head, she has to be seen to be taking action, or otherwise what does that look like? You know how hot the issue of bullying is among parents and it wouldn't take much for them to lose confidence in her.'

I give him a sideways look. 'Well, sorry, but she's not using our daughter to make a point. Because that *is* my point. She *has* got a case of bullying on her hands and is very obviously looking the other way.'

'Thea, we don't actually know what happened. Lauren was beside herself and we only got about two sentences out of her the whole time we were there. Certainly not enough to know what actually took place. I'm not saying she got it wrong, but we need to talk to her tonight before we go jumping to conclusions. Otherwise we're simply doing what the head wanted to accuse us of – backing our daughter regardless.'

'So you don't think Leo was bullying Tilly?'

'I didn't say that...'

'Okay... But you weren't there on the first day of school when Leo came racing out of school, barged past Tilly and nearly sent her flying. Now, I don't know whether it was deliberate or not, and Anna tried to make light of it at the time, but Leo's mum really laid into him. If he didn't have an issue with Tilly then, I'm pretty certain he's got one now; no child likes being told off like that in public and Tilly was the reason for it.'

Drew stops walking for a moment. 'Are we saying that Tilly is obviously being bullied because... well, because she's an easy target?'

'No!' I glare at him. 'That's not what I'm saying at all. I'm making no more assumptions about this than you are, but Lauren's behaviour today was completely out of character. She must have had a good reason for what she did. And yes, on the face of it, Lauren seems like she's the only one who's done anything wrong, but bullies are often experts at hiding what they do. So, if you were the parent of a disabled child, who had been singled out for abuse, verbal or physical, would you rather everyone just ignored it so you couldn't be accused of making a fuss? Or, would you rather the child's friend stood up for them? Because if I were Anna, I think I'd be rather pleased that Lauren is loving and loyal and brave enough to take a stand.'

'Of course I'd rather someone stood up for them, but that isn't the point here, Thea. We don't know that Tilly *is* being bullied. All I'm saying is that it's probably not a good idea to assume she is, or the whole thing could get blown out of proportion. Besides, if Tilly is being bullied, then isn't that Anna's issue to deal with?'

I raise my eyebrows.

'Anna and Rob's,' Drew corrects himself.

Better, but that's not my only complaint. Bullying is a big deal and I've seen it swept under the carpet too many times.

Drew takes a deep breath. 'Thea, I'm really proud of Lauren for trying to do the right thing, but she did go about it in the wrong way and, as her parents, we have to help her to understand that. I'm as unhappy about the way that this has been dealt with as you are, but try not to let yourself get upset about it. Or go thinking all the staff at the school are the problem. The girls have only just started school here for goodness' sake, we don't want them, or us, labelled as troublemakers.'

He starts walking again and I let him go one or two paces before I carry on myself. Somehow walking by his side no longer seems to be the right fit. *Don't get upset about it*, he said. But I am. I wanted Drew's total support on this and I'm surprised I didn't get it.

CHAPTER NINE

I almost miss Lauren as I enter her bedroom, but when I do spot her, the sight stops me in my tracks. It could be me tucked up on the window seat, partially hidden behind the curtain, but instead it's our eight-year-old daughter who has found her way there, just like I used to do when I was her age. It was my place of refuge back then, when I wanted to read or to draw, or simply stare out of the window lost in a daydream. It's also where I used to take myself when I needed to cry.

'Is everything all right, sweetheart?'

Lauren turns at the sound of my voice and nods, her face pale and solemn.

'I'm sorry, Mummy.' Her sad little voice is scarcely more than a whisper.

'Oh, Lauren…' I kneel on the floor beside her, my arm sliding around her small shoulders. 'You're not in any trouble, I promise. What you did today was very caring and very brave, but Daddy's right when he says that hitting people isn't the right thing to do, even when it seems like there's nothing else you *can* do. And all you have to remember is that there's always an adult you can talk to. Whether that's one of us at home, or someone at school; they'll know how to help. And as long as you tell the truth, you'll never be in any trouble for trying to help your friends.'

She nods, but to my horror a slow tear makes its way down her cheek. I reach out to wipe it away. 'So there's no need to be sad, little wren.'

There's a small smile but if anything the tears come even faster.

'But I didn't,' she says, her head hanging down. Her hands are fiddling with a fold of paper on her lap, turning it over and over, first one way and then the other. I watch her for a second, mesmerised.

'Didn't what, sweetheart?'

She sniffs and a sob breaks free. 'I didn't tell the truth…'

I can feel my back stiffen. 'About Leo?' I ask, gently.

She doesn't reply.

'Lauren…? Whatever it is you need to tell me…'

'But I'll be in trouble.'

I can't lie to her, but it's breaking my heart to see her so forlorn. 'Maybe,' I say. 'But it's always worse if you don't own up to things. What didn't you tell the truth about?'

The seconds tick by until I reach out a hand. 'What's that, Lauren?' I touch a finger to the bright-pink envelope she's been fiddling with.

'It's a letter. From Tilly. She gave it to me at school.' And she draws it away, tucking it under the edge of her legs.

'Oh… And are you going to write a reply? You can give it to her in the morning.'

She shakes her head, a tiny movement. 'But that's how I know I wasn't telling the truth. Because Tilly explained what happened, and I got it wrong. Leo wasn't hurting her at all, not really.' Her face lifts to mine. 'I'm sorry, Mummy…'

And with another sob she hurls herself into my arms.

'Oh, Lauren…' I say, my hand stroking her hair. It's so obvious what's happened here, but how can I tell her the truth of the situation? I'll effectively be calling her friend a liar, and Tilly's certainly not that. She's just a scared child playing down an incident because she doesn't want to make things worse for herself. It's Anna I need to speak to, not Lauren. So instead, I just hold her, telling her it's going to be all right until her tears subside.

I can still see the edge of the pink envelope peeking out from beneath Lauren's legs. 'You know, when I was your age I used to write down any worries I had, a bit like Tilly has, only you write a letter to yourself, not to another person. I don't know why, but I found it helped. And then once you've done that you put the letter away for a bit and try to forget about it. I always found that when I read the letter a little while later, the thing I was worried about had disappeared. Maybe you could do that too and find somewhere to keep the letters safe.'

There's a gulp of breath and the smallest of nods. 'I will.'

'Good girl.' I tilt my head to one side. 'Now, why don't you come and have a nice bath and then we can read for a while. How's that?'

And it's not until much later when I'm undressing, sitting on the edge of the bed in a room where my parents once slept, that I allow myself to remember what it was like to be a child with a secret.

*

We're running late for school the next morning, which suits me fine. It means there's no time to stand around worrying about whose eyes are on me in the playground or, worse, have a conversation with Leo's mum about what happened yesterday. I will have to at some point, I know that, but not today. There's no sign of Anna or Tilly either. They went on ahead of us and I hope this means that Anna is already inside discussing her own concerns. So I kiss the girls goodbye, give Lauren an extra big hug and head for home. I have work to do but I'm also very aware that there's a jumble of thoughts building inside my head and I need a little time to straighten them all out. And Drew, I need to talk to Drew. If anyone can make sense of it all, he can.

Except that when I get back, going straight through to the studio, I find he's got his jacket on, and is patting his pockets for his car keys and phone.

'I got a bite,' he says, grinning, gesturing towards his laptop. 'So, I'm going to strike while the iron's hot before they change their minds.'

This is brilliant news. 'Who?' I ask.

'It's only a small charity, in the Brecon Beacons, but it's a start,' he says. 'And they just responded to a newsletter I sent out on spec, which is even better. At least it means I'm getting something right.'

I put my hands either side of his head and kiss him square on the lips. I can feel him grinning. 'More than most,' I reply, as his hands slide around my buttocks. 'Go, knock 'em dead,' I add.

He checks his watch. 'They're a good two hours away,' he says. 'So I have no idea when I'll be back.'

'Go,' I say, nodding at him. 'Don't worry…'

He's distracted now. Already thinking about what he needs to do, what he needs to say.

'Just go and be brilliant,' I add.

He beams at me and plonks a kiss on my nose. 'Love you.'

'I love you too.'

Seconds later he's gone and the rush of his energy departing the room leaves it feeling strangely empty. I drift through to the kitchen to make a drink. Perhaps a little caffeine is all I need to get the day flowing but, even as I sit back at my desk sipping my coffee, I realise that it's not going to help. I try holding one of my brushes, usually the thing that starts my creative juices flowing. Yet, despite the way I've been feeling about my work the last few days, the journey to that space feels laboured this morning. Even though a part of me is eager to continue with my work, I feel oddly inert and yet restless at the same time.

I look at the clock. There are hours ahead of me. I should be glad for the chance of uninterrupted work, it's usually something that makes my fingers tingle with excitement, but today it's almost as if I don't want to be left alone with my thoughts. The brush stills in my hand. That's exactly what it is. If I'm left alone with them, I'll have to admit to what I'm thinking and I really don't want to do that. I need to keep busy, but it's not my work I need right now. I need industry of a different kind.

Rachel and Gerry will be here at the weekend and the spare room needs some work if it's going to be a comfortable place for them to stay. A damn good clean will make the world of difference but the furniture is a bit of a hotchpotch too; random items left there from when we moved. Still, with a bit of effort I should be able to make it look presentable. I swallow the rest of my coffee and head back to the kitchen for some cleaning materials.

Except that, as I cross the landing, I'm drawn back into Lauren's room, not at all surprised to find myself heading towards the window seat.

I was amazed to find it still here when we moved in, certain it would have been ripped out in an effort to modernise. Even more astonishing has been the way that Lauren has gravitated here, just as I did, and to see her occupying this same space yesterday brought forth a powerful emotion. And when I realised that the envelope on her lap was the same one I had hidden away all those years ago, it almost took my breath away.

A picture book rests on the seat cushion and I place it carefully on the bed before returning to yank the cushion from the seat and hurl it to the floor. Underneath the wooden lid is a useful storage cubby where Lauren has packed away some of her dolls and I pull them from the dark interior, the slightly musty smell of the old wood seeping through the cracks of my memories. My hands seek out the corner plank on the floor of the cubbyhole, testing, feeling. Out of sight, out of mind. For all these years.

I press the end closest to me, feeling the corresponding lift from the far end and, although my fingers are much larger than they used to be, with a bit of scraping of nails and jiggling of the wood I'm able to work it free, revealing the cavity beneath. The secret hiding place of my childhood.

I sit back on my haunches, my skin prickling with sudden heat as I recognise where I'm at. There's a threshold here that once I cross there will be no going back from. If there's anything still here. I take a deep breath, all at once realising that I desperately want there to be.

I should get a torch really. The space isn't big, but it's big enough to have filled with spiders and unmentionables of almost every variety. My fingers gingerly start to explore. At first there is nothing, a cold draught, something soft on the floor of the space, but then I touch the edges of a smooth surface, and I know that Lauren has replaced the envelope exactly where she found it. The pink envelope that came with a birthday card one year and in which, for reasons I forget now, I always placed my darkest fears. Maybe I thought that nothing could ever be that bad if I enclosed it in something so relentlessly cheerful.

There should only be one piece of paper inside it now. All the others I threw away as time rendered the petty upsets of my childhood innocuous: the day my pet hamster died; the time I ripped the hem of my party dress and was devastated; when I got into trouble for spilling blackcurrant juice all over the white tablecloth when my grandma came to stay. All gone, except this last one, a page torn from my favourite notebook and left with the house for safekeeping. It had seemed like the right thing to do when we moved; I hadn't wanted to take it with me. And truly, up until now, I can't remember ever thinking about what I had written. I didn't need to – nothing like that had ever happened again.

My hands are trembling as I lift the envelope clear of the space that, until recently, has kept it hidden for twenty-three years. I was eleven when I wrote the letter. I don't remember exactly when, but sometime in the weeks before we left and the golden, magical time that was Pevensey was over.

There are two other sheets of paper in here now – Tilly's letter and perhaps a reply from Lauren – but I won't read them. They're private, and I know without looking which one's mine. The paper is pale yellow, made crinkly around the edges from the damp space, and I open it up, the handwriting achingly familiar. It's large and round, innocent. And it's as if my old self is sitting here beside me now, except that she already knows what's written on the piece of paper, and she's waiting for me to read it so that we can compare notes. Did she feel the same back then as I do now?

> I've had weird butterflies in my tummy all day today. Like when you know you're in trouble or something bad happens. And I don't think I've ever seen mummy crying before. She tried to pretend she wasn't but her face was all red so I know she was because that's just how mine goes.
>
> I think it was because she and daddy were arguing. She shouts at me sometimes, but I've never heard her shout at him and he looked like he was crying too.
>
> But I'm too scared to ask what's wrong. Because when Drew's mum was crying once, he asked her what was wrong and it was because his grandad had died. And I don't want anyone to have died.

I stare at the words again. It's not as if I remember them exactly, but I remember the feel of them. And she's right, I have had weird butterflies in my tummy all day, just like she did. I've been trying to ignore them, but they're there.

I never did find out why my mum was crying, or what she and Dad had argued about, but I guess it didn't matter. People cry all the time. They argue too, and she and Dad were married right up until the day he died, so whatever it was couldn't have been that serious.

I lower the paper to my lap. Perhaps that's why I'm here today. To be given the proof by my younger self that, just because we feel something is wrong, doesn't necessarily mean it is. Or at least it's something that blows over, a storm in a teacup as my mum used to say. Maybe all I needed was to get things into perspective. To recognise that what felt important enough back then for me to write down and leave in my secret place turned out to be just a childish anxiety. I stare out the window, at the gilded trees outside. That would make sense.

Except… I shake my head, because there is something there, niggling me at the back of my mind. This isn't just a memory I can close the door on, because there's something stuck there, keeping it ajar. I look down at the envelope once more. It's incredible that Lauren even found it in the first place, but she's so like me at times it hurts. I wonder what she felt when she first discovered my letter. And when she read it. Has she worked out that I'm the little girl who wrote it? Has it made her feel safe, knowing that her worries are tucked away next to mine?

But I've lied to her. I told her that if she wrote them down they would disappear, and yet mine are still here, the ghostly fingers of their memory reaching out to me, ruffling the hairs on the back of my neck. A shiver ripples down my back and I thrust the letter inside the envelope, suddenly wanting it as far away as possible.

It takes only a moment to return it to the hiding place of my youth, to work the wooden slat into position and pile Lauren's dolls back inside the cubbyhole, closing the lid. The cushion slides neatly over the top and, as if by magic, it's just a reading seat again. As if the last few minutes never happened and the picture-postcard view of my childhood is no longer torn in two.

I'm about to leave the room when I remember Lauren's book. I retrieve it from the bed, trying to recall how it was placed on the seat so that she won't know I've been here. Something flutters from it to the floor. It's a sheet of newspaper and, as I bend to pick it up, the butterflies in my stomach take flight.

CHAPTER TEN

The newspaper is yellowed with age, the edges rippled where it has succumbed to the damp, just like my letter.

The page facing me carries a huge advertisement for Butlin's holiday camp, and I harbour a brief hope that it has been left behind for purely innocent reasons, a bit of fun maybe, like unearthing a time capsule in the garden. But I know that's not going to be the case. Because the spot where Lauren found it is a place where secrets were kept.

A heavy thudding fills the centre of my chest as I open up the folded sheet to see what's at its heart. Spread in front of me are pictures of the village from my childhood: the school still with its old sign in place, the church, the lane looking lovely with its summery gardens. And for a moment I believe that this might really be just a memento after all. Until I see the headline.

Because these photos aren't in the paper to announce that the village has won an award for Britain in Bloom, or been voted one of the best places to live. They're there as a reminder to people, to jog their memories in case they might be able to shed some light on who could have dragged a thirteen-year-old girl into the bushes on a warm summer night as she walked home from Guides.

I close my eyes and swallow. There is a faint clicking noise coming from some distant corner of the house, most likely the hot water system settling. Closer to me are the sound of blackbirds outside, trilling from the roof. But apart from these small reminders of normality, everything else has irrevocably changed. Because this newspaper is here, in my old house, and has been hidden alongside my letter in the bright-pink envelope, and I really don't want to think about why that might be.

I scan the paper for clues; there are no names, just a date in June, but nothing to indicate which year and, as I turn the paper this way and that, I realise there's no other date anywhere. I peer at the photos again, trying to work out when they would have been taken, but there's no doubt in my mind that this is the incident that Anna had referred to. A crime where the perpetrator had never been found. I rack my brains, trawling my memory banks for the name Anna mentioned – Georgia Thomas – but there's nothing. Not a single thing to tell me why this newspaper is here. My hand flies to my mouth as I suddenly realise what I've been reading. And, more to the point, who else has. There isn't much detail in the article but the thought of Lauren looking at what little there is makes me feel sick.

I hurriedly replace the picture book on the seat where I found it, refolding the newspaper, before taking it away. Tucking it inside my bedside-table drawer where it can no longer poison the air with its words. I have no idea what to do now. Do I speak to Lauren about it, or not? I certainly don't want her asking questions of her friends, but neither do I want to bring this thing into our home any more than it already is.

I don't know how long I sit there, perched on the edge of my bed as I try to make sense of the last few minutes. Because one thing's for sure; the newspaper clipping was only the start of something, not the end. What came next I have no knowledge of, but I can imagine. And it's something I'm going to have to find out. Maybe I should go and speak to Anna again, and see what else she knows. But, even as I think it, I know I won't, not yet anyway. This whole thing needs to stay at a distance, where I can keep an eye on it.

My laptop screen flickers into life as I boot it up and I'm amazed to see it's only just gone ten. A little over an hour since Drew left. He won't be home for ages yet but I just want him here so that I won't be on my own, wondering why someone has hidden the details of a child-abuse case in our home.

There's not much to go on. After an hour of searching the internet in every way I can think of, I'm left with little more than I already knew. It's obviously very old news and took place long before social media existed. Reporting was done the old-fashioned way, in print, and very little of it has been archived. I can find nothing that might help me.

Georgia is okay though. And by that I mean she's alive and, I'm assuming, well. A trawl of Facebook allows me to discover that she's living near Hereford, although there's no mention of family. But there are no further details about the incident when she was thirteen other than those in the newspaper. She was sexually abused but her attacker was never found. Several local men were questioned, but they all had substantiated alibis and, without DNA evidence to go on, it seems the investigation ground to a halt.

As a child I'd been to Guides once or twice until I decided it wasn't for me. Meetings were held in the local community hall, at the other end of the village from Pevensey, and if Georgia lived locally her walk home would have taken only a matter of minutes. That's all it had taken to change her life forever, but there was still a life out there that had continued almost unaltered, someone who knew that they were guilty. And it made me wonder who else might know. Perhaps the person who had hidden the article away, maybe as a reminder, or maybe to bide their time. I sit up straight. Damn, why hadn't I thought of that before?

We'd been gone from the village for twenty-three years and I had no idea who had lived in the house after we moved. It could have been one person or it could have been ten for all I knew. But the decor is still very dated and it seemed logical that if the house had changed hands more recently that some of the work we still needed to attend to would have already been completed. And I can't help but think of Anna's description of its most recent occupants: a man who gave her the creeps, who didn't like children, and his wife, the opposite, perhaps long-suffering…

But my questions have no answers and I can't begin to think how I can find out. I pace the house like a caged animal until it's time to go and collect the girls from school. They hurry home with me, lured by the promise of an impromptu baking session.

It's nearly seven o'clock by the time Drew returns. I'm sick with longing to have someone to talk to about all of this, yes – but mostly to be folded into his arms and told that everything is going to be okay. But he's buzzing when he arrives, a grin stretching from ear to ear as he shrugs off his jacket and throws down his folder onto the kitchen table.

'I've bloody done it!' he exclaims, as he sweeps towards me, arms outstretched so that I can share in his joy. 'My first order… Oh God, Thea, honeycomb houses are going to be a thing… I've had to promise all sorts to get it, but I don't care!'

He whirls me round, but it feels weirdly like it's happening to someone else and I don't know how to be. Drew has been working towards this for years and I've thought so many times about what this moment will feel like for him; the realisation that this could be what changes everything, what brings the dream that bit closer. But all I can think of is, not now… not when there seems to be so many other things to think about. Not when I want to talk to him. And I hate myself for it.

So I pretend. I have to. And I grin back at him and make whooping noises that bring the girls running. 'I told you!' I say.

'I knew it was just a matter of time.' And I beckon the girls in. 'Come and give your amazing daddy a big hug.'

We dance a weird entwined jig around the kitchen until Chloe breaks away. She fetches the tin from the side and shows her father the muffins we'd ended up making earlier. 'Look, Mummy said we should make these for you so that we can celebrate,' she says proudly.

'Aha!' he replies. 'Well how clever of Mummy to know we'd be needing them.'

His eyes light up as he grins at me and I don't disagree. I'd forgotten I'd even said that and I marvel that I could still be that person without even thinking about it.

'Which reminds me,' I add, as another thought comes to me. And this was something I *had* consciously planned, a while back in fact for this precise moment. I'm very grateful for it now.

I cross to the pantry and bring forth the bottle of champagne that I'd stashed there. It isn't ice-cold, but it's been on the marble slab for days and is pretty chilly.

'Ta-dah!'

Drew does that thing with his eyes that melts me from the inside out and he pulls me in to press his lips against mine. 'What did I ever do to deserve you?' he says. And I can't possibly answer.

He hasn't eaten yet and, now that his elation is settling, he's suddenly ravenous and wary of drinking the champagne on an empty stomach. So I rustle up a quick plateful of beans on toast, leaving him to eat it as I chivvy the girls to have their bath. Half an hour later, I'm eating a chocolate chip muffin and drinking champagne as I sit and listen to Drew talk. It's the only thing to do but the contrast of his mood against mine tastes bitter.

'So, who is this charity then?' I ask. 'Come on, tell me all about it.'

He shoves in a mouthful of his cake before replying. 'They're only small, an organisation that runs short-break, respite holidays for people with disabilities. They've just received a grant to allow them to expand and want to create a woodland centre on a parcel of land which they've been able to buy. However, access isn't great at the moment and there's not a lot of cash left over to build anything the traditional way.'

'Which is where the honeycomb houses come in...'

Drew nods. 'They want two to start with, but in time hopefully more, the beauty of them being of course that they can all slot together. They'll use one for sleeping and eating and the other will be somewhere their service users can have access to the nature that's all around them.'

'So what else did you have to offer them to secure the deal? Don't tell me you've got to sleep with the managing director...'

Drew grins. 'Damn, I didn't think of that,' he replies. 'If I had maybe I wouldn't have had to give them a discount.' He chews thoughtfully. 'Still, I made sure that in return I can follow the project from start to finish and use it for publicity. It will mean a bit of to-ing and fro-ing, but worth it in the long run. Let's just hope everything goes according to plan.' He finishes his muffin, crumpling up the paper case and dropping it onto his empty plate. 'Anyway, what sort of a day have you had? How are the girls? Is Lauren okay? She seemed all right when I came in.'

I look at him, puzzled by his question. The events of yesterday seem so far away and I'm struggling to make any reply that isn't vague.

Drew looks at his watch. 'I'd best go and listen to the girls read,' he says. 'I could use a shower too, but after that, I'm all yours...' And he drains his glass of champagne with an unmistakable look in his eye.

And so time slips further and further away and there no longer seems to be a moment when I can possibly release the fears I'm holding deep inside of me. It wouldn't be fair.

But I know that Drew will notice something soon, when his euphoria wears off and other things start to nibble at his consciousness. Because I can't keep up the pretence that everything is fine for long.

It's night-time now and he's turned away from me, onto the side he generally favours when he's deeply asleep. His breathing is quiet and even and, although I've willed myself to relax, I know that my current state of wakefulness is as good as it's going to get. And I silently begin to count the hours until morning.

CHAPTER ELEVEN

It's been an odd couple of days. Like there's something in the water. I smile at my choice of words as I empty the washing-up bowl of suds and hang up the dishcloth to dry. It's like when you catch something out of the corner of your eye but, when you look, there's nothing there. So I'm probably just imagining the hush that has fallen as I walked past a group of mums, or caught someone looking at me with more than a passing glance... It feels as if the questions endlessly circling my own head are being repeated by everyone else. Who left the newspaper clipping in our house? What really happened? What does it mean? But I know that they can't be asking these things because I still haven't told anyone else about my discovery, not even Drew...

And now the weekend has arrived at last, and for that at least I'm grateful, because that means Rachel. And hugs and good conversation. I hadn't realised I'd missed her quite as much as I have until I'm faced with the prospect of seeing her again. I've been constantly rushing to check the front window for the last half hour, and listening out for their car, but now they're finally here and I can't contain my excitement.

By the time I fling open the front door, they've already pulled up outside and spilled from the car, stretching legs and laughing. Then hugging Drew and the girls, who were playing outside, but came running at the sound of tyres on gravel.

Rachel is staring up at the house, shielding her eyes from the sun. Her hair is shorter than the last time I saw her but her smile is the same as she spots me coming towards her. We pause for just a second, feeling distance occupying the space between us, but then it's gone, vanished by the memory of our friendship that fills it.

'Thea, look at this place!' she exclaims. 'You said it was gorgeous, but I didn't realise it was *this* gorgeous. The photos don't do it justice at all.' She throws up her hands. 'In fact, this whole place is magical. I think I'd forgotten the countryside even existed. You know, green spaces that don't suddenly stop the other side of a handful of trees. The green here goes on forever.'

Gerry comes forward and hugs us both. He looks tired, his face grey and puffy in comparison to Drew's, which glows golden in the afternoon sun. He's grinning at us, taking in what he sees. 'You're never coming back to London, are you?' he says. 'We must be mad thinking you would.'

I give Rachel a quizzical look.

'For some bizarre reason we thought you might get bored, with all the endless gorgeous scenery,' she says, pulling a face. 'Or fed up with the peace and quiet... the fresh air, no traffic jams, no commuting...'

Gerry breathes in deeply, the swell of his round stomach expanding. 'As if you would... Still, you never know, maybe this will be the weekend when we decide we've had enough of London too.'

Drew grins at him. 'We do have paramedics in the country, Gerry,' he says. 'You could do a lot worse.'

Rachel looks away, a wry smile on her face. This isn't a new conversation. In fact, I'd bet it was a topic of discussion for most of their journey here.

'Anyway, come on in,' adds Drew. 'Let's get you something to eat and drink. And then, I can show you to your room.' He rolls his eyes. 'I've always wanted to say that...'

I take Rachel's arm. 'Anyone would think he's lord of the manor,' I say. 'We do have five bedrooms now, but they're not *that* big.'

She laughs. 'I was wondering when we'd get to meet the butler…'

Admittedly the hallway is a bit of a conversation-stopper. With its beautiful tiled floor and mahogany panelling either side of the staircase which sweeps upward to the galleried landing, it's very *Homes & Gardens* but, fortunately, Rachel and Gerry know us well enough to see beyond that and the relaxed chatter continues unabated.

Half an hour later, having done the tour, I'm back in the kitchen making a pile of sandwiches as Rachel comes in from the garden.

'Honestly, you should hear those two out there, like a couple of old men,' she says.

Drew and Gerry have set up camp for the afternoon by the look of things. The deckchairs are out, the beers are set up on the table and they don't look as if they're planning on moving any time soon.

'That's okay,' I reply. 'At least it will mean I can have you all to myself for a while.' I turn to hug her. 'Oh, it's so good to see you again, Rachel.'

Her eyes are shining. 'I know!' She sighs dramatically. 'This week has gone so slowly and, if anything, I think Gerry has been worse than me.'

She glances back out through the open door. 'He misses Drew something chronic, not that he'd admit to it, of course…' She breaks off. 'He's had a bit of a rough time at work actually, and his mates in the service are great, but he and Drew always used to swap stories about how bad each other's jobs were. Perversely it used to make him feel better.' But then she grins. 'Or perhaps it was the beer… Anyway, it's good to see you too, Thea. It feels like you've been away forever.'

I brighten my smile. 'So, come on then, tell me all your news. How's your business going now that term has started again? I bet the dinner-party season will soon be in full swing.'

Rachel rolls her eyes. 'Yep. But you know me, Thea, I love it and hate it both at the same time. But actually, I've been asked to do some teaching at a local deli that's just opened. They were looking for a way to get some more punters through the door and the owner asked me if I'd do some classes there. I don't think it's going to be particularly lucrative but—'

'It could lead in all sorts of directions, Rachel. I think that's brilliant news.'

'Unless his business is a total flop, of course.'

I tut. 'Yes, but with you doing your thing, how could it be?'

Rachel has automatically taken over the buttering of the slices of bread I've cut. She grins. 'I hadn't thought of that.' She scoops up another curl of butter from the pot. 'It will be nice to do something a little different though, and good experience too.'

'For when you move to your farmhouse in the country, you mean? And run your brilliantly successful cookery school.'

She blushes, peeping across at me from under her lashes.

I stand back to look at her better. 'You're actually thinking about this, aren't you?' I say. 'I mean, really seriously thinking.'

'Oh, I don't know, Thea. Sometimes I think we are and then we talk ourselves out of it again. I guess it's just that now you two are gone, London seems... Well, London is like it's always been, but maybe I'm just more aware of its shortcomings now. You get so caught up in everyday life that you simply carry on, like a hamster in a wheel – can't get off it – and haven't got time to look at what might be around you either. Or you're too afraid to. Sometimes it takes a change in someone else's life to make you take stock of your own.'

She puts down the knife. 'And you guys look so well, and happy. Relaxed, tanned, carefree... Do I need to go on?' She grins again. 'You are, aren't you? Please tell me you are...'

'Yes, we are,' I reply, laughing. 'It hasn't all been plain sailing, nothing ever is, but being here again feels right. Like it was meant to be.' I ponder the look on her face. 'Your interest in our welfare is lovely, Rach,' I say. 'But why do I get the feeling there's more to this conversation than just plain curiosity?'

Her face lights up in excitement. 'Possibly because the reason why we left Jamie with his nanny and grandad is so that Gerry could take Monday off as holiday and we can spend the day exploring.'

I let out a little squeal. 'Exploring with a view to house-hunting?'

Rachel just smiles. 'We can stay in a hotel though if…'

I silence her with a fierce look. 'You will not,' I say. 'Don't be so silly. You're more than welcome to stay here, especially if that's the reason.'

'You're going to think we're stalking you.'

'As if…' I nudge her arm. 'Come on, you've got me all excited now. Let's get these sandwiches made, and then I can show you around the village. Not saying you have to move *here* of course, but…' I wink at her as she continues buttering the bread.

Come two o'clock it's absolutely boiling and I wonder if we're in for another storm. After the rain midweek, a mini heatwave has arrived as predicted, causing Drew and Gerry to drag their chairs across the lawn into the shade from the willow. They both look as if they could fall asleep at any minute. Taking pity on them, Rachel and I decide to take the girls with us on our walk and, lured by the promise of an ice cream and a paddle in the stream, they readily agree.

We're just heading out of our gate when I spy Anna walking back up the lane with Fergus and Tilly trailing behind. Neither of them look pleased to have been for a walk. Fergus I can understand – his tongue is lolling out and he looks hot and thirsty – but it's unusual to see Tilly looking so dispirited.

I wave and wait for them to reach us.

'Hi Anna, what a gorgeous day!' Lauren is already dancing around Tilly and Anna smiles a little, relieved perhaps to see her daughter looking happier, but it doesn't completely hide her obvious tension. I stand back. 'This is my friend, Rachel, from London.'

'I've heard all about you,' Anna replies, easily enough, but I can't help but wonder if she feels a bit awkward in the face of my friendship with Rachel. I hope not.

'We're just off out for a walk,' I add. 'Round the village and then down to the Sawley brook for a paddle. I can take Tilly too, if she'd like to come.'

Anna darts an anxious look at her daughter. 'Maybe not today,' she says. 'I didn't realise it was so hot and we've just been out for quite a long walk.' Her voice falls to a near whisper. 'She's a bit down in the dumps for some reason, so I'd best take her home.'

But Anna's quiet words are still loud enough for Tilly to hear. 'Oh, Mum, please can I go? I'm not tired, honest.' Tilly's face looks brighter and I can see Anna is torn. Unwittingly, I've put her in a difficult position.

'I don't want her to be a nuisance,' Anna replies, unusually reticent, even though we both know that the girls will play far more happily if they're all together.

'Mum, please…'

Lauren comes back to my side, looking up at me with a pleading face, but it's not my decision to make. I'm struggling for a way out that doesn't leave Anna in a worse place when she glances across at Rachel and smiles back at me. 'Actually, that would be lovely, Thea. As long as you don't mind?'

'Not at all. I'll make sure we head back if Tilly looks too hot or tired.'

Tilly's already dancing about in her slightly jerky, lopsided way, but she doesn't look lacking in energy, far from it.

'You'll need your wellies, Tilly,' Anna says. 'Do you want to go run and get them?' Her daughter doesn't need a second invitation and the three girls race off as Anna mouths a thank you at me. She drops to her haunches to give Fergus a fuss. 'Even you're worn out today, aren't you boy? I think we're all a bit out of sorts.' He's taken the opportunity to flop in the dusty lane and, although he raises an eyebrow at being addressed, it's clear he has no desire to move. The seconds tick by.

'Thea tells me you live next door,' says Rachel. 'That must be so weird knowing that Drew lived there as a boy and must know your house almost as well as you do.'

Anna straightens. 'We've only lived here for five years and I gather it's changed a bit since, but yes.' She looks along the lane towards her house, passing the dog lead from one hand to the other as she does so. 'I'm not sure I'd like to go back to the place where I grew up.'

She pauses for a moment. 'In fact, I'm sure I wouldn't. But then I don't think my memories are as happy as yours are, Thea.' She smiles, wistfully, or simply with sadness, I can't tell.

To my relief, there's a shriek as the girls come hurtling back towards us, their feet making the odd waffling noise that only running in wellies can produce. Fergus gets to his feet as if sensing movement is imminent.

'Right, come on then you lot, let's go,' I say. 'And poor Fergus can have a proper rest.' I turn to Anna. 'We might be a couple of hours, is that okay? But we'll see how we go.'

She nods and passes a hand over Tilly's hair. 'Behave yourself, you,' she says. 'I'll see you later. Lovely to meet you, Rachel,' she adds. And with that she turns, her thick ponytail swinging as she walks away. She's only gone a few paces when she stops and glances back. 'Oh, and enjoy your walk. Bye...' She waves, smiling.

The girls are already walking on ahead. 'Mind the road,' I say automatically as Rachel and I follow behind.

'She seems nice,' says Rachel.

'Oh, she is,' I reply. 'They've been such lovely neighbours since we moved in.' I pause for a second. 'Although, she was a bit quiet today.' I nod at the girls' backs in front of us. 'I think she might be a bit worried about Tilly actually,' I murmur. 'I'll tell you in a bit...'

We turn out onto the main road through the village where the full force of the sun hits us after the relative shade of the lane. 'Blimey,' I say. 'Ice creams before we paddle, or after?' I ask, grinning at Rachel. 'Or both?'

There's a predictable chorus from the girls and I laugh. 'We'll see,' I add.

The village is quiet, although the soft strains of organ music drift out from the church as we walk past. 'Did I tell you that Anna's husband, Rob, is the local curate?' I ask. 'He has a christening tomorrow, as well as the usual Sunday service. I would imagine they're having a practice.'

Rachel nods. 'It's lovely.' She takes a deep breath and sighs. 'That's what I really like about villages,' she says. 'That whole community thing. Where everyday ordinary things are a big part of people's lives. It happens in London too, I'm not saying it doesn't, but the cycle of life here seems more...' She searches for the right word. 'Meaningful somehow. People are involved on a different level.'

I smile at her. 'You really have been bitten by the bug, haven't you?' I say. 'But you're right, it's nice to feel a part of things. And the children just love it here.' I'm conscious of Lauren's altercation with Leo as I say it, particularly as we're now nearing the school.

'Well, they've obviously made friends easily enough. Have they settled in okay?'

'Yes, fine,' I reply, skirting the subject. I would love to talk to Rachel about it, but it doesn't seem fair. She's come for a weekend away, not to listen to my worries. 'Of course, it's helped having Tilly on our doorstep. They all hit it off straight away.'

Rachel nods, directing her look in front of us. 'It must be incredibly difficult for Tilly,' she says, softly. 'But she manages very well, doesn't she?'

'Testament to Anna and Rob,' I reply. 'They don't treat her as if she has a disability so I don't think Tilly really ever gives it a thought. She just gets on with life, and she's such a confident little thing that it's good for Lauren too – who dotes on her, as you may have noticed,' I add, grinning.

'I don't think I'd be quite so well adjusted about it as they seem to be,' remarks Rachel. 'I think I'd be completely neurotic if it were Jamie and be reaching for the cotton wool every five minutes.'

I nod. 'Me too. But then I guess we never know what we're capable of until we're faced with it.'

'You mentioned that Anna was worried about Tilly though…' She lets the sentence sit between us.

I'm about to answer her, but we're nearly at the shop. 'Let's get some ice creams first,' I say.

I wasn't expecting to see Jackie here today, seeing as it's the weekend, but I can hardly march everyone back out now that the children have crowded around the freezer trying to decide what to buy. I stand back for a minute, letting them have first pick, and try to catch Jackie's eye. She's determinedly straightening some perfectly aligned cereal boxes.

'Was everything okay the other day?' I ask.

She looks up, doing the 'who me?' face. But she can't pretend for long, I'm staring right at her.

'The other day,' I repeat. 'When you had to bring Chloe home early.' I smile. 'I haven't really seen you since then, but I just wondered if everything was all right. It wasn't bad news, I hope, only you did look worried.'

Jackie frowns as if trying to remember, but then her expression hardens. 'No, everything's fine, thank you.'

She's not a particularly good liar.

I turn my attention back to the girls. 'Come on, Chlo, move over. I can't get a look in and I want an ice cream too.' I playfully nudge her out of the way with my hip, but the whole time I'm choosing I'm conscious of Jackie's eyes boring into my back. Or perhaps it's just my imagination.

As soon as we each have an ice cream in our hands, Rachel scoops them from us. 'My treat,' she says, holding them out of my reach. 'And don't argue, it's the least I can do.'

I know from experience that Rachel won't enter into any discussion on the subject, so I move to the back of the shop to give her some room. It doesn't take long to pay, we're the only customers in there, and, as soon as we're back outside, I help Rachel hand out the lollies that the girls have chosen. Lauren automatically takes Tilly's and unwraps it for her, without so much as a glance passing between them, and I realise again how close they've become in such a short space of time.

'Blimey, do I smell or something?' asks Rachel, holding up her arms and sniffing dramatically.

I give her a puzzled look. 'Not to my knowledge, why?'

'Only I thought village shops were supposed to be friendly places and yet the woman in there was giving me the evils the whole time. You too actually.' She grins at me, rolling her eyes. 'Oh, I get it, it's because you're not local, isn't it? Nine generations of your family weren't born in the village, or something like that.'

I smile at Rachel's assessment, although a part of me is dismayed to know I was right in feeling an atmosphere. 'Oh, take no notice of her, Rach. I think she's one of the village gossips…' I purse my lips. 'As I'm just beginning to find out.' I take a bite of my choc ice, lips scrabbling as a piece of chocolate cracks and almost falls away.

'You mentioned one or two teething troubles,' she replies. 'Is that what you meant?' Rachel never misses anything. She gives me a searching look, one I've come to know very well over the years.

I sigh. The girls have walked on a little way ahead so it's okay to talk. 'Lauren had a bit of an altercation with a boy in school, and I think his mum has taken great delight in painting Lauren, and therefore by implication, me, as the villains of the piece.'

'Why, what happened?'

'She punched him.'

'Lauren?' says Rachel, eyes wide. 'Blimey, what made her do that? I can't imagine Lauren punching anyone.'

I shrug. 'She was just standing up for Tilly,' I say. 'And there's no doubt Lauren hit Leo but, from what she's said, he was goading her, daring her to hit him, and unfortunately Lauren took him at his word.' I give a wry smile. 'Sadly however, the head thought it was a good opportunity to make an example of Lauren, and threatened us with exclusion.'

'But that's ridiculous. Excluding Lauren? Doesn't she have eyes in her head?'

'Ah, but she only has our word for what Lauren is normally like,' I reply. 'And we parents are completely unreliable when it comes to assessing our offspring apparently. Plus, Lauren's official school records haven't arrived yet, so how could she possibly know.'

Rachel snorts. 'It sounds as if she's the type of head who treats all her parents as if they're idiots. And you got hauled in to see her, did you? I bet that went well.'

'We tried to make our point, but Lauren's only been there a week, Rach, so I couldn't say too much. Probably not wise to make an enemy of the head just yet. But poor Lauren, she was absolutely beside herself.'

Rachel throws an affectionate glance in Lauren's direction. 'I can imagine. Oh, that's horrible. But what happened to the boy? Did he get threatened with exclusion too? Is that why his mum has got it in for you?'

I shake my head. 'Nope. As the "victim" he got off scot-free.'

Rachel slides me a look. 'Oh come on… really?'

'Believe me, I'd be the first to reprimand Lauren if I thought she'd done something wrong, and I'm not saying that hitting another child is ever right, but she says that Leo was hurting Tilly and I believe her. I've never seen her so upset.'

Rachel looks between me and the girls. 'Then good for her, I say. I wish more people stood up to bullies. And I bet Anna was grateful, she's obviously still rather worried about Tilly.'

I nibble the edge of my ice cream to hide my expression. 'We haven't really had a chance to talk about it yet.' That's not strictly true; for some reason we haven't spoken about it at all. 'But, yes, I think so, even though Tilly's trying to pretend that nothing happened. Lauren's somewhat changed her story now and I'm convinced it's because Tilly is worried about the repercussions if she makes a fuss.'

Rachel is quiet for a moment. 'So how come we got the silent treatment in the shop then?' she asks. 'Was that Leo's mum?'

'No, a friend of hers though. All I can think of is that she's been a bit vocal about what happened and—'

'The village jungle drums are doing the rest.'

'Yes, something like that.'

Rachel nudges me gently. 'Well I'm sorry you've had that to contend with but I hope you haven't let it put a dampener on things here, not when everything else is so perfect.'

CHAPTER TWELVE

There's a bit more of a breeze down by the brook and we walk for a while before the lure of the water gets too much for the girls and we have to give in to their requests to paddle.

It's hardly changed at all down here since I was a girl. The trees are taller, the hedges thicker, but the little bridge over the brook into the meadow beyond is still the same. The river is just as I remember it too, right down to the little beach where the water runs shallow over a raised bed of stones.

Chloe is wading across it and studying the ground intently, looking for treasure. Every now and again she brings me bits of polished glass she's found, worn smooth by the water. Tilly and Lauren, on the other hand, are dancing about in the shallows, pretending to catch fish, but it's just an excuse to put their hands in the water and splash each other. Lauren has a distinct advantage over Tilly but she doesn't seem to mind at all, taking Lauren's hand every now and again to steady herself.

'Ah, this is the life,' sighs Rachel.

We're sitting a bit further along the bank, sandals thrown off, our bare feet turned to the sun. I wonder how long we'll be able to do this before some proper autumnal weather arrives.

'And it's all of ten minutes from your house,' adds Rachel. 'I'm so jealous.'

I catch a blade of grass between my fingers. 'I used to spend half my life down here as a child; fishing for minnows, playing Pooh sticks. I never imagined for one minute that I'd get to bring my own children here.'

'Jamie would love this.'

Rachel's not looking at me, but instead staring straight ahead, lost in thoughts of how her and Gerry's future might be.

'I think Jamie's mum and dad might love it too,' I remark, looking at her pointedly. 'So do it, Rach... Why not? Jamie is at the age where transitioning to a new school wouldn't be a problem.'

'I know,' she replies. 'It's just all the other stuff, isn't it? My parents for one. It's handy at the moment having them so close and, what with Dad's health scare last year, it makes me worry about being too far away from them.'

'I know. It's easy for me to tell you to move when I don't have that problem, but you know I bet if you asked them, they'd say the same thing.'

'They probably would,' she agrees. 'How is your mum anyway? Has she come around to the idea of you being here a bit more?'

Too late I realise that this is territory I didn't want to stray into. My mum's reaction was the only thing that marred our coming here.

'A little, I think. But I know I upset her. I was so excited about coming back here I didn't stop to consider what our news would mean for her. I guess it brought back too many memories of Dad. It hasn't been that long since he died, after all.'

'She'll come round,' says Rachel, understanding my feelings about it. 'Just give it time. I bet once she gets used to the idea she'll be really happy for you.'

'I know... I hope so. After Dad died I thought we might be able to regain some of the closeness we had when I was younger. I know I idolised my dad, but she always seemed so happy to take a back seat and that hurt. I thought that with him gone she might want to try to close the gap between us, but then she went and moved miles away from home and that kind of put paid to that.'

Rachel smiles and rubs my arm. She's heard this all before. 'People deal with grief differently though, Thea. Perhaps that was just her way of coping with it. Don't give up though, coming here could be just the opportunity you need to get things back on track.'

She's not the first person to say this, I realise, as I think back to Anna's words. Maybe I should go and see Mary Williams after all. She and Mum are obviously much closer friends than I thought and she could well prove to be the link between us. It certainly wouldn't hurt to get someone else's point of view.

'And meanwhile, I might have to keep you busy helping us to house-hunt,' Rachel adds.

She's teasing, trying to take my mind off thoughts about my mum, but, as I think about her words, I know I'd love it if she and her family did move closer. Perhaps I'd just like to know I have an ally in my camp.

I glance up, realising that the noise Tilly and Lauren were making has stopped. In fact, they're no longer in sight. I pause, listening, but apart from birdsong and the sound of Chloe's feet crunching over the stones, it's silent. They haven't gone past us, the view is open along the straight stretch of the brook, so perhaps they've doubled back. I sit forward, but I still can't see round the big bushes at the bend in the river.

'Chlo?' I call. 'Have the girls walked back behind you?'

She lifts her head and scans the riverbed. 'No...'

I get to my feet. It's the silence I don't like.

Rachel follows suit and in seconds we're standing on the bank, but no matter which way we turn there's no sign of either girl. It's ridiculous, they can't just have disappeared. We'd have seen them. There's nowhere for them to go.

I'm about to shout out when I hear a muffled giggle coming from away to my right and, all at once, a memory assails me. I smile at Rachel, putting a finger to my lips as I make my way silently down the bank and into the shallow water beside Chloe.

I pick my way along the stony surface, careful not to make a sound. I'm not sure if I can be seen, but the giggles have disappeared now and I get the sense that breath is being held. The brambles are thick with leaf and from the field side appear dense and impenetrable. It's only from the river that you appreciate their secret; a peculiarity of their growth, coupled with their age, has allowed a cavern to form around their thick, gnarly trunk. Growing on the edge of the bank has only served to heighten this natural phenomenon. In some of the older bushes, a ten-year-old child could stand upright inside the 'cave', or easily lie down, and I know this for a fact. It's where Drew and I and countless other kids used to hide out.

Back then, despite having to approach it from the water's edge, the entrance to the hollow was always quite clear, but today it's barely discernible. Perhaps it's the passage of time, or the fact that children don't play out like they used to, but, even knowing how these bushes have formed, I'm still struggling to see where the girls are hiding. In fact, were it not for Tilly's bright-pink tee shirt I don't think I'd have spied them at all.

I'm not an especially large person but if this is going to work I need to have the element of surprise. So I take my time, judging how I'm going to do this. I even straighten at one point and turn in the other direction, calling loudly for Lauren. Behind me, Rachel and Chloe are watching with bemused faces, but I think Rach has twigged where the girls have gone. She motions for Chloe to stay quiet beside her.

I plant my feet a little further apart than usual, stabilising my balance and trying to lower my centre of gravity. Then, when I think I can manage it successfully, I drop to my haunches, lifting aside a large frond of greenery and roaring like a monster as I do so.

Screams rapidly dissolve into fits of giggles as the girls are found. The laughter is quickly followed by groans of dismay at having been discovered, but already Lauren is shuffling forward to come and meet me, tales of their hiding ready on her lips. Rachel and Chloe are beside me now.

'Let me look, let me look,' says Chloe, anxious not to be left out, and I lift up the branch again so that she can see inside.

'Oh, that's so clever,' she announces.

I grin. 'Isn't it?'

Chloe offers a hand to pull Lauren out as I try to hold back the brambles for Tilly who is right behind her, struggling a little to avoid the prickles. 'We could have stayed in there for ages,' she says, scrambling forward.

I wait until Lauren drops down beside me, leaning back in to help Tilly.

'Ouch,' she exclaims. 'Blooming thorn.'

The back of her shoulder is caught up and I make her wait a second while I try to unhook her clothing. 'Careful,' I warn. 'Don't pull or you'll rip it.' Eventually she's free and the two of them stand in the water, puffing from the exertion of their adventure.

'Phew,' says Tilly. 'I didn't think we were ever going to get out of there.' But she's grinning just as broadly as Lauren is.

'Isn't that the best hiding place ever?' says Lauren. 'You can see out but no one can see in, it's brilliant! And there was bags of room.' She looks up at me, frowning. 'But Mummy,' she adds. 'How did you know we were there? That's not fair... We thought you'd never find us.'

'Ah...' I tap the side of my nose. 'Magic!'

'Oh, go on, tell us...' says Tilly. 'Please... Was it because I was giggling?'

'Were you?' I say, smiling at her. 'Well, I didn't hear you...'

The two girls are looking at one another, trying to work out how I knew, and I let them dance about a bit before laughing.

'Oh, all right then,' I say. 'It's not magic after all... although it kind of is. Would you believe I used to hide there when I was a little girl. All the children did.'

Lauren's eyes are round. 'Wow,' she says. 'That's so cool...'

Rachel's amazed. 'That's incredible. Fancy it being the same after all this time.'

'It was pretty much just as it is now,' I add. 'Maybe not quite as big inside, but two of us still used to be able to crawl inside, I can remember that. We came down here by ourselves all the time and no one thought anything of it.' I shudder. 'I can't imagine that happening now, thank goodness, but it's still astonishing that it hasn't been bulldozed away or something.'

Tilly is wriggling, shrugging her shoulder as if she has an itch she can't scratch. 'Are you all right?' I ask.

'Something's still prickling me,' she says. But she can't reach it. She has no arm on the other side to investigate for her.

'Hang on, let's have a look.' I lift up the sleeve of her tee shirt, peering at the fabric. I can see where she's been scratched but it's only a little one, nothing serious. I run my hand over the top of her shoulder and brush at the cotton before lowering it back down again. 'How's that? Any better?'

Tilly gives an exploratory wiggle and nods but then almost immediately shakes her head. 'No, it's still there.'

'Okay, we'll give your tee shirt a shake. Arms up.'

She's facing me as I ease the material up her body and gently over her head in case whatever is caught there scratches at her face and, as I do so, Tilly turns slightly to one side.

I glance at Rachel, my breath catching in shock. I want to check she's seen it too. Along the back edge of Tilly's deformed arm is a row of spiteful-looking bruises. They're fresh; still a vivid blue. And almost certainly made by two fingers pinching hard at the soft flesh. My movements stutter to a halt and I stare at the tee shirt in my hand as if I suddenly have no idea what to do with it.

'Is it a thorn?'

It's the innocence of Lauren's question that makes my stomach flip. Because she knows about the bruises but they're past history compared to this new hurt. She's not concerned about them at all now. She *was* concerned at the time. In fact, she was beside herself, but she's been taught that they don't matter. *We* taught her that they don't matter, and it's this acceptance of the damage that has been done to Tilly that shocks me even more.

I look down at her inquisitive face as she tries to see what the problem is and her concern forces my hands to move, turning the tee shirt inside out to check for prickles.

'There, Mummy, look.' Lauren points to a tiny reddish-brown thorn, clinging to the fabric, and I pull it free, dropping it into the water away from me. I can't tear my eyes away from Tilly's arm, but neither do I want to look at what has been done to her. I swiftly turn her top the right way out and ease it back over her head.

'I think that should do it,' I say, as brightly as I can manage.

Tilly beams happily. She has no idea that there's anything amiss and my heart goes out to her. How can we have let this happen? How can we have let our children think this doesn't matter? By not following up on what happened with Leo we as good as told Lauren to forget about it too, and I never thought to check again if Tilly was okay. I should have, particularly given that I now know she was trying to play down things out of fear. Never mind not wanting to get on the wrong side of the head teacher, I should have made a huge issue out of this, not been happy to settle for her complacency.

There's a boiling fury rising inside of me that, for the moment, must stay hidden and so, as Rachel lays a hand on my arm to show her support, I smile. Despite the fact that the languid pace of the afternoon feels gone, I remind myself that the girls have done nothing wrong and I'm determined that Tilly's day, in particular, should not be soured.

A check on my watch shows that it's getting on for half past three. I did say to Anna that we'd be a couple of hours but I know she'll be fine if we're back a little later. She would have said if she had anything planned. I kick my foot in the water, sending splashes over Lauren's feet.

'Right then,' I say, grinning. 'Seeing as you two girls were so naughty and started playing hide and seek without us, why don't we have a proper game and all join in. What do you reckon, Chloe? Do you think you could find an even better place to hide than these two scallywags?'

She darts a look around her. 'Oh yeah!' she says, eyeing up the numerous trees and bushes.

I look at Rachel. 'Right, rules,' I add. 'Everyone will get to the count of one hundred to hide but no one is allowed to go into the field on the other side of the river, or beyond this one, okay?' I wait for the answering nods. 'And if we can't find you then either Rachel or I will shout "Time's up" and wherever you are you have to come out. So, who's going first? Chloe?'

She gives an enthusiastic nod of her head, already seeking out potential hiding places.

'The rest of us, gather round into a circle, heads together, eyes closed and no peeking! Are you ready, Chlo?' I wait for everyone to settle themselves and begin counting. 'One… two…'

*

It's almost five by the time we traipse back up the lane, hot, thirsty and a bit tired, but we've had a great afternoon and I really don't care about these minor irritations. The girls have smiles on their faces and that's all that matters. I didn't say anything to Rachel but she joined in our games with as much gusto as I did and I know she picked up on my intention, when she stops just shy of the house, hanging back a little.

'Tilly looks so much more cheerful than she did earlier,' she comments. 'Do you think she's all right?'

'I hope so,' I reply. 'I'll have a word with Anna when I take her home, but she's a brave little thing, I'm sure she'll be fine.'

Rachel nods and waves at my two. 'Come on then, Lauren, Chloe, let's go and get a drink.' She waits while the girls hug goodbye and then scoops them off, leaving me to walk the rest of the way with Tilly. Anna's in the front garden watering some pots still full of geraniums when we arrive. She looks up at my greeting.

'I was just about to send out the search party...' she says, straightening. The comment sounds light-hearted enough.

'Oh I know, sorry! We were just having too much fun, weren't we, Tilly?'

Tilly beams and I expect to see the same expression on Anna's face but although she smiles, it stops halfway. I check my watch, widening my eyes as I do so.

'Oh, crikey, Anna, sorry. I really didn't realise it was this late.' It's a little white lie but it's unusual for Anna to be out of sorts.

She opens her mouth to say something but then closes it again, and there's a tiny pause before she does speak.

'No, it's okay. I'm glad they've all had fun.' And then she does smile, properly. 'I hope Tilly wasn't any trouble?'

'Of course not. She never is,' I reply, wondering how I can broach the subject of Tilly's bruises. I need Anna to know that I'm on her side. I'm so angry with myself for not following it up when Lauren got into trouble. 'They all played so well together.'

There's a sharp bark as Fergus comes running around the corner from the garden, no doubt investigating the voices, and soon begins his usual ecstatic quiver on seeing Tilly. Anna pushes at his head as he tries to lick the drops on the watering can.

'Ugh, Fergus, no… that's dirty. Tilly, can you take him inside and get him some more water, sweetheart? And get yourself a drink too!' she calls after her. 'Silly dog won't go and lie in the shade. Honestly, sometimes I think he needs more looking after than Tilly does.'

I smile. 'Maybe that's just because Tilly's so sensible.' I pause for a moment, but maybe it's best just to say what's on my mind instead of beating around the bush. 'Listen, Anna,' I begin. 'I just wanted to say sorry for the other day, for not coming to check on Tilly after school when I should have done. You must have thought it was really off.' I realise belatedly that this might be why Anna has seemed a bit distant. 'It's just that Lauren was so upset and well… anyway, that's no excuse.'

Anna looks confused.

'Somehow it all ended up being about what Lauren had done, instead of Leo. Tilly's name hardly came into the conversation at all, which is what makes me really angry about this whole thing, given what happened to her. Anyway, I just wanted to let you know and—'

'I'm sorry, Thea, I haven't a clue what you're talking about…'

'Oh.' She must have. Surely? I bite my lip, the conversation becoming increasingly awkward. 'The other day at school, when Lauren hit Leo and we got dragged up to see Mrs Faulkner…'

'Oh that, don't worry about it, Thea, honestly.'

I frown. 'Yes, but I did ask at the time if Tilly was okay, only the head was so busy trying to sweep the actual bullying under the carpet and make an example out of Lauren that she seemed scarcely bothered about Tilly at all. And then Lauren was so upset afterwards that I didn't think to come and check on Tilly, and now I've seen the bruises on her arm… Well, anyway, I just wanted you to know that I'm sorry.' I try a brighter face. 'And not that you need anyone to help you fight your battles but, if you do, I'm your woman.'

There's an odd expression on Anna's face, a tightening. 'What bruises?' she asks.

And I realise my mistake.

'Sorry, that sounds really nosey, I should have explained… The girls were playing hide and seek and Tilly got her tee shirt caught on some brambles. Something was prickling her and when I slipped off her tee shirt to see what was causing it, I saw the bruises. Not that Tilly made a fuss or anything, I mean she's not like that, is she? But they looked pretty nasty.'

Anna nods. 'I see, well, thank you, that was very kind. But Tilly's fine. No harm done.' She looks back in the direction of our house. 'Is Lauren all right?'

'Yes, she's okay… concerned about Tilly, but…'

And I'm wondering why Anna is deliberately trying to make light of this. No harm done…? I've seen it with my own eyes. The beats of silence stretch out between us. Anna is looking at her feet. I'm looking at Anna looking at her feet and I don't understand why there's this change in her.

She gives a sudden sigh, an impatient venting of exasperation that so clearly says I couldn't possibly know anything about any of this, and I feel immediately ashamed. Because I don't. I've never had to experience what Anna has. I've never had to fight for my child day in, day out, just for a chance for them to be considered 'normal'. Coping with the likelihood of daily taunts must be bad enough, but then having to justify yourself to all and sundry who think they know better must be a nightmare. And here I am, joining their ranks. I reach out an arm.

'Anna, I'm so sorry. You must be fed up with people like me, sticking their oar in, doing the whole righteous indignation act as if you weren't capable of doing it yourself. I really don't mean—'

She looks up. 'That's okay, Thea.' She smiles, but it's tinged with sadness and… resignation. 'I know you didn't mean anything by it. It's just that I've learned not to make a big thing about issues like this. It only seems to make the matter worse, and Tilly understands that she's… different from other children, and that not everyone can be as loving and compassionate as she is.'

I'm not sure what to say. I understand her point of view, but surely—

'And I'm not excusing it,' continues Anna. 'But sometimes drawing attention to behaviour of this kind just reinforces how different Tilly is. I've had people accuse me of getting things out of proportion, making mountains out of molehills, you name it, they've said it. Like we're looking for special dispensation, or sympathy even.'

'But that's ridiculous!' Except that even as I say it, I know that Anna isn't making it up. I know what people are capable of. 'We're talking about bullying,' I reply. 'If something is wrong, something's wrong, irrespective of the situation.'

'It should be… But sadly I've found that isn't always the case. You'll have to take my word for it,' she adds, growing defensive.

I hold her look. I don't want to disagree with her, but there's a voice in my head telling me that underneath all this is a child, and surely that's more important than anything else.

'Thea,' she says pointedly. 'I'm also the curate's wife.'

Her eyebrows are raised, challenging me to argue, but I understand. I understand completely.

'So, what? Love and understanding at any cost, is that it?'

Anna looks away. And the seconds tick by.

'You see?' she says suddenly. 'See how it is? Even you… You came here out of concern, wanting to help, and yet we've ended up arguing. That's what always happens. So is it any wonder that I prefer not to talk about it? Just you wait until you're on the receiving end of all the village gossip, then you'll know what I mean.'

Her eyes widen, partly at the shock of what she's just said, but something else too. And this time it's my turn to raise my eyebrows.

'I just mean that there's always something. It's a village, Thea, people gossip.'

But that isn't what she means and we both know it.

I inhale a deep breath. I didn't come here to argue though, Anna has got that much right, and I don't want to lose her as a friend either. She and Rob have been good to us since we moved in. I like them both, but more than that I should be offering my support in whichever way Anna needs it, not in the way I think she does.

'You're right,' I say, trying to soften my voice as much as I can. 'And I don't want to be "people", Anna, who think they know best and don't listen, intent on peddling their fixed point of view. So, if I've offended you, I'm sorry… And I'm not sitting in judgement either. I do want to help, if I can, and if you need it. Otherwise I'll just keep my big mouth shut.' I grin at her and hope it's enough.

The hard look on her face dissolves in an instant.

'No, I'm sorry, Thea. I get so… so frustrated by it all… But I shouldn't take it out on you.' She opens her arms and we hug. 'And thank you for taking Tilly out this afternoon, really. I know she'll have had a great time.'

I nod. 'Okay… but please Anna, promise if it all gets too much, you'll come and talk to me about it?'

'I will…' She picks up the watering can. 'Enjoy the rest of your evening,' she says.

'You too.'

I turn to go and she gives a little wave, watching me as I leave. There's a smile on her face, but I have a horrible feeling I've just made a big mistake.

CHAPTER THIRTEEN

'Jesus! Don't you have a go at me as well.'

Drew holds his hands up in a 'who me?' gesture and grins at Gerry. 'Have you met my wife, the diplomat?'

I bash his arm. 'That's not funny.' I pull a face. 'Okay, so maybe I was a little heavy-handed, but what would you have done?'

'Erm, not got involved,' replies Drew as if it's the most obvious thing in the world.

I roll my eyes at Rachel. 'Men,' I say. 'What are they like?'

She looks over at Lauren and Chloe who are having a whale of a time running through the park, stopping at every horse chestnut tree to look for conkers.

It's Sunday and we've come out to Shrewsbury with Rachel and Gerry to show them the county town, starting the day with a walk along the river that threads its way through the centre. I've no idea how we got onto the subject of my conversation with Anna yesterday, but I really wish we hadn't. I did enough thinking about it last night.

'Well, you weren't there, were you?' says Rachel, directing a look at my husband. 'They were really nasty bruises. And I think Thea is quite right to call it out.'

Drew laughs. 'So do I. I just wish she hadn't alienated our neighbours in the process.' He beams at his audience but for once I'm not finding it funny.

I turn away. The girls are shrieking with laughter and so it's easy to pretend I'm captivated by them. But there's something about this conversation that doesn't sit right. It's light-hearted for sure, but I'm not feeling it. What I'm feeling is rebuked. I'm used to Drew teasing me, it's not that. In fact, I've always loved this aspect of our relationship – we both give as good as we get – but he wouldn't normally mock me, not over a subject as important as this.

'Oh dear, well, I might just have blown it then,' I reply. 'Given that half the village is already talking about us.'

'Are they?' Drew's reply comes quickly.

His look is a little more direct than usual and I'm surprised to feel slightly glad to have jolted him from his levity. 'Well if the daggers we got in the village shop are anything to go by, then yes, definitely.'

I could mention the article I found, but I won't. The timing isn't right but more than that I need to work out its significance first.

Rachel laughs. 'She's right, the woman in there yesterday looked like she'd been sucking on lemons.'

'Jasmin's mum,' I supply for Drew's benefit. 'You know, the woman who brought Chloe home early that time, because "something" came up? She's a bit of a gossip apparently.'

'So what are they talking about?'

'I have no idea. Do they need a reason?' I'm trying to make light of it now, but it's Drew that doesn't want to let it rest; the tone of his voice dropped at least an octave as he replied. 'However, I would imagine it's because our daughter is a wanton thug,' I add.

He looks quizzically at me.

'Jasmin's mum is friends with Leo's mum,' I say.

'Oh, is that all.' He looks relieved.

Gerry blows air out from between his teeth. 'I'm beginning to wonder if this moving to the countryside lark is such a good idea after all…'

'I know,' agrees Rachel. 'Who knew it was such a hotbed of scandal and intrigue?' She smiles at me. 'I reckon they're just trying to put us off, Gerry. I don't think they want us to move up here at all...'

I grin. 'Busted.'

'Well, tough,' she says, sticking out her tongue. 'Seriously though, if we are considering it...' She stops to slide a look at Gerry and then grins. 'Okay, as we *are* considering it, we need to think about location, particularly for Gerry and his job. We've no idea of the best places to look. And, much as you love us, you probably won't want us right on your doorstep.'

'That's very true,' I reply, laughing, and glad to be changing the subject. 'Well, as far as location goes, I think anywhere around here would be pretty much perfect. The hospital's just on the outskirts of town and there's another about a half hour's drive away. Why don't we go and do some window shopping in a bit? None of the estate agents will be open but we can always give you a few pointers and then tomorrow you can go off by yourselves and have a tour around a few other places.'

Rachel looks at Gerry for agreement. 'Sounds like a good idea,' she says, swinging Gerry's hand as she scuffs through a pile of leaves. She points to an ice cream stand obligingly stationed to catch passers-by. 'Right, I reckon it's about time we had another one of those, don't you?'

I glance up at the sky as the first in a line of black clouds drifts across the sun.

'Best make it quick,' I say. 'I'm not sure how long it's going to be before we get spectacularly wet.'

'It wouldn't dare,' replies Rachel. And I'm surprised to find myself wishing I had her optimism. Where did that come from?

It isn't far to the town centre and we take our time ambling through the beautiful park and up through the formal gardens that sit at its middle, stopping for a few minutes to finish our ice creams. The surrounding streets are old, lined with handsome period houses and quirky independent shops that are good for tourists and natives alike, and I can see that Rachel and Gerry are pleased by what they see. There's one street in particular where a row of estate agents have set up office and we move from window to window, checking the details in each.

The door to a gallery on the other side of the street is invitingly open and I drift across to peer in the window, calling to say that I'll catch everyone up. It's rather an occupational hazard, but I can't pass by an art shop of any kind without stopping, whether it's to look at finished artwork or to drool over papers, brushes and pristine tubes of paint. I haven't been in here before, but a wonderful collection of hand-drawn illustrated maps draws me in.

There are several different designs, each of a particular local town and its distinctive features; Ludlow and its castle, Bridgnorth and its funicular railway, their interesting points of note beauti-fully depicted in pen and coloured ink. One in particular takes my eye. Not a street map this time, but the whole of Shropshire, very cleverly executed as a pictorial guide to the county. I realise immediately that it would make a wonderful gift for Rachel and Gerry; the perfect accompaniment to my friends' house-hunting.

On impulse, I pluck the mounted print from its stand and take it over to the counter to pay. The woman who greets me is dressed in a beautiful pale-green tunic, over the front of which hangs a huge oval pendant – silver, with what's unmistakably the palest blue sea glass. But it's her array of silver rings which ultimately catches my eye, the number and size of them stirring a memory deep inside of me. A tinkly laugh, the flash of silver in sunlight… people. I don't want to stare, but the more I look, the more she seems familiar.

'Hi,' she says, smiling. 'These are lovely, aren't they?' Her hand goes out to receive the print. 'Are you only visiting for the day?'

'No, no, I live just south of here but I'm buying this for some friends…' I hand over my purchase, meeting her smile. 'They're thinking of moving this way so I'm hoping it might turn out to be a bit of a good-luck charm.'

She nods and touches a hand to a small leaflet stand on the counter beside her. 'I only asked because the artist is going to be here next Saturday, working live in the shop on a new map. If you or your friends want to come and meet her, feel free to pop in, any time.'

I peer at the name on the notice. Heather Atwood. She's not an artist I know but that's hardly surprising given I haven't had time to suss out the local network yet. This could be a good opportunity though. 'My friends are only here for the weekend, unfortunately, but I might pop along. I'm only in Ditton Batch so I'm not far.'

'Ditton Batch…'

I meet her eye. 'Yes, do you know it?'

She looks away, turning to the till. 'I used to live there once… Are you paying by cash or card?'

'Oh… um, card please.'

She taps in the price of the print, silver rings glinting.

'That's so weird… Do you know I thought there was something about you I recognised when I came in.' I break off, trying to study her face. 'I actually used to live in the village years ago when I was a child. At Pevensey House, maybe you know it? My husband and I have just moved back there, to the same house in fact, would you believe. When did you live there? Maybe we were in the village at the same time.'

'I shouldn't think so, it was years ago.'

'Yes, me too.' I do the maths in my head. 'We left in 1996.'

The hand holding the print stills as her head turns towards me. Her eyes widen as the colour drains from her face, her mouth parting. It closes again as she swallows.

'Oh my God…'

Heat flickers up my neck. Her reaction is not at all what I'm expecting. 'Are you all right, I…'

I hear the sound of laughter again. No, it's not laughter, someone's crying…

'I'm sorry. You probably don't remember me at all. I—'

'No, I know who you are.'

I stop dead at the sudden ice in her voice, so chilling. The eyes that regard me are cold and lifeless. They look so out of place amid her glowing complexion and bright clothes.

I look around me, neck prickling with foreboding. 'I'm sorry,' I manage. 'I think… maybe there's been a misunderstanding…?'

I wait for her to enlighten me, but she remains silent.

The beam of sunlight slanting through the window is cut off as a cloud passes overhead and I stare at the print on the counter.

She holds out her hand and I can feel the burn of her gaze as I fumble with my purse, pulling ineffectually at my debit card. Eventually I manage to pull it free and pass it over.

I think for one weird moment that she's going to keep my card, or refuse to serve me at all, but then she slides it into the reader and wordlessly turns it to face me. My mind has gone completely blank. I can't even remember my PIN number.

'I'm really sorry… I've obviously upset you, but I… Maybe you're thinking of someone else…? We lived at Pevensey, behind the church…'

I punch in the number without thinking. Her hands are shaking as she turns the reader back towards her.

'And my husband, Drew, you might remember him, he lived next door…?' My voice trails away. I'm not sure why I'm still trying to speak to her, but I'm desperate to show her she's made a mistake, that whoever she thinks I am, she's got the wrong person. That whatever she's feeling can't possibly be directed at me.

But it isn't going to work, I can see that. Because the look in her eyes tells me that she's absolutely certain. I can feel the hatred surrounding her almost as clearly as if I can see it. She places the print inside a bag and then plucks my card from the reader before holding both out to me, pinned together by a thumb and forefinger.

I swallow and reach out to take them, trying to grip them with fingers that feel numb. Just as I make contact she gives them a tug, a sharp jolt to make her final words even more cutting.

'Don't ever come in here again,' she hisses, shoving the package at me.

My debit card slides away and flies across the floor and I feel dizzy with shock as I scrabble to pick it up. I'm gulping for air by the time I reach the door, the breaths I've been taking somehow failing to supply my lungs with oxygen. And yet the street looks normal when I stumble outside. I can see my family, my friends, just metres from where I'm standing, carrying on as if nothing has happened. Their blissful ignorance is something I'm no longer able to share.

I have no idea what just took place, but it's one of a series of things I'm desperately trying to ignore. I can't think about any of this, not today, and certainly not right at this moment. But I'm struggling to push the woman's words from my head, the memory of the harshness in her voice. I look down at the card in my hand. This is something I can do; the practicality of stowing it away in my purse creating a link back to the normal, the everyday. That done, I hurry after everyone. The one thing I can't be right now is alone.

'Sorry about that,' I say, my voice breathless, catching in my throat as if I've just run a huge distance. 'I'm a bit of a sucker for an art shop as you know.'

Rachel looks up from where her head is practically resting against a window as she peers inside. She eyes the paper bag I'm holding. 'Oh, did you get something nice?'

I'm about to answer when there's a subtle shift in her expression. 'Are you okay, Thea? You look as white as a sheet.'

I touch a hand to my cheek as Drew pivots towards me, but I can't meet his gaze just yet.

I smile. 'I think so… maybe it's just the price of the art supplies in there… sheesh… eye-watering.' My fingers are plucking at the edge of the paper bag. 'I did get this though.' I hand over the print, smiling at Gerry. 'I thought it might be either a nice incentive or a nice memento, possibly both.' I perhaps shouldn't have given it to them just yet, particularly as I've just realised the price sticker is still on the back, but I needed to do something.

I watch while Rachel opens it and peers inside, smiling at her exclamation as she pulls the print free.

'Oh, look at that, it's gorgeous!' She angles the print to show Gerry, trying to find some light to illuminate the detail. The street is narrow here and, with tall buildings either side and the sun determinedly behind a cloud, in shadow.

Drew has hold of both the girls' hands but he lets them go as Rachel passes the illustration to him. He smiles up at me. 'Yes, I definitely approve. Is it someone you know?' he asks, turning the picture over to see the artist's details.

I shake my head. 'Someone local though.'

He looks back up the street towards the shop. 'Not a million miles away from your style,' he comments. 'Perhaps you should approach them to sell some of your work.'

'No.' The word escapes my mouth before I have a chance to soften its tone. 'I mean, these prints are lovely, but there really wasn't anything else in there to write home about. Besides, I'm far too busy at the moment.'

Drew grins at Gerry. 'Have you met my wife? She's a very important illustrator.'

Rachel rolls her eyes and pokes at Drew's arm. 'Don't be so mean. I think Thea's absolutely right. And the print is lovely, but your work is way better than this. Besides, when we move to the country and I'm running an incredibly successful cookery business, I shall be so busy and important that folks will have to make an appointment just to speak to me.' Her voice has adopted a very plummy tone. 'Just ignore him, Thea. Beastly man.'

There are laughs all round and, whether it was intentional or not, I'm grateful to Rachel for moving us forward.

'Anyway, how are you getting on?' I ask, gesturing towards the agent's window.

'Aw…' Her face softens. 'Just look…' She points to a photo dead centre in the agent's window. 'How magical is that?'

The property for sale is a traditional stone farmhouse, in a small village about a twenty-minute drive from Pevensey. Huge swathes of lavender adorn the front garden and there are even roses around the door.

'And I bet there are sheds and barns and all sorts,' adds Rachel. 'Just perfect for converting into a workspace. I can't believe we can even afford a place like this. It makes you wonder why we haven't thought of moving before.'

Gerry smiles but exchanges a look with Drew before replying. 'Affording it in the first place is one thing, Rach, being able to afford living there on a daily basis is quite another. We'd need to be very sure we had money coming in from the get-go, so I'd really need a job to come to at the very least. Your income would be zero to start with.'

She pulls a face. 'I'm not daft, Gerry. I do know that. But it's like we said, this is just window shopping until we want to think about it seriously. We have to start somewhere.'

'And there is a very good place to start,' I reply, pointing at the card in the window. 'That's a lovely village too,' I add. 'Just saying…'

*

'Are you worried about money, Drew?' I ask, later in the evening when we're on our own. 'Because you needn't be.' I try to make my voice sound as casual as I can. 'We're fine at the moment, and your work will pick up. It isn't as if you're short of enquiries.'

He looks across at me from the chair where he's reading. 'What makes you say that?'

I could say, *Well your defensiveness for one*, but I don't. 'Nothing really, just the comment that Gerry made about moving when we were in town and the fact they'd need to guarantee they had money coming in first. He looked at you just before he said it and I wondered if it's something you'd been discussing.'

'We've talked about it, yes. It's a valid point. They have a young son.'

'Yes, of course. I rather meant… are *you* worried?' It rankles slightly that he might have been discussing it with Gerry and not me.

'It's taking up more of my thoughts than it usually does, yes,' he replies. 'Given that I'm not really doing anything right now. Enquiries are one thing, but pointless if they don't translate to actual work. I have one order in the bag, Thea, and that's it. I'm not about to get carried away.'

'But they're speculative, you know that. People often want to check the cost of something before coming to a decision and it can take them weeks to do that.'

'Yes, but even so you're talking about extensions and conservatories, conversions over the garage… Thea, I didn't make partner at Franklin and Wilks to spend my life building twee additions to people's houses.'

'No, I know.' I sit on the arm of his chair, my hand running along his shoulder before resting my lips against the top of his head. 'You're better than that.'

He's silent for a moment and I wonder what he's thinking. There's no point in uttering bland platitudes. I know the score as well as he does.

'You know, maybe you should have a think about selling your work. Maybe not straight away, but you could do a lot worse than places like that shop in town. Your commission's going to last a while yet and it'll hopefully give rise to more, but there's no guarantee. I don't think it would hurt to keep your options open, that's all. The last few weeks have made me realise how precarious our life could be.'

He has a point, but it irritates me. He's worried about his work situation so he's putting his anxiety onto me about mine – when I've never had an issue finding work. Okay, so I had to take jobs I didn't really want when I first started, but I still took them. And I've lived with the precarious nature of being self-employed for years, it's the nature of the beast, but, through it all, I've more than held up my side of the financial burden.

'I might,' I say. 'But only when I think the time is right or I want to explore some different ways of working. I've been treading a steady path towards book illustration for a long time, and you know that's what I've always wanted to do. I'm not about to give all that up on a whim, certainly not when there's no need to. Besides, if I did want to think about selling my artwork elsewhere, it definitely wouldn't be in a place like that.'

'Why? What was wrong with it?'

What was right with it? The very thought of what happened when I bought the print is tying my stomach in knots. I really don't want to have to think about it and I certainly don't want to talk about it.

'Do you remember a woman from the village when we were younger, who used to wear lots of big silver rings?' I ask. The question surprises me. I hadn't even considered I was about to ask it.

Drew frowns, his eyes flickering. 'I don't think so.' He makes a show of trawling though his memory banks. 'No, not that I'm aware of.'

He's studying me, wondering if he should ask the next question. I'm quite interested to see if he does.

'Why do you ask?' he says, giving me my answer.

And now I'm wondering if I should continue, because something about this conversation isn't sitting right. 'Because that's a description of the woman who served me in the shop today. And the vague thoughts I had that there was something familiar about her proved to be exactly right when she all but threw me out. Not surprisingly, I have absolutely no idea why, but I thought somehow that you might have.'

'Me? Why would I know?'

I raise my eyebrows. 'Call it intuition…'

Drew fidgets in the chair. 'Why, what did she say?'

'Nothing much, it was more the way she said it. Like I was something she was desperate to scrape off the bottom of her shoe. And what started as a perfectly normal conversation changed the minute she found out that we used to live here. She hardly spoke after that and then hissed at me never to go in the shop again.'

I still can't see Drew's eyes because of the angle at which we're sitting and I get to my feet. 'So you tell me, what was all that about? No wonder I'm not falling over myself to go back in there. Although I've a good mind to demand to know what she meant by it.'

Drew is looking at his lap, staring at the page of his book. 'Just leave it, Thea,' he says quietly.

I stare at him for a moment. 'But it was completely weird,' I argue. 'Wouldn't you want to know what she meant by it?'

'Not really. I think I'd just rather stay out of her way. She sounds mental to me.' He glances up but his gaze descends just as quickly and the seconds tick by. This is a conversation he really doesn't want to be having.

I cross the room to the chair where I was sitting earlier in the evening, to my own book which rests on the seat. The newspaper article slips out effortlessly from between its pages. 'Ordinarily

I'd be inclined to agree with you. But I came across this the other day.' I hand it to him.

His interest is piqued by the age of the paper, I can tell, but his face remains studied as he reads. 'Where did you get this?' he asks, handing it back. 'Rather old news.'

'I found it. Here in the house.' I'm not about to tell him where. 'Bit odd, don't you think? Bit much of a coincidence?'

'A coincidence…? I don't see how. What's it coinciding with, Thea? Some crazy woman in a shop?' He glances at my hands. 'I can imagine that whenever this attack happened it would have been pretty big news round here, but what's it got to do with us?'

'Oh, I don't know, maybe the fact that I found it in our *house*…'

He rolls his eyes. 'Thea, at the time, everyone who had the newspaper delivered would have had a copy of it. And as soon as it became yesterday's news, someone used it to line the shelves in the pantry, I don't know.'

'But it hadn't been discarded,' I argue. 'It had been hidden. And that makes it completely different.' I weigh up what to say next. 'I wondered if it had something to do with the people who lived here before us. Only Anna said how she found the man incredibly creepy. What if his wife hid the paper?'

Drew stares at me. 'What if she did? Thea…' he warns. 'Look, I have no idea, and how on earth are you ever going to find out? More to the point, what difference will it make? It's past history, done and dusted, and I should leave it that way if I were you. Start thinking about the present, there's quite enough going on here.'

I'm still watching him, my lips pursed together as I bite back what I want to say. Because I really don't want to do this, not now, not when our friends are sleeping in a room above us and will hear every word of our argument.

'I'm going to bed,' I say. 'Are you coming?'

'In a bit,' he replies, finally meeting my eyes. 'I'm just going to read for a little while.'

'Okay…' I get to the threshold of the door before turning. 'Drew? Are you sure you're all right…? Only you've seemed, I don't know… a bit tense the last couple of days.' I let out the breath I hadn't realised I was holding.

But he smiles as he makes a show of thinking. 'Maybe I am, a bit… Yes, you're right. Sorry, Thea, I think I'm just more wound up about this whole money thing than I realised. Probably just because I see how it is for Rachel and Gerry now that they're thinking of moving. But I'm okay though… I promise.'

*

I haven't written in my journal for a long time. It's been in my bedside table drawer, forgotten about mostly, but I take it out tonight, rooting around for a pen. My thoughts have got to go somewhere. Maybe I'm reading too much into it, but Drew's face was studiously impassive as he read that article tonight. It talks about child abuse, for goodness' sake, and he's a father of two daughters. Surely there ought to have been some flicker of emotion?

CHAPTER FOURTEEN

The dash to school the next morning is mercifully short. It's teeming with rain and everyone has their head down, loath to hang around. It probably explains why Rob seems to ignore me as he runs past the bottom of our drive on his usual morning jog. I expect he just didn't see me, intent on settling into the rhythm of his strides. Perhaps he was wearing headphones and didn't hear us. Perhaps, perhaps...

I also don't want to think about the look in Stacey's eyes as I pass her on the playground, or the fact that she and another mum seem to deliberately move away from where I'm standing. Even Anna didn't wait to walk to school together as we normally do. She left a little earlier to see one of the teachers. And I'm sure that's the case, I can see her now, leaving the building and walking towards another mum in the playground. Pastoral business no doubt. She does a lot of that.

So, I kiss the girls and watch them dash straight inside – no early-morning playtime today on account of the rain – and then turn to make for home. I promised Rachel and Gerry I'd cook a special breakfast for them this morning and I'd rather be at home doing that than standing here wondering about things that I wish weren't in my head.

I've gone about a quarter of the way back when I hear pattering steps behind me.

'Thea!'

I turn to see Anna hurrying to catch me up and for some reason it makes me feel absurdly happy. I haven't seen her since our rather awkward conversation on Saturday.

'What a day,' I remark. 'Thank heavens I can just go home and batten down the hatches. Do you reckon that's it for the summer then?'

She frowns. 'I've no idea.' Her hands are thrust into her coat pockets and she looks cold and pinched. 'I'm glad I've caught you,' she continues. 'Only, well... it's a bit awkward actually...'

I keep my face as neutral as I can.

'I've just come from a quick meeting with the head teacher and the chair of the PTA committee about the arrangements for the Harvest Festival. I'd asked her if she could help me out with a couple more volunteers for the supper and, well, I think there's been a bit of a misunderstanding.'

'Go on...'

Anna's face freezes. I have a horrible idea I know what she's going to say. 'Well, she's done a wonderful job of recruiting people, except that wasn't exactly what I asked her to do. And now, instead of letting me have the names of a couple of people who might be interested, she's drawn up a full list of helpers.'

'Ah... and let me guess. I'm not on it.'

Anna's expression is pained. 'I did point that out but she refused to alter it. You're not a member of the PTA, you see, so—'

'No, not likely to be either, am I? Just out of interest, who *is* the chair?'

Anna flinches slightly. 'It's Jackie... and she's not the easiest person to deal with. When I suggested that she could just add you as well, she said that everyone had volunteered out of the goodness of their hearts and if she went and chopped and changed things now, people would quite rightly assume that they weren't wanted after all – her words not mine – and I'd end up with no volunteers at all.' She drops her head. 'I'm sorry, Thea. Ordinarily I'd argue the case, but I'm not that keen to raise my head over the parapet just now. Stacey's on the list, you see, and—'

'Stacey?' I concentrate on the road ahead for a few steps before stopping. 'I see... *now* I'm beginning to understand. It's okay, Anna, it's not your fault. I would have thought they'd be only too happy to get some new blood involved, but I guess mine must be the wrong colour or something...'

Anna nods as she stares down the street. 'She and Jackie suddenly seem to be thick as thieves and I don't want there to be any unpleasantness over the supper, it's always been such a fun family event. It isn't right, but...'

'Anna, I understand. Don't worry.' I try a weak smile. 'Their loss, eh?'

We walk a few steps in silence. 'Thank you,' she says. 'Not everyone would be so understanding.' She heaves a sigh. 'This is one of the things I hate about being a curate's wife – so many damn committees, and I always seem to get caught in the middle. Anyway... How have your friends got on with their house-hunting?' she asks. 'Are they definitely going to move this way?'

Anna's obviously trying to change the subject and, however much it hurts, dwelling on the subject now wouldn't be fair to her at all.

'I think they'd like to,' I reply. 'But first they'd need to work out jobs and a million and one other things; you know how it is. But, if all that falls into place, then yes, it could well happen. They're going off today on their own to have a look around the area, so if it would stop raining that would be great.' I grimace at the weather. 'But then again, maybe it's better to see the place when it's gloomy. If they like it on a day like this, they're certainly going to like it when it's sunny.' I groan inwardly. What an inane thing to say. The conversation seems stilted now but Anna doesn't seem to have noticed. Too lost in her own thoughts.

We walk in silence the rest of the way and I pause automatically by our gate to say goodbye, just as Anna turns to me.

'I'm really pleased your friends might be coming nearer,' she says. 'That would be lovely for you, wouldn't it? To have Rachel around for support.'

It would, but I don't want Anna to think that our friendship means nothing to me. 'We'll see what happens,' I say. 'But, listen, I'm in all day and this rain is enough to drive anyone mad. Pop over if you fancy a coffee.'

She raises a hand in farewell. 'Thanks,' she says. But I'm none the wiser as to whether she'll appear or not.

The house rings with laughter as I open the front door and it's in such direct contrast to the world outside that I follow the sound to the kitchen as if under a spell. Gerry is recounting one of his madcap adventures from life as a paramedic. I'm sure they're not madcap, not really, but he makes them sound that way. Like the time a man with a prosthetic limb was involved in a minor road traffic accident and one of Gerry's junior colleagues genuinely thought the man's foot had been wrenched off.

I've missed today's story but it doesn't matter, the room is filled with smiling faces and the air hums with good humour. Drew looks up as I enter, laughter still etched in the creases around his eyes, which deepen even further when he sees me.

He darts a look out the kitchen window, pulling a face at me as my mac drips water onto the floor. 'Shit, is it still raining that hard? Well, now I feel guilty for not offering to do the school run.'

'So you should,' I reply, grinning. I hold my arms out as if to hug him and he jumps backward to avoid getting wet before coming and wrapping his fingers around mine.

'Your hands are freezing,' he says, kissing me. 'Come and have a coffee, it's just brewed.' He holds out his arms for my coat and I shrug it off so that he can hang it in the utility room. I watch him as he walks away, his rear view deeply appealing, and chastise myself for becoming so maudlin. Our best friends are here, in a place we love, and we have so much to be grateful for. Drew and me. Me and Drew.

'I can't believe the weather,' I say. 'That's such bad luck. It's been absolutely glorious up until now.'

But Gerry is sanguine. 'It won't spoil the day. Far nicer to be touring the countryside in the rain on a day like this than stuck in London. Besides, better to see somewhere when it's not looking its best.'

I smile, his response echoing the words I'd cringed at when talking to Anna only a few moments ago. Here, they don't seem incongruous at all.

'Right, well, I'll get some breakfast on the go and then at least you'll be set up for the day. Full English, Gerry?' I catch Rachel's eye and wink as Gerry holds his stomach and groans.

An hour and a half later we wave them goodbye, with hugs and kisses and promises to keep us posted with any developments. They've certainly caught the moving bug, I can see it in the excitement on both their faces. But now the house is quiet again, hushed with expectancy as the rest of the day stretches out ahead of us.

I haven't thought about my work all weekend but now it's as if a magnet is drawing me back to it and I recognise the need to immerse myself. The washing-up is done, another pot of coffee has been brewed and I carry two mugfuls of the fragrant brew through to the studio. Drew is already there, head bent to his screen, and I take my seat beside him.

I'm not sure how much time passes before I lay my brush back down and get to my feet, taking down one of Kathryn Talbot's old books from the shelf behind me. I've made a good start on a new illustration but there's something missing from it, something I'm striving to capture but can't quite translate. The book is one I've read dozens of times, and a real favourite of the girls. Every word and every detail of the illustrations is as familiar to me as the freckles on my face. But it isn't the words I start to read. Instead it's the story the pictures tell that I'm interested in, or, more importantly, how they make me feel. What clues they give me about the narrative, its humour, the tone of whatever is happening. I'm looking for something but I don't know what, only that I'll know it when I find it. I look up, thinking, seeing not the rain outside but instead a particular illustration in my mind. Flipping the pages forward, I realise it's not one from this book at all and I place it back on the shelf.

It's very neat and tidy in Lauren's room, but I'm not here to do the housework. Either side of the chimney breast are shelves of books and that's where I'm heading. All the rest of Kathryn's books are here, lined up in an organised row, and I've remembered which story holds the illustration I'm after. Taking it down, I cross to the window to read. I sink onto the seat but the moment I do I'm suddenly very conscious of where I'm sitting. And in that second all thoughts of the illustration evaporate.

How can I possibly sit here knowing that underneath me a secret has lain hidden; here in my house. And for how long? And at the heart of that secret is a young girl, a victim of a crime that has never been solved. I gaze around the room at my own daughter's things – at her beloved bear, Mr Blue, at the book in my hand, her slippers by her bed – and I realise that I can never let this rest now. I owe it to both Georgia and whoever hid that article to find out what happened. And I think I may know just where to start.

I duck my head around the studio door, letting Drew know that I'm popping around to see Anna. He's concentrating hard on something and scarcely reacts beyond a muttered goodbye, but that's okay. I don't want to have to explain myself just yet.

Anna is baking, her kitchen worktops covered with an array of ingredients.

'Do you mind if I carry on?' she says as she leads me into the room. 'Only I thought I had more time than I have.'

I wave a hand to show that she should, but I'm hesitant now. 'I can come back another time,' I volunteer, not quite sure where I should position myself.

But Anna ignores my comment. 'Have your friends gone now?' she asks, taking eggs from a dish.

She's busy, I can see that, but Anna's the curate's wife and a master at making small talk. Her remark seems thoughtless somehow; of course they've gone, it's almost lunchtime.

'Oh yes, ages ago. I've been trying to work since they left but I've ground to a bit of halt... Actually I've got one or two things on my mind, and I wondered if I might talk to you about them.'

Her back is to me but her movements stall as she hears my words and she pauses for a moment before turning around. Almost as if she's trying to compose herself.

'Yes of course,' she says. 'Is everything okay?'

I take a deep breath, thinking carefully about how to start. 'Can I ask you something?' I begin, not waiting for a reply. 'Only the first time we met you mentioned the couple who lived at Pevensey before us. I just wondered how much you knew about them. How long they'd lived there?'

She looks almost relieved at my question and I can't help but wonder what she thought I was about to ask. 'Who, the Campbells? Oh goodness, well not much, I'm afraid. Like I said, I didn't really have much to do with them and—'

'Yes, well that's kind of why I'm asking really. I got the impression you didn't particularly like them, the man especially?'

Her eyes narrow slightly. 'I found him a bit odd, that's all.'

'You said you thought he was creepy.'

Anna looks startled. 'Did I? Well, yes, I suppose... in a way.' She stops for a second. 'He just had a way of looking at you, for slightly too long... Does that make any sense? It was off-putting. Or sometimes when I was talking to Miriam – that was his wife – I'd find he was watching me, really quite intently.'

I nod. 'And do you know if other people thought the same way?'

'I've really got no idea.' She looks at me curiously. 'It wasn't as if I made a habit of talking to people about him,' she says. 'It was just a personal observation. But that doesn't mean there was anything to it. Why do you want to know?'

But I don't want to reveal why just yet. 'I wondered if they'd lived here a long time,' I say. 'Because the house is still really quite dated in parts. As if someone older had been there for years and seen no reason to introduce anything more modern.'

'I've no idea.' She strokes her top lip with a finger. 'I got the sense it was a few years, not for any specific reason, just things that were mentioned from time to time. I know he worked locally – he was a civil servant – and then retired from that job maybe ten or twelve years ago, something like that. Whether they lived at Pevensey the whole time though, I'm afraid I don't know.' She stops to think, but then shakes her head. 'No, I can't think they ever said anything more specific. You're going to have to tell me why you want to know though, Thea.'

'I found something, hidden in the house,' I reply. 'I just wondered who had put it there, that's all.'

She smiles. 'Sounds intriguing…'

'Not really,' I say, lightly. 'It's of some age, I'm just curious to know when it dates from.'

'Well, whatever it is that has made you think it might be the Campbells has also made you think about them in certain way.' She tilts her head and studies me. 'And I suspect not in a good way, otherwise you wouldn't be asking me these questions.'

I smile. 'Probably not,' I reply. 'So do you have any idea when they moved in?'

But Anna refuses to let me change tack. 'I bet it was behind the panelling in the hall, wasn't it? I've always wondered if there were any secret compartments in there… What was it, a blood-encrusted dagger?'

'Blimey, Anna, how old do you think the house is? Besides, it's hardly big enough to have a secret compartment – although I must admit I've never looked. But don't worry, it's nothing quite so dramatic.' Except that as soon as I say it I realise that it might as well be.

Her face falls. 'So what was it then?'

And I realise I'm going to have to tell her just at the same moment I'm wondering why I don't want to. 'It was a newspaper article actually, but there's no date on it. I've a rough idea but that's why I was wondering about the previous owners of the house.'

'Again, why do you think it was them that left it there?'

I'm beginning to squirm. I can't say why without mentioning what the article was about. And I really don't want to have to admit it. I sigh with frustration. I'm going to have to tell her.

'Because it seems an odd thing to have hidden,' I begin. 'And finding it in our house has made me feel uneasy. It gives me the creeps actually, and I remembered that's exactly what you said about the man who lived here before us.'

Her look intensifies. 'Go on,' she says.

I swallow. 'It was about that girl who was attacked, from years ago.' I give a weak smile. 'Of course that could be nothing to do with it. There was an advert on the back for a Butlin's holiday camp, but somehow I don't think the desire to take a trip to Skegness is a secret worthy of hiding.'

There is a sudden stillness in the room. Anna's face freezes and, although she recovers herself, the split second it takes her to do so sends a shiver of unease rippling through me.

'How long ago did it happen, Anna?'

She attempts a nonchalant expression but doesn't quite manage it. 'Oh, crikey. I don't exactly know. Fifteen years ago, maybe, a bit longer... possibly twenty.'

'And you don't know how long the Campbells lived at our house?' I ask. 'Could they have been here then?'

'Well it's possible of course, but—'

'So who *would* know?' I ask.

Anna's eyes are wide. 'What are you trying to say, Thea? You can't go around suggesting that he was responsible. Me saying he gave me the creeps was just my opinion, and not based on anything concrete. It certainly wasn't intended as damning evidence.'

'But it's a bit of a coincidence, you have to admit?'

She stares at me, a look of horror on her face. 'No… No, I don't think it's that at all. Because you're making a huge assumption here and besides—'

The silence between us blooms.

'Besides what, Anna?'

She shakes her head. 'No, I'm sorry, I'm not having this kind of discussion. It's quite wrong. And just the way these sorts of horrible rumours start. People say all kinds of things and then before you know it everybody's talking and the whole thing gets completely out of hand…' She comes to a halt.

I try to hold her look but she drops her gaze. 'But a crime *was* committed,' I reply. 'One where the guilty party was never found. Maybe it's just as wrong to ignore it,' I say, mildly. 'However, I wasn't thinking of accusing anyone, Anna. Just trying to think logically about what I found.'

She shakes her head again and, as she looks away, it suddenly strikes me that we're now talking about two different things, and it's Anna who is concerned about rumours, not me.

I lean forward slightly. 'The other day, when we spoke about Tilly being bullied, you said that I should wait until I was on the receiving end of the village gossip. You meant it to sound like a throwaway comment, but because you're far too honest to lie, it didn't quite have the conviction it should have had. So you tried to cover up your slip by saying that all villages are rife with gossip. That may well be the case, but now I'm wondering what you meant by it. Were you talking about yourself, Anna? Or was it me?'

She slides me a nervous look.

'Only I'm not daft,' I continue. 'The hush that falls when I walk past people, the curious looks that linger just that little bit too long, even you look uncomfortable today... Or am I just imagining it?'

Her breath stills as she looks at me, the seconds ticking by, before her shoulders suddenly slump. 'No...' she says, eventually. 'No, I'm sorry, you're not.'

'Then would you at least do me the courtesy of telling me why everyone seems to be talking about me? I've only just arrived in the village for goodness' sake; I haven't done anything and yet the welcome mat isn't exactly being rolled out.'

I didn't actually mean by her, but Anna's guilt speaks for her. 'That's hardly fair,' she says. 'You've no idea how difficult...' She trails off.

'Look, all I want to know is what people are saying,' I reply. 'Forget anything else for a minute. Don't you think it's only fair that I do?'

Anna glances at me, but her gaze drops to the floor and stays there. 'I've heard some things, that's all,' she says.

'What things? I know if anyone's privy to what goes on around here, it's you.'

She looks up then. 'Yes, and do you know what that's like?' she retaliates. 'Being the keeper of everyone's secrets because of who I am. It's exhausting. I don't know how Rob does it, but even though everyone seems to think it's okay to wash their dirty linen in my presence, I don't then go around airing it elsewhere. Whatever is being said, it didn't come from me.'

'Anna, I never said it did, but please, I just want to know what it is.'

She folds her arms across her chest and it's clear she isn't going to tell me. I get to my feet. 'Fine,' I say. 'I reckon I know who started all these whispers so I'll go and ask Stacey... that's right, isn't it?'

Anna doesn't reply, which is all the confirmation I need.

'Thea, wait!'

But I'm already walking out the door.

CHAPTER FIFTEEN

It would have been too easy to simply find Stacey in the shop. Too easy and wholly inappropriate, considering what I want to say. Jackie isn't in there either. Instead it's a much older woman I don't recognise and my mention of Stacey's name elicits no sign of recognition. But I know roughly where she lives and that will have to be enough.

The estate is two roads of modern houses that must have been built about ten or so years ago. They certainly weren't here when I was a child; back then it was all just fields. They're right at the other end of the village but, even so, a five-minute walk is all it takes to find myself staring at the rows of near identical houses which pretty much all look like they're occupied by families. I walk down the road a little way and pick a house at random on my left. A bright-red scooter lies on its side near the front path.

My knock brings a harassed-looking woman to the door with a toddler on her hip. When I explain who I'm looking for, my carefully rehearsed and very plausible lie as to why tripping off my lips, I'm rewarded with a pointing finger and the words 'Number eighteen.' The door closes seconds later.

I have no real idea what I'm going to say should Stacey actually answer the door, but the look on her face as she finds me on her doorstep would seem to be a pretty good indicator of how the conversation is going to go.

'You'd best come in,' she says, flicking a glance down the street. She stands back to let me enter the narrow hallway before openly looking me up and down.

'I'm sorry for coming unannounced, only I had no other way of contacting you.'

She peers at me suspiciously. 'Yeah well, you're lucky I'm in. I should be at work but my boss rang early to swap my shift.'

I smile graciously.

'What do you want anyway? I haven't got time to stand here talking about the good old days.' There's a sneer in her voice that sets my teeth on edge.

'Do you know I still can't place you,' I reply. 'And yet you obviously know me…'

I'm subjected to further scrutiny. 'I know *of* you,' she clarifies. 'My older sister, Claire, was in your class at school.'

We're still standing in the hallway. There's not much light but enough to see the open disdain on Stacey's face. I struggle to think. I can't remember the names of half the girls in my class at school. But then a memory stirs. 'Claire… Sunderland?' I ask. 'Is that your last name?'

'It was. I'm Brooks now.'

I nod. 'Yes, I do remember. Claire used to be really good at netball, didn't she?'

'She still is. She played on the county side for a few years.'

'Oh…' I trail off. I'm still not sure where this is all going and Stacey clearly isn't going to help me out. But then again, why would she, when she's hardly made a secret of her dislike for me? And I'm beginning to find it *very* irritating.

I move further down the hallway and through the first door I come to, a sitting room. I'm aware it's rude but I don't want to say what I need to cramped in the hallway with Stacey, I need some space between us.

'Right, what's this all about then?' I begin, as she marches after me. 'Cause I'm getting fed up of all the sly looks and silences. You, Jackie, and the rest…'

She gives me a stony look.

'Okay… well you obviously have something you feel the need to talk about, something that involves me. And since we've only just moved here and I don't know any of you, I'd like to know what all the whispering is about.'

'Yeah, well what do you expect when you go around calling my son a thug? Just because I'm on my own and don't live in a big posh house. Doesn't mean you can go spreading lies.'

My mouth drops open. 'Who told you that?' I counter, fully prepared to brazen this out. "Cause I've done no such thing. I'm quite happy to admit that my daughter punched Leo but that's because she doesn't like seeing her best friend getting bullied. And while I'm furious that it happened in the first place, and that my daughter seems to be the one who's ended up in trouble, what I haven't done is shared any of that with anyone else. I certainly haven't been gossiping about it.' I glare at her. 'And I don't really give a stuff whether you have a problem admitting your son is a bully, but trying to throw up a smokescreen by making out I'm the one at fault here is just pathetic.'

Stacey draws in a breath. '*I* can't admit to it? Well, that's bloody rich coming from you. When we all know why *you're* bad-mouthing me.'

'I'm doing what?'

'Trying to make out I'm a bad lot when you're literally the spawn of the devil.'

A gobbet of spit lands on my face from the force of her words. I feel like I've been stung.

I take a step backward, pulse beating hard against my neck. But Stacey hasn't finished.

'Surprised?' she sneers. 'And there's you, looking and talking like butter wouldn't melt. Well, living in a big house isn't going to help you now, is it? What did you think, that it meant you were untouchable…? Oh dear.' There's a horrible gleam in her eye. She's actually enjoying this.

'Or maybe you didn't think that there would still be people here who remember what happened. Well, there are, especially when it's something like this, people have *very* long memories indeed.' She looks me up and down again, her face contorted. 'I don't know how you have the nerve to show your face around here again, pretending like nothing happened. Not after what your dad did.'

The breath catches in my throat as it constricts. 'My dad? What on earth has any of this got to do with my dad?' I can feel the first dark rumblings of dread gathering in the pit of my stomach.

'So when I mentioned earlier that my sister Claire was in your year at school, I "forgot" to mention that I have another sister too, one who's even older. Hayley was two years above you. And do you know who her best friend was…? Well I'll tell you, shall I? It was Georgia. Georgia Thomas. Remember her, Thea?'

'No. No I don't…' I shake my head, fear pricking at my neck. 'I don't know what you're talking about.'

But I do. Of course I do.

Nausea washes over me at the mention of Georgia's name, and I'd give anything to flee Stacey's horribly hypnotic gaze, but I can't. I'm rooted to the spot.

'Well maybe this will help you to remember.'

Stacey crosses to a small table set with chairs in one corner of the room and picks up a piece of paper left there. From its position I'd say it's one she's been looking at recently. She brandishes it in front of her, her face a distorted mask, and my stomach drops away in shock as I see what it is.

She unfolds the newspaper in front of me, relishing her slow and deliberate movements until the full spread is revealed.

'See…'

Stacey jabs the paper towards me and I take the yellowed sheet, acid burning my throat as I begin to read.

> … *a thirty-seven-year old local man is still being questioned, although an arrest has not yet been made. Meanwhile police are urgently appealing for anyone who may have any information relating to the case to come forward…*

'See that?' she spits. 'Where it says a local man is helping the police with their enquiries – that was your dad, Thea. Your dad.' I can feel her gaze burning the side of my face, and then she laughs. 'What… you didn't know? Ask anyone, Thea. It's the truth.'

I swear in that moment my heart nearly stops. Its chaotic pounding in my chest is matched only by the way the thoughts are careering through my head. But the moment I manage to catch hold of one, it shatters like glass and sharp needles of pain from its splinters pierce my heart.

I don't remember leaving Stacey's house. Nor do I remember my passage through the village, except that it must have been swift and uncaring because now my only reality is the solid wood of Pevensey's front door and my race up the stairs.

I only just make it to the bathroom. But even the spew of vomit which hits the toilet bowl can't cleanse me of my thoughts or the images in my head. My father. Touching. Even the possibility makes me heave. The thought that he could, that anyone would… I'm thinking as a mother, about Lauren, about Chloe, but more than anything I'm thinking as a daughter, about my own childhood and the fact I have to acknowledge: that it was all a lie.

I rest my cheek against the toilet seat, scarcely caring that this isn't the most sanitary place for it to be. It's the least of my worries. I'm searching my memories for any inkling that something was out of place, any suggestion that there might have been… and then I stop. What am I doing?

I sit up straight, tucking my hair back behind my ears. How could I even consider such a thing? My father was the most kind and loving and perfect dad anyone could ever wish for. There's no way he could have done anything like this; he'd have abhorred what happened to Georgia as much as I do. I was heartbroken when he died; my daddy, the man who had been there for me through everything, the good times and the bad. Yes, he'd hugged me, and kissed me, ruffled my hair, stroked my face. But I'd been glad of it, just as I am when I see Drew with our girls, just like a father should be. And I'm suddenly rocked by grief and anger that anyone might have thought these things about him. That he'd had to endure the torture that all this would have brought. That he died and I no longer have him to comfort me.

It takes a while for my tears to subside to the point where I can even think of moving. I reach for the toilet roll and wipe my face, flushing the loo and getting unsteadily to my feet. I gulp water from the tap, swirling it around my mouth and spitting it into the sink, watching it disappear as I run fresh water to wash it away. My insides feel scoured out, like I've swallowed acid.

'Thea?' Drew's voice is hesitant, wary with anxiety.

But the sound of it still explodes into the quiet house. I freeze. I had forgotten he was even in the house. But what do I say? What *can* I say?

He moves closer. 'Thea?' he says again. His hand slides around the back of my neck. 'Hey, what's wrong?' And, turning me round, he wordlessly pulls me in.

'I'm sorry.' I shudder, trying to hold back my emotion, and I really am. I'd give anything not to do this now, but his love is breaking a hole in the dam that's been holding back all my fears and worries from the last few days.

'Hey, come on now. What's this all about? Did something happen with Anna?'

I sniffle against his chest, confused momentarily by his words, until I remember that's where he thinks I've been. I still have my jacket on. But my conversation with Anna seems so far away, it's as if it happened to someone else. And yet… Her words come rushing back to me and the realisation that she knows about this too hits me like a blow. I can feel the images in my head building again, the words forming in my throat. Words that I need to get out and off my chest where they've been lying heavy. But how do I say them? If I speak them it will make them real.

Drew's hand is stroking my hair. He can feel the rising tide within me. 'Thea, sweetheart. Jesus, you're scaring me now. What's this all about? Has something happened. One of the girls…?'

I manage a shake of my head.

'Then what? Come on, Thea, tell me.'

'I knew I was right,' I begin, looking up at him. 'I knew something was wrong… people in the village… everyone really… even Anna. And now I know why…'

'Thea, love, that doesn't really make any sense…'

'How is that possible? That other people could know when I didn't? My own dad, Drew, how could I *not* know?' My voice is rising as I speak, beginning to stumble over the words.

His arm stiffens slightly. 'What are you talking about?'

'I knew that people were talking about us. You made out that I was imagining things, but I knew I wasn't. And the article too… It was hidden, Drew. Someone left it in our house. Someone who knew its secrets…' I stare at him. 'Oh, but that's it! Stacey doesn't know about that… so she has it all wrong…' I feel a surge of hope flare. 'It was the Campbells, don't you see? I knew I was right.'

Drew's grip on my arm strengthens. 'Thea…' His face is close to mine. 'I know you're upset, love, but you're babbling… And I can't make head nor tail of what you're saying. Start at the beginning.'

A rush of breath escapes me. 'For goodness' sake, there's no time… I have to go back and show Stacey. Tell her what Anna said about Mr Campbell, prove to her that this couldn't have anything to do with my dad…'

But Drew isn't about to let me go. 'Thea…'

'Okay… Look, I met Stacey in the village shop just after we'd moved in. She's lived here all her life and it was clear she remembered me, but I couldn't work out why she's been looking daggers at me ever since. Even before what happened when Lauren hit Leo, I knew there was more to it than that. And when I was over at Anna's this morning she told me that I was right; people *are* talking about us. And I'd had enough… so I went to see Stacey and she… well, she…' The words catch in my throat. I look up at Drew, swallowing hard. 'She showed me this.'

I'd been clutching the yellowed sheet of newspaper as I'd run back to the house and at some point it must have fluttered to the floor. I pick it up, the movement causing my head to swim.

'It's a newspaper article about that girl that was molested, a bit like the one that I showed you. Except that it must have been from later on because it said that a man was being questioned about what happened. My dad, Stacey said… But he can't have been, Drew, I mean that's *ridiculous*. My dad would never…' My voice is rising, but it sounds strangely like it belongs to someone else. 'In any case it wasn't him because it must have been the man who lived here before us – Mr Campbell – don't you see? Anna said he was really creepy and his wife must have been the one who hid the newspaper I found. It all makes sense…' I trail off, my words chasing each other around my head.

Drew looks like he's about to cry. 'Thea, why are you doing this to yourself? You're chasing shadows, trying to prove a point that isn't even there.'

He stops suddenly, eyes widening as he realises what he's said. 'And I know why you're doing it… So do you, if you'd only admit to what you've been thinking.'

A tear rolls down my cheek.

'This isn't going to go away, and no amount of wishing is going to make that happen. Think about it logically for a minute. If Stacey has a newspaper article about the attack on Georgia and she mentioned your dad, that dates it to when they were living here. So how can it have anything to do with these people, what did you call them, the Campbells…? Because if it did it would mean that they were living at Pevensey the same time as your mum and dad. That's not possible, Thea.'

I'm watching his lips. I can hear his words but they're not making sense. I shake my head. 'No, that's not right…'

Except that it is. I know it is. My heart contracts with fear.

'What did you say?' I ask slowly. 'About the article. What did you say?'

Drew frowns. 'I don't… I just said that if Stacey has an article about Georgia then—'

'Yes… Georgia. You said Georgia, except that I didn't mention her name just now…'

'Didn't you?' His brow furrows. 'Well then I must have remembered it from before.'

It's possible, I suppose. But even as I think it, something clicks within me, like a circuit completing itself. I raise my eyes to look at him. I never mentioned her name before.

We're close. One of his hands still cradles the back of my neck, the other enfolds my hand against his chest. We're locked in and there's nowhere for either of us to go.

'You *knew* about this?' The words tear from my lips. 'You *knew* and you didn't tell me?'

He's not looking at me. Not properly, his eyes are ever so slightly adrift. Just like everything else.

I push at his chest, scrambling to be free. His answer explodes inside my head and I can't think straight.

'Thea!' He pulls against me, trying to keep me close to him. 'Oh God…' His hands are clutching at me. 'How could I possibly have told you, Thea? I didn't find out until after your father died, I swear. Before then I was just as in the dark as you.'

I slap at his arms, eyes wild. 'That's no excuse and you know it! How could you even think of keeping something like that hidden from me? I was his daughter for Christ's sake.'

But Drew's voice is broken. 'Thea, your father had just died, what was I supposed to do? Just drop it into conversation one day... Oh, and by the way your father was accused of being a child molester... You took his death hard enough as it was, how could I possibly have added to your grief?' His words are choked off. 'I don't think I could have borne hurting you that much.'

'My father was not a child molester,' I hiss, my jaw aching with the force with which I'm clenching it shut.

'Thea...' His voice is soft, pleading. 'I loved him too...'

A sob breaks free. 'I just don't know how you can live your whole life and not know something like that,' I say. 'How does that even happen? Was I really that stupid, that blind to what was going on around me?' I want to ask if I'm *still* that blind, but I don't.

'You were a child, Thea. Why *would* you know?'

I think back to the letter written by my eleven-year-old self. One that I had also hidden for safekeeping. 'But I did know,' I say. 'I knew something was wrong, and I did nothing about it. I was too scared...' I tremble as I say it. I'm still scared.

Drew's head dips in resignation. 'I think my mum was terrified when your dad died. As if his death would be a catalyst, drawing attention to speculation about what had happened all over again. Only this time the whole story would come tumbling out and you would find out in the worst possible way.' He paused, swallowing. 'She told me so that I could tell you... protect you.'

'But you didn't tell me... you didn't protect me.'

'No... I didn't. But I never asked for her to pass the mantle of safekeeping to me either. And I wish with all my heart she hadn't.'

There is silence between us. I know I'm hurting him, but I'm hurting too and I need to find a way to understand how we got here.

'So where was my mum in all of this, Drew? Why didn't she tell me? She just left me to carry on like nothing had happened, and instead I had to hear it from someone else. I could understand it when I was a child, but I stopped being a child a long time ago.' I stare at him, knowing he's not going to answer. 'I've never had a proper relationship with her, now I know why... Is it any wonder when she—'

'She was doing what mums do, Thea; trying to protect you.'

'Really? Is that what it was? Or was she too afraid to say anything for fear of it getting out again? Too cowardly to stand up for what she believed in.' I trail off. 'Or maybe she never believed in him at all,' I say, bitterly.

'Thea, don't. Your mum loved your dad. Still does.'

I let his words sink in. I want to believe them, but my only thought is that the person who attacked Georgia was never found. 'Do *you* think it's true?' I ask quietly. 'Could my dad have been involved in what happened to Georgia?'

'No!' Drew's reply is instantaneous. 'Don't go thinking that...' He breaks off and gives me an odd look as a sudden light gathers in his eyes. 'You don't know, do you?' he asks, his voice picking up. 'Listen, your dad couldn't have been involved because he was with my parents that entire evening. They both were, your mum and your dad; they'd gone around to mine for supper. Thea, your dad had an alibi.'

I stare at him, a tiny spark of hope catching fire. 'But the papers didn't say... Actually the papers didn't say anything...' I think about the implications of his words. 'So what did happen then? Why was my dad even accused in the first place?'

Drew sighs. 'I don't know why,' he admits. 'Only that the police were asking questions about your dad a couple of days after

Georgia was…' He can't bring himself to say the words. 'Well, after she… Anyway, that's about all there was to it because my parents told them straight away that your dad was with them all evening. Plus, someone else corroborated the story too, so that was that. They'd been visiting the churchyard and seen your mum and dad walking round to mine. I think the police had been following up a few other enquiries as well and maybe they got a lead elsewhere, I don't know, but after a few weeks it all petered out. My mum didn't know what happened ultimately, the papers stopped reporting it and obviously no one was privy to the police investigation so… All we know is that Georgia's mum kind of… lost it a bit, started accusing your dad of all sorts. I think she was even warned about her behaviour by the police but in the end your folks just decided to move. I guess it was easier than having to live with that.'

'And yours did too…'

I can feel him watching me, trying to deduce what I'm thinking. 'Yes, but not for a couple of months after.' He pauses for a moment. 'Thea, there's nothing wrong with that… Haven't we just had Rachel and Gerry up here for the weekend looking to move this way?'

I nod. 'I know…'

'But what? Jesus, Thea, don't go looking for trouble where there is none.' He softens his voice again. 'Look, I know how horrible this is… You can't even begin to come close to getting your head around it, and yes, you should have known. But don't let your feelings about your dad change. The memories you have of him are the only ones you need.'

He's right, I know he is. But I can't help the way I'm feeling now.

'The trouble is, Drew, it's not just me, is it? Stacey has been going around spreading rumours about this, I know she has. And saying that I've accused her son of being a bully to try to cover this up. It started almost as soon as we moved here and it's getting worse.' I hold his look. 'You should have told me,' I say bitterly.

I can't help it, I feel let down. 'For God's sake, Drew, we've only just moved here. This was supposed to be a dream move for us and now I have no idea where this is all going to end.'

He pulls away from me. 'Oh no, no you don't. Don't you try to put all the blame on me when all I've done is try to protect you. You're the one who brought us here.' But his anger hurts even more.

'Because it was the right thing for us to do!' I retaliate. 'Or at least I thought so at the time, but then I didn't exactly have all the information I needed to go on, did I? Because *you* chose not to share it. And actually, *I* didn't bring us here, we both agreed that moving was the best thing for our family. The difference between us is that I made my decision in good faith. You could have said something. You *should* have said something.'

'I said plenty, Thea, you just weren't listening. I tried to ward you off gently, made a few comments about how coming back might not be such a good idea. I even showed you the details of a few other houses I'd found, but no, you ignored it all. Short of blowing a hole right through the middle of your childhood, what else was I supposed to do?'

'That's not how I remember it.'

'No, of course it isn't, because once you get an idea in your head, Thea, there's no shifting you. And you *never* listen! Maybe I should have just told it to you straight… But I couldn't do that to you. Do you have any idea how hard it was for me? Listening to you babbling on about Pevensey, day in, day out; the dream house and the idyllic childhood. You were so excited, your work was taking off like never before, and all I wanted was for things to be perfect for you.'

'Like they are now?' I hiss. 'We ought never to have come back here, Drew, and you should have stopped us.' There, I've said it.

His eyes spark with anger. 'No, we shouldn't have. But whose fault is that? If I'm guilty of anything, it's of loving you, Thea, that's all. I know what this place means to you, what it means to us. It's where we were made for heaven's sake. So ask yourself, if the shoe were on the other foot, what would you have done? Would you have told me? Or would you have done what I did, and assume that what happened to Georgia took place so long ago that there was no reason for it ever to come to light again?'

'I wouldn't have taken that chance,' I say sadly. '*Because* I love you. Were you ever going to tell me? Or were you going to let me live my life, day by day, hoping that I'd never find out? Praying that you'd never have to watch my life implode?'

'Oh, for God's sake, Thea, now you're just being melodramatic. I'm sorry no one told you about what happened, okay. And I'm sorry that you found out the way you did. But let's be logical about this a minute. Your dad wasn't actually involved in what happened to Georgia, so don't get so het up about the fact that you should have known – that's not really the issue here, is it? Nothing's really changed.'

'Well if you can't see that it has, then you're even more deluded than I thought. Everything has changed. I can feel it… But isn't the real issue here about trust, Drew? I didn't think we would ever have secrets from one another, but it seems I was wrong. You should have told me about this, long before we even thought of moving, and certainly before it ever got as far as it has.' I break off as emotion threatens to overwhelm me. 'And whatever happens now as a result is down to you, and I'm not sure I'm ready to forgive you for that just yet.'

He holds my look for a moment before glancing away. My heart thumps in my chest for several more seconds before he finally turns back to me. 'Yes, well we're here now, so what are we going to do about it?'

But I have no answer for him.

CHAPTER SIXTEEN

I can't remember ever spending a night like that before. So close to Drew and yet further away from him than I ever thought possible. An uneasy truce had developed by the time we went to bed but, as soon as we climbed in beside one another, the intimate arrangement of limbs that usually came so naturally had become a journey we had no map for. It felt wrong, and all it had taken was this slight shift to widen the gap between us into something we were unable to traverse. Our speech felt stilted and, as the minutes ticked past, the silence formed an impenetrable barrier. Now, in the early morning, it has become the elephant in the room – an object to be circumnavigated warily, and neither of us know how to achieve this. We've never argued like that before.

I get up when I can no longer bear to lie in bed and, once I've tidied the kitchen, made tea for us both and packed lunches for the girls to take to school, there's nothing left for me to do but confront my thoughts. I still can't believe I didn't know any of what had happened but what haunts me the most is the fact that if something like this could be hidden from me for so long, then so could the truth.

Drew gets up and tries to start a conversation a few times, but it stalls after the first sentence. He doesn't know how to make things right between us and I'm not sure I want to let him just yet. To find out those things about my past is bad enough, but to discover that they've been kept from me by someone who I thought shared everything is proving the hardest pill to swallow. Because this isn't just about me.

I have a sudden vision of my mother as I go to wake Chloe. Is this what it was like for her? Putting on a brave face in the aftermath of the accusation, pretending as if everything is normal? I feel like I'm looking at myself from the outside in; as if someone else is occupying my body and I'm just an observer. And it strikes me that I had no idea what Mum was going through either. How she felt. And I know I'm going to have to talk to her.

'Come on, sleepyhead,' I cajole, cuddling up to Chloe's warm body as I sit on the side of her bed to nudge her awake. She's always been the hardest one to shift in the morning. Lauren, on the other hand, is generally up with the lark and is already downstairs having her breakfast. I pass my hand over Chloe's hair, lingering for a moment to stroke it away from her face. I know how much she likes it, she's just like me in that regard, always comforted by the sensation. I'd give anything to climb into bed alongside her, to hold her close and breathe her in, hoping that time will stand still and she will never be hurt, never be scarred by life.

Reluctantly, I draw away. However much I want to preserve this moment, the hands of the clock are moving and the last thing I want today is to have to nag her about being late. Whatever else happens, I'm determined that she will have the best of me this morning, that's all I can give her, Lauren too.

Drew is chatting quietly with her in the kitchen, sitting side by side at the breakfast bar, their shoulders touching. He looks up as he sees me walk in and I know he feels it too, the heartstring-tugging pull of responsibility we have for these two small people. That we're the only ones who stand between their happiness or sadness and we have to get it right. He smiles warily, in acknowledgement.

I've already asked him to take the girls to school this morning and he readily agreed, taking over the chivvying and checking that everything is ready for the day ahead. For so long it's been a routine that he took no part in but, now that he's working for himself, it's something he hopes to change. I have to wonder how any of this is going to work out.

He's by the door now, collecting coats and school bags, handing them out as the girls come to kiss me goodbye. And then they're out the door, into the damp fresh air to wait for Tilly. It surprises him when I collect my coat from its hook.

'Oh, are you coming with us?' he asks, but I shake my head.

'No. I'm going to see Anna. She doesn't teach first thing on Tuesdays because Rob takes assembly first. In fact, he'll be walking Tilly to school this morning, which means she'll be on her own.'

I thought my voice was light but Drew arches his eyebrows. 'Is that wise?'

'Maybe not, but I'm going anyway. And you can look at me like that all you want. Anna has definitely heard some of what's been said, and I want to know how much. I also want to know what she thinks. If we're about to have our lives made hell then forewarned is forearmed.'

'I see, and that's my fault too, is it?'

'Well, we wouldn't have moved here if I—'

'Hadn't been so blinkered in your determination,' interrupts Drew. His voice is barely above a whisper but there's a hard set to his jawline.

I ignore his comment and watch them go, standing in the hallway for a few moments until I can no longer hear Lauren's chattering down the drive. The silence of the house echoes around me. I close the door quietly, suddenly feeling incredibly small. And very alone.

I'm not sure that going to see Anna this morning is such a great idea either. It seems a little like rubbing salt into the wound but, the more I think about how she behaved yesterday, the more I realise that Anna knows exactly what's been said, and, more to the point, she's already formed an opinion on it. I have to know where I stand.

Anna is obviously enjoying the quiet solitude of an undisturbed cup of tea as she leads me into her kitchen. A mug sits on the table, an open magazine beside it. Although she refills the kettle to make another, I'm surprised to see a look of resignation on her face. I don't think that would have been the case, before. It annoys me.

'Actually Anna, don't worry about making me a drink, I've not long had one.'

She frowns, possibly at my tone, possibly at the recognition of her own thoughts. 'I wondered if I might see you today,' she says, slipping back into her seat. 'When you left yesterday, I…' Her gaze drops to the table where her fingers play with the edge of a coaster. 'Did you go and see Stacey in the end?'

I sit down opposite, tucking my hair behind my ears. 'I did,' I reply. 'And I wondered if I might talk to you about it.'

'Yes of course.' She adjusts her position, resting her hands one on top of the other, and I realise that this is a side of Anna I haven't yet seen – the listener, fulfilling the obligations of her pastoral role. But it isn't a stance I thought I'd ever see her adopt with me.

'Could we not do this?' I say. 'I'm not here as just another parishioner, Anna. I came here as a friend.'

She sits up a little straighter. 'Yes, of course you did, sorry, force of habit.' She gives a tight smile but her position doesn't alter.

'You've obviously heard about my dad,' I begin. There's no point in beating about the bush.

Anna fidgets nervously. 'It's a lot to take in, Thea, I—' She catches my expression and stops. 'It's just a shock, that's all. I really never thought that it would involve…'

'Well, that makes two of us.'

Her eyes meet mine.

'I'm not joking... Really, Anna. Up until yesterday I had no more idea than you.'

She looks away. 'Shit,' she says quietly.

'Yeah, bit of a bastard, isn't it? Finding out that your whole childhood might have been a lie. That your dad wasn't who you thought he was.' I pause for a moment. 'Did you think I already knew, is that it? Jesus, did you honestly believe I could have come back to live here knowing that?'

'Well I... I didn't know what to think.'

'You still don't.'

'No, not really,' she admits.

'Well again, that makes two of us.' I give a weak smile. 'But I promise you, Anna, I don't remember anything about this from my childhood. We moved away when I was eleven... Now, at least, it's obvious why. But at the time, I had no idea that anything out of the ordinary had happened. I came back to Pevensey in good faith, wanting what's best for my family. A new life for us in the country...' My voice catches as tears begin to well. 'In a place where we'd all been so happy. I can't believe I could have got it so wrong...' I lift my chin a little.

Anna is rubbing one thumb along the top of the other. She has no idea what to say.

'What did Stacey actually say to you?' I ask, eventually. 'Is it all round the village...?'

Anna grimaces in reply. 'I'm sorry, Thea, maybe she just said it to spite me, knowing that we're neighbours, I don't know, but I couldn't ignore it.'

I open my mouth to speak then suddenly close it again, confused. 'Hang on a minute. Why did she want to spite you?'

A tightness passes over Anna's face. 'Never mind,' she says. 'That has nothing to do with this.' She shakes her head. 'Besides, I don't think people like Stacey need a reason to say the things they do, but it was what she said, Thea. People are… Well, we're all parents. I think they're a little bit freaked by it.'

'People…?' Heat prickles at my neck. 'What did Stacey actually say?'

Her head drops as a wave of colour rushes up her neck and over her cheeks. 'I'm sorry, Thea,' she whispers. 'But she said your dad was a child abuser.'

No speculation. No reference to the fact that he was questioned but that's all. No mention that he was never charged, that he had an alibi. Just a bald statement of Stacey's opinion. She has proclaimed herself judge and jury.

It's even worse to hear someone else say it. Bad enough to have those words reverberating in my own voice, but to hear them said by someone else… It makes them real. And suddenly more dots are joined; the bigger picture is becoming clearer. My anger flares into life.

I look down at the grain on her table, letting my eyes trace its whorls and curves. 'And you think it's true?' I say finally.

She peeps across at me, trying to gauge my reaction. 'I didn't say that.'

'You have actually, Anna. Pretty much you have. By everything you've said and done since you spoke to Stacey. Before that even, when you maybe heard little whispers.' She looks away and I know I'm right. 'You know, what would have been really nice was if you'd come and spoken to me about it. Did it not occur to you that I didn't even know?'

Her eyes widen.

'But what's almost as bad as having my whole childhood and the memory of my father called into question is that someone could use what they know, or rather think they know, for their own ends. That doesn't just make me upset, Anna. I'm bloody furious… Who the hell does Stacey think she is to say those things?'

'I think she's just like that,' says Anna quickly. 'I don't really know how the subject came up, I just… Well, I was in the shop…'

She breaks off, her face still flushed. 'Thea, I'm so sorry. I can't begin to understand how something like this must feel, but I wasn't fishing for information. Believe me, I really didn't want to know…'

'Then why was I even a topic of conversation?'

Anna is quiet for a minute, she's trying to think. 'I'm not even sure,' she admits. 'But gossips don't need a reason, do they?' She studies me. 'Besides, what does this have to do with anything? What does it matter why it was said, isn't *what* was said more important?'

'My father was not a child molester,' I hiss. 'And whatever else this is, it's nobody's business but my family's. My dad was never charged. In fact, he has an alibi for the night it happened, but I shouldn't even have to tell you that. And I'm damn sure that Stacey isn't going to mention it either. If we hadn't come back to Pevensey no one would be thinking about any of this. No, there's a reason this has come up now, and it's got something to do with Stacey.'

Anna frowns.

'Oh, come on… Can't you see it? She as much admitted to me yesterday that she's quite happy to spread malicious lies about me in retaliation for calling her son a bully, when in fact I've done no such thing. Not outside of my own four walls anyway. And yet she's taken that decision… Do you know what I think? Maybe I'm wrong, but I reckon it's easier to go around spreading lies about someone else than having to admit the truth about her own son's behaviour. It very nicely deflects all the attention from her. And, let's face it, who'd want to challenge her about it when you run the risk of becoming victim to her vicious rumours.'

'Thea, you can't just say stuff like that! Listen, I know you're upset but—'

'I haven't even started yet,' I reply, grimly, warming to my theme. The more I say, the more it seems to make sense. 'It makes Stacey untouchable, doesn't it? No one wants to take her on and so we hand her all the power, keeping quiet, never challenging her about Leo's behaviour. We make it really easy for her to ignore it too. Why acknowledge it if you don't have to? Yeah, she knows what she's doing all right. It's knowing and it's calculated. And I'm sorry, Anna, but by keeping quiet about what her son did to Tilly you've fallen right into her trap.'

The colour has left Anna's face, all except for two pinpoints of red in the centre of her otherwise pale cheeks.

She struggles to her feet. 'I think you should leave now, Thea,' she says. 'I'm sorry. I can see how angry you are, but it's hardly fair to come around here and take it out on me – or worse, make up stories about someone else, which is exactly what you're accusing *her* of. I don't think Stacey is a particularly nice person, but that's all there is to it.'

Her face shows her struggle for control. 'And I think you're actually going to make it worse if you carry on thinking the way you are. I don't really know how you start to put something like this behind you, but making more of it than is necessary isn't going to help, especially where Stacey is concerned. And, despite what you say, I don't think I've allowed myself to fall into her trap. I think I'm just being sensible,' she finishes rather stiffly, standing over me and clearly wondering whether she should sit down again.

I don't really want to go, but I stand up anyway. I'm desperate to find a way to reach Anna, to have a friend to confide in, but I may well have blown it, just like Drew warned. It's just it seems so obvious to me what's happening. Maybe Anna's right, maybe I am exactly like Stacey, throwing up a smokescreen so I don't have to admit what I'm feeling about my dad, but I'm disappointed by Anna's reaction, I can't help it. This is her house though and I shouldn't have got angry. The realisation brings the threat of tears instead.

'Anna, I'm so sorry...'

We stand and look at one another for no more than a second, but even that feels too long. The easy manner we had has gone and I know that's my fault.

'I really didn't want to upset you. I'll go but… please can you just remember who it is we're talking about here? My father, not me, not Drew and not my girls. We're just the same as we've always been.' I bite my lip. 'You even said it yourself, Anna, that Stacey told you what she did because we were neighbours. Neighbours, you said, not friends. An unintentional slip perhaps, but…'

Anna's face softens a little. 'What did you expect me to do though, Thea? Just blank it from my mind? You can't hear something like that and not react.'

'I didn't expect you to ignore it, no, but I had hoped your reaction wouldn't be quite so predictable. I've done nothing wrong, Anna. And neither has my father; he had an alibi, remember.'

A tortured look crosses her face. 'Thea, it isn't that simple.' She vents a sigh of frustration. 'I know you've done nothing wrong, it's not that… it's just… Look, Rob is a curate… not the vicar, but just his assistant. The vicar has four parishes locally and someday, well, Rob hopes to have his own. Church-going is already on the decline and it's taken him a long while to build trust in the community. He—'

'Can't have that tarnished by anything "nasty"… not in his back yard… Yeah, I understand. I understand perfectly.' I start to move towards the hallway before my tears get the better of me.

'Thea, wait!' Anna takes a step towards me. 'For goodness' sake, I'm Rob's wife, the curate's wife, it's my duty to support him.'

'What, at any cost?'

She glares at me. 'Well, what do you expect me to do? What would you do if you were in my shoes?'

'What would you do if you were in mine?' I counter. 'Have a little self-respect, Anna. You are allowed to have an opinion of your own, you know.' I dash a hand across my cheek. 'I'll let myself out.'

I've almost reached the front door, aware that Anna has followed me, before I suddenly remember that there was something else I wanted to say.

'Do you know, Anna, I'm sorry. I'm sorry you feel the way you do. I'm sorry you feel the need to choose the lies you're being peddled over what's right, but I'd still like you to remember that my door is always open, should *you* need to talk any time.'

The tears are coursing down my face by the time I make it back to the sanctuary of my kitchen. I stand for a moment, staring out the window, looking at the garden where I played so happily as a child, before I break down into choking sobs. 'Oh, Mum… why didn't you tell me?'

CHAPTER SEVENTEEN

I don't know how long I stand there before I feel Drew's arms go around me. I hadn't even heard him come in, but suddenly he's there, the only thing that feels solid in my life right now. How on earth did we get here?

I don't mean to stiffen, it's an automatic response to the thought that has flashed through my head. But, before I can rectify it, Drew pulls away. I turn in his arms but the closeness has already gone and the gap between us increases.

'Drew… I—'

'My mistake,' he says coldly. But there are tears in his eyes too as he takes a step backward. 'I've got work to do,' he adds and, before I can stop him, he's turned on his heel, making for the studio.

I should go straight after him, but I don't. Because what would I even say? My body gave away what I was thinking, however subconsciously, and to deny it would only make things worse. Drew would see through it in a moment. But I don't want to stay here either, so close to where he is and yet so far. I feel trapped.

There's a band of pain tightening around my head that is growing worse with every passing minute and I know from experience that fresh air and some exercise to release the tension are the only things that will help. Except that I've been denied those too. There's no way I can leave the house; I've become a prisoner. And I should be working.

Indecision roots me to the spot until, unable to bear being inside my head for a minute longer, I creep upstairs to do the only thing that seems left to me: submit to the oblivion of sleep. If it will let me.

I'm halfway across the landing when I catch sight of Lauren's bed through her open door. Mr Blue, her bear, is propped against her pillow and it draws me towards it like a magnet. I'm suddenly desperate to be a child again, swamped by a wave of nostalgic longing, for what I don't know. Perhaps it's a yearning for a time when things seemed simple, the comfort of not having to make decisions, of being looked after and protected, but the force of the feeling brings renewed tears to my eyes. I crawl beneath the covers, pulling the bear down with me, and curl into a ball.

*

I feel the emptiness the moment I awake. A hollow that's no longer just inside of me but has leached out until it's spread throughout the house. It's silent and heavy, an oppressive stillness that weights the air. Something is missing and I know exactly what it is.

I walk through the rooms like a stranger, one by one, until I reach the kitchen with its sheet of white paper in the centre of the table, a note that confirms what I already know. Drew has gone.

A shockwave of panic pulses through me and I force myself to breathe, to read the note, and make sense of what is written there. There is a meeting. Drew will be back later, he doesn't know when. But he'll be back later... I read it again. He'll be back later... And the tears spring to my eyes. I cannot be without Drew. I don't know how.

But, for the moment, the house is empty, and I stand in the kitchen for several minutes before conscious thought returns. I rub at my face, at my sleep-drugged eyes, my skin, which feels like putty. My headache has gone, but in its place is a leaden feeling that makes even the simplest of decisions feel out of reach. My clothes are rumpled and my mouth parched. A crust of dried saliva feels rough on my chin.

The tap water is cold, but I drink it greedily, splashing it over my hands and face, the shock of it bringing me back to the present. It's nearly eleven o'clock. What on earth am I going to do now? The day feels like it contains an impossible amount of time to fill, but I have to do something. I drift through to the studio but, although I lift the cover on my sketchbook, the work feels alien, there is nothing to connect me with it. I sit on the stool and stare out into the garden.

All at once I cannot bear to be inside – in this house that once promised me the world but has now snatched it away from me. I push the doors open, flinging them back as far as they will go and breathing in the cool air. The grass is damp and my bare feet lay a trail through it as I walk, ignoring the path, heading for the table and chairs which sit under the trees to the rear. The church clock chimes the hour as I sink onto one of the chairs, hugging my arms against the stiff breeze.

The house and gardens lie in front of me. Beyond them the church, the lane which wends its way to Rose Cottage, the fields behind, the school, the shop, a crossroads with houses, farms on the outer reaches, and I feel utterly insignificant in the face of it all. The village which once felt like home, welcoming and enfolding, now seems otherworldly, a hostile prison whose secrets haunt me. My chin drops towards my chest and I close my eyes.

I've no idea how long I sit there before I become aware of someone calling my name. I drag myself back to the present, opening my eyes to a light that seems incredibly bright and jarring. So much so that I have to squint to make out the figure coming across the lawn towards me.

'Thea, whatever are you doing?'

The words take me instantly back to the past again and I sit up; it's what I always used to do.

'Mary…' I can't say any more.

She makes a clicking sound with her tongue. 'Heavens, aren't you cold?'

I stare at her. I am, I'm freezing.

'Sorry,' I say, getting to my feet. 'We should go inside, out of the wind.' I must look deranged, I think, suddenly shivering. And I'm ashamed that my old head teacher should find me looking like this. Sitting in the garden with no coat on, no shoes either. What must she think of me?

I apologise again. 'I wasn't feeling well.' It's a small lie, but I'm not myself, that much is true. 'I just needed to get some fresh air.'

We enter the studio and I close the doors firmly behind me. The room feels frigid, but Mary stops by my workbench and peers at the paper there.

'You're forging quite the career for yourself, aren't you?' she says. 'Justifiably so; I can see why your mother is so proud of you.'

'Is she?' The words are out of my mouth before I can stop them. I'm about to apologise again when I'm struck by the look on her face as she looks around her in wonder.

'This is new,' she says. 'Well, of course it is. Everything must be new… It's so long ago since I was here but… Oh, I always did love this house, so wonderful to be back.' She looks at the door which leads to the living room. 'May I?' she asks.

I nod, following her as she moves from one room to another, her face lighting up as memories come flooding back. We end up in the kitchen where she takes a seat at the table. I join her in a daze, I don't know what else to do.

She smiles at me. 'Your mother's kept me up to date with all your news, obviously, and so I know you have two little girls now as well.' Her fierce blue eyes twinkle back at me as she shakes her head in amusement. 'Goodness, to think that you and Drew used to sit outside my office, as punishment for talking too much in class. Quaking in your shoes, you were, but inseparable even then.

In fact, I often used to think that if one of you got into trouble, the other followed suit just to keep them company.' She smiles at me. 'And now look at you, all grown up.'

I fidget awkwardly, embarrassed by the way I must look. I'm hardly doing a very good impression of a competent adult.

'I don't see many stories from my time at the school as successful as yours, but you and Drew... There always was something special about you.'

I swallow, my throat constricting with emotion. What she says is true, and I can't bear the thought that it could ever be any different. But I still don't know why she's here. After our last meeting we'd made no definite promises to see one another and a trip down memory lane seems incongruous at best.

'Sorry, where are my manners,' I mutter. 'Would you like a cup of tea?' I look around the kitchen vaguely as if I haven't the first idea how to make one. 'I've been in bed,' I add, as if that explains things. 'In fact I haven't long been up...'

The blue eyes linger on mine for a moment. 'I should make you one,' she replies, pausing for a moment to continue in her scrutiny. 'Is everything all right, Thea?' But then she shakes her head. 'No, of course it isn't... how could it be?'

She sighs. 'It hasn't been easy, has it, moving back here? I can see why you wanted to, of course. And Drew too... Pevensey is such a wonderful house. It broke your parents' hearts when they had to leave and I'm not sure your mother ever really got over it. Never felt settled, she told me. But she certainly didn't think that you would ever move back here – that came as quite a shock, as I'm sure you can imagine. No doubt it was a decision you made with the best of intentions for your family but, unfortunately, as is the way of these things, it was only a matter of time before people made the connection between your family and what happened to Georgia. You weren't to know that of course, but sadly it was rather inevitable.'

'Yes, well perhaps I wouldn't have been in such a rush to come back here if I had known about Georgia…' I can feel my anger rising again but I force it back down. Mary has done nothing wrong. And of course she knows all about it. It's only me that doesn't.

She raises her eyebrows. 'You always think that too much water has flowed under the bridge, and that no one could possibly remember, but all it takes is one person and a whisper, and then what starts as a trickle turns into a flood. I had hoped this wouldn't be the case, but… Oh dear, I am sorry.'

My mouth drops open. 'I should have been told,' I reply, eyes blazing. 'But instead everyone seems to think that there wasn't a right time to tell me, or that it all happened so long ago people would have forgotten about it. None of that is any help to me now, is it? If I *had* known then I would never have come back here. Even Drew knew and yet… How long will it be before my own children hear the gossip-mongering and start asking questions? That's what I want to know.'

The steely gaze I remember so well is turned on me. 'Thea, what are you angry about? That information was kept from you, or that your dad was accused of something so awful in the first place? Because it sounds very much to me as if it's the former…'

I open my mouth to argue but a wave of shame washes over me and my eyes lower to the table.

'Hmm, I thought so.' She pushes her chair back from the table and levers herself up, breath sighing through her teeth as she does so. 'Don't ever get old, Thea, I don't recommend it. Now I shall make you some tea and we can talk some more. Sensibly.'

I would argue, but years of being told not to are hard to over-turn, and so I sit meekly, thoughts freewheeling around my head, while my old head teacher moves assuredly around my kitchen. My head is beginning to pound again.

A short while later a hand is placed gently on my shoulder and a mug set before me. The hand lingers a while, the touch warm, and oddly understanding.

'But you're not having anything,' I remark.

There's a quick smile. 'When you get to my age there is little else to do besides drinking endless cups of tea in between the small actions that punctuate daily life. Believe me, it's quite a relief to go without.' She retakes her seat. 'Now then, where were we?'

I wrap my hands around the mug. 'I think I was just being an obnoxious six-year-old again,' I reply.

'Perhaps... But then when we're faced with the depths we thought our lives would never sink to, it's surprising how tempting a good tantrum can be. Life *is* unfair at times. I don't think there's any doubt about that.' Mary watches me as I blow across the surface of my tea. 'But, as a friend rather than your old head teacher, I would like to ask you a question, Thea, and please think very carefully before you answer.'

I manage a small nod, wondering what on earth is coming next.

'I can see that you've been very upset and angered by this nasty business and I would imagine that, particularly given where we're currently sitting, it's caused you to question the life that you lived here as a child. Would I be right?' She doesn't wait for me to agree. 'So, I'm wondering whether you think your past is what's wrong here, or simply your knowledge of it?'

I close my eyes briefly, willing her question to make sense, but just when I think I grasp the point she's trying to make, it skitters away from me.

'I'll put it another way,' she says. 'Was Georgia Thomas molested when you were eleven?'

I stare at her. 'Well, we know she was.'

'And was your father, if not accused of that, then at least connected with it?'

I don't answer.

'And yet, before you moved back to Pevensey, you were not aware of either of those things. So did they happen or not?'

'Of course they did…' My brain is moving interminably slowly.

'So the only thing that has changed, the only thing making you so upset and angry, is the knowledge of a particular thing.'

And finally I understand the point she's making. 'But that's absurd.'

'No, Thea, it's not absurd. It's currently the difference between your life carrying on the way it has, happy and successful, with two beautiful daughters and a loving husband, or sliding into something you clearly wish you could run away from.'

My fingers are still curled around my mug which rests on the table and she wraps her own around mine.

'I can see this is difficult for you, but you mustn't blame your mother for not wanting your life to change. It's bad enough that hers had to. And as little as ten minutes ago you asked me when your own children were going to start asking questions, so you see you're no different after all. Your fears now are exactly the same as your mother's were all those years ago. She did everything she could to protect you, just like you would if it were your own children. More than that, she ensured that the memories you have of your father were never diminished. Your mother is one of the strongest women I know, Thea, and, if I'm not much mistaken, you're a chip off the old block. You'll get through this, I know you will.'

I look at Mary Williams, sitting in my kitchen, as she must have done countless times before. Her mind is still as sharp as it ever was and her friendship with my mum just as strong, despite their distance apart. Maybe I do need to see things from a different point of view. I've only ever looked at my relationship with my mum from one angle, but I can see now that I need to widen my perception to take account of all the sacrifices she must have made for me. The silent suffering that she endured for years just to protect me. It's a humbling thought. And what's true of my mum, I realise, is also true of Drew.

'Thank you,' I whisper, suddenly incredibly touched that this woman, who I haven't even thought of in years, should take the time to tell me these things. 'You must think me incredibly rude…'

But the smile I receive in reply is warm with compassion. 'Teaching is a hard profession, Thea, but one thing I learned from it is never to be judgemental. I've seen too many facets of too many lives to be shocked by how people react to the crises they face. We're all different, and often what you see on the outside is no real indicator of what's going on inside.'

'Is that a yes or a no?' I ask, a wry smile crossing my face for an instant.

'It simply means I understand,' comes the reply. 'And that in saying it perhaps you won't feel quite so alone.'

Mary's kindness touches something deep inside of me. 'Are you sure you wouldn't like something to drink?' I ask. 'It doesn't seem right for you to take the trouble to come and see me and not even have a cup of tea. I feel I should offer you something.'

She shakes her head. 'No, that's very kind, but there's really no need. There's no debt to repay and I should get going – I think you could use some time alone with your thoughts.' She gives my hand another squeeze. 'But if you do want to talk some more, you know you can come and visit, don't you?'

I nod.

'Good,' she replies firmly, a warm smile on her face. 'Because I shall be keeping an eye on you…'

CHAPTER EIGHTEEN

As soon as Mary has gone, I drain the last of my tea and carry my mug to the sink to wash. A thought came into my head as I was waving her goodbye and now I'm in a hurry to pursue it.

The boxes of photos are in one of the spare bedrooms, untouched, exactly where we left them when we moved. Some while before I'd bought a load of albums with the intention of sorting them all out, but I still haven't got around to it – teasing out the pictures we want to keep on hand from those we don't. All of them memories but, since Dad's death, some more precious than others. But that isn't really the point today. Now I just want to surround myself with them, to feel close to my dad again, to see if the photos look as they did when I was packing them up to move.

Just a few short weeks ago I had looked at these pictures of my childhood as a reminder of what I was about to return to. Now I'm looking to see if they were a lie. If they were staged snapshots of the life we were pretending to have rather than the one we did. I can't believe that my memories are false, but I have to face the fact that they could well be. Despite what Drew said, and despite everything I feel about my dad with every fibre of my body, I don't know for certain what his involvement was with Georgia. I have to consider the possibility, however slight, that he was not the man I thought he was.

The photos aren't in any particular order. I could be aged two in one picture, closely followed by a shot of me on my eighth birthday. But, in a way, that helps because I want to see if anything changed over the years. I spread them out on the floor around me, sorting them into loose piles.

It's odd, but I've never realised before how relatively few photos there are of my mum and, as I cast my eye over them now, I understand why. In so many of them she would have been the photographer instead of the subject.

I hate taking photos. I'm not that keen on being in them either but throughout our girls' early lives I've always had the feeling that I should have been taking more – to preserve those moments and give us, or them, something to look back on when we're older. But the trouble is that I've always preferred to be in the moment rather than the recorder of it. It doesn't seem right to be viewing the action from a distance. I want to be immersed in it, to feel it, and I wonder if my dad was the same. And if maybe my mum was too...

I pick one up, a Christmas gathering showing a blend of my family and Drew's, all of us wearing party hats and pulling crackers. I don't remember it particularly, but it's typical of so many others. My dad is leaning in towards me as if to share some joke or other and I can almost feel the warmth of his shoulder against mine. Another shows Drew, on the evening he broke his arm, grinning bravely as a nurse works a plaster cast around it. I didn't find out until the morning after it happened but I remember being furious with him for being so careless. In the next, it's years earlier, a day in summertime, and my dad is teaching me to ride my bike, one hand on the back of my saddle, the other on my shoulder. I'm in the lane outside, just about to go around the bend, and my mum must have stood in the gateway to the churchyard to take the shot. The view is side-on but you can still see my grin stretching from ear to ear.

I pick pictures up then put them down, looking for a sign of anything untoward. Are people frowning when they should be smiling? Does anyone look awkward or uncomfortable? But they don't, the photos are just as I remember them, relaxed snapshots of family life, easy and spontaneous. Nothing has changed. The relief is almost overwhelming and a swell of hope begins to build. Perhaps it's all still okay.

Time passes without my even noticing. I'm lost in my memories, set free from any constraints the day held over me, existing solely in a space where everything is as it should be. Images of my dad float and settle around me, comforting and peaceful, and my childhood returns to the happy place in my heart I always thought it occupied. I shift my legs out from under me, stretching away the stiffness and running my hands over the piles of photos that litter the floor. It's only lunchtime, and I have plenty of hours ahead of me to make a start on the task I'd originally planned. And now I want to take my time. I want the albums to be the best tribute they can be to my dad, and to my mum, who so diligently recorded all of this for me.

I start to gather the pictures together, to stack them into piles so that I can begin sorting. Drew's young face is grinning up at me from the top of the one nearest and I stop for a moment, laying a finger against his cheek. Even as a boy there was something golden about him, and I always knew that what we had was special. I remember my fear when I first saw his plaster cast, and learned that he had fallen out of a tree. How much worse his injuries could have been. A broken back, a cracked skull, things that would have changed his life and mine forever. The thought had terrified me even then.

I lay the picture back down again and pick up the next, trying to decide how I want to order the photos – by date, by subject… I know I won't get it exactly right, but I can almost certainly sort them into rough chronological order. I glance back down, noticing as I do so a detail I hadn't spotted before. There's a date stamp in the corner of the photo I'm holding and, now that I look, quite a few of the pictures have it. The discovery makes the decision easy and Drew's photo goes to the top of the pile as a marker for all those which will need to come before it or after. I peer closer, checking the date.

I must have got it wrong. One of those occasions when you get numbers muddled, back to front. Or the memory of it misfires. That's all it will be. But the hairs on the back of my neck are rising…

I sit, holding the photo in my hand, completely unable to move, growing hotter and hotter as the seconds tick by. I should check, put myself out of my misery, but the voice in my head is starting to cry.

I walk silently across the landing and into our bedroom where I take out my journal and open it. The newspaper article I took from Stacey is right where I left it, and I'd give anything at this moment to have thrown it away. I thought about it. My hands are shaking as I unfold it, the chant in my head becoming louder and louder. *Please be wrong, please be wrong, please be wrong…*

I check the date mentioned in the paper. The day on which Georgia Thomas was attacked. Tuesday 25th June 1996…

And then I look back at the photo, at Drew and the young nurse bandaging his arm, his mum by his side.

The dates are the same.

Which means that Drew and his parents were at the hospital the same evening that Georgia was walking home from Guides.

There's no way they would have been having my mum and dad round for supper.

They had lied.

And my dad had no alibi.

*

I have to wait another forty-seven minutes before Drew comes home. I hear the front door open from where I'm still sitting, sprawled on the floor of the spare bedroom. I retreated back here after my anger spent itself, after I had raged backwards and forwards across the landing, after I had kicked the bedroom door so violently it feels like I've broken my toe, and after my scream of rage had given way to near hysterical sobbing. Now I'm just numb.

There are photographs everywhere. No longer in tidy piles but, instead, scattered across every surface, under the bed, anywhere and everywhere they could travel when I'd hurled them. All but one, which I still hold in my hand.

I hear Drew's footsteps cross the hallway, keys jangling in his hand as he heads for the kitchen. There's a pause before I hear him again, re-entering the hall from the living room after completing a circuit through the studio. He checks that I'm not in the dining room, or the small sitting room, although why he thinks I would possibly be there is beyond me. He stops then and I can almost imagine him at the foot of the stairs, looking upward, anxiety playing across his face as he tries to decide whether he wants to come up to find me, and if he does what mood I'll be in. I could even still be in bed where he left me.

But he's going to find out soon enough as I scramble to my feet just as he steps onto the bottom tread. He's nearly halfway up by the time I make it to the top, standing on the precipice, swaying gently.

'Thea…?'

The confusion in his voice is tinged with something else, fear perhaps… Or can he feel the remnants of my anger vibrating in the air?

I can hear my voice, but it's as if it's coming from someone else's mouth. Or as if the words are in another language. But then I understand that there are no words at all, just a sound, the rise and fall of a keening cry that echoes around the hallway. It can't be me at all, instead some animal, wounded, but, as I turn my head towards the noise, I realise that it's my pain I can hear after all.

Drew is thundering up the remaining stairs, his feet heavy on the treads, but I don't want him near me. I back away along the landing, warding him off with my hands. He reaches me and I can see the exact moment when he understands the significance of the snapshot I'm holding in my hand. It's as if time has slowed into a series of photographic stills, each recording a minute detail of his expression as it changes to show his compassion, his anxiety, his alarm – and then the sure and certain knowledge of what's coming next.

'Thea, I'm so sorry, so sorry,' he murmurs, trying to pull me closer as I fight to push him away. I can't think with him so near. He doesn't want to look at me but I have to know I'm right.

'Thea, don't do this,' he warns, eyes wide, but it's too late. His response gives me all the confirmation I need.

I am free of him, my eyes burning into his, frightened and beseeching.

'You bastard!' My slap glances off the taut muscles of his arms, and the feebleness of my action enrages me even more. I shove Drew away from me, scrabbling at his arms. 'You lied to me,' I yell. 'There's no way your parents could have given Dad an alibi when they were at the hospital with you, and you knew that, didn't you? Why did you even bother to tell me they had in the first place, you've just made everything so much worse!'

'Worse?' he shouts. 'How could it be worse? You asked me if your dad was guilty, Thea, what was I supposed to say? Probably not, but don't tell anyone, only my parents gave him a false alibi. I was only trying to make you feel better.'

'Yeah, and how do I feel now, Drew?' I reply, eyes blazing. 'Haven't I been lied to enough already? Something else you were hoping I would never discover. It was bad enough finding out that you knew what happened with Georgia and you could have just left it there. In fact, you should have. But no, you had to go and volunteer information that you knew was a lie. Don't you see how much worse that makes it? You gave me hope... actually you gave me a certainty that Dad wasn't guilty, and now you've snatched that away from me again. Well, you've really excelled yourself, Drew. Congratulations, you've made him seem guiltier than ever.'

My hand flies to my mouth. 'Oh God, this is serious… it's criminal… Your mum and dad, they…'

Drew grabs my arm. 'No, Thea, they didn't. Your dad wasn't guilty of anything. He was at home with you and your mum all evening on the night that Georgia was attacked, but when the police were looking to make an arrest, to put away someone guilty of something so dreadful, what kind of alibi would that have been? None at all. All my parents did was make sure that there was no question of his innocence.' He looks down at the photo I'm still holding. 'Christ, I'd forgotten we even had that.'

I tear it into tiny pieces, hurling them at him in frustration. 'Well, it's a bloody good job no one ever found it, isn't it? Because if they had my dad would almost certainly have been convicted of abusing Georgia. A false alibi is bloody serious, Drew. And not only would it have incriminated my dad, but your parents would have been implicated too. Can you imagine what our lives would have been like?' I break off as my throat closes at the sickening thought of what might have been.

Drew's face contorts with sorrow. 'Thea, your dad's dead…'

'Exactly! So he isn't even here to defend himself. If anyone ever finds out that your mum and dad lied, it will be an open-and-shut case. Dad will be found guilty because that's the obvious solution, and now no one can prove otherwise.'

'For goodness' sake, that would never stand up in court.'

'It doesn't need to,' I scream at him. 'It's what people will think!' A sob catches in my throat at the thought.

Drew takes a step towards me. 'Thea, you're still talking as if you think your dad was guilty. And he wasn't! Nothing's changed, Thea, nothing at all.'

I thrust a finger into his chest. 'Well, you'd like that, wouldn't you? How convenient for you if it would all just stay the same. Well that's where you're wrong, Drew, because everything has changed. I trusted you. And you lied to me. Keeping information from me I could just about accept, but not this. I'd nearly got my head around the idea that any of this even happened at all, that a massive chunk of my childhood teetered precariously on a secret kept from me my whole life. I'd even pretty much accepted that there may have been valid reasons for keeping the information from me, and I'd convinced myself that I knew the truth, that my dad could never be guilty. But now? Now, I don't know what to think...'

'Yeah, and whose fault is that, Thea? You brought us here!'

'You could have stopped us!'

We glare at one another across a hostile space that neither of us is going to breach.

'I thought I knew everything there was to know about you,' I add. 'That if there was one person I could trust in my life, it was you. That you would never, ever, do anything to hurt me. How could you, when neither of us know where I finish and you begin? It would be like hurting yourself.'

I shake my head, bitter tears sliding down my cheeks. 'But now I can't believe how wrong I was. You deliberately misled me. Misled me and betrayed my trust, and I promise you it's the last time you'll ever do it.'

Drew's eyes widen, fear peering out at me. 'What are you saying?' he asks, his whole body going limp.

I could blow us apart.

I could detonate a grenade in the centre of our marriage. An explosion so large it would leave only splinters, or dust. I could do it right now...

Instead I walk away.

CHAPTER NINETEEN

I leave the next morning, as soon as the girls are safely at school. I make Drew take them; I've no desire to see anyone. Besides, I want him out of the house while I pack.

'Thea, this is crazy, listen to me.'

'Why is it, Drew? From where I'm standing it's not crazy at all. I want some answers and I'm clearly not going to get them from you.'

We're standing in the hallway and he's not exactly blocking the front door, but close enough.

'But what about Chloe and Lauren? What am I going to say to them?'

'I'm sure you'll think of something.'

He goes to answer but then closes his mouth, his eyes fearful.

'What? Scared I won't come back?'

Drew doesn't answer and I can't say I blame him. I'm angry and I'm upset, but I'm not vindictive. Not yet anyway, but I can feel the potential for it just waiting for me to give it the green light. 'I'll be back tonight, okay?'

'Yet you're taking a bag...'

'I'll be back, Drew,' I repeat. 'Just tell the girls that Grandma is a bit poorly or something and I've had to go and see her.'

He hesitates and then nods slightly. 'Does she even know you're coming?'

I pick up my bag. 'I'll call on the way. Three hours is far too much notice to give of my arrival. I don't want to hear a whole heap of excuses, I want to hear the truth.'

'Thea, please… don't go like this. I understand you wanting to see your mum, I actually think it's something you should do. But don't go when you're angry and upset, when we're… Look, if you wait a couple of days, maybe we can get something sorted out and I could come with you.'

'And at what point am I going to stop being angry and upset, Drew? Answer me that. Two days isn't going to make any difference to how I feel. I've had this kept from me almost my entire life and I'm not prepared to wait any longer. It's bad enough being lied to, but what's worse is that the one person in all of this I want to talk to isn't here any more. So, I'm going by myself, Drew. I want to make up my own mind about things. I need to know… And the truth is just something I'll have to deal with.'

He doesn't answer but takes the bag from my hand and carries it outside to the car. 'Please make sure you drive carefully, Thea, and ring me when you get there.' He breaks off, clearing his throat. 'I need to know you're okay… And I'll be here when you get back, we can talk then, and I…' He stops, swallowing.

I look up at him, at the face I know so well. But I can't think about us now.

'I love you,' he finishes, close to tears, and I blink hard, trying not to remember the aching empty space in the bed last night. The dip of my waist without the familiar weight of his arm, my knees nestling into the crook of his as I turn over. The way our fingers would link automatically. All of it missing. Apart from when the girls were born it's the only time we've ever slept apart. And I missed him more than I thought possible.

'I'll ring you,' I say, keeping my eyes on the car. If I look at him I'll never be able to do this. I stare at the road ahead as I pull out of the drive. I know he's standing there, watching me leave long after the car is out of sight. But my heart is already breaking, I don't need to see the expression on his face to know that his is too.

In the end I don't even let Mum know I'm on my way. I can't, it's all I can do to keep driving. If I stop then thoughts will sneak around the barriers I've put up and I can't have them do that, not yet anyway. Not until I'm ready.

The traffic is light and I make good time, turning into the end of her road a little before noon. I'm busting for a wee and gagging for a drink, and I realise now how stupid it was not to tell her I was coming. I could have a very long wait ahead of me if she isn't home. But seconds later, I spot her bright-red Mini and I pull onto the drive behind it.

I reach down to collect my handbag from the passenger footwell before climbing from the car. My overnight bag is still on the back seat and my hand rests on the door handle for a moment, undecided. I have no idea yet whether I'm going home tonight.

A seagull cries overhead as a gust of wind carries the salty tang of the sea towards me. The scent reminds me how ridiculous this situation is. My mother lives in a beautiful part of the country. She's moments from the sea itself, a pretty harbour on one side and a sweeping bay on the other… Chloe and Lauren would absolutely love to come and stay here and yet, in the years since my dad died, I think we've been here twice, that's all. It seems obvious now why not and I realise that the repercussions of our sordid family secret have extended far beyond just me.

Of all the emotions which cross my mother's face, I think relief is the one that stays there the longest. I wonder how often she's thought of this moment, finding me on her doorstep.

'Darling,' she says, holding out her arms, but then she checks herself. 'Oh, are you on your own?' There are multiple scenarios crossing her mind, but only one which makes any real sense. 'Is everything all right…? You and Drew, you're not…?'

It's the easiest conclusion to jump to, but I don't have any answer for that particular question. 'I'm not here because of Drew, Mum,' I say.

'No,' she says. 'But I'm glad you are here.' She draws me in and I'm surprised by the strength of her hug.

Her hair is much longer than when I last saw her, but it suits her. Still a burnished chestnut, not as dark as mine, but with it just tipping onto her shoulders, she looks... rather incongruously, relaxed. And I remind myself to breathe.

'I made a cake this morning,' she adds, as I follow her into the kitchen. 'I must have known you were coming. Either that or it's my turn to do refreshments at the bowling club. But no mind, I can make another. It's not until tomorrow.'

'I know, I'm sorry. I should have rung really, it's just that—'

'If you'd stopped to think about it you would never have come.'

'Something like that,' I admit. I watch her as she takes the kettle to the sink to fill it with water. 'You don't seem very surprised,' I say.

Her hand freezes for a second and then she continues with her task, still facing away from me. 'Thea, you moved back to Pevensey. It was only a matter of time.'

Not a criticism as such, more resignation.

'Were you ever going to tell me?' I ask.

'No.' Her reply is immediate. And definite.

She places the kettle back on its stand to boil. 'And if you want to know why, it's because I took very great care to ensure that you never knew. And having made that decision once, I intended to stand by it. There was no need for you to know, what difference does it make?'

'How can you say that? It makes a hell of a difference!'

'To what exactly?' She holds my gaze. 'What benefit has it brought you?'

I open my mouth but close it when I realise that I have no answer for her.

'Thea... I hope it will come as no surprise to you to learn that this is something which has occupied a great deal of my thoughts over the years. And I don't intend to "chat" about this in the kitchen, it's rather too important for that. Besides which, you've driven a long way, and no doubt need a wee and something to eat and drink. Once we've addressed those things, I think we should take a walk and I will tell you everything you want to know. But not before.'

I nod, chastened. 'I'm sorry,' I say. 'You're right. And thank you, I'd like that.'

Mum smiles and I suddenly feel time slip away from me. Despite my age and my own motherhood, I'm still her child.

'I hope that the manner in which you found out was at least... kind?' she says. 'That perhaps Drew was able to pick a good time, and break the news gently...'

'Hardly...' I heave a sigh. 'I found an article about Georgia that someone had hidden in the house, and Drew said nothing... I thought it might have had something to do with the previous owners of Pevensey so I started asking questions, and still Drew said nothing. The whole village has been talking about us, Mum. I practically got thrown out of a shop by someone who I now realise must have been Georgia's mum, and the whole time Drew still said nothing. It wasn't until I'd had the truth of it all actually shoved in my face that he finally admitted he knew about it. So no, it wasn't kind, or gentle, and I don't think I'm ever going to be able to forgive him for that.'

'Harsh words, Thea. I hope you don't mean them.'

I stare at her back as she turns to take down a couple of mugs from a cupboard. 'Well, how do you think I feel? When my own husband keeps secrets from me. He should have told me right at the beginning when he had the chance. But no, he let it get so much worse. He didn't even tell me about the ridiculous farce of an alibi straight away. But instead, he let me find out about it in the worst possible way. I'm furious with him, Mum. Angry. Upset. But most of all I feel betrayed. He's taken any trust I had and smashed it to smithereens.'

She is silent for a moment, digesting my words. And I know that these are conversations she must have had with herself over so many years. Her reply is dispassionate.

'Yes, I feared as much. Unfortunate, but not a surprise. If you want my opinion, Drew should never have been informed either.' She frowns. 'Had I known that his parents were going to tell him I would have argued strenuously against it. But people always feel that they should do something when they hold information like this. As if it's the proverbial hot potato that will burn a hole in their pocket unless they pass it on. But of course the option always remains to do nothing. To merely set it down and let it cool. It's a pity more people don't use it.' She searches my face for a moment. 'And I can see how it's made things difficult between you and Drew.'

My silence is all the confirmation she needs.

She sighs. 'He'll be hurting too, Thea. It wasn't fair to tell him, it's a burden he should never have had to carry.' She shakes her head. 'But I cannot change that either, more's the pity.'

She waters the teabags and her face rearranges itself into a bright expression. 'Now, while we have our tea, tell me what else has been happening. How are the girls?'

We spend the next half hour talking about the trivia of our lives. How Chloe and Lauren are liking their new school, how my work is coming along, how Mum is enjoying the new life she has carved out for herself. But it's necessary. It gives us time to adjust to being with one another, space to settle our nerves.

'Did you bring a coat with you?' Mum asks as I finish my drink. 'It's a bit blowy out there today.'

'No, I didn't think to, I…'

'You can borrow one of mine.' She raises her eyebrows. 'That's if you can bear to be seen in one of my old lady coats.'

I smile. There's nothing old lady about my mum.

She fetches two jackets from the cupboard under the stairs and I slip on the bright floral raincoat, quite similar to the one I have at home. She changes her shoes and there's a moment when we stand, face to face, contemplating each other in the hallway. Her hand reaches out to tuck my hair behind my ears and she leaves it there for a second, her thumb resting on my cheek.

'Come on,' she says brightly, and I trail after her, my eyes unexpectedly filled with tears. 'We'll head down to the harbour, I think. I find the coming and going of everyone's lives there most conducive to thinking about one's own.'

We walk in silence for most of the way. It's turned into a beautiful day here – the cloud lifted just as I arrived and now the fresh wind has chased away the last remnants of it. I'm happy to simply drink in the views, so different from those at home, and the peace, but I also have no idea how to start the conversation we need to have. The progress of my visit is already straying far from how I imagined it would be.

As we turn into the harbour itself, Mum heads straight for a bench, where she sits, not looking at me, but straight out past the sea wall to open water. I take a seat beside her.

'I'm not sure how you wanted me to be, Thea,' she begins. 'But I always knew that I was such a huge disappointment to you while you were growing up.' She turns to me, her gaze frank and oddly accepting.

I swallow, a deep shame beginning to stir.

'But I fear I was as much to blame for causing that as you were in thinking it. So perhaps I should explain and maybe now you might see why I behaved the way I did. You see, if I have any regrets at all, it's that, as you grew older, you and I never quite managed the relationship I wanted us to have. It's something which has brought me its fair share of heartache over the years, but when the thing with your father happened, I took a decision, and I've stuck by that for all these years.' She smiles wistfully. 'But perhaps, if there's any good to come of all of this, it's that maybe the time has come for things to change. I hope so.' She slides her hand across the bench, laying her fingers over my own. They're freezing.

'I really don't remember much about the night that Georgia was attacked. In that it was a perfectly ordinary evening, but the next day was the single worst day I have ever lived through, with the exception of the day your father died. My entire life, everything I believed in and valued, was thrown up in the air and then came crashing down around me. And at first I refused to believe it, that it was even happening at all; it all seemed so ridiculous. But then I realised that it wasn't going to go away and that my life had been irrevocably changed. And I had to decide how I was going to live with that.'

Her voice is steady, but her face betrays the deep sadness she still feels. I nod, curling my fingers around hers.

'It was one of the bleakest times of my life and it would have been so easy to have slobbed about in bed all day, to let my hair grow lank and greasy, to wear clothes I hadn't changed in days. I would have welcomed it, would have loved to wallow in my self-pity. I almost felt as if I deserved it. But then, there you were, and you were too important to let down. I didn't want you to have those sorts of memories, or be the kind of mother who seemingly didn't care when, in fact, the very opposite was true. And so I put aside my feelings, forbade myself to cry when you were around, tidied my hair and put on my make-up and, one by one, I got through the days, although the pretence took every ounce of my strength. In fact, I almost didn't make it... and had it not been for one single fact I don't think I would have.'

I tip my head at her. 'And what was that?'

'Your dad,' she said simply. 'Because I truly loved him. And one day I realised that the only way I would get through any of it was to decide what I felt, for good or bad, and act accordingly. And so I sat, one day when you were at school, and I thought about your dad. About all the things he'd ever said and done, our life together, and I examined it all. And when I'd done that I realised I couldn't conceive of your father being guilty of what he'd been suspected of. Your dad had said he was innocent and I had to make up my own mind whether I believed him or not, to listen to my own judgement and no one else's. After that it became easier and I was able to dismiss the doubts I had, and the fears.'

I think about her words for a moment, but there's something I still don't understand.

'But why was that ever in question?' I ask. 'I know that Drew's parents gave Dad a false alibi because they were at the hospital, but if Dad was at home with you that night, what was there to even consider?'

As soon as I say it I realise there can be only one response. I don't think I can bear any more.

'Oh, Thea... I thought you knew...' Her eyes fill with tears. She seems to struggle to marshal her thoughts before taking a deep breath. 'You'd gone for a sleepover at Millie's house the night Drew broke his arm, do you remember? And so I don't think you ever really heard the story of what had happened – not surprising under the circumstances. Your dad had seen Drew climbing the tree just as he turned into the driveway as he came home from work. That big horse chestnut just inside the gate to the churchyard.'

'It's still there,' I remark.

'Well, of course, what he should have done was warn Drew that it probably wasn't a good idea to climb it, whereas in fact what he did was just wave at him, grinning. An easy thing to do when he was tired from work, and simply looking forward to his dinner and a Friday night at home. Of course when Sarah came running round later to tell us that Drew had fallen from the tree, your dad was distraught, saying it was his fault, that he could have prevented it. You can imagine how he felt. And so Alex and Sarah carted Drew off to the hospital and, a bit later on, not being able to settle, we popped round to theirs to let their dog out for a wee and then your dad went off to get a bit of fresh air...'

I can see where this is leading now.

'And so you see, he *was* out for a little while, only half an hour or so but...'

'Long enough to sow seeds of doubt,' I reply.

'Yes,' says Mum quietly.

'And so you don't actually know if Dad was innocent.'

'Thea, in the absence of any absolute proof, how can anything be certain when it's one person's word against another? But in here...' She taps her chest. 'In here, in the only place it matters, I know. Your father said he was innocent, and I believed him.'

'So why was it necessary for Alex and Sarah to give him an alibi? That just makes it worse, surely?'

She pauses, her memories reminding her of what she'd been through, the struggles against things beyond her control.

'It wasn't something we planned,' she replies. 'So please don't think that. I can see how this makes it sound sinister, but it really was quite innocent. I think what happened simply was that Alex panicked. When the police asked him about your dad he told them that we'd had dinner with them the previous evening. You have to understand, Thea, that when things like this happen, things with... children, that people don't think straight. From that moment it became something we had to go along with. Otherwise we'd have been in really deep water.'

I raise my eyebrows. 'Oh, and that didn't sound suspicious? Christ, it's a wonder they didn't lock up Dad straight away and throw away the key.' But I can see how it happened. People aren't thinking straight today, let alone twenty-odd years ago.

'There was talk at the time of a man who had been seen a few times driving very slowly through the village. No one recognised the car, or knew who he was, and I think he became the focus of the police enquiries, but of course we never heard what happened.'

I nod, staring across at a small fishing boat that has just entered the harbour. I watch it make its way to the quayside, safe now, homeward bound.

'But no one knows about Drew's broken arm? Or rather the timing of it?'

She shakes her head. 'We just told everyone it had happened a day later, on the Saturday.'

I think of the photograph I ripped to shreds and threw at Drew. How could our parents have all been so stupid? The outcome could have been very different indeed if it had come to light. I'm still holding my mum's hand and I move a little closer.

'I'm so sorry,' I say. 'I have no idea how you coped with all of that, any of it actually. To even contemplate that Dad could be involved in something like that is bad enough, but to have everyone talking about you as well.'

She smiled sadly. 'In many ways it was the worst thing. We'd lived in the village for years and yet people who I thought were my friends crossed the street rather than talk to me. But I couldn't be responsible for what everyone else thought, Thea, only myself. And as long as I was able to stay true to what I believed in then nothing else mattered.'

'But we still moved away...'

'Yes... In my naivety I thought things would get better after a while, but they didn't, and so we chose to move away. Not because I was scared of people, or ashamed – I would have fought them all day long to protect your father's good name – but because when they could see that I didn't care what they said, they decided that you were a much easier target. And you weren't capable of standing up for yourself, or arguing back, and I couldn't bear to have your childhood ruined. So I did what every parent should do and I protected you.'

My tears are flowing freely now. I'd had no idea that my mum had done this for me and I'm forced to examine my own feelings. Have I gone through my whole life blaming Mum for taking us away from Pevensey? Is that why we've never quite had the relationship we both wanted, or even why I'd been so adamant to return back there, to the house I'd always felt torn from?

'Oh, sweetheart...' She loosens her fingers to turn and take me in her arms. 'I'm sorry too.' Her lips rest against my head. 'I can see now that trying to keep all this from you was stupid but, at the time, I truly thought it was for the best.'

My speech is fragmented. 'You did everything you could have for me... and I never even knew... That's what hurts, that I blamed you when I shouldn't have.'

She strokes my hair, pulling back slightly to look at me. 'And I should have told you when you were older, when you could have understood, but your father begged me not to. It was the only thing we disagreed on in the end. He couldn't bear the risk of you not believing him. And, as daughters often gravitate towards their fathers, I took a step back, when I could, so that your relationship with him became even deeper. Showing him how much I believed in him was the only way to heal the tear that doubt had ripped in the fabric of our family.'

'You must miss him so much.'

'Oh yes,' she says, 'every minute of every day.' Her voice is warmed by her love. 'But I get by,' she adds. 'I do things. I talk to people, I go out, pretend I'm having fun, and it helps. Sometimes I even fool myself.' Her smile is sad. 'Your father was the most remarkable man I ever met, Thea. Being without him is completely unacceptable.'

There's nothing I can add to that except to pull her close once more. There's a painful nuance to my grief now, weighted with the understanding of Mum's devotion, not just to my dad, but to me as well. I never once gave her credit for the sacrifices she made for us. Sacrifices she made over and over and which I never noticed, seeing instead only what I wanted to and not the truth. It feels as if a lifetime passes in the next few minutes as the images and memories of my childhood shift and readjust.

'So now you also have a decision to make,' she says eventually. She smooths my hair, tucking it back behind my ears before her thumbs gently wipe away the tears from my eyes. 'You have to decide what you believe, Thea. You, and no one else. And once you have decided then you hold that belief close to you and you don't let anyone change your mind. Not ever.'

'I'm so sorry, Mum,' I reply, looking up at her through my lashes. 'I've behaved appallingly. At a time when you really needed my help. And not much better now… I've been an awful daughter to you.'

But she shakes her head and rises from the bench, holding out her hand. 'Don't be silly,' she says. 'How could I love you so much if you were?'

CHAPTER TWENTY

Lauren's hand is cool against my forehead. 'Are you still feeling poorly, Mummy?'

I can hardly lift my head from the pillow, and the look of gentle concern in her eyes sends another wave of guilt sliding over me.

'Do you know, I think I feel a bit better now,' I reply. 'It must be seeing you. Have you got everything ready for school?'

She nods, an uncertain smile on her face.

'Well, you have a lovely day, and I'll see you later, sweetheart. In fact, I'll probably be up and about by then.'

'Will you?' Her eyes light up.

I don't want to lie, but she doesn't deserve this. 'Blow me a kiss because that will definitely make me feel better.'

I smile as she reaches the doorway, giving a little wave before she puts her hand to her lips in reply.

'Bye darling.'

I lay my head back on the pillow and close my eyes.

Nearly a week has passed since Drew and I argued. After I returned from Mum's my mood morphed into a melancholia that left me listless and de-energised. The slight croakiness in my throat intensified into raw agony, accompanied by a high fever, and it's left me wiped out. Allowing grief to hit me like a wall. It's as if I've lost my father all over again – the all-pervading pain that I will never be able to talk to him again is the very worst thing. Would he have thought about all of this in the last few hours before he died? Would he have wanted to tell me? To reassure me that, even though he would no longer be with me, I could remember him always the way he was. Because, despite what Mum said, even though I know her words make sense, there is the knowledge that no one has ever been caught for the crimes committed against Georgia. And that means there is still doubt.

I must have drifted back off to sleep again after Lauren left but I'm suddenly awake as the creak of a floorboard cuts into my consciousness.

Drew is carrying a cup of tea and a plate of toast which he slides onto the bedside table. He's about to perch on the edge of the bed before he changes his mind and straightens again. 'You should try to eat that,' he says, walking towards the door. 'You've hardly had anything the last few days.'

I can't bear the stilted conversation between us. We move around each other with polite detachment, like two wounded animals wary of further hurt. At times, when the girls are around, we're almost animated as we slip back into the easy practicalities of parenthood and, for a little while, it feels like we've forgotten what happened. But it doesn't last long. And, each time we withdraw, the shores on which we stand seem even further apart than before.

I struggle upright, clearing my throat which still feels thick. 'No, that's okay… I need to get up.' He's almost at the door when I call him back. 'Drew?'

He turns.

'Have Lauren and Chloe been all right?' I ask.

There's a slight softening of his face as he nods. 'They're okay, Thea. A little confused I think. Chloe especially, but this friend of hers… Beth… seems very sensible. I'm not aware that they've heard anything they shouldn't…'

That wasn't really what I meant.

'And Lauren?'

'Quiet…'

It's her I've been worried about the most, particularly as Anna and I parted on such bad terms. 'But Tilly…?'

Drew holds my look. 'Anna knows how well Tilly and Lauren get on and I don't think she's going to let anything get in the way of that. What would be the point?' He hovers by the doorway a moment longer. 'Anyway…'

I nod. 'Yes, sorry. You must have things to do…'

And just like that he's gone from the room, the echo of our conversation hanging like stale air.

My hair feels rank, my body both stiff and jelly-like at the same time, but I have to get up and out of this bed. If I don't do it today, I fear it may never happen. I lift my mug from the bedside table with a shaking hand and drink my tea. Then I swallow every mouthful of toast as if it's medicine I can't live without and, taking in a deep breath, swing my legs over the side of the bed.

The shower has always been a favourite place to think. And today, I need it more than ever. Because it isn't enough to start simply behaving like a wife and mother again. I need to think like one. I have moved my family to Pevensey and, if we're going to stay, then I need to change the way I've been feeling – about Drew, my dad, everything that makes our life here worthwhile.

It takes an age to get dressed, to clean my teeth and dry my hair. My fingers tremble as I put on my mascara and I almost give up on the whole thing and sink back onto the bed again. But I have to be better than this. By the time I'm done I think I vaguely resemble my former self. I pick up my mug and plate and prepare to go downstairs. There are some things I need to say.

I start to rehearse them in my head as I walk across the landing, but a glance in through the open doorway of the spare bedroom sends my head reeling and tears springing to my eyes. Sometimes it's the smallest things that crack your heart wide open.

Leaving my plate beside the sink, I begin to make a pot of coffee. I'm desperately thirsty, but I'm also stalling for time before I go through into the studio to speak to Drew. I know he's in there; I can feel his sadness even if I can't see him. I carry the coffee through when I'm done, my caffeine-laden peace offering.

'You've tidied up all the photos,' I say. 'Thank you… I…' But I can't finish the sentence.

Drew is sitting at his computer but his fingers are unmoving on his keyboard, the mouse beside it untouched. He's staring out of the window. It seems an age before he turns away from it.

'I couldn't bear to see them like that,' he says. 'Like they were unloved.' He swallows. 'And whatever else they are, they're our memories, Thea. I thought they deserved better.'

I nod, and a tear spills down my cheek.

'They do… I was angry,' I add, lip trembling.

'And what are you now, Thea?' he asks, his eyes holding mine.

I think for a moment, trying to find the right word. 'Sorrow,' I say eventually. 'I am sorrow.'

His lips part slightly. 'Me too,' he replies.

I so desperately want him to get up from his desk, to cross the room and hold me, but he doesn't and he isn't going to however much I want it. The distance between us is still too great.

'I made some coffee,' I say, placing down the pot. 'I thought you could probably do with another… How are things going?'

The day that Drew got his first order was only just over a week ago but it feels as if several months have passed.

'Okay,' he replies, glancing at the coffee. There's an empty mug beside him on the desk. 'Thanks,' he adds. 'I don't remember even drinking the last one.' He hits a key on his laptop, awakening the screen. 'Actually, Thea, I… No, it's okay, it doesn't matter…'

'No, what is it?' I ask. 'Come on, tell me.'

Drew is being very careful but I still hear the slight sigh of frustration. I wait a few more seconds but his gaze remains on the screen and I know he isn't going to tell me. He can be as stubborn as I am at times.

My desk is exactly as I left it and I'd like to sit down and try to remember how to draw. But I feel self-conscious, as if I'll be in the way. I did the odd little bit before I got ill, but it was as if someone else was holding the brushes and I long to feel the deep connection I have to everything when I'm working well. Colours seem brighter, sounds richer, and the earth reveals itself in so much glory some days the poignancy almost hurts. More than anything it makes me feel alive and is where my energy comes from. I could certainly use some right now. I trace a finger along the edge of the desk but I don't think I can do this today, there are other things to attend to first.

'Anyway…' I say, moving towards the door. 'I'll leave you to get on, but don't worry about picking the girls up from school today, I'll do it. I'm sure you'll appreciate not having to stop what you're doing.'

Drew's hand stills on his keyboard. He wants to say something but he doesn't know how.

'What is it?' I ask again.

He hesitates a fraction. 'No, don't worry, I can sort it. I really don't think you're well enough yet.'

'Drew, I have to go sometime… and the longer I leave it, the harder it's going to be.'

He picks up the pot of coffee and pours some into his mug. 'Aren't you having one?' he asks.

'No, I'll get one… in the kitchen, in a minute, I'll just have an instant…'

His look softens slightly. 'Sit down,' he says. 'I'll get you a mug.' He returns moments later.

'Here,' he says, pouring me a drink. 'It shouldn't be too hot now.'

I sip it gratefully. 'What is it you need to sort?'

His response is guarded. 'Just the offer of a meeting, but it's okay, I can go another time, when you're feeling better. It's really short notice and besides, I had thought when you were feeling up to fetching the girls again that I really should come with you but...'

His eyes dip away and I suddenly realise what he's getting at. It isn't the meeting that's the problem, it's the picking up the girls from school. Fear takes hold before I can even think about it and the hand that's holding my mug shakes a little. Automatically, Drew reaches out to steady it and, in that second, I see what I've become: not a wife, an equal partner, Drew's cheerleader, his best friend and soulmate, but instead a burden. And Drew doesn't deserve to be my carer.

'Has it been awful?' I ask, eyes wide.

He surveys me for a moment before nodding gently. 'Not all the time,' he replies. But I know the score.

'What time's your meeting?' I ask.

He pulls a face. 'If I'm going to make it I'll have to leave in an hour or so and I need to put the finishing touches on my presentation.' He checks his watch. 'I probably ought to go and get ready... But you still look very peaky, Thea, you really don't need to do this.'

Except we both know that I do.

'I'll manage,' I reply, trying a wan smile. 'So go on, go and get yourself sorted.'

I put down my mug and edge my fingers towards his, willing him to take them. But my invitation is ignored and instead Drew rises from his desk. His eyes linger on mine for just a moment before he leaves the room and the heavy silence left behind wraps itself around me like a cloak. I take a sip of my coffee to hide my emotion and try to pretend that I'm okay.

He leaves an hour later and I wait until he's gone before returning to the studio and sinking onto my stool. Somewhere in this room is my muse and, apart from anything else, I damn well need to find it. My head is beginning to pound again and I force my shoulders down, trying to recall the lightness that flows through me when I draw. I pick up a pencil and begin to doodle, quickly sketching what I can see through the window. It might be the only thing I manage today, but it's a start.

It's only when a bird flies close to the window, startling me, that I realise I've been talking to my dad for at least ten minutes. It started off as a conversation in my head but now I'm speaking aloud, waiting for him to answer a question. One that I'm sure he answered for my mum over and over again. What was he doing on the night that Georgia Thomas was dragged into the bushes? He replies, pretty much straight away, giving me his full attention just like he always did, *just walking, Thea, just walking*. And I wonder how long it will be until I stop feeling the need to ask him this question.

I stare out into the garden, thoughts swirling around my head, because it's just like my mum said. It almost doesn't matter what I think, whether I've made up my mind what I believe or not. After all, that wasn't what drove my family from the village. It was what other people thought…

My head still feels as if it's full of thick fog, but there's a thought in there somewhere, trying to materialise through the mist. I sit a little straighter, willing it to attain solid form, a ghostly apparition made corporeal. And then I see it.

I don't just have to change the way I've been thinking, but folk in the village too. I'm under no illusion that it will be easy but I have to challenge Stacey's behaviour. I know I can't change the past, but I can try to ensure we have a future. Despite everything that's happened, this is still the perfect place for us, and our children. I want them to have just the same loving and carefree childhood as I had.

My mum and dad did all they could to ensure mine and if I don't stand up to Stacey and her lies now it will have all been for nothing. My own family will have to go through everything they fought so hard to protect me from, and the events of the past will perpetuate themselves long into the future.

CHAPTER TWENTY-ONE

At least it's not raining, but I'm glad of my jacket as I walk up the road to school. It gives me somewhere to put my hands, which are thrust deep into the pockets. My shoulders are tensed, lifted up somewhere around my ears, but it helps to make me feel slightly more in control, the shaking slightly less obvious. It's far easier to feel like someone who can change the world in the privacy of your own home.

I've deliberately timed my arrival so that I'm not one of the first on the playground. In fact, I'm later than most and there is already a gaggle of mums inside and outside the gates. No one notices me at first but I'm not daft enough to think that I'll get away with this scot-free. Sure enough, a conversation stalls as I stand just inside the gate. It's irritating but not my primary concern right now, because I've just spotted what is over by the far wall of the playground.

Stacey's standing with Jackie and another two mums, and I wonder how long it will take them to see me as I walk across the yard to stand next to them. Not among them, not looking at them either, but close enough that I'll be able to hear their every word. Funnily enough though, no one seems to be talking.

I don't actually want to speak to Stacey, all I want today is to make a point. To stand my ground and show them I can't be intimidated. But it's taking all my willpower not to turn and run.

I want my very presence to unnerve them, for them to know that something has changed and that, whatever it is, there's more of it coming. Though my heart is pounding so hard I'm surprised they can't hear it.

The silence continues for a few moments longer and maybe it's just my imagination but I'm sure there are conversations grinding to a halt all over the playground. Or maybe it's just that the tone of them has changed, from a relaxed burble to an expectant buzz. There's a definite shift in the atmosphere and, close to where I'm standing, a tension, as if breaths are being held. And then, all of a sudden, Stacey laughs. A loud brash sound and the words 'child abuser' float out behind it. Clear as a bell. And loud enough for the whole playground to hear.

No one says a word.

I feel physically sick, but I dig my fingernails into the palms of my hands and try to picture one of my favourite photos of my dad. I want to experience the contrast between how looking at it makes me feel – suffused with love, pride and happiness – to how Stacey wants me and everyone else to feel – sickened and disgusted. I want to feel a burning sense of injustice build within me, letting it grow, unleashing a surge of anger, and it does, fury rolling over me in a wave.

More than anything I want to slap Stacey, to hear a single sharp retort as my palm meets with her skin, to feel the cleansing sting of the pain. There's a moment when I think I might. Can feel my muscles twitching all the way down my arm. Instead I walk over to Stacey until I'm standing inches from her.

'Don't.'

The word is loud, imbued with far more confidence than I'm feeling, and she can see the coiled spring of violence within me, only just under control.

She takes a backward step, her eyes darting to either side. 'I'm sorry, love, did you say something?'

I can hear the tremor in her voice, the surprise that someone has challenged her. She's trying to shrug it off, make light of it, even looking for support from her fellow coven members. But she won't get it, I can see by the looks on their faces.

'Don't,' I say again, just as loud. 'Don't ever talk to me. About me. Or my family ever again.'

Her face contorts into a vicious sneer.

'Yeah…? Or what?'

But I don't answer. My silence is far more powerful than my words could ever be.

I give Stacey one last look before returning to my original position, staring out across the playground, head held as high as I can muster. A pulse is beating in my ears, and I focus on breathing in and out until the roaring subsides. But I have done it. First step taken.

I daren't look either left or right, even though I can feel the stares of countless parents, and among them, Anna. I glimpsed her when I first came in, chatting to another mum, but I don't want to talk to her yet, not here. It's neither the time nor the place. So instead I concentrate on maintaining my stance just in case Stacey should feel she needs to have another go. But she doesn't. I'm still very much in their space and it doesn't take long for them to move slowly away until I'm on my own again, but I don't care. Let folks have a good look at me. I've got nothing to hide.

The atmosphere changes again as the first children come out from school, their bright chatter cutting through the subdued conversations. And, all at once, there is movement, normality, and a more purposeful air. I spot Lauren and Chloe almost immediately, their anxious faces scanning the groups of parents, and I'm so happy I did this today. They need their mummy back. Lauren breaks from Chloe's side and comes running across.

'Mummy! Oh, you're here, are you feeling better?' Her face is lit with happiness.

'Yes, sweetheart, I am.' And I realise it's true. 'Have you had a lovely day?'

She screws up her face. 'S'been all right… Tilly got top marks in our maths test and I came second, so that was good.' She pauses for a moment. 'We didn't cheat though, honestly…'

I laugh. 'I wouldn't have supposed you did for one minute.' I pull her to me, wrapping her in a big hug. 'And is Tilly okay?'

Lauren pulls back, looking up at me with her familiar earnest expression. 'She's very sad at the moment, Mummy.'

I stroke a hand over her hair. 'Is she?' I say. 'Well then, we'll just have to do what we can to make her happy again, won't we?'

Her face brightens. 'Can I go and play, just until teatime?'

I glance across to where Anna is standing, already making to leave. It would be a good opportunity to talk to her. 'Let's just see, shall we,' I say. 'I'll have a chat with her mum in a bit.'

I scoop Chloe into my side and give her a squeeze, knowing that she's far too old for a full-on show of affection in public. 'All right?' I ask, and she burrows into me, her face pressed against my breast. 'Come on then, let's get home.'

The crush of people slows us down as we near the gates but I wait our turn, conscious that most of the mums are, if not actually avoiding me, anxious not to make eye contact. The few that do, I meet with an open smile and a friendly greeting. Where Stacey is among the throng I have no idea, but in a few moments we're out of the bottleneck and into the lane. Anna is somewhere behind us but we walk on. I don't want to rush things and I'm happy just listening to the girls' chatter about their day.

By the time we get home, the usual routine of stowing bags, hanging up coats and collecting a drink and biscuit swings easily into action and I'm grateful. The day is far from over and I need the sustenance that this normality provides.

Drew isn't home yet, but I check on the dinner and am about to sort out another load of washing when there's a knock on the back door. I open it to find Tilly standing there.

'Would Lauren and Chloe like to come and play?' she asks. 'And Mummy says that she has some cake for us all, so if you'd like some too you're very welcome to come over.' She pauses, mouth pursed, hoping that she's delivered her message correctly. The girls are already bouncing at my side so I've no need to ask them what they think. I'm just inordinately pleased that Anna has invited me round too.

'Thank you, Tilly, that would be lovely. Would you mind passing on a message to Mummy for me? Say that I just need to pop to the shop but I won't be any longer than ten minutes and then I'll be right over.'

She thinks for a second and then nods, happy that she can deliver my reply intact. I close the door behind me as all three girls race off across the lawn towards Rose Cottage, leaving me to skirt the path around to the front of the house and into the lane.

I've already rehearsed what I want to say and, all too predictably, there are several people crowded around the shop counter. I don't intend to stay long and it looks as if I won't have to; the bodies part like the Red Sea, leaving me standing in the middle of the aisle with a clear line of sight to Jackie's astonished face.

'Fabulous,' I say. 'The more the merrier.' I march up to the counter, the biggest smile on my face that I can muster. 'Hi, Jackie, I'm so glad I caught you. I just wondered if you could do me the biggest favour...?'

She looks like she's swallowing crushed glass.

I don't give her the chance to refuse. 'You see, I've been thinking... Back in the playground earlier Stacey asked me what I might do should she decide she wants to keep spreading malicious gossip about me... So you see, the thing is Jackie, this is where I'm at...'

I break off to smile at the faces around me. 'I've had enough of someone I don't even know telling other people things about me that are simply not true. Now, I reckon I've worked out why she's decided to do that, but the rest of you... maybe you're not bothered. Maybe you're more concerned with staying on the right side of her than behaving like decent human beings yourself... Still, I guess it's up to you how you sleep at night.'

I clear my throat, willing my voice to stay steady. 'But, it's really lovely to find so many of you here all having a little chat, because I'm hoping that one of you at least has a conscience... Plus, of course, you're all witnesses to the fact that I'm not screaming or shouting, or swearing, or, heaven forbid, threatening anybody. All I'm doing is asking you to pass on a message for me, Jackie.

'You see, I'm sure Stacey thinks she knows all about what happened to Georgia Thomas all those years ago but, apart from the fact that my father is entirely innocent of the crime that was committed, she also seems to think that somehow this... "wickedness" has permeated down the years to infect my whole family. Which frankly is so utterly ridiculous I'm amazed no one has told her to stop being such a prat. There really is no reason to treat us all as if we're the devil incarnate, not when we've done nothing wrong. We're different people, you see. Jeez, it really is very simple...' I shake my head in bemusement as I take a step back. 'Is that okay, have you got all that?'

There's a slight snort off to one side and I'm aware of heads swivelling between myself and Jackie, wondering what comeback there's going to be, if any.

'Anyway,' I add, backing away from the counter. 'That's all I wanted to say, thanks so much.'

'Well I don't know what the bloody hell you need to tell me for,' grumbles Jackie, finally finding her tongue. 'I'm not your skivvy.'

I smile again. 'No, that's true, but I thought I'd tell you because you're Stacey's friend… Or maybe I got that wrong. Maybe you're nothing like her at all…'

I'm almost at the door to the shop now, but Jackie's not about to let me go without a fight.

'Stupid cow… I don't know who you think you are coming in here and making out like you're better than the rest of us. Not when your dad was a lying paedo…'

I guess I was asking too much for her not to resort to easy insults. But I meant it when I said I'd had enough.

I round on her. 'And you know that for a fact, do you? You think it's okay to say things like that when my dad was never even formally questioned, let alone arrested or charged. Or maybe the truth doesn't bother you? It seems to me that the only so-called facts you've been listening to are ones put about by someone who's a low-life bully. And for the record, no, I don't think I'm any better than the rest of you… Or, I didn't. Now I'm not so sure…'

'Yeah, and why would Stace even bother with someone like you? Stuck-up poncey artist in your big bloody house. Who do you think you are?'

I've been walking back up the aisle as she was speaking and am now only inches away from her.

'Shall I tell you why Stacey bothers with people like me? Because in her world you dish the dirt first. Isn't that the first rule of fighting dirty? Create a nice little smokescreen so I'll think twice about making trouble for her. Well, tough – her son is a thug and a bully and it's about time people stopped looking the other way. He's been making a little girl's life a misery and everyone just ignores it because they're scared of her. Not hard to see where her son gets it from, is it?'

Jackie practically spits at me. 'You can say what you like, but you're just as bad as her… Anna… You make a right pair, going around accusing people.' She juts out her chin, the irony of what she's just said completely lost on her. 'Maybe she shouldn't be so concerned with trying to blame other people for her precious daughter's bruises, maybe she should look closer to home... or even next door... '

Too late I see the danger as she trails off, a triumphant sneer on her face. I've pushed her too far.

'Yeah... I reckon that's right,' she continues. 'Stacey said that you and Drew used to be neighbours, that your families were the best of friends. Well, I wouldn't mind betting they were all in it together, thick as thieves the lot of you, just like you are now. They say the apple never falls far from the tree, don't they? Huh, they got that right.' Her eyes are shining as she grins at everyone around her, full of gloating.

A surge of heat races through me and I slowly move until I'm standing right in front of her. My eyes lock with hers.

'You lot are pathetic,' I hiss. 'No, you're sick... How you could even think such a thing about Rob is beyond me. A man you know, who'd do anything for you, as would Anna... And my Drew has done nothing either. For God's sake, just listen to yourselves.' I look at the gawping faces around me. 'And wouldn't you all love it if I said I was going to do everything in my power to take Stacey down? Well, sorry, but I couldn't bring myself to stoop so low. Stacey's welcome to the gutter, I just hope the rest of you manage to pull yourselves out of it.' I push myself away from the counter and storm from the shop.

CHAPTER TWENTY-TWO

I don't remember any of the walk back down the lane until I reach the gate by the churchyard and grasp hold of it, panting for breath. What have I done? Poor, poor Anna, now I've dragged her into this as well. How on earth have things reached the point when seemingly perfectly normal, perfectly nice people, start spreading such awful lies? Do we really all need to belong so much that we're prepared to take the side of someone like Stacey just so they'll let us be in their 'gang'? Talk or be talked about, maybe that's just how it goes. No, I can't believe that, I won't believe it. We're better than that, we have to be.

Anger is still surging through me, but the rush of adrenaline that fuelled it is now ebbing away, leaving my stomach hollow and my legs feeling like jelly. I'm not even sure I can manage to walk to Anna's, but I will. If she's heard any whisper of this I can't possibly leave her on her own.

I look up at the sky through the canopy of trees that have been the backdrop to a huge part of my life. There's little wind today, but they rustle gently, a moving picture of fading greens, bright russets and golds, and still beautiful despite the poison that seems to have leached into the air of late. I'm not giving any of this up; this is my home, that of my husband, my children and my friends. I take a deep breath, determination helping me to find my feet, and I follow the sound of the girls' shrieks of laughter.

The back door of Rose Cottage is slightly ajar when I reach it, and I tap lightly before walking in. Anna is at the sink, staring out across the garden, but something about the way she's standing makes me realise she's not seeing anything. She turns when she hears me enter.

Neither of us say anything for a moment. I had planned to, something warm and apologetic, given the way we parted, but I'm shocked by how dreadful Anna looks and it dries my words. She looks as if she's barely clinging on, her eyes huge in her pale face.

'Drew said you'd been ill and I…' She pauses. 'I meant to come and see you before to ask if you needed anything… but Drew said he had it covered and—'

'Jesus, Anna, you look dreadful!'

She bites her lip, smiling uncertainly. 'So do you, actually…' Her words end in a wry smile before she bursts into tears.

'I'm so sorry,' she says, backing away. 'I know you don't need this… You really don't need to stay, it's just I…'

But I catch her sleeve. 'I'm not going anywhere,' I reply. 'Don't be so bloody stupid.' And I pull her into a hug which makes her cry all the harder.

'I've got some tissues somewhere.' She sniffs, eyes searching the room.

'Here.' I hand her the box from the side and she slides them onto the table, plucking out a handful before sitting down. I sit silently on the seat opposite, giving her some space to compose herself. Her face is blotchy, red spots livid against the paleness of her skin, and this isn't the first time she's been crying either. I can see it in the tightness around her eyes.

'I've treated you appallingly,' she splutters.

But I hate that she can even think this way, not after the way I've behaved. 'No, no you haven't. It's me that needs to apologise, Anna. For heaven's sake I questioned everything you are, as a wife and a mother. I should never have said the things I did. It was rude, judgemental and… well, just vile actually. How else were you supposed to respond after I'd backed you into a corner?'

She looks up, sniffing. 'Yes, but I didn't understand then… And you were right all along. Trying to pretend that something isn't happening doesn't stop it from being so.' She opens her mouth to say more but just the act of recalling what she needs to say brings a fresh bout of tears. She swipes at her nose with a tissue. 'I can't believe people could even think such a thing. I mean, what kind of depraved…? I know things like that happen, I'm not that naive, but…' And then she stops dead and looks at me, horrified at what she's just said. And I no longer know whether she's talking about me or her.

'Can I get you some water, Anna? Or something else…' I cast about the kitchen for something, anything, that will make her feel better.

But she shakes her head, fingers shredding the tissue. 'How have you coped?'

I might not be sure what she's talking about but I can still answer the question. 'Well, I haven't, clearly. I've blown a hole in my marriage, argued with a good friend, and then taken to my bed for nearly a week to pretend that the outside world doesn't exist.'

Anna's mouth drops open. 'Oh…' She wipes a tear from her face. 'But I saw you today at school,' she says. 'You were… fierce…'

I smile sheepishly. 'I didn't feel like it,' I reply. 'I was terrified.'

'But at least you're standing up to her. I've tried… but now I just seem to have made things so much worse.' She pauses to marshal her thoughts and I know she's wondering how to tell me.

'I've just come from the shop,' I say, holding her look. 'I know what they're saying, Anna.'

He mouth gapes open.

'And I may have just shot my mouth off…' I recount the conversation, wincing as I hear my words all over again. 'I'm sorry, Anna, I just couldn't help it. What an absolute load of bollocks, I've never heard anything so ridiculous.'

To my surprise a smile flits across her face. 'Actually, I should thank you, Thea. You wouldn't believe the people who have hesitated, looked at me just a little bit longer than necessary, taken just that little bit too long to come up with a response. People who I thought were my friends. People whose children Rob has christened, even married in a couple of cases.'

I can feel my anger building again. Because this is exactly what happens when our emotions are toyed with, when our maternal fears are jerked like the strings of some evil puppet; we start to see shadows where there are none. And I can see how easily we begin to distrust our own instincts. Rob is no more capable of hurting Tilly than my dad was capable of abusing Georgia. But the seeds have been sown, and in fertile soil they've started to grow…

'How is Tilly…?' I prompt, reaching forward to give her hand a squeeze.

It takes a while for her to even start explaining. It's too raw, too present, and it's bad enough having the thoughts inside her head, let alone having to put them into words. But eventually she finds a place to start and draws in a deep breath.

'You were right,' she begins. 'About Tilly being bullied. I thought it was just the one time, when you saw the bruises. And I let myself believe that was it. But it's not just the odd shove here or there, or teasing getting out of hand. It's targeted, almost daily acts… insidious…'

'Leo?'

She nods. 'And I'd been doing my best to ignore all the warning signs… trying to persuade myself that it was all a storm in a teacup and there was no need to make a fuss but…' She visibly shakes. 'Now I know the extent of it.' She looks straight at me, her face taut with anger, but something else too. And I know that look well, it's guilt.

'Tilly is… very independent as you know, but there are still quite a few things that she needs help with, personal things like washing her hair, and to start with I thought that perhaps she was getting a little self-conscious, growing up, you know. And she's always understood she's different, but maybe her perception of her disability was changing, maybe she was becoming more aware of it herself.' She breaks off to shake her head. 'But really all I was doing was just pretending there was no problem.' Her lip begins to tremble. 'I've let her down so badly…'

'No, no you haven't, Anna. You have a beautiful, well-adjusted daughter who has only good things to say about people. And that's because you and Rob always strive to let her be the best she can.'

She thinks about my words for a few seconds before clearing her throat. 'I don't have a faith, Thea,' she continues. 'Not like Rob does, but I do believe that generally people are good and kind and if you believe that then… Except now I think maybe I've got it wrong. That I've set Tilly up to fail somehow because she expects that from people too.'

'Oh Anna, that's the only thing to believe. Imagine how awful life would be if we didn't hold onto that. Some people just hide their goodness very deep indeed…' I break off, thinking of Leo and his mum. 'Or, they've never been taught that it's okay to let it out. Worse, that only bad behaviour gets you attention…' I watch Anna's face as she wrestles with herself. 'Were there lots more bruises?' I ask gently.

She hangs her head. 'Her poor little body… all up the insides of her arms, especially around her stump, pinch marks mostly, but right where the skin is softest…'

'And right where it's not obvious…'

Anna's head jerks up. 'Yes… I hadn't thought of that.' Her eyes dart around the room as she takes in what I've just said. 'But that still doesn't excuse it. I should have noticed, I'm her mother for goodness' sake. And Tilly's been quiet, even withdrawn on occasion. You know what she's like, she never complains, and I just thought maybe she was coming down with a bug or…' She holds my look, her own one of abject despair.

'Anna, you don't need to explain, not to me.' The irony of what I'm about to say almost makes me smile. 'You're not the one at fault here, don't forget that.'

Apology flashes across her face. 'I'm so sorry, Thea. I should have been the one reminding you of that fact. The way you've been treated is appalling. You've had the most awful time of things, haven't you?' she says.

My head is still swimming, crowded with conflicting emotions; anger, regret, sadness, but maybe just a little hope too.

'Are you sure you don't want a cup of tea or something, Anna?' I ask. 'Only… I think I could do with one…' I hold out my hand to show my still trembling fingers.

Her expression changes immediately. 'Oh God, sorry, Thea… you must be feeling awful.' She jumps up and, as she looks at me, she smiles properly for the first time since I got here and I feel the foundations of our friendship begin to re-shore themselves up. 'Actually, I can do better than just tea. Hold that thought,' she says with purpose. 'I'll be back in a sec…'

She arrives back just as the kettle is beginning to boil, carrying an enormous cake tin which she plonks down on the table.

'And before you say anything, yes I know we're not a huge family.' She cranks off the lid to reveal an enormous chocolate cake, made in three layers, which stands about ten inches tall. 'This isn't the first one of these I've got through this week either.' She eyes me over the table, a challenging look on her face.

It's in such contrast to the mood of just a few minutes ago that a snort of laughter escapes before I have time to contain it. 'Oh, amen to that!'

I clap my hand over my mouth but Anna just laughs. 'Half each?' she asks.

And suddenly, when just a short while ago eating anything seemed like a massive chore, my mouths fills with saliva and I think I probably could finish the entire cake.

Anna hands me two plates and a knife, leaving me to portion the cake however I see fit, while she finishes making the tea.

Neither of us speaks for several minutes while we steadily work our way through the first few mouthfuls, forks delving into the gooey richness of the soft sponge. This is serious business and can't be rushed.

I wave my fork at her. 'So, what are we going to do about all this?' I ask, licking icing from my lips.

For a moment I think Anna might be about to cry again, but then she raises her chin a little and a defiant look comes into her eyes. 'Thank you for including yourself in that statement,' she says. 'I don't think I can do this by myself…'

My hand reaches across the table. 'Listen, anyone who can bake a cake like this must have special powers,' I say, taking another mouthful. 'Blimey, this is good. Besides, what are friends for?'

She smiles at the compliment but then her face falls again. 'Except that I don't think I've been much of a friend.'

I'm rapidly learning that guilt and blame are very happy bedfellows, but there is no place for either of them at times like these. 'You've had quite enough on your own plate to cope with, Anna,' I reply. 'And if I'd thought about it more I would have understood how this whole business with my dad put you in an awkward situation. Rob's position in the village is unique, and he has a responsibility to everyone in it, not just his friends or neighbours. I'd underestimated the constraints that places on you both, or rather I'd ignored them. Besides, he's your husband. It's only right that you should want to support him.'

Anna's face crumples at the mention of Rob's name. 'That's just it,' she replies. 'I'm terrified about what's going to happen now and it's only the beginning… The thought that he could… That other people might think…' She breaks off and shudders. 'I don't know how you've coped with it, I really don't. God, Thea, what am I going to do…?'

Her words remind me of just how bad things have become. 'And now it isn't just Rob,' I say, lips trembling. I take hold of both of Anna's hands and force her to look at me. 'This business with my dad… it's worse than you think,' I say quietly.

She looks up, a single tear tracking down her face.

'I still don't really know many more details than I've told you before. My dad *was* questioned about what happened to Georgia but, because he had an alibi for the night it happened, nothing ever came of it.' I'm still struggling to bring myself to say it. 'Except that what's worse is that I've now discovered my dad didn't really have an alibi at all. Oh God, Anna you have to swear not to tell anyone, please, not even Rob…' I swallow. 'Drew's parents said he was with them, *not* because he needed an alibi, but because I think they panicked. Drew swears blind it doesn't change anything, that my dad is still innocent, but—'

'Of course it does!' Anna's face is angry, her cheeks blazing with colour once more. 'For you it makes all the difference…'

She squeezes my hands and I'm relieved to see that her anger is not directed at me. Instead her watery eyes are full of compassion. 'Oh, Thea, I'm so sorry… How do you even begin to process something like that?'

'No one knows about this, only our families, and Drew…' His name comes out more bitterly than I had intended. 'He knew the whole time, Anna, he's known for years. He just couldn't bring himself to tell me, so he let us move back here… We've had a massive row and I don't know how to make any of this better. Not when I can't trust him to tell me the truth.'

I wipe away a tear that has spilled down my cheek. 'But I realised today that if I don't challenge what people are saying, none of this is ever going to change. It will go on and on, just like it did for my mum and dad until they had to move. I don't want that, Anna. I couldn't bear it. So I thought that if I could stand up to Stacey, to let her and her gang know that they aren't going to beat me, that it would at least be a start. But all I've done is manage to make things even worse.'

I pull a face. 'It was my own fault. I backed her into a corner and she had no way out but to retaliate, but to suggest that both our families are now locked in some sort of age-old conspiracy. It's so ridiculous but...'

Anna gives a weak smile. 'Here we are...' she says.

And suddenly a white-hot anger burns away the last remnants of fog in my brain. 'I've had enough of this,' I say. 'I don't know what Stacey's game is but I'm damn well going to find out. And in the meantime, you and I are going to finish our cake and then we're going to think how to put an end to all the lies and bully-ing. It's game over as far as I'm concerned.' I stick my finger into the top of the sponge and transfer a blob of icing to my mouth, savouring the dissolving sweetness. 'Is Rob at home now?' I ask.

She gives me a curious look. 'No, he's been out for most of the day. He's gone to a meeting at the diocese; something to do with the board of education. But I've no idea how to tell him, Thea. He'll be absolutely distraught.'

'So then we have a little while to work out what to say. I feel so awful, Anna. If we'd never come back to Pevensey then none of this would have happened. With Tilly I mean, or Rob. The thing with my dad is different. That was just waiting in the wings ready to burst out from behind the curtain at any time, but now it's involved you and—'

'No,' says Anna firmly. 'You mustn't think that. If Tilly wasn't the one getting picked on, then some other poor child would be on the receiving end. I'm quite convinced about that. I've been up to the school on several occasions and I've seen which way the land lies. The head doesn't believe she has a bullying problem in her school, therefore there isn't one. This isn't going to stop unless someone stops it.'

I think back to the reception we received the day Lauren punched Leo. 'Yeah, I got that impression too… So, we need to sort out how we're going to tackle this.'

Anna eyes the remaining cake still on her plate and picks up her fork. 'Good,' she says. And then her hand stills once more. 'Except that I don't think it's going to be that easy. I have another problem.'

'Go on,' I say somewhat warily.

'The Harvest Festival Supper, which is this weekend…'

I'd forgotten all about it.

'Jackie and Stacey are on the committee. I've got a horrible feeling there's going to be more trouble.'

CHAPTER TWENTY-THREE

'That's the third one this morning,' wails Anna, putting down her phone. 'And if anyone else pulls out, I'm going to scream.'

It's Thursday and I'm sitting in Anna's kitchen, ostensibly helping with the arrangements for the Harvest Supper, but the way things are going it doesn't look like there will even be one. But there has to be. I owe it to the memory of my dad, and everything he fought for in this village to make sure it happens. I can't let him down.

'And you wouldn't believe the excuses that people have come up with, either,' continues Anna. 'Anyone would think people were averse to working with the daughter of a paedophile and the mother of a domestic abuse victim.'

Her words are meant to sound light-hearted but she can't quite pull it off. She stops for a moment to reflect on what she's just said, mouthing sorry at me, before visibly pulling herself together. A steely gleam of determination replaces the look of misery in her eye. But we're neither of us convinced that it's going to be enough.

'Okay,' I say. 'Run it all by me one more time and let's see what we can do.'

But it's hopeless, we can both see that. I stare morosely out of the window at the sheets of rain being hurled against the glass. 'Is this going to carry on all day?' I ask idly. 'A ray of sunshine wouldn't go amiss.'

Anna looks up from the notepad on the table in front of her and follows my gaze. She looks as if she's never seen rain before.

'Damn,' she mutters, pulling her phone towards her. 'With everything else going on, I haven't even given a thought to what the weather's going to be doing. If it's raining we won't be able to have the traditional children's procession to carry all the donations from the church to the village hall. Everything is displayed on tables during the meal and then taken to the local food banks the next day. Since Rob's been curate here I can't remember a year when that hasn't happened.' Anna checks her phone and pulls a face. 'Tomorrow looks brighter, but there's heavy rain forecast for the weekend, look.' She angles the display so I can see it.

'Yes, but that could all change in day or two, surely?'

'Possibly, but we need to know what we're going to do if it doesn't. Apart from anything else we'll have to arrange to get all the donations to the hall ourselves.' She looks through the kitchen doorway to the hallway and the study where Rob is busy working. 'But I don't really want to worry Rob about this today,' she says. 'He's making plans, a new project for the diocese, and I'd rather he just concentrate on that. I think it might do him more good just now.'

Her eyes betray a feeling I recognise all too well, the peculiar pain of a hurt carried for another.

'Is Rob okay?' I ask gently.

'I think so,' she replies. 'He's angry mostly, which is not an emotion he often gives rein to. After all, he's supposed to be an advocate for compassion and forgiveness, but that's a little hard when you're the one who needs to find it.'

'I would imagine it is. He's only human though, I hope he remembers that.'

'It's the first time his faith has been properly tested.' She smiles a little awkwardly. 'And even though the accusations hurt, in a rather perverse way I think he's welcoming the challenge this is presenting him with.'

'Every cloud has a silver lining…?'

'Something like that.' She grins suddenly. 'What doesn't kill you makes you stronger…?'

'Yes, lovely sentiments but utter rubbish.'

She arches her eyebrows. 'Aren't they?' She gives me a look that shows she understands just how I've been feeling. And, despite the situation we're both in, it's a bond between us, and I like that. She picks up her pen and draws a line under the list she's made on her pad. 'Right, that's enough of that,' she says. 'I refuse to think about it any more today.'

But she will, I know she will.

I'm about to reply when a quacking duck heralds the arrival of a text message to my phone. And I can guess straight away who it's from when I see a row of smiley face emojis.

Bloody hell, Thea, I think we might just have sold the house!!
Trying to get hold of Gerry, speak soon! R xx

I stare at the message, stunned. I've been meaning to ring Rachel, but somehow, with everything going on here, I hadn't given any more thought to their house-hunting. I'm beginning to type out a quick reply when I stop, looking back across at Anna, now doodling on her notepad. There's a cunning plan forming at the back of my mind and, without stopping to think about it any further, I delete my message and dial Rachel's number instead.

*

'You don't believe in making life easy for yourselves, do you?'

Rachel is standing with her hands on her hips in the village-hall kitchen staring at the table in front of her. It's laden with produce and boxes of foodstuffs.

It's now late on Saturday afternoon, the day before the Harvest Festival Supper, the day we discover whether we really can do this thing or not. Without Rachel's expertise it won't be possible. She didn't take much persuading to come and help us out, particularly given that she and Gerry are now officially looking for a place to live. The speed at which everything seems to be happening is making my head spin but – apart from when I relayed the catalogue of recent events to Rach – she hasn't stopped grinning since they both arrived.

'So what's supposed to happen?' she asks, frowning. 'At Jamie's school we just donate things for the Harvest Festival and they get shipped off to those in need. But, apart from a special assembly to mark the occasion, that's about it.'

Anna runs an anxious hand through her ponytail. 'Well, traditionally the supper began not only to celebrate the successful harvest but also as a means of ensuring that the older people in the parish, or the weak and infirm, were provided for. Surplus produce would have also been distributed at the supper, after an evening of giving thanks, and celebrations…' She breaks off to grin. 'Most likely an awful lot of ale, riotous singing and bawdy games… Nowadays our donations go to the local food bank but the supper is a major fundraiser for the upkeep of the hall. The whole village is invited and most of them turn up.'

'We nearly lost this place when my mum and dad lived here,' I add. 'Some developers wanted to flatten it and use the land for housing, but my dad got the whole village fighting against them and they managed to save it, and all the land behind. This hall really is the centre of the community.'

'Ah…' says Rachel, understanding instantly. 'So this supper is important for all sorts of reasons.' She gives me a tender look.

Anna nods. 'It's an old building and it costs a lot to maintain but, by using donated goods, and having volunteers do all the cooking, serving, washing up, and everything else, every bit of money raised from the sale of tickets goes directly to the hall.' She eyes the table with a disconsolate expression on her face.

'And it's that help which you don't appear to have…'

'Er, no.' Anna pulls a face. 'The PTA committee have made sure of that.'

'Then they need a bloody kick up the arse,' says Rachel. 'What the hell did they think was going to happen? That their supper was just going to be magicked out of thin air?'

Anna looks at me and grimaces. 'I think they just decided that with everything that's been going on, the kitchen was going to get mighty hot and they'd rather not get burnt. Several of the members have been quite, er, vocal…'

'Yes, I've heard.' Rachel is unrepentant. 'Cowards,' she adds. 'The whole lot of them.' She scratches her head. 'Right, well I suppose there's no point whinging about it, is there? We've got a meal to pull together and I guess we'd better get our thinking caps on… How many did you say we're catering for?'

'Over a hundred…' whispers Anna.

Rachel's staring at the table again, dishes from every buffet, dinner party and christening she's ever catered for running through her head.

'And is this everything?' she asks.

'Heavens no,' answers Anna. 'Most of it's still at the church. But we try to use as little as possible for the meal so that the majority can go to the food bank. I know that's not ideal, but…'

Rachel nods. 'No, I'll make it work, don't worry. It would just be helpful to have a look at what else we can use.'

I pull a face. 'There's another slight problem,' I say. 'The procession might have to be cancelled because of the rain that's forecast. If it is, it means we'll also have to ferry all the donations over here ourselves. Today. There won't be time tomorrow.'

Anna nods. 'Rob was just on his way around to the school when we left. If this weather doesn't improve I can't see how on earth we can go ahead as usual, but it will be up to him and the head to decide. Shall we go and see how he's getting on?'

The rain hasn't abated one iota and we're standing for a moment in the doorway to the village hall, contemplating a mad dash through the puddles to Anna's car, when Drew pulls up. He gets out and runs around to open the boot.

'I've just seen Rob on his way back from the school and it's been decided. All the donations are going to have to be brought here before tomorrow, I'm afraid. I think Gerry is bringing his car around as well, a couple more loads each should do it. Can you give me a hand to empty the boot?'

Between us it takes only a few minutes to bring everything inside before Drew is despatched to collect the next load. Gerry and Rob turn up moments later and before too long the kitchen is filled with even more tins, packets and jars, alongside a growing pile of fresh produce.

Rachel pounces on some parsnips and apples with undisguised glee. 'Oh, I was hoping for some of these…' She places them to one side and continues her inspection.

The men disappear once more and I leave Rachel to her thoughts, joining Anna in the main hall. It's a familiar room and hasn't changed much since I was a child; a large oblong with windows down both sides and a polished wooden floor, which lends the room its particular smell. There's a stage at one end, scene of countless school and amateur dramatic productions, and on either side of it are two smaller rooms with a connecting corridor behind, used as backstage areas or storerooms, depending on need. One of the rooms is full of folding tables and chairs, all of which will have to be set up before the supper tomorrow.

I cross the room to stand beside Anna. She looks peculiarly lost. 'Penny for them?' I say.

It takes a moment for her focus to include me. 'How are we ever going to manage this?' she asks eventually. 'It's not just the food, Thea, it's all of this…' She waves a hand at the airy space in front of us.

'I'm sorry, Anna, I'm not following you. I know it seems like a tall order, but Rach is amazing. She does this for a living, don't forget, she'll come up with something.'

But Anna shakes her head. 'I wasn't thinking of that,' she replies. 'You've been to these suppers when you were a child here, haven't you?'

I nod.

'So, it's a bit hard to have a party in a room which looks like this, isn't it?'

And I suddenly realise what she means. The room is neat and tidy, it's actually very pleasant, but that's where it stops. It's certainly not festive. At all.

'Ah…' I grimace. 'Yes, I see what you mean… So what's happened about decorations in previous years?' But as soon as I say it I know what the answer is. 'Jackie and the committee…' I say. I don't even have to wait for Anna's answering nod.

'I didn't even think about this,' she adds. 'It's normally just done. And I'm busy helping Rob, and manning the kitchen…'

It's the resignation in her voice which fires my anger. 'Then we'll do what we can,' I reply. 'And what we can't do, won't get done. You can't do everything, Anna, they're bloody lucky to have you and Rob at all.' I link my arm through hers. 'Let's all have a cup of tea and a brainstorm. Some brilliant idea will come to us, you'll see.'

She smiles. 'You're such a shit liar,' she says. 'But thank you…'

*

Rach has made a list. In fact, Rach has made a list of lists and we're all headed back to Pevensey with several bags of vegetables among other things. A takeaway is on the cards, as is a rather long night of food preparation but, before it gets dark, there's one more thing I have to attend to.

I have no idea whether my idea will actually work, and there's really only one way to find out. So, armed with several carrier bags, I leave Drew to make some tea and take Gerry outside to collect as many leaves from our Virginia creeper as we can. They're soaking wet but for what I have in mind they'll be literally hung out to dry, so it hopefully won't matter.

'If all this works, your place as honorary members of the village will be pretty much guaranteed,' I say to Gerry as he passes me another handful of the leaves. 'But I'm very grateful to you and Rach, you're supposed to be house-hunting…'

Gerry grins. 'Which we will be,' he replies. 'Come Monday. Nothing is open tomorrow anyway and besides…' He stares at his hands, which are rapidly turning white with cold, just as mine are. 'We wouldn't be having half as much fun if we stayed at home.'

'Yeah, right…'

He stops and watches me for a second or two. 'Actually, I mean it. I know things are… difficult just now. But this is the place you were made, Thea, you and Drew, the children, all of it. And it's still so perfect for you all. I can see that now.' He wipes away a droplet of water from his nose. 'I worried at first that our coming here was too much of a shift from our lives in London, but now I can see that's exactly why it could be right for us too. I don't know whether it's because we see it in you and Drew, or whether Rach and I have only just realised what's been missing from our lives, but… it feels right to be doing it.'

He breaks off, laughing. 'God, listen to me. I don't normally come over all philosophical but it's like…' He stares up at the creeper, his fingers tracing the outline of one of the stems. 'How can you ever grow if you don't have roots?'

And all at once I'm taken back to the playground of St Hilda's school on the last day of term, just before we moved. It was the day when Rach had told me that she couldn't ever imagine having childhood memories like mine, her words echoing Gerry's. I'd smiled and told her that two years from now she'd get her dream too – a farmhouse with roses around the door and her own baking empire – but it was just something I'd said, knowing that our paths were about to split in different directions. I didn't really think for one moment that it would come true. Just as I never really believed that I would ever have the kind of life my childhood had led me to believe I could. But what's the point of ever having dreams if you don't believe in them?

'Roots… and space and sunshine and a little rain…' I say, smiling up at the sky and blinking as the raindrops hit my lashes. 'Although, not too much rain, I've had enough of that just lately. It's time for the sun to come out again.'

'It will, Thea. This is… a storm. It will blow over, I'm sure of it.' Gerry holds my look for longer than is necessary. 'You and Drew will be okay.'

I shiver. 'Come on, let's get back inside. My fingers are so cold I can't feel them.' I glance down at the full bags we're carrying between us. 'I reckon we have enough of these now anyway.'

CHAPTER TWENTY-FOUR

I slip my fingers into Anna's as she stares out across the village hall from the kitchen doorway. 'You okay?'

She gives a slight nod. 'Terrified,' she replies. 'You?'

'I feel sick.' I turn to look at her and smile. 'Just remember that in a few hours this will all be over,' I say. Although we both know that's a lie. Somehow I think it's going to take a lot more than a good meal to convince the locals that our families don't need to be chased from the village by an angry mob bearing pitchforks.

I follow the line of her gaze to where Drew is busy laying out jugs of squash and water down the rows of trestle tables that all but fill the space.

'How are things?' she asks quietly.

'He doesn't want to be here any more than I do,' I reply.

'No… but he is,' says Anna. 'And you're talking…'

'Not about anything that matters though. It's like we're strangers making polite chit-chat.'

She nods. 'He's incredibly proud of you. You do know that, don't you?'

I shrug. 'Maybe, but…'

'No, I mean it. He said as much to Rob, who, if he manages to curtail his anger today…' She smiles. 'He said you were always the strong one, the one who righted wrongs, even when you were children.'

'I don't think so, that was always Drew, he…' And I trail off, lost in memories. Drew was always the one who brought out the best in me, who quashed my doubts with his steadfast love. I squeeze Anna's fingers back. 'I might just go and…'

And she nods, waving me away.

Drew has already laid out the crockery, glasses, cups and saucers alongside a line of greenery which I placed down the centre of each table earlier. It's holly and ivy mainly, interspersed with the bright-coloured heads of as many dahlias as I could find in the garden. He looks up as I approach, the predictable tentative smile on his face.

'It looks good,' he says.

Above our heads my leaf 'bunting' cascades like streamers from the central chandelier light fitting, fanning out like the spokes of a wheel with each end anchored to a point on the wall. Strung on the virtually invisible nylon thread that I use for my pictures, each leaf seems to hang as if by magic and, with the lights lit, the colours glow from the palest lemon to the deepest vermillion and every shade in between.

'It's something at least,' I reply. 'It seems mean not to have any decoration at all. Just because the committee want to make a point today, I don't see why everyone else has to suffer. The Harvest Supper isn't for them, or us, it's for the villagers.'

He nods. 'And I'm sure they'll be grateful for the lengths that have been gone to on their behalf. Today wouldn't have happened at all if it weren't for you, Anna and Rachel.'

'I hope so. Although somehow I doubt it.' I look around the room. 'Sorry, Drew, I'm just not feeling hugely optimistic that today is going to change anything.'

'You never know,' he says quietly. 'We can but try.'

There's a wistful note to his voice that catches at my heart. I'm about to reply when I hear my name being called. Rachel is waving at me frantically from the kitchen doorway.

I turn, a rueful smile on my face. 'I'd better…'

'Yes,' he says. 'I'll… people will be here soon. Gerry and I will need to man the teapots…'

We smile at each other and it's all we can do. For now.

In all the time I've known her, I've never actually seen Rachel in action as a caterer, but she's incredible and I can see why she's always so busy. Calm and efficient, organised and methodical, she's been a whirlwind of energy and enthusiasm since early morning, giving directions, making endless decisions and always keeping on top of everything that's going on, never once allowing any of her metaphorical plates to stop spinning. The result is a kitchen full of the most amazing smells and a dinner almost ready to serve that I didn't think would ever be possible. It won't suit everyone, but maybe it's a change for the better. Only time will tell.

'How's it going?' I ask as I reach her.

She hands me a wooden spoon. 'Okay, everything's almost ready, but can you come and stir for me? Otherwise we're going to have a large amount of very lumpy custard…'

Behind us the front door bangs as the first of the villagers begin to arrive and my eyes fly straight to Anna's. Nothing will officially start until Rob has made his way here from the church but, as he'll be one of the last to appear, we need to make sure that everyone gets settled in first with a hot drink, happy to be inside from the incessant rain once again. It's time for Anna to take centre stage – not as the saviour of the Harvest Festival Supper, or as sous-chef, bottle-washer, mother, friend, or any of the other roles she has taken in her stride – but this time as the curate's wife.

Two hours later there is a happy hubbub of noise and the hall is filled with conversation and laughter. The children, set free from the confines of the dinner table, have sought out the empty spaces to play their games while their parents and the older villagers remain seated, nattering happily and enjoying the food.

Rob and Drew have brought nothing but good comments back to the kitchen over the change to the menu this year. Gone are the dishes of coleslaw and pasta salads and, in their place, Rachel has provided bowls of piping-hot leek-and-potato soup with home-made croutons and spiced, toasted pumpkin seeds – perfect comfort food for such a wet and miserable day. A rich chickpea and roasted vegetable stew followed, fragrant with warming spices and piled over buttery couscous, and finished with apple crumble and custard. It was an eclectic mix, Rachel was the first to admit, but I'm so proud of her. And happy for her too. I can't think of a nicer way for her to start off a new life and she might even end up with a queue of ready customers for her new business once they move.

Given the success of the day so far, I could quite easily pretend that everything is okay were it not for Stacey, Jackie and the other committee members all sitting in a row with their families. I'm watching them now. How they even have the nerve to show their faces here is beyond me, and I don't think it occurred to any of us that they actually would. I can't imagine how Anna must have felt, having to serve Stacey and Jackie their food, but she did so, head held high.

And now it's my turn. I'm doing circuits of the hall, collecting empty glasses and cups and ferrying them back to the kitchen for washing. So far, I've managed to avoid their table but I can't keep doing it, and I won't. I can't spend the rest of my life as if I'm apologising for something I haven't done.

A slight tug on my jumper distracts me for a moment. It's Chloe, with a frown on her face. 'Do you know where Lauren is?' she asks.

I look up, scanning the hall. 'She was with Tilly in the kitchen a few minutes ago,' I reply, not seeing her. 'She's probably still there.'

But she shakes her head. 'No, I've just been in there.'

Stacey is laughing at something although I'm too far away to hear what.

'Oh…' I smile down at Chloe. 'Then I don't know, love. She'll be with Tilly somewhere. Have you looked in the room at the back? I should try there.'

'Okay.'

I watch her make her way through the tables, then give Stacey one last look before scooping up a pile of empty cups from the nearest table and taking them through to wash. True to their word, Drew and Gerry are busy at the sink and my presence elicits a predictable groan.

'I can't believe there are still cups we haven't washed,' says Drew. He rolls his eyes and looks at Gerry, a pained expression on his face. 'Did I volunteer us for this?' he asks, nodding as he does so. 'Yes, I thought I did…'

'So, what happens now though?' asks Gerry. 'Do people just drift away or what?'

I glance at the clock on the wall. It's gone three and, although the rain has stopped, the view from the window is dark and gloomy.

'It varies,' answers Anna. 'Rob will give a bit of a speech soon and that's pretty much the signal for everyone to finish up, but some years, when the weather's been better and the kids are playing outside, folks stay on for a bit. It's all done and dusted by the time it's dark though, and I think today people will just want to get home.'

Drew nods. 'No offence, but let's hope so,' he says.

'Then I'll go and chase up the last of the cups.'

I slip back out the door just as two elderly ladies pass me on the way to the cloakroom. I smile automatically only to be greeted with a frown.

'Course that kind of thing would never have happened back in my day,' says the first, moving away. 'I might be old, but I know what's right, and buying someone in to do all this is just plain disgraceful. Whatever happened to everyone pitching in together?'

I take a step backward, turning to follow the sound of the voice. It sounded very much as if the words were entirely for my benefit, the voice slightly raised above a normal speaking level. But they must be talking about something else. Surely not…

The lady who had spoken stops for a moment to pull her cardigan around her. 'Not sure I'll bother coming next year if it's going to be like this.'

Her friend nods, looking back at me. 'Me neither. Goes against the spirit of the whole thing.'

I shoot a glance back out to the hall where people are still milling, chatting and finishing their drinks. It all looks just as it did half an hour ago. And then I look back. I can't let this pass.

'Um, excuse me…?'

Two heads turn my way.

'Sorry,' I say, stepping forward. 'I couldn't help overhearing what you were saying… Were you talking about today? About the supper here?'

The first lady pulls me in with a disapproving stare. 'That's right,' she says. 'Your friend, I think…' I follow her line of sight to where Rachel is sitting talking to two other women. 'The one that did all the cooking.'

'Yes…?'

'From some fancy catering company…' Her eyebrows are raised. 'You might have only just arrived in the village, but really, that's not how we do things here.' She breaks off, tutting. 'This is supposed to be a community event, not an opportunity to line the pockets of your friends.'

'What?'

I look between the two of them, feeling my stomach flipping in shock. 'Who told you that?'

But I didn't need to ask, it's obvious. Colour races over my cheeks. 'No, that's not how it is,' I continue. 'My friend does run a catering company but she came here today to help, and only because everyone else pulled out!'

I spin on my heels to face the room. 'I don't believe it,' I say. 'Is that really what people are saying?'

The two women look at one another, now very aware that they've just started something they wished they hadn't. My face must be puce.

'I've bloody well had enough of this,' I say, marching forwards, just as I catch sight of Anna's anguished face through the kitchen door. Drew and Gerry are hot on her heels.

'Thea, wait!' Anna's voice is distraught.

But I'm done waiting. I will not let my friends be treated this way. I can see Anna moving across to Rob out of the corner of my eye. He's standing talking with the head teacher and, if I'm not mistaken, about to make his speech any minute now. I have to be quick and I march across to Stacey's table before I can change my mind.

'What have you been saying about Rachel?' I demand, looking from one to the other. 'Well?'

'Well, what?' Stacey looks up, an idle sneer on her face. 'You accusing us of something? Again…?' She smirks at Jackie. 'Almost seems like she can't keep away, doesn't it?'

'Because it's bad enough you trying to trash my family and Anna's too, but to have a go at my friend when all she's done is try to fix the mess you and your cronies have created…'

'I don't know what you mean?' She frowns. 'Do you understand what she's talking about, Jackie?'

'Maybe you'd like me to tell everyone?' I threaten. 'Explain how you and your friends deliberately pulled out of helping, knowing it would make today almost impossible. And not content with that, you're now bad-mouthing the person who stepped in to help out of the goodness of her heart. Anyone would think you didn't care about the people in this village at all…'

I've forced my voice deliberately low but she can hear my fury and, even as I finish, I realise that the relaxed chat around me has stilled. And Stacey has noticed too. Her eyes flick nervously to one side. She looks to her friends for reassurance, but bit by bit the sound in the room drops away and eyes begin to turn on me. My heart pounds as I realise what I've done, staring out at the sea of faces, the breath catching in my throat… This is neither the time nor the place to air a very private grievance. There are children here for goodness' sake.

And I nearly bottle it, nearly run for cover to the safety of the kitchen and away from prying eyes, but Drew has come to stand by my side. And he smiles, a slow, warm smile that travels up from his boots to light his eyes, meant for no one else but me. He gives an almost imperceptible nod, never breaking eye contact. And then I see Rob take a step forward to stand beside Anna and Rachel too as Gerry touches her arm.

'Hi… everyone… sorry, can I just have your attention for a minute…'

There is an instant hush at the sound of Rob's voice, and in the space it creates, all I can hear is my mum, urging me to make up my mind of what I believe in. Telling me to hold it close and never let it go. And I see now that I have. I know what I believe, and not just about my dad, but also, finally, what I believe about Drew.

A memory comes rushing back. Of Drew standing on the driveway of Pevensey House, hands on hips as I'd accused him of fancying another girl, just because he'd given her apples from his parents' garden. We must have been all of ten years of age.

'Thea Bradley,' he'd said. 'I shall never marry you if you're going to turn into an enormous green-eyed monster. Have you forgotten who I am, or do you need a reminder?' And with that he had crunched across the gravel and kissed me hard on the lips. I had been so mad but, seconds later, I was helpless with love and admiration for this luminous being. In one fell swoop, Drew had reminded me of what I'd always known; that I could trust him because he only ever did things for the right reasons. Even at such a tender age I'd known that. So how come I'd forgotten it now? Or maybe I've remembered it, just in time.

I glance across at Drew but his attention is focused on Rob. In fact, the whole room has fallen silent.

'So I guess by now you've all realised that today's supper has been a little different than in previous years, but judging by all the clean plates and bowls coming back to the kitchen you've all enjoyed it.' I'm happy to hear murmurs of appreciation.

'It's been different in other ways too,' he continues. 'And because the Harvest Festival has always been such a strong community event, I'd like to remind everyone of how strong our community actually is. You see, you almost didn't have a celebration of any kind today…'

Somewhere in the audience a throat is cleared, loudly and with purpose. He ignores it. 'And I could say that it's no one's fault, just one of those times when a series of unfortunate events unfold…' He pauses for a moment, smiling out across the room. 'So today nearly didn't happen at all because one or two of the organising committee became ill, I think one had to make an emergency visit to a sick relative, another's husband was really poorly and she couldn't leave him, and… oh, yes, a burst pipe to contend with, I think. Except that none of these things are the truth. They're excuses made up by people who don't care about their community at all. People who are quite content to live in one where lies and gossip are the currency rather than honesty and empathy.'

A collective breath is held and I risk a look around me. Judging by the looks on people's faces, they're not used to Rob making comments like this. Anna looks shocked. She's standing right beside him and it's clear from her face that this wasn't what she was expecting.

Rob breaks into a big grin as if to soften his words. 'But, as you might expect, I'm a firm believer in clouds having silver linings and it's made me realise that I'd forgotten what *I* should be doing here, as your curate. And that instead of doing what I ought to, I've settled for being what I thought people wanted – the kind of vicar who steers a middle course, who doesn't rock the boat, who performs his duties with a smile, doesn't make his sermons too long, and is at the beck and call of anyone who needs him. But what price is popularity and security when you have to sell your soul to achieve it?'

He shakes his head. 'My family and friends have been on the receiving end of some very nasty comments over recent days. Hurtful comments that strike at the very heart of who we are as people. It doesn't matter that they aren't true, what matters is that folk felt it was okay to make these accusations. That they could condemn so quickly, judge so falsely, instead of seeking the truth.'

There is a collection of murmurs from somewhere and I see Anna turn and smile at Rob with an expression on her face that would melt even the hardest of hearts.

And all the while Rob has managed to look like he's about to award first prize for the largest marrow at the village fair. But his face darkens now. 'What's going on in this village is wrong and it needs challenging. I'm sorry if you wanted the kind of vicar who was prepared to look the other way and not stand up for the things he believes in, but that's not me, and now seems a good a time as any to tell you that I intend for things to change.'

He casts his eyes around the hall, looking expectantly at the faces that surround him before looking directly at me. I can feel myself beginning to blush under his intense scrutiny.

'And in a way maybe they already have… You see, today shouldn't have happened. It would have been cancelled were it not for some exceptional people. People who have also been on the receiving end of some appalling gossip, but who have risen above it, and put others before themselves. And everything that has happened here today has been down to them. And I do mean everything.

'So, I'd like you to put your hands together to say a massive thank you to my wife, Anna, our good friends, Thea, her husband, Drew, and their friends, Rachel and Gerry. In fact, it's Rachel who's been responsible for the amazing meal you've all enjoyed today, a meal borne out of determination, ingenuity and the goodness of her own heart.'

He lets the tumultuous applause speak for itself, joining in himself for a few minutes until he judges that the noise is dying down a little. He holds up his hand to gain everyone's attention. 'Anyway…'

The applause dies a little more and he waves his hand.

'Anyway,' he shouts, and the last of the clapping peters out. 'I also want to thank all of you – for coming, for being so generous with your donations as you always are, and for remembering what the Harvest Festival is all about: celebrating the bounty and richness of our community. In fact, sharing a meal here today is a good reminder that this wouldn't even be possible were it not for the efforts of Thea's father. A man who, as many of our older villagers will remember, was instrumental in saving this building from demolition so that we could continue to come together as a community for many years to come. Today could have seen the end of that, but I hope that this reminder of what we're really all about will see us all safely through the coming months. Together.'

'Hear, hear!' The loud shout comes from someone to my right, but I can't for the life of me see who it is. Someone close to Anna, for she turns and beams at them, smiling down at Chloe who has gravitated awards her. A little embarrassed perhaps to have her parents made the centre of attention. And then Drew's hand slips into mine and nothing else really matters anymore.

An expectant hush falls as the seconds tick by, as if people are waiting for Rob to say more, but he's nodding and smiling at those around him and gradually normal sound begins to creep back into the room. Out of the corner of my eye I can see a few heads swivelling, perhaps as the import of his words sink in and they begin to seek out those committee members who have just been called to shame. But I can see them, I'm looking straight at them; Stacey and Jackie, sitting motionless, faces like thunder.

Rachel comes to join us. 'I think they got away lightly, don't you?'

Drew smiles. 'Perhaps, but I think Rob said all he needed to. They've got the message and by saying what he has here, in front of everyone, he's managed to bag a great deal of support at the same time. I think he played it very well. Look!'

He directs our attention back to where Rob is standing, a crowd of people around him, congratulating him on the day and saying their thank yous before taking their leave. In fact, I can see a few people around the room putting coats on, and gathering their children to them. Just like Anna said, it looks as if everything is going to wrap up, and a surge of relief washes over me. I think we might just have got through it.

'I can't thank you enough though, Rach,' I say. 'We could never have done this without you.'

She beams. 'Would you believe I actually enjoyed it? It felt good to be doing something that mattered and I've stretched myself today.'

'Well, I'm proud of you,' I say. 'You didn't have to help out. Actually, I'm proud of all of us,' I add. 'And I'm so happy for Anna and Rob; they've been such lovely neighbours and friends from the minute we moved in. They didn't deserve to be treated the way they have.'

I just want to get home now, to be back at Pevensey, relaxed and among friends, but I know that there is still plenty of work to do before we finally get to shut the doors of the village hall behind us. Most people seem to be on their feet now and I try to search out Anna among them. But I can't see her anywhere, nor Chloe. My eyes scan the tables for them, but they're not sitting down, nor have they moved to stand beside someone else. There's a bunch of children from school tidying away some board games they were playing with and, crouched beside one of them, is the head teacher. But there's something about her pose that strikes me as odd and, without even really knowing why, everything else that's going on in the room falls away.

I'm now not just scanning the room, I'm interrogating it, my eyes moving from one person to the next, systematically and thoroughly. My eyeline is suddenly blocked as Gerry homes into view, placing a hand on my arm.

'Well, wasn't that bloody brilliant! I really thought—'

'Sorry, Gerry,' I say, leaning out so I can see past his shoulder. 'It's just that…' I'm distracted but he's standing right in front of me. I drag a smile back on my face. 'It was, wasn't it. All in all, I'd say it was a roaring success. Mostly down to your wife's culinary talents of course…'

I can see a few children still running around, others being made to put coats on and gather together their things in readiness for leaving but…

'Had it been left to me to do the cooking, things would have turned out very differently indeed,' I add.

Rachel grins. 'And with any luck, even though today was something of a baptism of fire, I might even persuade one or two people to pay for my skills once we move up here. I know it wasn't planned, but all this may turn out to have been a blessing.'

I wave at Rob as he walks towards us, feeling Drew's fingers entwine with mine. And I want to drink in this moment and everything it means for us. But I can't.

I look between the faces of my husband and friends, relaxed and happy. 'When was the last time you saw Lauren?' I ask.

CHAPTER TWENTY-FIVE

Drew spins around. 'Well she was... just...' His eyes find mine, and then Rob's. 'Where's Tilly?'

My heart begins to clamour as I try desperately not to jump to conclusions, but my alarm is infectious and I'm beginning to panic.

'I saw Anna with Chloe a few moments ago... Oh, Christ, Drew...' I break off, remembering Chloe's question to me from a while ago. I'd completely forgotten about it. I'd dismissed it.

'Chloe couldn't find them either, I...' I'm trying to remember when it was. Before the speeches, but how long before?

'When, Thea? When was this?' Drew's face looms in front of me.

I shake my head. 'Don't, I'm trying to think... I was on my way to the kitchen...'

Anna is hurtling towards us with Chloe in tow. 'Thea, I can't find the girls. I've looked everywhere and no one knows where they are.'

My eyes fly to the doors at the back of the hall. Someone has opened them as a few people begin to leave. 'No! We mustn't let them. We need to ask.'

Rob senses my thoughts in a second. He throws up his arms, striding into the centre of the room. 'Everyone,' he shouts. 'Please! Can everyone just wait a moment!'

There's a startled hush after the camaraderie of the minutes before.

'Please!' shouts Rob, a little less loud. 'Hang on a minute…' He gestures to the door where a young family are making their way out, only to find their path suddenly blocked by Gerry. I look around and I can already see Rachel crouching and talking to people. 'This is really important please, before any of you go. Has anyone seen Lauren? Or Tilly? They're always together, they…' He breaks off, anguish catching at his throat.

Everyone is looking at someone else. And any minute now there'll be a call, or a cry to let us know where they are. Or Lauren will pop her head up from somewhere wondering what all the fuss is about. Any. Minute. Now.

But the call never comes. And heads are shaking. Expressions are worried. A child coughs and it's as if a gunshot has gone off. I can't hold my breath any longer.

It's only seconds, but each one feels like a thousand. I pull Chloe towards me. 'It's okay, sweetheart, it's okay. We'll find them.' I drop to her height. 'I'm so sorry I didn't listen before.' She's properly crying now, frightened, and I have to bite back a sob of my own. Lauren's only eight…

And suddenly a shout echoes across the hall. It's Beth's mum, holding tight to her visibly shaken daughter. 'They were outside,' she says, looking at Beth for confirmation. 'Not that long ago. A crowd of them from Tilly's class.'

Beth's looking at a friend beside her and even from here I can see the pleading in her eyes. *Go on*, she's saying, *tell them*, and slowly a hand is raised in the air. 'We were just playing…' comes a voice.

'No one's in trouble,' says Rob. 'It's okay to be playing, but we just need to know where the girls are. Did you see them come back inside?'

The girl shakes her head. 'We were playing tig, and then we came back inside to play hide and seek.' Her eyes fly to the window. 'Because it was getting dark… But I didn't see where they went.'

Rob smiles. 'Thank you, Ellie, that's really helpful.' He looks back around the room. 'So was anyone else playing hide and seek? It's okay to say,' he reminds them. 'No one's in trouble.'

But there is silence. Furtive looks and nothing more.

Everything is taking so long. And I want to scream, but I know I can't because the only thing that matters right now is where Lauren and Tilly are. Whatever I feel isn't going to help. I grip Anna's hand.

'We'll find them,' I say. 'I promise. They won't be far. And you know what they're like, they'll be together…' Because I can't begin to think how it would be if they were on their own. How they would be feeling. I choke off the thought.

Gerry is coming back towards us. 'Right, I reckon they're still outside somewhere and, although I don't like the thought of all these people here, having them leave will be a nightmare. They're going to have to stay until we've checked.

'Rachel, do you think there's any way you can go around and explain this to all the parents. Let's keep everyone occupied – there are too many children here and I don't want them getting upset. Rob, and Drew, we need to get folks together who can help us look outside. As soon as we can.'

He doesn't need to say any more. And I'm suddenly immensely grateful for Gerry's paramedic training. My ability to think has just deserted me. Drew's body is solid and reassuring, and his fingers wind ceaselessly around mine, but he's pulling away and I have to let him go.

He drops to his haunches in front of our eldest daughter. 'You go with Mummy, Chlo, and help look after everyone, okay? I'll be back in just a minute.' She nods and I lead her away, following Rachel, and still holding tight of Anna's hand. Her face is ashen. She's hardly said a word, but she doesn't need to. Guilt has silenced my tongue too.

Someone has made way for us at one of the tables, but I can't sit down. I should be doing something. I want to be out there, but

I need to be in here. And the pain of feeling torn is unbearable. Anna suddenly pulls away, muttering something about torches, and I watch as she runs towards the kitchen. And all I can see is the dark outside the windows.

Chloe is shivering by my side and I wrap my arms around her, holding her as close as I can. My thoughts are skittering from one thing to the next but I can't concentrate, every fibre of my being is waiting, my senses strung tight, alert for any vibration of change. Just at the moment when I realise that Anna hasn't returned to the table, I hear a shout from the other side of the hall.

'How can you even sit there?' It's Anna, leaning over Stacey, her face twisted with rage.

'While all this is going on, pretending like it doesn't have anything to do with you. I don't even want you breathing the same air as me. With your lies and gossip, making out like we're to blame, when all the time it's your son who's been making Tilly's life a misery. My daughter's out there somewhere, and it's all your fault!'

'Oh, shit.' It's Rachel, getting to her feet.

But, as I stare between her anguished look and Anna's tear-stained face, it's as if everything else is pushed to one side and I'm left with a vision, right smack bang in the centre of my brain. And it's of Leo. And he's sitting right by his mum's side, his eyes resolutely glued to the table.

I release my grip on Chloe. 'Wait here, sweetheart.'

But I'm too late, Stacey has sensed the danger she's in and there's no way she's going to back down without a fight.

'You sure about that, are you?' she snarls at Anna. 'You want to think carefully about that before you go around accusing people, especially when you've got no proof. So what if your husband's the vicar, think he's better than the rest of us, do you? When everyone knows that vicars are the worst... touching up kiddies all the time, it's sick. So don't you go round saying my Leo's to blame for your precious daughter's bruises when you need to start asking questions a lot closer to home.'

I throw Rachel a horrified look. Oh dear God. How can Stacey even say those things? Not after everything that Rob said. And not here, not in front of everyone.

Anna looks like she's about to throw up.

'You really are an evil cow,' I say, rounding on Stacey. 'It's bad enough that your son's an utter thug, without you trying to pin the blame on other people just so you don't have to face the truth. It's about time you woke up to yourself, Stacey, because before too long people are going to find out the truth, and where will that leave you? Alone in the gutter, that's where.'

'Well, that's rich coming from you,' she spits back. 'The daughter of a known child molester.'

Every sound in the room stops dead.

And for a moment I feel as if I might pass out. My vision is blurring, and the tether that's holding me here is becoming gossamer-thin. I can feel every eye in the room on me, but I've come too far to let them win, to influence what I believe. I pull myself straighter.

'You'll have to do better than that, Stacey. Because I have nothing to fear from the truth. And do you really think I'd be stupid enough to come back here if my dad was guilty of such a crime? He was made a victim too, and one day they'll find out who really attacked Georgia when we were kids, and why you're so bloody obsessed with something that happened over twenty years ago…' I break off. I've held her gaze the entire time I've been speaking, her eyes alive with scorn. But there's a change now, some other emotion, and I'm shocked to recognise it as fear. Something ripples through me but it's gone so fast I can't catch it. But it's important and…

Stacey snorts, sending anger coursing through me once more. Rachel touches my arm – a gentle warning – but I shake her off.

I'm not letting these women get away with treating people the way they have.

I stare at the faces in front of me. 'And if I really was as depraved and nasty as you've been trying to make out, not only would that be so utterly ridiculous I can't even be bothered to explain why, but wouldn't I be the one going around spreading lies and making people's lives a misery? But instead, here I am, just going about my business, trying to raise my family and do right by this community. Not like you, and all your friends who were quite happy to leave us in the shit today. But you've been outed, shown up for who you really are...' I lean towards Stacey again. 'And now, as much as I've enjoyed our little chat, you're wasting my time. I want to know the truth and you're going to help me get it.' I turn to Leo. 'Were you outside with Tilly and Lauren?' I ask. 'Playing hide and seek?'

There's no reply.

'Leo...! I asked you a question,' I add, my voice dangerously low. 'Were you playing outside with Tilly and Lauren? Yes or no?'

Stacey pushes her chair back from the table with a hideous screeching sound. 'Don't you dare talk to my son like that.'

'It's important,' I hiss. 'Two children are missing for God's sake.' My eyes burn into hers and for a moment I really don't think there's any level on which I can get through to her, but I'm inches away from doing something we'll both live to regret and she knows it.

She elbows Leo roughly. 'Answer the lady,' she says.

I drop to his side. 'Please, Leo, we just want to find them. Do you know where they've gone?'

There's a tiny shake of the head. 'They ran off,' he murmurs. 'I didn't do nothin'.'

'So why did they run off?' I ask. 'They must have had a reason...'

He raises his head slightly, peeps at me from under his lashes, but then his head drops again.

'Leo, it's dark outside. Think how you would feel if you were outside, all by yourself, in the dark and cold.'

I turn my gaze back to Stacey, I'm pleading with her this time.

'What did you say?' she warns. 'And you'd better bloody tell me… Leo…?'

He huffs. 'I didn't know they were going to run off, okay. I was only joking.'

'What did you say?'

'That they'd better find a really good hiding place, that's all, otherwise…' He stops dead and looks at me. 'Otherwise everyone would know how rubbish they were at playing the game.'

There's something in what he's saying, and I narrow my eyes trying to pick up on it, but it's not right, it doesn't make sense. And everything I know about this child makes me think that he's very good at not getting caught.

'I don't believe you,' I say. 'I don't think that's any kind of threat. Lauren would just laugh at you if you said that. So, try again Leo, what did you really threaten them with?'

A sly grin comes over his face as he looks up and very slowly draws a finger across his throat.

I stare at him, reeling, the room spinning round me as the storm in my head builds. The waves are swamping me, pulling me under but, just when I think I can stand it no longer, it passes and the sea calms. I'm in the eye of the storm and it's quiet here, and strangely peaceful. There's room to think. And in that instant, it comes to me.

'I know where they are,' I say, incredulously, staring at Anna's astonished face. 'I do, I know where they are,' I repeat and then I bolt for the door.

I almost crash into Drew and Gerry as I hurtle outside.

'Hey… hey…!' It's Drew, trying to halt my flight. 'Thea, slow down, it's okay, I've got you.'

I stare up at his face. The last of the light is falling on one side of it, giving him an eerie look. It's almost completely dark now, how can it possibly be all right?

I struggle from his hold and instead pull at his arm. 'No, I know where they are… We have to go, come on.'

His eyes widen. 'Where? Thea, we've checked all the places there are to hide. I think Gerry's right, we need to call the police now. It's getting cold and neither of the girls had their coats on. There's no time to waste.'

'I know!' I pull at his arm again. 'Please… For God's sake, Drew, come with me.'

'Thea?' It's Anna, with Rachel by her side. 'You said you know where the girls are?' Her voice is rising hysterically.

'And I do, I promise you, Anna.' I pull her into my arms, feeling her body tremble against mine. 'I'll bring them back, I swear.' I pull away to look at Rachel. 'They're at the brook, Rach, you remember, don't you, that day we went paddling…?'

'The brook?' She's looking about her, trying to remember where it is. 'Thea, they could be anywhere… Maybe we ought to stay here?'

'No! It's the perfect place to hide. That's what Lauren said, remember? The perfect place to hide. I know how her mind works, Rach, and if she wanted to protect Tilly at any cost… that's where she'd take her.'

I can see her weighing up my words. I look at Drew, at Gerry and back to Anna again. I'm pleading with them. We haven't got time to argue.

'Go,' says Anna, nodding suddenly. 'You're right, I know you are. Go!'

'Stay here!' I call, already pulling Drew away. 'With Rob, in case they come back…'

'We'll be ready for you,' says Rachel resolutely, her arm already around Anna whose eyes meet mine, one mother to another.

'God speed,' she says.

'I'm coming with you,' says Gerry. 'Which way?'

He flicks on a torch, playing the beam in front of us as I grab Drew's hand and run across the car park. A thin drizzle has started up and I pray that there's no more rain. The girls will be cold and probably wet. The brook will have risen— a wave of terror constricts my throat, forcing me to slow down as I gulp air into my lungs. Don't think, just move…

We stop as we get to the road, Drew automatically pulling me to the right. 'No,' I pant. 'Left… follow the road, we'll break our necks otherwise.'

He steers the course, knowing I'm right. Running across the uneven field in the dark is asking for trouble and it's not that much quicker. Our steps thunder down the lane, the torchlight bouncing off the road surface as Gerry runs behind. I can see very little, but I don't need to. I've walked this way so many times in my life before and Lauren and Tilly are pulling me along. They're at the end of it. They have to be.

Drew crashes into the gate that leads onto the footpath down to the bridge, fumbling with the catch. My breath is burning in my chest, forcing me to cough, and behind me Gerry is puffing hard. But there's something else and I struggle to listen, my hand on Drew's arm, holding him still a moment.

'Oh, dear God, the water!'

I can hear it crashing against the concrete struts that support the bridge. It's much narrower at this point of the river, and two days of torrential rain will have swollen the brook to double its volume. I just pray that the girls are high enough up the bank. Lauren's sensible, she's… But they're in the dark. They'll be frightened…

The noise is much louder down by the bridge and I race across and out into the field beyond, stopping dead. I can't see a thing.

In the dark there are no markers, no landmarks, save for the dark shapes of the bushes. I run forward, but I can't tell where I am.

'It's along here… but I can't see where. Gerry, can you play the torch on the water. We need to find the beach…' But even as I say it I realise that it will no longer be there, covered over by the swell of water.

'Lauren!' I yell. 'Tilly!'

'What are we even looking for?' shouts Gerry, trying to make himself heard above the noise of the water.

'There's a bush,' I shout. 'With a hollow middle where you can hide. It's right at the water's edge.' I've reached a gap between two dark shapes. 'I need to get in the water!'

'What…? No, Thea, it's too dangerous.' Drew is pulling me back, but he knows I'm not going to give up. He grabs both my shoulders until I'm facing him, rain or tears glinting wet on his face. 'Together,' he puffs. 'I'm not losing you too. Together… or not at all.'

'Then give me your hand,' I say, leading him down to the water's edge. 'Hold me.'

I inch forward but there's no way to do this carefully, the water level is too high and the darkness makes it impossible to judge. The torchlight barely gilds the surface. I'm going to have to trust in faith and, tightening my grip on Drew's hand, I jump. The breath leaves my body as I splash, stumbling slightly on the uneven riverbed, freezing water slopping midway up my thighs.

'Lauren…! Tilly…!' Drew's voice is hoarse, and the sound is snatched away by the wind and the tumult of water.

'Pass me the torch…'

I play the beam at the water's edge, looking for the gaps that I know should be here. It's just so hard to make anything out, it all looks so different at night. 'Lauren!' I shout with all my might, straining to listen.

There's a crash behind me as Drew lands in the water, followed by Gerry.

'Christ!' Gerry hisses, the expletive is right in my ear. 'Thea, this is crazy, they can't be here, there's nowhere to go...'

'Yes, yes there is,' insists Drew. 'We used to play here as children... Thea's right, we just need to find them. They'll be safe up under the bushes...'

'Shhh! I need to listen.'

And then I hear it, faint and a way in front of me. But unmistakable.

'Mummy...?'

CHAPTER TWENTY-SIX

'They're here…! Oh, Lauren, keep shouting sweetheart, as loud as you can, tell us where you are!'

'Mummy, quickly!'

I can hear the panic in her voice, and I almost fall, trying to push myself through water that pushes right back. But Drew's got me, his grip firm and steady. I can barely see the entrance to the hiding place, the water is right up over the bank and there's no way to enter it without getting almost submerged.

The brambles tear at my hands as I try to pull them to one side, flashing the torch through the gaps, trying to see. 'Are you okay?'

'We can't get out, Mummy, quickly…!' She's crying now, the pain of her sobs far worse than the brambles that rip my hands as I try to pull them away.

And then I catch a flash of Lauren's white fleece, think I see the gleam of her eye. 'I see them, Drew, help me, please… I can't…'

'Jesus,' Gerry hisses from behind, crashing against the bushes. I can hear him grunting with effort as he uses virtually his whole body weight to rip the branches aside.

And then Drew is past me, hauling himself up on the bank by whatever means possible, thorns scraping at his skin. 'It's okay, Lauren, Daddy's here, it's okay.'

The noise of her crying increases now that she's so close to rescue. And I shine the torch forward, trying to give Drew as much light as possible. 'Tilly!' I call. 'It's okay, sweetheart... Is she okay?'

'She can't stand up, it's too slippy...'

Drew reaches them, pulling both children onto his lap as he collapses in a heap, his feet still scrabbling for purchase on the muddy bank. The water is almost to the top of the cave, the last remaining two feet the only part to stay dry. Behind them is the dense thicket of brambles and what would have been their only way out. But in the dark, scared and disorientated...? They wouldn't have had the strength, let alone anything else. I shudder as a sob breaks free from my throat, knowing how close they came...

Gerry is beside me, measured and calm. 'Let's get them out, fast as we can now. Pass them down your legs, Drew, and keep them out of the water if you can. I'll lift from there.' He looks to me but he doesn't need to ask.

'I can carry her,' I say, my teeth gritted with determination.

I can hear Drew murmuring but I can't make out what he's saying above the noise of the water. But then, clear as a bell: 'No, Daddy, Tilly first, she's very cold.'

I haven't heard Tilly speak yet and I don't need to look at Gerry to know what he's thinking. 'Quick as you can now, that's right,' he says. Arm out, Tilly, we've got you, we've got you. Take my hand... there...'

I heave the branches upwards and away from her as best I can as Gerry bodily hauls her from the space. Only when they're clear do I let them drop so he can scoop her upward and into my waiting arms. Her eyes are open, wide and terrified, but she still hasn't spoken. I clasp her trembling body to me.

'It's okay, darling. Talk to me, sweetheart, are you okay...?' There's the teeniest of nods, just a slight movement against my neck. 'Are you hurt?'

'No…'

I'm kissing the top of her head, rubbing her back. She's like ice. And however high I hold her, her legs are still in the water. Gerry takes one look at her and dips his head.

'Drew, hang on, I'm coming back. I need to get Thea and Tilly to the bank and out of the water.'

I feel his arm around my back, his hand gripping my elbow as he steers us safely to the edge. He hauls himself out and then, kneeling, lifts Tilly clean out of my arms, as I scramble up the bank and flop to the grass.

'Go!' I shout. 'I've got her, go!'

I hear the splash as Gerry crashes back into the water. I have Tilly, but I need to see Lauren, to hold her. It's pitch-black, and I'm sitting, my legs splayed on the grass. I'm trying to remember what Tilly was wearing, trying to feel how wet she is, but my hands are too cold to feel anything.

'Hang on, Tilly, let me just take this off.' I have a tee shirt on under my fleece, and Tilly needs the warmth far more than I do. I wriggle off my outer layer, gasping as the cold hits my wet skin, and pull Tilly to me. She needs no encouragement to cling on and I spread the fleece across her back, pulling it round her as best I can. 'It won't be long now, darling, I promise.' She whimpers against me but I'm just glad to hear the sound, any sound.

A beam of light plays against my leg.

'Mummy!'

'I'm here, darling. I'm here…'

I can't see much but I know Lauren's free, that she's in Drew's arms, that she's safe. And then they're beside me, hugging and kissing, crying… Drew's hands are in my hair, the rough of his cheek against mine.

'I told you I'd protect her, Mummy. I looked after her, all the time. It was Leo, he was really going to hurt her.'

'I know, darling. You were so brave… But you don't have to worry about that now. It's all over… You're safe now, I promise.'

And it's a vow I will keep until my dying day.

'Come on now, let's move,' says Gerry, helping me to my feet. He goes to take Tilly from my arms, but I can't let her go.

'It's okay, I'll take her, for as long as I can.'

Tilly's legs are wrapped around my waist, her one arm curled tight around my neck. She feels as light as a feather but I know how hard it's going to be to carry her back. My legs already feel leaden. But I'm not letting go of her either and so I put one foot in front of the other, chest burning, muscles fighting me every step of the way until we reach the car park.

A shout goes up. 'I can see them! They're here…! All of them!'

And in front of me, moments later, a rectangle of bright light splits the night as the doors to the village hall open, filling with silhouettes.

Anna is the first to reach me and, as I hand her daughter to her, I know I will never again in my life give anyone anything so precious. She's openly crying, unable to speak beyond murmurs and endearments as she clasps Tilly to her, but there's a moment when her eyes meet mine, and she says all she will ever need to.

Rob's arms go around them both. 'Thank you, dear God, thank you,' he says.

And then I turn to hold my daughter, my legs almost giving way. Rachel brings out Chloe, and together with Drew we make a human sandwich, stumbling towards the hall, entangled and crying and laughing both.

The hall is still full of people and the release of tension as we enter is palpable, a collective breath no longer held. The children have been taken home, but others have stayed, unwilling to leave until there was news. One way or the other. And I know how close we were to disaster.

A space has been cleared for us, and amazingly there are blankets and warm coats, jumpers, fleeces, mittens and hats, together with hot chocolate and sweet tea, a huge plate of biscuits and some chocolate Mini Rolls. Rachel pulls us down to sit, stripping off socks and wet clothes with little regard for privacy, but no one cares.

There are trails of blood all across Gerry's face and arms, from where the thorns dug deep, but he doesn't stop until he's checked the girls over. Quickly, calmly, methodically. He asks Tilly in particular a load of questions, but she's becoming more alert by the minute and I know he's happy when he turns and gives me the faintest of nods. Then, and only then, does he remove his own sopping boots and clothing and succumb to Rachel's ministrations.

No one really notices as people leave, but I guess folks figured we needed time to be on our own, and space to acclimatise to what has just happened. And so, after a little while, I realise that there's pretty much just us left. Us and, perversely, half of the committee members who have made it their business to finish the washing-up, tidying everything away.

A few of them come to stand in front of us now, Jackie at their forefront offering me another cup of tea. It makes me want to laugh for some strange reason.

'I owe you an apology,' she begins.

And that does make me laugh. Or someone sounding suspiciously like me does.

'Somewhat of an understatement…'

She dips her head. 'Yes, well… I'm sorry, anyhow.' She sniffs, turning her head slightly and I follow her line of sight. Sitting at a table, on her own save for Leo beside her, is Stacey. Even from a distance it's clear to see she's been crying.

'We've all told her we want nothing more to do with her,' she says. 'It should never have gone this far but… well, a few other mums have come forward as well…'

A woman to her right shuffles into view. 'You don't want to make a fuss, do you, but my Jess has been on the receiving end of Leo's bullying once or twice, her dinner money mainly but...' She looks behind her. 'And Carrie's daughter too...' Another woman takes a step forward.

'We've spoken to the head,' she says. 'Just now, there's a few of us actually.'

'And none of you thought to mention any of this before?' asks Anna, shaking her head. 'You're unbelievable.'

'We didn't know,' argues the woman. 'We all thought our children were the only ones... and besides... well, we're all friends with Stacey and our kids have always got on with Leo before. This is a recent thing and I thought, hoped I suppose, that it would all blow over. Stacey had enough on her plate and no one wants to kick a person when they're down...'

I look up, puzzled. 'What do you mean?'

'She's been in a hell of a state, since her dad died back in the spring,' answers Jackie. 'They were very close and she took it really hard. Her old man left not long after too. She's had a right time of it.' She eyes us nervously. 'Not that that's really any excuse, mind, but... Anyway, I'm glad your girls are all right.'

I can see Rachel looking at me out of the corner of her eye, wearing her protective mantle. 'You've got a bloody nerve,' she says. 'It's a bit late for that.'

I smile. 'No, it's okay, Rach.' And it is, because somehow it really doesn't seem to matter any more. Some things are simply more important. I get slowly to my feet. I'm taller than Jackie and for one moment I think she actually believes I'm going to hit her. And I enjoy leaning forward until my face is right up close to hers.

'Apology accepted,' I say.

Her eyes widen in shock.

'And you know why, Jackie? Because this stops, right here, and right now. I'm not about to start giving you a hard time because you're going to have a hard enough one coming to terms with what you've done. You and all your friends. Now, get your shit together and start behaving like a decent human being. For all our sakes.'

*

I sink onto the sofa, feeling the weight of the day heavy on my limbs, and pull Mr Blue towards me. Lauren must have left him there when the girls were watching the television earlier, but I bury my nose in his warm fur before tucking him under my chin. I don't think Lauren let go of Tilly's hand for more than a few minutes the entire evening. Or Tilly didn't let go of hers. It's hard to tell exactly which way round it was. They're just like Drew and I were at that age, inseparable.

We all congregated back at Pevensey for a while after returning from the village hall. Food was eaten, hot baths were taken and the men opened a bottle of whisky. But the girls are all tucked up in bed now; Tilly back at Rose Cottage with Anna and Rob, and Lauren snuggled in beside Chloe.

Everyone knows there are questions to be asked and discussions to be had, but it's like I said to Drew earlier: it feels as if we've already moved on. The only thing that matters just now is that we're all together. Safe and sound. Even so my head feels like it's ready to explode and I remind myself that it's okay to relax now. Seconds later I'm asleep.

I'm still cradling Mr Blue in my arms when I wake, glancing at my watch to see that I've been asleep for well over an hour. I struggle upright and kiss the bear's nose before swinging my legs onto the floor. Lauren won't want to be asleep without her faithful friend and he certainly seems to have done me the world of good.

A slight noise catches my attention and I turn to see Drew hovering in the doorway, carrying a mug. His expression is tender, tentative…

'I came in before but... How are you feeling?' he asks, but all I hear is, *I love you.*

I'm across the room in seconds and he searches around him for a moment, looking for somewhere to put down the mug. Then I'm in his arms and it's like it always used to be; neither one of us solid, but merged somewhere in the middle.

'We'll get through this, Thea,' he murmurs. 'I promise.'

But I can't speak. Wave after wave of relief is coursing through me. That he might actually be right and all we have to do is cling onto our rock for just a little while longer until the stormy seas are calm again. And for now just feeling him hold me is enough. There have been times over these last few days when I never thought that would happen again.

'I'm sorry,' he says, stroking the back of my head as he pulls it to his chest. 'I just didn't know what to do... So I did nothing and then so much time went past it became impossible to do anything.'

'I was vile,' I murmur. 'Hateful. I can't believe the things I accused you of when I knew you would never...' I trail off. I don't think it needs to be said any longer.

'It's not your fault...'

'It's not yours either. No one's fault, a responsibility, but one we share...'

We stay entwined for a few more moments before I gently pull away. 'I should take Mr Blue back to Lauren,' I say. 'You know what she's like otherwise.'

But he takes the bear from me, smiling. 'She came down a little while ago,' he replies. 'But when she saw you were cuddling him, she said that you had far more need of him than her just now. You have the loan of him,' he adds. 'Just for the one night, mind.'

His words bring tears to my eyes. 'How did we get to have such wonderful kids, Drew?' I say.

'Luck?' he suggests. 'But more than likely, love...'

I sniff. 'It makes me sad. That there are children in the world who don't get that…'

'Children like Leo, maybe…' He sighs. 'But we don't know their circumstances, Thea, so we can only be true to ourselves and what we believe.'

I stare at him. 'That's just what Mum said.'

He smiles. 'Then it must be right.' He holds out his hand. 'Come on, let's get to bed. It's been a very long day…'

And that night his foot slips against mine, his arm slides around my waist and his skin sears a line of heat the entire length of my body.

CHAPTER TWENTY-SEVEN

The girls went back to school this morning. Undeterred, unafraid and, so it would appear, not in the least bit unhappy. We could learn a lot from their resilience and courage. Perhaps we already have.

We spent the day together yesterday after we'd waved Rachel and Gerry off to go house-hunting. Rob, Anna, Tilly, me, Drew and the girls. Two families out together for the day having fun. And it was absolutely the most perfect thing to do. There was an almost holiday mood, carefree, full of gratitude for a day set free from anything but our desire to be together and enjoy ourselves. And this morning it's as if a line has been drawn in the sand, one which we all stepped over, relishing the prospect of life on the other side. Not delusional, just hopeful.

It's how I feel as I open the studio door. It would be hard not to, it's flooded with sunlight. Drew is already there, intent on his computer screen, and I love to see this expression on his face. When he's drawing like he is now, it goes much deeper than mere concentration. There's a fervour to how he looks, an excitement which he holds in check, releasing bit by bit as he completes each aspect of the design. I've often wondered if this is what I look like when I paint. But he breaks off what he's doing as I enter and his smile meets mine.

His gaze returns to his work as I settle myself, opening my notes and my sketchbook with preliminary drawings in it, before finally bringing out the illustration I've been working on. I need to know whether the studio can still feel like it once did.

'That's better,' he says, his attention still on his computer, but then he turns to me. 'We've missed you,' he adds. 'It hasn't been the same.'

'We?' I query.

'The house and I,' he replies. 'You've been gone a while, Thea, it's good to have you back.' His expression is warm. It's not an accusation, but an observation of an honest feeling.

'It's good to be back,' I reply, looking around the room, and I realise how much I've missed being in this space. Sitting alongside Drew, working, these ordinary moments forming the links in the chain of our everyday lives. Its strength binding us together. It's what will carry us on into the future.

I pick up my pencil, feeling its smooth wood, warm and balanced in my hand, and I begin to draw.

I don't know how long it is before I stop, feeling Drew's fingers sliding around the base of my neck. It's a sensation as familiar as breathing, as he dips his head to look over my shoulder at the work on the page in front of me. I raise my head, eyes flicking left and right, the change in focus allowing me to 'see' the picture for the first time. And I'm astonished by what I've drawn.

Drew's breath is audible in my ear. 'Jesus, Thea,' he murmurs. 'That's incredible.'

The scene is the first in which Weasel appears, a devious trickster who delights in making mischief. Here, he is planning to sabotage Rabbit's picnic and, from the haughty sneer on his face to the malevolent gleam in his eye, every nuance of his character is clear to see, but wrought with such expressive detail that the drawing dances with energy and life. It will make every child who sees it root even harder for Rabbit, and long to see Weasel's downfall. He'll be the villain that everyone will love to hate and my heart leaps in recognition of what I've done.

I lean back into Drew's body, feeling the warmth of his weight behind me. 'I thought it had gone,' I say. 'That I had lost it...' My words bring tears, unbidden, springing to my eyes. My hand reaches upwards, seeking out his.

Drew's reply is immediate. 'No, never,' he says. 'Something that strong can never be broken...' His fingers twine with mine, his lips are in my hair and we both know we're no longer talking about the character on the page but, instead, the character of our love.

We stay like this a few moments more until Drew slips away to make us both a drink and I sit gazing at my work, feeling the renewal it has brought, the rebirthing of energy and purpose. And with it comes certainty. I slip from my stool as Drew places down a mug of tea by my side and cross to stand behind his chair.

'Is it going well?' I ask, seeing that his own drawing has come to life, far bigger and more complex than his original honeycomb house.

He regards it for a moment before a slow smile crosses his face. 'Yeah...' he says. 'I reckon it is.'

'This is different though...' I add, pointing at the screen.

There's a rueful smile. 'There hasn't really been an opportunity to tell you about this, but—'

'You've got another job? Drew, that's brilliant!'

'Unexpectedly so. God really does work in mysterious ways...'

I look up at him, bemused at his comment, and my expression is met with laughter.

'So you'll never guess what Rob did before he decided to join the clergy.'

I raise my eyebrows. 'Somehow I don't think you're about to say he was a lion tamer... Go on, tell me, what did he do?'

'He was a quantity surveyor. Not for long, mind, but...' His words are an invitation.

I look at his smiling face, trying to decipher the piece of information he's so obviously wanting to share, but which I haven't yet worked out.

'And so when I went to a meeting at the diocesan board of education recently…' He's trying so hard not to laugh. 'Funnily enough, I met Rob there… And we might be near the point of working out a deal for me to supply the diocese with a range of school buildings, not dissimilar from my honeycomb houses… Didn't he say he might be working on a project that I could help him with?'

I stare at Drew as he grins from ear to ear, remembering Rob's words from the very first day we met him. 'Oh my God, that's such brilliant news!' I nudge his hip. 'Why didn't you tell me?' But of course I already know the answer.

He looks back down at his drawing, still smiling. 'If I've understood the brief correctly, and I think I have, then it should be perfect for what the diocese needs. It's combining the best of both worlds, a tailor-made solution at a fraction of what a traditional building would cost them.' His eyes are dancing with excitement. 'It could be the start of something I'd be really proud of. And it gives what I can offer a whole new dimension. If they go for it I'm going to have to think about how I do things because I could be really rather busy…' He trails off but I can already see where this might be headed because Drew is one of the most generous people I know.

'And so Rob…?'

Drew merely raises an amused eyebrow. 'We don't know yet, because much will depend on conversations he has with the diocese. His position as curate here has to come first, but there might be ways he could help out on a consultancy basis. It's a win-win situation as far as I can see.'

'And now that it would seem we're no longer in danger of being chased from the village by an angry mob carrying pitchforks, it couldn't have come at a better time. For all of us.' I check my watch. 'I wonder how Rach and Gerry are getting on?'

'They're going to love the house, Thea, you know it as well as I do. I've never seen them so excited.'

'Rachel said she'd ring once their viewing was over. What if they want it, Drew? They've sold their house – this could all happen very quickly.'

'Almost as if it's meant to be…'

I pat my back pocket, feeling for my phone, but I must have left it upstairs. 'Back in a sec.'

The phone is on my bedside table and I snatch it up, checking the screen in case I've missed her call, but it's blank. I'm halfway to the door before something makes me stop and double back. I sit on the edge of the bed, thinking. And then, with a trembling hand, I reach forward to pull open the drawer. Today seems like the right day to do this. To clear away the past.

I slide both newspaper articles from my journal and sit with them on my lap for a moment. I don't read them, I don't need to, I've already memorised their contents. They will fade from my mind over time but I no longer need these reminders, they're unimportant now.

I rise to my feet just as the thought comes to me. I don't know why I didn't see it before, and I stare at the papers in my hand. It seems so obvious now.

Drew is back at work as I pop my head around the studio door. He probably wouldn't even notice I've gone for a while but I tell him I'm just popping round to see Anna. He grins.

'More cake?'

'Probably,' I reply before slipping back out of the room.

*

Stacey doesn't even look surprised to see me. She nods and there's even the trace of a smile as she leads me straight into the front room, a conciliatory gesture as she indicates that I should take a seat.

She perches on the edge of a chair opposite mine, her fingers twisting the tissue that's balled in her fist.

'How do you know?' she asks softly.

I lay the newspaper article down on the coffee table in front of her. 'Because of this,' I reply. 'I have one pretty much the same at home. Same age, same newspaper probably. It's what got me thinking in the first place. Why had it been left there, hidden in my house? Who had left it? Because you don't just hang onto something like that, not for all these years, unless it has some very deep significance, do you?'

Stacey doesn't reply.

'You see, I know in my heart that my dad wasn't guilty of attacking Georgia, and I was actually going to destroy these articles today. To put all this hateful business firmly in the past and leave it there. But as soon as I saw the clipping, it made me wonder why *you* had the article in the first place. Why *you* had kept it for all these years... or if not you, someone else in your family. I realised then of course. Because what was true for my mum is also true for you, isn't it?' I pause, letting the question form fully before I say it out loud. 'When did you find out, Stacey? When he died?'

A tear rolls down her cheek. 'It was among Dad's things. We found it when we were going through them, along with a note...' Her voice cracks. 'Asking for forgiveness.'

'Oh, Stacey...'

'And none of us knew. Had any idea. Not my mum, nor me, nor my sisters.' Her hand covers her mouth as if she's going to be sick. 'And it was my sister's friend for God's sake, Georgia... she was always round our house when we were younger.' A tremor shakes her shoulders. 'Oh God...'

I close my eyes and swallow, expecting to feel relief, and yet how can I, in the face of someone else's pain? I've been where Stacey is now. Every feeling running through her head is one I've already experienced. Except for her, there is no escape. There is no doubt. There will be no reprieve.

'So when I came back you thought you could blame my dad instead of yours…'

She's crying openly now. 'I thought it would make it all go away! That it wouldn't have to be true. I knew it was wrong, but I thought if I could make other people think it was your dad then I wouldn't have to admit—'

'Stacey, it doesn't work like that.'

'I know!' Her voice has risen, her eyes wild with fear at the understanding of what she needs to accept, what she must accept.

And, inexplicably, I find myself holding Stacey in my arms, this woman who has caused my family and friends so much pain, letting all the hurt and sorrow wash out of her.

'What are you going to do?' she whispers, a few moments later.

I gently release her. 'Would you like me to get you anything?' I ask. 'A drink, or…?'

She shakes her head. 'I'm having trouble keeping anything down.' Her body is still trembling.

'Do you have anyone you can talk to… about all of this? You shouldn't be on your own.'

'My mum and sisters help a bit, but they're feeling it too. There's no one else. Not since… My bloke left too. He couldn't cope with it, didn't want anything to do with me, or Leo…' Her voice fades away and there's nothing I can say. She has to make peace with herself and her friends. Her son too. No one else is going to do it for her.

I watch her for a moment. 'Just now you asked me what I was going to do about this.'

She raises fearful eyes.

'And I'm not going to do anything… I've been through hell, Stacey. I know what it feels like, but I reckon for me that might be over, on its way at least. I thought I hated you for what you've done to my family, but I don't. I feel sorry for you because your suffering isn't over, not by a long chalk. And you've got a long way to go yet before you find any peace.' I take hold of her arms. 'But I think you know what will help you to find it. You and your son. Do the right thing and tell the police, Stacey. Give Georgia and her family some closure, that's all I ask.'

'But I just want it to stop!' she pleads.

But I can't make it stop.

All I can do is hold her.

And tell her that I forgive her.

EPILOGUE

Thea

Stacey moved away a few months later. Where to I don't know, and I didn't ask. She came to say goodbye and I hugged her and wished her well. What else could I do? She has a tough time ahead of her. She didn't volunteer the information and the question wasn't mine to ask, but I know it's in the hands of the police now; the papers have been full of it. I bumped into Jackie a week or so ago too, and she told me that Stacey and Leo are getting the help they need, and that's the main thing.

Life has almost got back to normal now. I no longer feel as if I have to hold up a sign which reads 'Nothing to see here, move right along'. We're just a normal couple, going about our business, raising our family, with the same hopes, dreams and fears as everyone else. Except that I don't think we're normal at all, I think we're extraordinary. Drew's business is going from strength to strength and, apart from the fact that he's finally realising his dream, I'm loving just having him here. He's the one person who brings out the best in me, who helps me to soar and yet who keeps my feet firmly on the ground. And one thing's for sure, I know that nothing can hurt us now.

So, was it a mistake to come back to Pevensey? Not in a million years. We've proved ourselves worthy of this house, but more than that we've found out what it is to come home. It's the place that made us after all; we belong here.

Drew

It's funny how, looking back before we moved, I was so scared that we would change, even though I thought I wanted us to. But I know now that the change was long overdue, and that we had outgrown our previous house and our lives. Because they were too narrow, too confined, and if we'd stayed in either of them we would never have grown. I don't think I ever expected us to blossom in the ways in which we have, but I know I have Thea to thank for much of that. For taking all our hands and leading us through it. She doesn't believe that of course. She smiles and just says that we were meant to come back to Pevensey for a reason and now we know why.

Maybe she's right. Who am I to argue when Pevensey has played such a huge part in all our lives? When I see her now, tucking her hair back behind her ears before she picks up her pencil to draw something so amazing it makes me catch my breath, and when I hear our girls, shrieking with laughter as they run barefoot in the garden, how could I ever have doubted that this was where we should live? Thea teases me now and says that the house is the real reason why I picked her all those years ago, but that's where she's wrong. I picked her because she was the girl whose heart was bigger than she ever realised. Always was, always will be.

A LETTER FROM EMMA

Hello, and thank you so much for choosing to read *My Husband's Lie*. I do hope you enjoyed it and, before I carry on, I should just mention that if you'd like to stay updated on what's coming next, please do sign up to my newsletter here and you'll be the first to know!

www.bookouture.com/emma-davies

As I write this we've just moved into another decade. Not only that, but on the 15th January 2020 I celebrated my four-year anniversary of leaving my old working life behind to become a full-time author. So it seems a particularly good time to take stock, and have a little celebration! It's also a brilliant opportunity to say a big thank you, to you my readers, who have made all this possible. To those of you who have been with me from the beginning, through all fifteen books (yes, fifteen!) and to those who have just joined me, it sounds a little corny to say it, but I really couldn't do it without you!

And *My Husband's Lie* has also proved to be quite a milestone for me in other ways. In some respects it's a return to my writing roots but, in others, marks the journey that I too have undertaken these past four years. Growing as a person and growing as a writer go hand in hand and this book has certainly provided some challenges. It's darker, more emotional and suspenseful than my other books, but it's been wonderful to write and now I'm here, it feels as if this is the place where I belong.

So I hope that readers of my past books will find even more to enjoy – I've been so grateful to have your company along the way and never lose sight of my loyalty to you. But to new readers, welcome, I hope you'll stay for the rest of my journey, it looks set to be another busy year.

I hope to see you again very soon and, in the meantime, if you've enjoyed *My Husband's Lie*, I would really appreciate a few minutes of your time to leave a review or post on social media. Every single review makes a massive difference and is very much appreciated!

Until next time,
Love, Emma x

 @EmDaviesAuthor

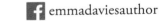 emmadaviesauthor

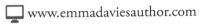 www.emmadaviesauthor.com

ACKNOWLEDGEMENTS

There's nothing like the moment when you pitch a new idea to your editor and within twenty minutes a reply comes back in block capitals shouting in excitement. But while that's magical, what often comes next can be quite the reverse as you actually sit down and try to write it. Because some books are just more elusive than others. They tease you, flirt with you, pretend to be something they're not, or just downright disobey you. And sometimes they do this so well that you don't even realise. Which is why I'm incredibly grateful to my editor, Jessie, for her wisdom and perspective, and for pointing out when this happens. For making sure that the story I was trying to tell turned out just the way I wanted it to. And for being so nice while she was doing it!

Printed in Great Britain
by Amazon